'Why stumblest thou, sorry jade ?   Scentest thou some ill ? '
The steed replied :

' Prince Ivan has come and carried off Marya Morevna.'

' Is it possible to catch them ? '

' It is possible to sow wheat, to wait till it grows up, to reap it and thresh it, to grind it to flour, to make five pies of it, to eat those pies, and then to start in pursuit—and even then to be in time.'

Koshchei galloped off and caught up Prince Ivan.

' Now,' says he, ' this time I will forgive you, in return for your kindness in giving me water to drink.   And a second time I will forgive you ; but the third time beware ! I will cut you to bits.'

Then he took Marya Morevna from him, and carried her off. But Prince Ivan sat down on a stone and burst into tears.   He wept and wept—and then returned back again to Marya Morevna. Now Koshchei the Deathless happened not to be at home.

' Let us fly, Marya Morevna ! '

' Ah, Prince Ivan ! he will catch us.'

' Suppose he does catch us.   At all events we shall have spent an hour or two together.'

So they got ready and fled.   As Koshchei the Deathless was returning home, his good steed stumbled beneath him.

' Why stumblest thou, sorry jade ?   Scentest thou some ill ? '

' Prince Ivan has come and carried off Marya Morevna.'

' Is it possible to catch them ? '

' It is possible to sow barley, to wait till it grows up, to reap it and thresh it, to brew beer, to drink ourselves drunk on it, to sleep our fill, and then to set off in pursuit—and yet to be in time.'

Koshchei galloped off, caught up Prince Ivan :

' Didn't I tell you that you should not see Marya Morevna any more than your own ears ? '

And he took her away and carried her off home with him.

Prince Ivan was left there alone.   He wept and wept ; then he went back again after Marya Morevna.   Koshchei happened to be away from home at that moment.

' Let us fly, Marya Morevna ! '

' Ah, Prince Ivan ! he is sure to catch us and hew you in pieces.'

' Let him hew away !   I cannot live without you.'

So they got ready and fled.

Koshchei the Deathless was returning home when his good steed stumbled beneath him.

' Why stumblest thou ? Scentest thou any ill ? '

' Prince Ivan has come and has carried off Marya Morevna.'

Koshchei galloped off, caught Prince Ivan, chopped him into little pieces, put them into a barrel, smeared it with pitch and bound it with iron hoops, and flung it into the blue sea. But Marya Morevna he carried off home.

At that very time the silver articles turned black which Prince Ivan had left with his brothers-in-law.

' Ah ! ' said they, ' the evil is accomplished sure enough ! '

Then the Eagle hurried to the blue sea, caught hold of the barrel, and dragged it ashore ; the Falcon flew away for the Water of Life, and the Raven for the Water of Death.

Afterwards they all three met, broke open the barrel, took out the remains of Prince Ivan, washed them, and put them together in fitting order. The Raven sprinkled them with the Water of Death—the pieces joined together, the body became whole. The Falcon sprinkled it with the Water of Life—Prince Ivan shuddered, stood up, and said :

' Ah ! what a time I ve been sleeping ! '

' You'd have gone on sleeping a good deal longer if it hadn't been for us,' replied his brothers-in-law. ' Now come and pay us a visit.'

' Not so, brothers ; I shall go and look for Marya Morevna.'

And when he had found her, he said to her :

' Find out from Koshchei the Deathless whence he got so good a steed.'

So Marya Morevna chose a favourable moment, and began asking Koshchei about it. Koshchei replied :

' Beyond thrice nine lands, in the thirtieth kingdom, on the other side of the fiery river, there lives a Baba Yaga. She has so good a mare that she flies right round the world on it every day. And she has many other splendid mares. I watched her herds for three days without losing a single mare, and in return for that the Baba Yaga gave me a foal.'

' But how did you get across the fiery river ? '

' Why, I've a handkerchief of this kind—when I wave it thrice on the right hand, there springs up a very lofty bridge, and the fire cannot reach it.'

Marya Morevna listened to all this, and repeated it to Prince Ivan, and she carried off the handkerchief and gave it to him. So he managed to get across the fiery river, and then went on to the

Baba Yaga's. Long went he on without getting anything either to
eat or to drink. At last he came across an outlandish bird and its
young ones. Says Prince Ivan :

'I'll eat one of these chickens.'

'Don't eat it, Prince Ivan!' begs the outlandish bird ; 'some
time or other I'll do you a good turn.'

He went on farther and saw a hive of bees in the forest.

'I'll get a bit of honeycomb,' says he.

'Don't disturb my honey, Prince Ivan!' exclaims the queen-
bee ; 'some time or other I'll do you a good turn.'

So he didn't disturb it, but went on. Presently there met him
a lioness with her cub.

'Anyhow, I'll eat this lion cub,' says he ; 'I'm so hungry I feel
quite unwell!'

'Please let us alone, Prince Ivan!' begs the lioness; 'some time or other I'll do you a good turn.'

'Very well; have it your own way,' says he.

Hungry and faint he wandered on, walked farther and farther, and at last came to where stood the house of the Baba Yaga. Round the house were set twelve poles in a circle, and on each of eleven of these poles was stuck a human head; the twelfth alone remained unoccupied.

'Hail, granny!'

'Hail, Prince Ivan! wherefore have you come? Is it of your own accord, or on compulsion?'

'I have come to earn from you an heroic steed.'

'So be it, Prince! You won't have to serve a year with me, but just three days. If you take good care of my mares, I'll give you an heroic steed. But if you don't—why, then you mustn't be annoyed at finding your head stuck on top of the last pole up there.'

Prince Ivan agreed to these terms. The Baba Yaga gave him food and drink, and bade him set about his business. But the moment he had driven the mares afield, they cocked up their tails, and away they tore across the meadows in all directions. Before the Prince had time to look round they were all out of sight. Thereupon he began to weep and to disquiet himself, and then he sat down upon a stone and went to sleep. But when the sun was near its setting the outlandish bird came flying up to him, and awakened him, saying:

'Arise, Prince Ivan! The mares are at home now.'

The Prince arose and returned home. There the Baba Yaga was storming and raging at her mares, and shrieking:

'Whatever did ye come home for?'

'How could we help coming home?' said they. 'There came flying birds from every part of the world, and all but pecked our eyes out.'

'Well, well! to-morrow don't go galloping over the meadows, but disperse amid the thick forests.'

Prince Ivan slept all night. In the morning the Baba Yaga says to him:

'Mind, Prince! if you don't take good care of the mares, if you lose merely one of them—your bold head will be stuck on that pole!'

He drove the mares afield. Immediately they cocked up their tails and dispersed among the thick forests. Again did the Prince sit down on the stone, weep and weep, and then go to sleep. The sun went down behind the forest. Up came running the lioness.

'Arise, Prince Ivan! The mares are all collected.'

Prince Ivan arose and went home. More than ever did the Baba Yaga storm at her mares and shriek:

'Whatever did ye come back home for?'

'How could we help coming back? Beasts of prey came running at us from all parts of the world, and all but tore us utterly to pieces.'

'Well, to-morrow run off into the blue sea.'

Again did Prince Ivan sleep through the night. Next morning the Baba Yaga sent him forth to watch the mares.

'If you don't take good care of them,' says she, 'your bold head will be stuck on that pole!'

He drove the mares afield. Immediately they cocked up their tails, disappeared from sight, and fled into the blue sea. There they stood, up to their necks in water. Prince Ivan sat down on the stone, wept, and fell asleep. But when the sun had set behind the forest, up came flying a bee, and said:

'Arise, Prince! The mares are all collected. But when you get home, don't let the Baba Yaga set eyes on you, but go into the stable and hide behind the mangers. There you will find a sorry colt rolling in the muck. Do you steal it, and at the dead of night ride away from the house.'

Prince Ivan arose, slipped into the stable, and lay down behind the mangers, while the Baba Yaga was storming away at her mares and shrieking:

'Why did ye come back?'

'How could we help coming back? There came flying bees in countless numbers from all parts of the world, and began stinging us on all sides till the blood came!'

The Baba Yaga went to sleep. In the dead of the night Prince Ivan stole the sorry colt, saddled it, jumped on its back, and galloped away to the fiery river. When he came to that river he waved the handkerchief three times on the right hand, and suddenly, springing goodness knows whence, there hung across the river, high in the air, a splendid bridge. The Prince rode across the bridge and waved the handkerchief twice only on the left hand; there remained across the river a thin, ever so thin a bridge!

When the Baba Yaga got up in the morning the sorry colt was not to be seen! Off she set in pursuit. At full speed did she fly in her iron mortar, urging it on with the pestle, sweeping away her traces with the broom. She dashed up to the fiery river, gave a glance, and said, 'A capital bridge!' She drove on to the bridge, but had only got half-way when the bridge broke in two, and the Baba Yaga went flop into the river. There truly did she meet with a cruel death!

Prince Ivan fattened up the colt in the green meadows, and it turned into a wondrous steed. Then he rode to where Marya

Morevna was. She came running out, and flung herself on his neck, crying:

'By what means has God brought you back to life?'

'Thus and thus,' says he. 'Now come along with me.'

'I am afraid, Prince Ivan! If Koshchei catches us you will be cut in pieces again.'

'No, he won't catch us! I have a splendid heroic steed now; it flies just like a bird.' So they got on its back and rode away.

Koshchei the Deathless was returning home when his horse stumbled beneath him.

'What art thou stumbling for, sorry jade? Dost thou scent any ill?'

'Prince Ivan has come and carried off Marya Morevna.'

'Can we catch them?'

'God knows! Prince Ivan has a horse now which is better than I.'

'Well, I can't stand it,' says Koshchei the Deathless. 'I will pursue.'

After a time he came up with Prince Ivan, lighted on the ground, and was going to chop him up with his sharp sword. But at that moment Prince Ivan's horse smote Koshchei the Deathless full swing with its hoof, and cracked his skull, and the Prince made an end of him with a club. Afterwards the Prince heaped up a pile of wood, set fire to it, burnt Koshchei the Deathless on the pyre, and scattered his ashes to the wind. Then Marya Morevna mounted Koshchei's horse and Prince Ivan got on his own, and they rode away to visit first the Raven, and then the Eagle, and then the Falcon. Wherever they went they met with a joyful greeting.

'Ah, Prince Ivan! why, we never expected to see you again. Well, it wasn't for nothing that you gave yourself so much trouble. Such a beauty as Marya Morevna one might search for all the world over—and never find one like her!'

And so they visited, and they feasted; and afterwards they went off to their own realm.[1]

[1] Ralston.

THE BLACK THIEF
AND KNIGHT OF THE GLEN.

IN times of yore there was a King and a Queen in the south of
Ireland who had three sons, all beautiful children; but the
Queen, their mother, sickened unto death when they were yet very
young, which caused great grief throughout the Court, particularly
to the King, her husband, who could in no wise be comforted.
Seeing that death was drawing near her, she called the King to her
and spoke as follows:

'I am now going to leave you, and as you are young and in
your prime, of course after my death you will marry again. Now
all the request I ask of you is that you will build a tower in an
island in the sea, wherein you will keep your three sons until they
are come of age and fit to do for themselves; so that they may not
be under the power or jurisdiction of any other woman. Neglect not
to give them education suitable to their birth, and let them be
trained up to every exercise and pastime requisite for king's sons to
learn. This is all I have to say, so farewell.'

The King had scarce time, with tears in his eyes, to assure her
she should be obeyed in everything, when she, turning herself in
her bed, with a smile gave up the ghost. Never was greater
mourning seen than was throughout the Court and the whole
kingdom; for a better woman than the Queen, to rich and poor,
was not to be found in the world. She was interred with great
pomp and magnificence, and the King, her husband, became in
a manner inconsolable for the loss of her. However, he caused
the tower to be built and his sons placed in it, under proper
guardians, according to his promise.

In process of time the lords and knights of the kingdom coun-
selled the King (as he was young) to live no longer as he had done,
but to take a wife; which counsel prevailing, they chose him a rich
and beautiful princess to be his consort—a neighbouring King's

daughter, of whom he was very fond. Not long after, the Queen had a fine son, which caused great feasting and rejoicing at the Court, insomuch that the late Queen, in a manner, was entirely forgotten. That fared well, and King and Queen lived happy together for several years.

At length the Queen, having some business with the hen-wife, went herself to her, and, after a long conference passed, was taking leave of her, when the hen-wife prayed that if ever she should come back to her again she might break her neck. The Queen, greatly incensed at such a daring insult from one of her meanest subjects, demanded immediately the reason, or she would have her put to death.

'It was worth your while, madam,' says the hen-wife, 'to pay me well for it, for the reason I prayed so on you concerns you much.'

'What must I pay you?' asked the Queen.

'You must give me,' says she, 'the full of a pack of wool, and I have an ancient crock which you must fill with butter, likewise a barrel which you must fill for me full of wheat.'

'How much wool will it take to the pack?' says the Queen.

'It will take seven herds of sheep,' said she, 'and their increase for seven years.'

'How much butter will it take to fill your crock?'

'Seven dairies,' said she, 'and their increase for seven years.'

'And how much will it take to fill the barrel you have?' says the Queen.

'It will take the increase of seven barrels of wheat for seven years.'

'That is a great quantity,' says the Queen; 'but the reason must be extraordinary, and before I want it, I will give you all you demand.'

'Well,' says the hen-wife, 'it is because you are so stupid that you don't observe or find out those affairs that are so dangerous and hurtful to yourself and your child.'

'What is that?' says the Queen.

'Why,' says she, 'the King your husband has three fine sons he had by the late Queen, whom he keeps shut up in a tower until they come of age, intending to divide the kingdom between them, and let your son push his fortune; now, if you don't find some means of destroying them; your child and perhaps yourself will be left desolate in the end.'

'And what would you advise me to do?' said she; 'I am wholly at a loss in what manner to act in this affair.'

' You must make known to the King,' says the hen-wife, ' that you heard of his sons, and wonder greatly that he concealed them all this time from you; tell him you wish to see them, and that it is full time for them to be liberated, and that you would be desirous he would bring them to the Court.   The King will then do so, and there will be a great feast prepared on that account, and also diversions of every sort to amuse the people; and in these sports,' said she, ' ask the King's sons to play a game at cards with you, which they will not refuse.   Now,' says the hen-wife, ' you must make a bargain, that if you win they must do whatever you command them, and if they win, that you must do whatever they command you to do; this bargain must be made before the assembly, and here is a pack of cards,' says she, ' that I am thinking you will not lose by.'

The Queen immediately took the cards, and, after returning the hen-wife thanks for her kind instruction, went back to the palace, where she was quite uneasy until she got speaking to the King in regard of his children; at last she broke it off to him in a very polite and engaging manner, so that he could see no muster or design in it.   He readily consented to her desire, and his sons were sent for to the tower, who gladly came to Court, rejoicing that they were freed from such confinement.   They were all very handsome, and very expert in all arts and exercises, so that they gained the love and esteem of all that had seen them.

The Queen, more jealous with them than ever, thought it an age until all the feasting and rejoicing was over, that she might get making her proposal, depending greatly on the power of the hen-wife's cards.   At length this royal assembly began to sport and play at all kinds of diversions, and the Queen very cunningly challenged the three Princes to play at cards with her, making bargain with them as she had been instructed.

They accepted the challenge, and the eldest son and she played the first game, which she won; then the second son played, and she won that game likewise; the third son and she then played the last game, and he won it, which sorely grieved her that she had not him in her power as well as the rest, being by far the handsomest and most beloved of the three.

However, everyone was anxious to hear the Queen's commands in regard to the two Princes, not thinking that she had any ill design in her head against them.   Whether it was the hen-wife instructed her, or whether it was from her own knowledge, I cannot

tell; but she gave out they must go and bring her the Knight of
the Glen's wild Steed of Bells, or they should lose their heads.

The young Princes were not in the least concerned, not knowing
what they had to do; but the whole Court was amazed at her
demand, knowing very well that it was impossible for them ever to
get the steed, as all that ever sought him perished in the attempt.
However, they could not retract the bargain, and the youngest

Prince was desired to tell what demand he had on the Queen, as he
had won his game.

'My brothers,' says he, 'are now going to travel, and, as I understand, a perilous journey wherein they know not what road to take
or what may happen them. I am resolved, therefore, not to stay
here, but to go with them, let what will betide; and I request and
command, according to my bargain, that the Queen shall stand on

the highest tower of the palace until we come back (or find out that we are certainly dead), with nothing but sheaf corn for her food and cold water for her drink, if it should be for seven years and longer.'

All things being now fixed, the three princes departed the Court in search of the Knight of the Glen's palace, and travelling along the road they came up with a man who was a little lame, and seemed to be somewhat advanced in years; they soon fell into discourse, and the youngest of the princes asked the stranger his name, or what was the reason he wore so remarkable a black cap as he saw on him.

'I am called,' said he, 'the Thief of Sloan, and sometimes the Black Thief from my cap ; ' and so telling the prince the most of his adventures, he asked him again where they were bound for, or what they were about.

The prince, willing to gratify his request, told him their affairs from the beginning to the end. 'And now,' said he, 'we are travelling, and do not know whether we are on the right road or not.'

'Ah ! my brave fellows,' says the Black Thief, 'you little know the danger you run. I am after that steed myself these seven years, and can never steal him on account of a silk covering he has on him in the stable, with sixty bells fixed to it, and whenever you approach the place he quickly observes it and shakes himself; which, by the sound of the bells, not only alarms the prince and his guards, but the whole country round, so that it is impossible ever to get him, and those that are so unfortunate as to be taken by the Knight of the Glen are boiled in a red-hot fiery furnace.'

'Bless me,' says the young prince, 'what will we do ? If we return without the steed we will lose our heads, so I see we are ill fixed on both sides.'

'Well,' says the Thief of Sloan, 'if it were my case I would rather die by the Knight than by the wicked Queen ; besides, I will go with you myself and show you the road, and whatever fortune you will have, I will take chance of the same.'

They returned him sincere thanks for his kindness, and he, being well acquainted with the road, in a short time brought them within view of the knight's castle.

'Now,' says he, 'we must stay here till night comes; for I know all the ways of the place, and if there be any chance for it, it is when they are all at rest; for the steed is all the watch the knight keeps there.'

Accordingly, in the dead hour of the night, the King's three sons and the Thief of Sloan attempted the Steed of Bells in order to carry him away, but before they could reach the stables the steed neighed most terribly and shook himself so, and the bells rung with such noise, that the knight and all his men were up in a moment.

The Black Thief and the King's sons thought to make their escape, but they were suddenly surrounded by the knight's guards and taken prisoners; where they were brought into that dismal part of the palace where the knight kept a furnace always boiling, in which he threw all offenders that ever came in his way, which in a few moments would entirely consume them.

'Audacious villains!' says the Knight of the Glen, 'how dare you attempt so bold an action as to steal my steed? See, now, the reward of your folly; for your greater punishment I will not boil you all together, but one after the other, so that he that survives may witness the dire afflictions of his unfortunate companions.'

So saying he ordered his servants to stir up the fire: 'We will boil the eldest-looking of these young men first,' said he, 'and so on to the last, which will be this old champion with the black cap. He seems to be the captain, and looks as if he had come through many toils.'

'I was as near death once as the prince is yet,' says the Black Thief, 'and escaped; and so will he too.'

'No, you never were,' said the knight; 'for he is within two or three minutes of his latter end.'

'But,' says the Black Thief, 'I was within one moment of my death, and I am here yet.'

'How was that?' says the knight; 'I would be glad to hear it, for it seems impossible.'

'If you think, sir knight,' says the Black Thief, 'that the danger I was in surpasses that of this young man, will you pardon him his crime?'

'I will,' says the knight, 'so go on with your story.'

'I was, sir,' says he, 'a very wild boy in my youth, and came through many distresses; once in particular, as I was on my rambling, I was benighted and could find no lodging. At length I came to an old kiln, and being much fatigued I went up and lay on the ribs. I had not been long there when I saw three witches coming in with three bags of gold. Each put their bags of gold under their heads, as if to sleep. I heard one of them say to the other that if the Black Thief came on them while they slept, he would not leave them a penny. I found by their discourse that everybody had got my name into their mouth, though I kept silent as death during their discourse. At length they fell fast asleep, and

then I stole softly down, and seeing some turf convenient, I placed one under each of their heads, and off I went, with their gold, as fast as I could.

'I had not gone far,' continued the Thief of Sloan, 'until I saw a greyhound, a hare, and a hawk in pursuit of me, and began to think it must be the witches that had taken the shapes in order that I might not escape them unseen either by land or water. Seeing they did not appear in any formidable shape, I was more than once resolved to attack them, thinking that with my

broad sword I could easily destroy them. But considering again that it was perhaps still in their power to become alive again, I gave over the attempt and climbed with difficulty up a tree, bringing my sword in my hand and all the gold along with me. However, when they came to the tree they found what I had done, and making further use of their hellish art, one of them was changed into a smith's anvil and another into a piece of iron, of which the third soon made a hatchet. Having the hatchet made, she fell to cutting down the tree, and in the course of an hour it began to shake with me. At length it began to bend, and I found that one or two blows at the most would put it down. I then began to think that my death was inevitable, considering that those who were capable of doing so much would soon end my life; but just as she had the stroke drawn that would terminate my fate, the cock crew, and the witches disappeared, having resumed their natural shapes for fear of being known, and I got safe off with my bags of gold.

'Now, sir,' says he to the Knight of the Glen, 'if that be not as great an adventure as ever you heard, to be within one blow of a hatchet of my end, and that blow even drawn, and after all to escape, I leave it to yourself.'

'Well, I cannot say but it is very extraordinary,' says the Knight of the Glen, 'and on that account pardon this young man his crime; so stir up the fire, till I boil this second one.'

'Indeed,' says the Black Thief, 'I would fain think he would not die this time either.'

'How so?' says the knight; 'it is impossible for him to escape.'

'I escaped death more wonderfully myself,' says the Thief of Sloan, 'than if you had him ready to throw into the furnace, and I hope it will be the case with him likewise.'

'Why, have you been in another great danger?' says the knight. 'I would be glad to hear the story too, and if it be as wonderful as the last, I will pardon this young man as I did the other.'

'My way of living, sir,' says the Black Thief, 'was not good, as I told you before; and being at a certain time fairly run out of cash, and meeting with no enterprise worthy of notice, I was reduced to great straits. At length a rich bishop died in the neighbourhood I was then in, and I heard he was interred with a great deal of jewels and rich robes upon him, all which I intended in a short time to be master of. Accordingly that very night I set about it, and coming to the place, I understood he was placed at the further end of a long dark vault, which I slowly entered. I had not gone in far until I heard a foot coming towards me with a quick pace, and although naturally bold and daring, yet, thinking of the deceased bishop and the crime I was engaged in, I lost courage, and ran towards the entrance of the vault. I had retreated but a few paces when I observed, between me and the light, the figure of a tall black man standing in the entrance. Being in great fear and not knowing how to pass, I fired a pistol at him, and he immediately fell across the entrance. Perceiving he still retained the figure of a mortal man, I began to imagine that it could not be the bishop's ghost ; recovering myself therefore from the fear I was in, I ventured to the upper end of the vault, where I found a large bundle, and upon further examination I found that the corpse was already rifled, and that which I had taken to be a ghost was no more than one of his own clergy. I was then very sorry that I had the misfortune to kill him, but it then could not be helped. I took up the bundle that contained everything belonging to the corpse that was valuable, intending to take my departure from this melancholy abode; but just as I came to the mouth of the entrance I saw the guards of the place coming towards me, and distinctly heard them saying that they would look in the vault, for that the Black Thief would think little of robbing the corpse if he was any-where in the place. I did not then know in what manner to act, for if I was seen I would surely lose my life, as everybody had a look-out at that time, and because there was no person bold enough to come in on me. I knew very well on the first sight of me that could be got, I would be shot like a dog. However, I had not time to lose. I took and raised up the man which I had killed, as if he was standing on his feet, and I, crouching behind him, bore him up as well as I could, so that the guards readily saw him as they came up to the vault. Seeing the man in black, one of the men cried that was the Black Thief, and, presenting his piece, fired at the man, at which I let him fall, and crept into a little dark corner myself, that was at the entrance of the place. When they saw the man fall, they ran all into the vault, and never stopped until they were at the end of it, for fear, as I thought, that there might be some others along with him that was killed. But while they were busy in-specting the corpse and the vault to see what they could miss, I slipped out, and, once away, and still away ; but they never had the Black Thief in their power since.'

'Well, my brave fellow,' says the Knight of the Glen, 'I see you have come through many dangers : you have freed these two princes by your stories ; but I am sorry myself that this young prince has to suffer for all. Now, if you could tell me something as wonderful as you have told already, I would pardon him likewise ; I pity this youth and do not want to put him to death if I could help it.'

'That happens well,' says the Thief of Sloan, 'for I like him best myself, and have reserved the most curious passage for the last on his account.'

'Well, then,' says the knight, 'let us hear it.'

'I was one day on my travels,' says the Black Thief, 'and I came into a large forest, where I wandered a long time, and could not get out of it. At length I came to a large castle, and fatigue obliged me to call in the same, where I found a young woman and a child sitting on her knee, and she crying. I asked her what made her cry, and where the lord of the castle was, for I wondered greatly that I saw no stir of servants or any person about the place.

' " It is well for you," says the young woman, " that the lord of this castle is not at home at present; for he is a monstrous giant, with but one eye on his forehead, who lives on human flesh. He brought me this child," says she, " I do not know where he got it, and ordered me to make it into a pie, and I cannot help crying at the command."

' I told her that if she knew of any place convenient that I could leave the child safely I would do it, rather than it should be killed by such a monster.

' She told me of a house a distance off where I would get a woman who would take care of it. " But what will I do in regard of the pie ? "

' " Cut a finger off it," said I, " and I will bring you in a young wild pig out of the forest, which you may dress as if it was the child, and put the finger in a certain place, that if the giant doubts anything about it you may know where to turn it over at the first, and when he sees it he will be fully satisfied that the pie is made of the child."

' She agreed to the scheme I proposed, and, cutting off the child's finger, by her direction I soon had it at the house she told me of, and brought her the little pig in the place of it. She then made ready the pie, and after eating and drinking heartily myself, I was just taking my leave of the young woman when we observed the giant coming through the castle gates.

'" Bless me," said she, " what will you do now ? Run away and lie down among the dead bodies that he has in the room (showing me the place), and strip off your clothes that he may not know you from the rest if he has occasion to go that way."

'I took her advice, and laid myself down among the rest, as if dead, to see how he would behave. The first thing I heard was

him calling for his pie. When she set it down before him he swore it smelled like swine's flesh, but knowing where to find the finger, she immediately turned it up, which fairly convinced him of the contrary. The pie only served to sharpen his appetite, and I heard him sharpening his knife and saying he must have a collop or two, for he was not near satisfied. But what was my terror when I heard the giant groping among the bodies, and, fancying myself, cut the half of my hip off, and took it with him to be roasted. You may be certain I was in great pain, but the fear of being killed prevented me from making any complaint. However, when he had eaten all he began to drink hot liquors in great abundance, so that in a short time he could not hold up his head, but threw himself on a large creel he had made for the purpose, and fell fast asleep. When I heard him snoring, as I was I went up and caused the woman to bind my wound with a handkerchief; and, taking the giant's spit, reddened it in the fire, and ran it through the eye, but was not able to kill him.

' However, I left the spit sticking in his head, and took to my heels; but I soon found he was in pursuit of me, although blind; and having an enchanted ring he threw it at me, and it fell on my big toe and remained fastened to it.

' The giant then called to the ring, where it was, and to my great surprise it made him answer on my foot; and he, guided by the same, made a leap at me which I had the good luck to observe, and fortunately escaped the danger. However, I found running was of no use in saving me, as long as I had the ring on my foot; so I took my sword and cut off the toe it was fastened on, and threw both into a large fish-pond that was convenient. The giant called again to the ring, which by the power of enchantment always made him answer; but he, not knowing what I had done, imagined it was still on some part of me, and made a violent leap to seize me, when he went into the pond, over head and ears, and was drowned. Now, sir knight,' says the Thief of Sloan, ' you see what dangers I came through and always escaped; but, indeed, I am lame for the want of my toe ever since.'

' My lord and master,' says an old woman that was listening all the time, ' that story is but too true, as I well know, for I am the very woman that was in the giant's castle, and you, my lord, the child that I was to make into a pie; and this is the very man that saved your life, which you may know by the want of your finger that was taken off, as you have heard, to deceive the giant.'

The Knight of the Glen, greatly surprised at what he had heard the old woman tell, and knowing he wanted his finger from his childhood, began to understand that the story was true enough.

' And is this my deliverer? ' says he. ' O brave fellow, I not only pardon you all, but will keep you with myself while you live, where you shall feast like princes, and have every attendance that I have myself.'

They all returned thanks on their knees, and the Black Thief told him the reason they attempted to steal the Steed of Bells, and the necessity they were under in going home.

' Well,' says the Knight of the Glen, ' if that's the case I bestow you my steed rather than this brave fellow should die; so you may go when you please, only remember to call and see me betimes, that we may know each other well.'

They promised they would, and with great joy they set off for the King their father's palace, and the Black Thief along with them.

The wicked Queen was standing all this time on the tower, and, hearing the bells ringing at a great distance off, knew very well it was the princes coming home, and the steed with them, and through spite and vexation precipitated herself from the tower and was shattered to pieces.

The three princes lived happy and well during their father's reign, and always keeping the Black Thief along with them ; but how they did after the old King's death is not known.[1]

[1] The Hibernian Tales.

THE MASTER THIEF

THERE was once upon a time a husbandman who had three sons. He had no property to bequeath to them, and no means of putting them in the way of getting a living, and did not know what to do, so he said that they had his leave to take to anything they most fancied, and go to any place they best liked. He would gladly accompany them for some part of their way, he said, and that he did. He went with them till they came to a place where three roads met, and there each of them took his own way, and the father bade them farewell and returned to his own home again. What became of the two elder I have never been able to discover, but the youngest went both far and wide.

It came to pass, one night, as he was going through a great wood, that a terrible storm came on. It blew so hard and rained so heavily that he could scarcely keep his eyes open, and before he was aware of it he had got quite out of the track, and could neither find road nor path. But he went on, and at last he saw a light far away in the wood. Then he thought he must try and get to it, and after a long, long time he did reach it. There was a large house, and the fire was burning so brightly inside that he could tell that the people were not in bed. So he went in, and inside there was an old woman who was busy about some work.

'Good evening, mother!' said the youth.

'Good evening!' said the old woman.

'Hutetu! it is terrible weather outside to-night,' said the young fellow.

'Indeed it is,' said the old woman.

'Can I sleep here, and have shelter for the night?' asked the youth.

'It wouldn't be good for you to sleep here,' said the old hag, 'for if the people of the house come home and find you, they will kill both you and me.'

'What kind of people are they then, who dwell here?' said the youth.

'Oh! robbers, and rabble of that sort,' said the old woman; 'they stole me away when I was little, and I have had to keep house for them ever since.'

'I still think I will go to bed, all the same,' said the youth. 'No matter what happens, I'll not go out to-night in such weather as this.'

'Well, then, it will be the worse for yourself,' said the old woman.

The young man lay down in a bed which stood near, but he dared not go to sleep; and it was better that he didn't, for the robbers came, and the old woman said that a young fellow who was a stranger had come there, and she had not been able to get him to go away again.

'Did you see if he had any money?' said the robbers.

'He's not one to have money, he is a tramp! If he has a few clothes to his back, that is all.'

Then the robbers began to mutter to each other apart about what they should do with him, whether they should murder him, or what else they should do. In the meantime the boy got up and began to talk to them, and ask them if they did not want a man-servant, for he could find pleasure enough in serving them.

'Yes,' said they, 'if you have a mind to take to the trade that we follow, you may have a place here.'

'It's all the same to me what trade I follow,' said the youth, 'for when I came away from home my father gave me leave to take to any trade I fancied.'

'Have you a fancy for stealing, then?' said the robbers.

'Yes,' said the boy, for he thought that was a trade which would not take long to learn.

Not very far off there dwelt a man who had three oxen, one of which he was to take to the town to sell. The robbers had heard of this, so they told the youth that if he were able to steal the ox from him on the way, without his knowing, and without doing him any harm, he should have leave to be their servant-man. So the youth set off, taking with him a pretty shoe with a silver buckle that was lying about in the house. He put this in the road by which the man must go with his ox, and then went into the wood and hid himself under a bush. When the man came up he at once saw the shoe.

'That's a brave shoe,' said he. 'If I had but the fellow to it, I would carry it home with me, and then I should put my old woman into a good humour for once.'

For he had a wife who was so cross and ill-tempered that the time between the beatings she gave him was very short. But then he bethought himself that he could do nothing with one shoe if he had not the fellow to it, so he journeyed onwards and let it lie where it was. Then the youth picked up the shoe and hurried off away through the wood as fast as he was able, to get in front of the man, and then put the shoe in the road before him again.

When the man came with the ox and saw the shoe, he was quite vexed at having been so stupid as to leave the fellow to it lying where it was, instead of bringing it on with him.

'I will just run back again and fetch it now,' he said to himself, 'and then I shall take back a pair of good shoes to the old woman, and she may perhaps throw a kind word to me for once.'

So he went and searched and searched for the other shoe for a long, long time, but no shoe was to be found, and at last he was forced to go back with the one which he had.

In the meantime the youth had taken the ox and gone off with it. When the man got there and found that his ox was gone, he began to weep and wail, for he was afraid that when his old woman got to know she would be the death of him. But all at once it came into his head to go home and get the other ox, and drive it to the town, and take good care that his old wife knew nothing about it. So he did this; he went home and took the ox without his wife's knowing about it, and went on his way to the town with it. But the robbers they knew it well, because they got out their magic. So they told the youth that if he could take this ox also without the man knowing anything about it, and without doing him any hurt, he should then be on an equality with them.

'Well, that will not be a very hard thing to do,' thought the youth.

This time he took with him a rope and put it under his arms and tied himself up to a tree, which hung over the road that the man would have to take. So the man came with his ox, and when he saw the body hanging there he felt a little queer.

'What a hard lot yours must have been to make you hang yourself!' said he. 'Ah, well! you may hang there for me; I can't breathe life into you again.'

So on he went with his ox. Then the youth sprang down from

the tree, ran by a short cut and got before him, and once more hung
himself up on a tree in the road before the man.

'How I should like to know if you really were so sick at heart
that you hanged yourself there, or if it is only a hobgoblin that's

before me!' said the man. 'Ah, well! you may hang there for me,
whether you are a hobgoblin or not,' and on he went with his ox.

Once more the youth did just as he had done twice already;
jumped down from the tree, ran by a short cut through the wood,
and again hanged himself in the very middle of the road before him.

But when the man once more saw this he said to himself, 'What a bad business this is! Can they all have been so heavy-hearted that they have all three hanged themselves? No, I can't believe that it is anything but witchcraft! But I will know the truth,' he said; 'if the two others are still hanging there it is true but if they are not it's nothing else but witchcraft.'

So he tied up his ox and ran back to see if they really were hanging there. While he was going, and looking up at every tree as he went, the youth leapt down and took his ox and went off with it. Any one may easily imagine what a fury the man fell into when he came back and saw that his ox was gone. He wept and he raged, but at last he took comfort and told himself that the best thing to do was to go home and take the third ox, without letting his wife know anything about it, and then try to sell it so well that he got a good sum of money for it. So he went home and took the third ox, and drove it off without his wife knowing any-thing about it. But the robbers knew all about it, and they told the youth that if he could steal this as he had stolen the two others, he should be master of the whole troop. So the youth set out and went to the wood, and when the man was coming along with the ox he began to bellow loudly, just like a great ox some-where inside the wood. When the man heard that he was right glad, for he fancied he recognised the voice of his big bullock, and thought that now he should find both of them again. So he tied up the third, and ran away off the road to look for them in the wood. In the meantime the youth went away with the third ox. When the man returned and found that he had lost that too, he fell into such a rage that there was no bounds to it. He wept and lamented, and for many days he did not dare to go home again, for he was afraid that the old woman would slay him outright. The robbers, also, were not very well pleased at this, for they were forced to own that the youth was at the head of them all. So one day they made up their minds to set to work to do something which it was not in his power to accomplish, and they all took to the road together, and left him at home alone. When they were well out of the house, the first thing that he did was to drive the oxen out on the road, whereupon they all ran home again to the man from whom he had stolen them, and right glad was the husbandman to see them. Then he brought out all the horses the robbers had, and loaded them with the most valuable things which he could find— vessels of gold and of silver, and clothes and other magnificent things—and then he told the old woman to greet the robbers from him and thank them from him, and say that he had gone away, and that they would have a great deal of difficulty in finding him again, and with that he drove the horses out of the courtyard. After a long, long time he came to the road on which he was travelling when he came to the robbers. And when he had got very near home, and was in sight of the house where his father lived, he put on a uniform which he had found among the things he had taken from the robbers, and which was made just like a general's, and drove into the yard just as if he were a great man. Then he entered the house and asked if he could find a lodging there.

'No, indeed you can't!' said his father. 'How could I possibly be able to lodge such a great gentleman as you? It is all that I can do to find clothes and bedding for myself, and wretched they are.'

'You were always a hard man,' said the youth, 'and hard you are still if you refuse to let your own son come into your house.'

'Are you my son?' said the man.

'Do you not know me again then?' said the youth.

Then he recognised him and said, 'But what trade have you taken to that has made you such a great man in so short a time?'

'Oh, that I will tell you,' answered the youth. 'You said that I might take to anything I liked, so I apprenticed myself to some thieves and robbers, and now I have served my time and have become Master Thief.'

Now the Governor of the province lived by his father's cottage, and this Governor had such a large house and so much money that he did not even know how much it was, and he had a daughter too who was both pretty and dainty, and good and wise. So the Master Thief was determined to have her to wife, and told his father that he was to go to the Governor, and ask for his daughter for him. 'If he asks what trade I follow, you may say that I am a Master Thief,' said he.

'I think you must be crazy,' said the man, 'for you can't be in your senses if you think of anything so foolish.'

'You must go to the Governor and beg for his daughter—there is no help,' said the youth.

'But I dare not go to the Governor and say this. He is so rich and has so much wealth of all kinds,' said the man.

'There is no help for it,' said the Master Thief; 'go you must, whether you like it or not. If I can't get you to go by using good words, I will soon make you go with bad ones.'

But the man was still unwilling, so the Master Thief followed him, threatening him with a great birch stick, till he went weeping and wailing through the door to the Governor of the province.

'Now, my man, and what's amiss with you?' said the Governor.

So he told him that he had three sons who had gone away one day, and how he had given them permission to go where they chose, and take to whatsoever work they fancied. 'Now,' he said, 'the youngest of them has come home, and has threatened me till I have come to you to ask for your daughter for him, and I am to say that he is a Master Thief,' and again the man fell a-weeping and lamenting.

'Console yourself, my man,' said the Governor, laughing. 'You may tell him from me that he must first give me some proof of this. If he can steal the joint off the spit in the kitchen on Sunday, when every one of us is watching it, he shall have my daughter. Will you tell him that?'

The man did tell him, and the youth thought it would be easy enough to do it. So he set himself to work to catch three hares alive, put them in a bag, clad himself in some old rags so that he looked so poor and wretched that it was quite pitiable to see him, and in this guise on Sunday forenoon he sneaked into the passage with his bag, like any beggar boy. The Governor himself and every one in the house was in the kitchen, keeping watch over the joint. While they were doing this the youth let one of the hares slip out of his bag, and off it set and began to run round the yard.

'Just look at that hare,' said the people in the kitchen, and wanted to go out and catch it.

The Governor saw it too, but said, 'Oh, let it go! it's no use to think of catching a hare when it's running away.'

It was not long before the youth let another hare out, and the people in the kitchen saw this too, and thought that it was the same. So again they wanted to go out and catch it, but the Governor again told them that it was of no use to try.

Very soon afterwards, however, the youth let slip the third hare, and it set off and ran round and round the courtyard. The people in the kitchen saw this too, and believed that it was still the same hare that was running about, so they wanted to go out and catch it.

'It's a remarkably fine hare!' said the Governor. 'Come

and let us see if we can get hold of it.' So out he went, and the
others with him, and away went the hare, and they after it, in real
earnest.

In the meantime, however, the Master Thief took the joint and
ran off with it, and whether the Governor got any roast meat for
his dinner that day I know not, but I know that he had no roast
hare, though he chased it till he was both hot and tired.

At noon came the Priest, and when the Governor had told him

of the trick played by the Master Thief there was no end to the
ridicule he cast on the Governor.

'For my part,' said the Priest, 'I can't imagine myself being
made a fool of by such a fellow as that!'

'Well, I advise you to be careful,' said the Governor, 'for he
may be with you before you are at all aware.'

But the Priest repeated what he had said, and mocked the
Governor for having allowed himself to be made such a fool of.

Later in the afternoon the Master Thief came and wanted to have the Governor's daughter as he had promised.

'You must first give some more samples of your skill,' said the Governor, trying to speak him fair, 'for what you did to-day was no such very great thing after all. Couldn't you play off a really good trick on the Priest? for he is sitting inside there and calling me a fool for having let myself be taken in by such a fellow as you.'

'Well, it wouldn't be very hard to do that,' said the Master Thief. So he dressed himself up like a bird, and threw a great white sheet over himself; broke off a goose's wings, and set them on his back; and in this attire climbed into a great maple tree which stood in the Priest's garden. So when the Priest returned home in the evening the youth began to cry, 'Father Lawrence! Father Lawrence!' for the Priest was called Father Lawrence.

'Who is calling me?' said the Priest.

'I am an angel sent to announce to thee that because of thy piety thou shalt be taken away alive into heaven,' said the Master Thief. 'Wilt thou hold thyself in readiness to travel away next Monday night? for then will I come and fetch thee, and bear thee away with me in a sack, and thou must lay all thy gold and silver, and whatsoever thou may'st possess of this world's wealth, in a heap in thy best parlour.'

So Father Lawrence fell down on his knees before the angel and thanked him, and the following Sunday he preached a farewell sermon, and gave out that an angel had come down into the large maple tree in his garden, and had announced to him that, because of his righteousness, he should be taken up alive into heaven, and as he thus preached and told them this everyone in the church, old or young, wept.

On Monday night the Master Thief once more came as an angel, and before the Priest was put into the sack he fell on his knees and thanked him; but no sooner was the Priest safely inside it than the Master Thief began to drag him away over stocks and stones.

'Oh! oh!' cried the Priest in the sack. 'Where are you taking me?'

'This is the way to heaven. The way to heaven is not an easy one,' said the Master Thief, and dragged him along till he all but killed him.

At last he flung him into the Governor's goose-house, and the geese began to hiss and peck at him, till he felt more dead than alive.

'Oh! oh! oh! Where am I now?' asked the Priest.

'Now you are in Purgatory,' said the Master Thief, and off he went and took the gold and the silver and all the precious things which the Priest had laid together in his best parlour.

Next morning, when the goose-girl came to let out the geese, she heard the Priest bemoaning himself as he lay in the sack in the goose-house.

'Oh, heavens! who is that, and what ails you?' said she.

'Oh,' said the Priest, 'if you are an angel from heaven do let me out and let me go back to earth again, for no place was ever so bad as this—the little fiends nip me so with their tongs.'

'I am no angel,' said the girl, and helped the Priest out of the sack. 'I only look after the Governor's geese, that's what I do, and they are the little fiends which have pinched your reverence.'

'This is the Master Thief's doing! Oh, my gold and my silver and my best clothes!' shrieked the Priest, and, wild with rage, he ran home so fast that the goose-girl thought he had suddenly gone mad.

When the Governor learnt what had happened to the Priest he laughed till he nearly killed himself, but when the Master Thief came and wanted to have his daughter according to promise, he once more gave him nothing but fine words, and said, 'You must give me one more proof of your skill, so that I can really judge of your worth. I have twelve horses in my stable, and I will put twelve stable boys in it, one on each horse. If you are clever enough to steal the horses from under them, I will see what I can do for you.'

'What you set me to do can be done,' said the Master Thief, 'but am I certain to get your daughter when it is?'

'Yes; if you can do that I will do my best for you,' said the Governor.

So the Master Thief went to a shop, and bought enough brandy to fill two pocket flasks, and he put a sleeping drink into one of these, but into the other he poured brandy only. Then he engaged eleven men to lie that night in hiding behind the Governor's stable. After this, by fair words and good payment, he borrowed a ragged gown and a jerkin from an aged woman, and then, with a staff in his hand and a poke on his back, he hobbled off as evening came on towards the Governor's stable. The stable boys were just watering the horses for the night, and it was quite as much as they could do to attend to that.

FATHER LAWRENCE, CONCEIVING HIMSELF TO BE ADDRESSED BY AN
ANGEL, FALLS ON HIS KNEES BEFORE HIM.

'What on earth do you want here?' said one of them to the old woman.

'Oh dear! oh dear! How cold it is!' she said, sobbing, and shivering with cold. 'Oh dear! oh dear! it's cold enough to freeze a poor old body to death!' and she shivered and shook again, and said, 'For heaven's sake give me leave to stay here and sit just inside the stable door.'

'You will get nothing of the kind! Be off this moment! If the Governor were to catch sight of you here, he would lead us a pretty dance,' said one.

'Oh! what a poor helpless old creature!' said another, who felt sorry for her. 'That poor old woman can do no harm to anyone. She may sit there and welcome.'

The rest of them thought that she ought not to stay, but while they were disputing about this and looking after the horses, she crept farther and farther into the stable, and at last sat down behind the door, and when once she was inside no one took any more notice of her.

As the night wore on the stable boys found it rather cold work to sit still on horseback.

'Hutetu! But it is fearfully cold!' said one, and began to beat his arms backwards and forwards across his breast.

'Yes, I am so cold that my teeth are chattering,' said another.

'If one had but a little tobacco,' said a third.

Well, one of them had a little, so they shared it among them, though there was very little for each man, but they chewed it. This was some help to them, but very soon they were just as cold as before.

'Hutetu!' said one of them, shivering again.

'Hutetu!' said the old woman, gnashing her teeth together till they chattered inside her mouth; and then she got out the flask which contained nothing but brandy, and her hands trembled so that she shook the bottle about, and when she drank it made a great gulp in her throat.

'What is that you have in your flask, old woman?' asked one of the stable boys.

'Oh, it's only a little drop of brandy, your honour,' she said.

'Brandy! What! Let me have a drop! Let me have a drop!' screamed all the twelve at once.

'Oh, but what I have is so little,' whimpered the old woman. 'It will not even wet your mouths.'

But they were determined to have it, and there was nothing to be done but give it ; so she took out the flask with the sleeping drink and put it to the lips of the first of them ; and now she shook no more, but guided the flask so that each of them got just as much as he ought, and the twelfth had not done drinking before the first was already sitting snoring. Then the Master Thief flung off his beggar's rags, and took one stable boy after the other and gently set him astride on the partitions which divided the stalls, and then he called his eleven men who were waiting outside, and they rode off with the Governor's horses.

In the morning when the Governor came to look after his stable boys they were just beginning to come to again. They were driving their spurs into the partition till the splinters flew about, and some of the boys fell off, and some still hung on and sat looking like fools. ' Ah, well,' said the Governor, ' it is easy to see who has been here ; but what a worthless set of fellows you must be to sit here and let the Master Thief steal the horses from under you ! ' And they all got a beating for not having kept watch better.

Later in the day the Master Thief came and related what he had done, and wanted to have the Governor's daughter as had been promised. But the Governor gave him a hundred dollars, and said that he must do something that was better still.

' Do you think you can steal my horse from under me when I am out riding on it ? ' said he.

' Well, it might be done,' said the Master Thief, ' if I were absolutely certain that I should get your daughter.'

So the Governor said that he would see what he could do, and then he said that on a certain day he would ride out to a great common where they drilled the soldiers.

So the Master Thief immediately got hold of an old worn-out mare, and set himself to work to make a collar for it of green withies and branches of broom ; bought a shabby old cart and a great cask, and then he told a poor old beggar woman that he would give her ten dollars if she would get into the cask and keep her mouth wide-open beneath the tap-hole, into which he was going to stick his finger. No harm should happen to her, he said ; she should only be driven about a little, and if he took his finger out more than once, she should have ten dollars more. Then he dressed himself in rags, dyed himself with soot, and put on a wig and a great beard of goat's hair, so that it was impossible to recognise him, and went to the parade ground, where the Governor had already been riding about a long time.

When the Master Thief got there the mare went along so slowly and quietly that the cart hardly seemed to move from the spot. The mare pulled it a little forward, and then a little back, and then it stopped quite short. Then the mare pulled a little forward again, and it moved with such difficulty that the Governor had not the least idea that this was the Master Thief. He rode straight up to him, and asked if he had seen anyone hiding anywhere about in a wood that was close by.

'No,' said the man, 'that have I not.'

'Hark you,' said the Governor. 'If you will ride into that wood,

and search it carefully to see if you can light upon a fellow who is hiding in there, you shall have the loan of my horse and a good present of money for your trouble.'

'I am not sure that I can do it,' said the man, 'for I have to go to a wedding with this cask of mead which I have been to fetch, and the tap has fallen out on the way, so now I have to keep my finger in the tap-hole as I drive.'

'Oh, just ride off,' said the Governor, 'and I will look after the cask and the horse too.'

So the man said that if he would do that he would go, but he begged the Governor to be very careful to put his finger into the tap-hole the moment he took his out.

So the Governor said that he would do his very best, and the Master Thief got on the Governor's horse.

But time passed, and it grew later and later, and still the man did not come back, and at last the Governor grew so weary of keeping his finger in the tap-hole that he took it out.

'Now I shall have ten dollars more!' cried the old woman inside the cask; so he soon saw what kind of mead it was, and set out homewards. When he had gone a very little way he met his servant bringing him the horse, for the Master Thief had already taken it home.

The following day he went to the Governor and wanted to have his daughter according to promise. But the Governor again put him off with fine words, and only gave him three hundred dollars, saying that he must do one more masterpiece of skill, and if he were but able to do that he should have her.

Well, the Master Thief thought he might if he could hear what it was.

'Do you think you can steal the sheet off our bed, and my wife's night-gown?' said the Governor.

'That is by no means impossible,' said the Master Thief. 'I only wish I could get your daughter as easily.'

So late at night the Master Thief went and cut down a thief who was hanging on the gallows, laid him on his own shoulders, and took him away with him. Then he got hold of a long ladder, set it up against the Governor's bedroom window, and climbed up and moved the dead man's head up and down, just as if he were some one who was standing outside and peeping in.

'There's the Master Thief, mother!' said the Governor, nudging his wife. 'Now I'll just shoot him, that I will!'

So he took up a rifle which he had laid at his bedside.

'Oh no, you must not do that,' said his wife; 'you yourself arranged that he was to come here.'

'Yes, mother, I will shoot him,' said he, and lay there aiming, and then aiming again, for no sooner was the head up and he caught sight of it than it was gone again. At last he got a chance and fired, and the dead body fell with a loud thud to the ground, and down went the Master Thief too, as fast as he could.

'Well,' said the Governor, 'I certainly am the chief man about here, but people soon begin to talk, and it would be very unpleasant

if they were to see this dead body; the best thing that I can do is
to go out and bury him.'

'Just do what you think best, father,' said his wife.

So the Governor got up and went downstairs, and as soon as he
had gone out through the door, the Master Thief stole in and went
straight upstairs to the woman.

'Well, father dear,' said she, for she thought it was her husband.
'Have you got done already?'

'Oh yes, I only put him into a hole,' said he, 'and raked a little
earth over him; that's all I have been able to do to-night, for it is
fearful weather outside. I will bury him better afterwards, but
just let me have the sheet to wipe myself with, for he was bleeding,
and I have got covered with blood with carrying him.'

So she gave him the sheet.

'You will have to let me have your night-gown too,' he said,
'for I begin to see that the sheet won't be enough.'

Then she gave him her night-gown, but just then it came into
his head that he had forgotten to lock the door, and he was forced
to go downstairs and do it before he could lie down in bed again.
So off he went with the sheet, and the night-gown too.

An hour later the real Governor returned.

'Well, what a time it has taken to lock the house door, father!'
said his wife, 'and what have you done with the sheet and the
night-gown?'

'What do you mean?' asked the Governor.

'Oh, I am asking you what you have done with the night-gown
and sheet that you got to wipe the blood off yourself with,' said she.

'Good heavens!' said the Governor, 'has he actually got the
better of me again?'

When day came the Master Thief came too, and wanted to
have the Governor's daughter as had been promised, and the
Governor dared do no otherwise than give her to him, and much
money besides, for he feared that if he did not the Master Thief
might steal the very eyes out of his head, and that he himself would
be ill spoken of by all men. The Master Thief lived well and happily
from that time forth, and whether he ever stole any more or not I
cannot tell you, but if he did it was but for pastime.

[1] From P. C. Asbjornsen.

BROTHER AND SISTER

BROTHER took sister by the hand and said : ' Look here ; we haven't had one single happy hour since our mother died. That stepmother of ours beats us regularly every day, and if we dare go near her she kicks us away. We never get anything but hard dry crusts to eat—why, the dog under the table is better off than we are. She does throw him a good morsel or two now and then. Oh dear ! if our own dear mother only knew all about it ! Come along, and let us go forth into the wide world together.'

So off they started through fields and meadows, over hedges and ditches, and walked the whole day long, and when it rained sister said :

' Heaven and our hearts are weeping together.'

Towards evening they came to a large forest, and were so tired out with hunger and their long walk, as well as all their trouble, that they crept into a hollow tree and soon fell fast asleep.

Next morning, when they woke up, the sun was already high in the heavens and was shining down bright and warm into the tree. Then said brother :

' I'm so thirsty, sister ; if I did but know where to find a little stream, I'd go and have a drink. I do believe I hear one.' He jumped up, took sister by the hand, and they set off to hunt for the brook.

Now their cruel stepmother was in reality a witch, and she knew perfectly well that the two children had run away. She had crept secretly after them, and had cast her spells over all the streams in the forest.

Presently the children found a little brook dancing and glittering over the stones, and brother was eager to drink of it, but as it rushed past sister heard it murmuring :

' Who drinks of me will be a tiger ! who drinks of me will be a tiger ! '

So she cried out, 'Oh! dear brother, pray don't drink, or you'll be turned into a wild beast and tear me to pieces.'

Brother was dreadfully thirsty, but he did not drink.

'Very well,' said he, 'I'll wait till we come to the next spring.'

When they came to the second brook, sister heard it repeating too:

'Who drinks of me will be a wolf! who drinks of me will be a wolf!'

And she cried, 'Oh! brother, pray don't drink here either, or you'll be turned into a wolf and eat me up.'

Again brother did not drink, but he said:

'Well, I'll wait a little longer till we reach the next stream, but then, whatever you may say, I really must drink, for I can bear this thirst no longer.'

And when they got to the third brook, sister heard it say as it rushed past:

'Who drinks of me will be a roe! who drinks of me will be a roe!'

And she begged, 'Ah! brother, don't drink yet, or you'll become a roe and run away from me.'

But her brother was already kneeling by the brook and bending over it to drink, and, sure enough, no sooner had his lips touched the water than he fell on the grass transformed into a little Roebuck.

Sister cried bitterly over her poor bewitched brother, and the little Roe wept too, and sat sadly by her side. At last the girl said :

' Never mind, dear little fawn, I will never forsake you,' and she took off her golden garter and tied it round the Roe's neck.

Then she plucked rushes and plaited a soft cord of them, which she fastened to the collar. When she had done this she led the Roe farther and farther, right into the depths of the forest.

After they had gone a long, long way they came to a little house, and when the girl looked into it she found it was quite empty, and she thought ' perhaps we might stay and live here.'

So she hunted up leaves and moss to make a soft bed for the little Roe, and every morning and evening she went out and gathered roots, nuts, and berries for herself, and tender young grass for the fawn. And he fed from her hand, and played round her and seemed quite happy. In the evening, when sister was tired, she said her prayers and then laid her head on the fawn's back and fell sound asleep with it as a pillow. And if brother had but kept his natural form, really it would have been a most delightful kind of life.

They had been living for some time in the forest in this way, when it came to pass that the King of that country had a great hunt through the woods. Then the whole forest rang with such a blowing of horns, baying of dogs, and joyful cries of huntsmen, that the little Roe heard it and longed to join in too.

' Ah ! ' said he to sister, ' do let me go off to the hunt ! I can't keep still any longer.'

And he begged and prayed till at last she consented.

' But,' said she, ' mind you come back in the evening. I shall lock my door fast for fear of those wild huntsmen ; so, to make sure of my knowing you, knock 'at the door and say, " My sister dear, open ; I'm here." If you don't speak I shan't open the door.'

So off sprang the little Roe, and he felt quite well and happy in the free open air.

The King and his huntsmen soon saw the beautiful creature and started in pursuit, but they could not come up with it, and whenever they thought they were sure to catch it, it bounded off to one side into the bushes and disappeared. When night came on it ran home, and knocking at the door of the little house cried :

' My sister dear, open ; I'm here.' The door opened, and he ran in and rested all night on his soft mossy bed.

Next morning the hunt began again, and as soon as the little Roe heard the horns and the ' Ho ! ho ! ' of the huntsmen, he could not rest another moment, and said :

' Sister, open the door, I must get out.'

So sister opened the door and said, ' Now mind and get back by nightfall, and say your little rhyme.'

As soon as the King and his huntsmen saw the Roe with the golden collar they all rode off after it, but it was far too quick and nimble for them. This went on all day, but as evening came on the huntsmen had gradually encircled the Roe, and one of them wounded it slightly in the foot, so that it limped and ran off slowly.

Then the huntsman stole after it as far as the little house, and heard it call out, ' My sister dear, open ; I'm here,' and he saw the door open and close immediately the fawn had run in.

The huntsman remembered all this carefully, and went off straight to the King and told him all he had seen and heard.

' To-morrow we will hunt again,' said the King.

Poor sister was terribly frightened when she saw how her little Fawn had been wounded. She washed off the blood, bound up the injured foot with herbs, and said : ' Now, dear, go and lie down and rest, so that your wound may heal.'

The wound was really so slight that it was quite well next day, and the little Roe did not feel it at all. No sooner did it hear the sounds of hunting in the forest than it cried :

' I can't stand this, I must be there too ; I'll take care they shan't catch me.'

Sister began to cry, and said, ' They are certain to kill you, and then I shall be left all alone in the forest and forsaken by everyone. I can't and won't let you out.'

' Then I shall die of grief,' replied the Roe, ' for when I hear that horn I feel as if I must jump right out of my skin.'

So at last, when sister found there was nothing else to be done, she opened the door with a heavy heart, and the Roe darted forth full of glee and health into the forest.

As soon as the King saw the Roe, he said to his huntsman, ' Now then, give chase to it all day till evening, but mind and be careful not to hurt it.'

When the sun had set the King said to his huntsman, ' Now come and show me the little house in the wood.'

And when he got to the house he knocked at the door and said, ' My sister dear, open ; I'm here.' Then the door opened and the King walked in, and there stood the loveliest maiden he had ever seen.

The girl was much startled when instead of the little Roe she expected she saw a man with a gold crown on his head walk in. But the King looked kindly at her, held out his hand, and said, ' Will you come with me to my castle and be my dear wife ? '

' Oh yes ! ' replied the maiden, ' but you must let my Roe come too. I could not possibly forsake it.'

' It shall stay with you as long as you live, and shall want for nothing,' the King promised.

In the meantime the Roe came bounding in, and sister tied the rush cord once more to its collar, took the end in her hand, and so they left the little house in the forest together.

The King lifted the lonely maiden on to his horse, and led her to his castle, where the wedding was celebrated with the greatest splendour. The Roe was petted and caressed, and ran about at will in the palace gardens.

Now all this time the wicked stepmother, who had been the cause of these poor children's misfortunes and trying adventures, was feeling fully persuaded that sister had been torn to pieces by wild beasts, and brother shot to death in the shape of a Roe. When she heard how happy and prosperous they were, her heart was filled with envy and hatred, and she could think of nothing but how to bring some fresh misfortune on them. Her own daughter, who was as hideous as night and had only one eye, reproached her by saying, ' It is I who ought to have had this good luck and been Queen.'

' Be quiet, will you,' said the old woman ; ' when the time comes I shall be at hand.'

Now after some time it happened one day when the King was out hunting that the Queen gave birth to a beautiful little boy. The old witch thought here was a good chance for her ; so she took the form of the lady in waiting, and, hurrying into the room where the Queen lay in her bed, called out, ' The bath is quite ready ; it will help to make you strong again. Come, let us be quick, for fear the water should get cold.' Her daughter was at hand, too, and between them they carried the Queen, who was still very weak, into the bath-room and laid her in the bath ; then they locked the door and ran away.

They took care beforehand to make a blazing hot fire under the bath, so that the lovely young Queen might be suffocated.

As soon as they were sure this was the case, the old witch tied a cap on her daughter's head and laid her in the Queen's bed. She managed, too, to make her figure and general appearance look like the Queen's, but even her power could not restore the eye she had lost; so she made her lie on the side of the missing eye, in order to prevent the King's noticing anything.

In the evening, when the King came home and heard the news of his son's birth, he was full of delight, and insisted on going at once to his dear wife's bedside to see how she was getting on. But the old witch cried out, 'Take care and keep the curtains drawn; don't let the light get into the Queen's eyes; she must be kept perfectly quiet.' So the King went away and never knew that it was a false Queen who lay in the bed.

When midnight came and everyone in the palace was sound asleep, the nurse who alone watched by the baby's cradle in the nursery saw the door open gently, and who should come in but the real Queen. She lifted the child from its cradle, laid it on her arm, and nursed it for some time. Then she carefully shook up the pillows of the little bed, laid the baby down and tucked the coverlet in all round him. She did not forget the little Roe either, but went to the corner where it lay, and gently stroked its back. Then she silently left the room, and next morning when the nurse asked the sentries if they had seen any one go into the castle that night, they all said, 'No, we saw no one at all.'

For many nights the Queen came in the same way, but she never spoke a word, and the nurse was too frightened to say anything about her visits.

After some little time had elapsed the Queen spoke one night, and said :

'Is my child well ?　Is my Roe well ?
I'll come back twice and then farewell.'

The nurse made no answer, but as soon as the Queen had disappeared she went to the King and told him all. The King exclaimed, 'Good heavens ! what do you say ? I will watch myself to-night by the child's bed.'

When the evening came he went to the nursery, and at midnight the Queen appeared and said :

'Is my child well ?　Is my Roe well ?
I'll come back once and then farewell.'

And she nursed and petted the child as usual before she disappeared. The King dared not trust himself to speak to her, but the following night he kept watch again.

That night when the Queen came she said :

'Is my child well ?　Is my Roe well ?
I've come this once, and now farewell.'

Then the King could restrain himself no longer, but sprang to her side and cried, 'You can be no one but my dear wife !'

'Yes,' said she, 'I am your dear wife !' and in the same moment she was restored to life, and was as fresh and well and rosy as ever. Then she told the King all the cruel things the wicked witch and her daughter had done. The King had them both arrested at once and brought to trial, and they were condemned to death. The daughter was led into the forest, where the wild beasts tore her to pieces, and the old witch was burnt at the stake.

As soon as she was reduced to ashes the spell was taken off the little Roe, and he was restored to his natural shape once more, and so brother and sister lived happily ever after.[1]

[1] Grimm.

PRINCESS ROSETTE

ONCE upon a time there lived a King and Queen who had two beautiful sons and one little daughter, who was so pretty that no one who saw her could help loving her. When it was time for the christening of the Princess, the Queen—as she always did—sent for all the fairies to be present at the ceremony, and afterwards invited them to a splendid banquet.

When it was over, and they were preparing to go away, the Queen said to them:

'Do not forget your usual good custom. Tell me what is going to happen to Rosette.'

For that was the name they had given the Princess.

But the fairies said they had left their book of magic at home, and they would come another day and tell her.

'Ah!' said the Queen, 'I know very well what that means—you have nothing good to say; but at least I beg that you will not hide anything from me.'

So, after a great deal of persuasion, they said:

'Madam, we fear that Rosette may be the cause of great misfortunes to her brothers; they may even meet with their death through her; that is all we have been able to foresee about your dear little daughter. We are very sorry to have nothing better to tell you.'

Then they went away, leaving the Queen very sad, so sad that the King noticed it, and asked her what was the matter.

The Queen said that she had been sitting too near the fire, and had burnt all the flax that was upon her distaff.

'Oh! is that all?' said the King, and he went up into the garret and brought her down more flax than she could spin in a hundred years. But the Queen still looked sad, and the King asked her again what was the matter. She answered that she had been walking by the river and had dropped one of her green satin slippers into the water.

'Oh! if that's all,' said the King, and he sent to all the shoe-makers in his kingdom, and they very soon made the Queen ten thousand green satin slippers, but still she looked sad. So the King asked her again what was the matter, and this time she answered that in eating her porridge too hastily she had swallowed her wedding-ring. But it so happened that the King knew better, for he had the ring himself, and he said:

'Oh! you are not telling me the truth, for I have your ring here in my purse.'

Then the Queen was very much ashamed, and she saw that the King was vexed with her; so she told him all that the fairies had predicted about Rosette, and begged him to think how the misfortunes might be prevented.

Then it was the King's turn to look sad, and at last he said:

'I see no way of saving our sons except by having Rosette's head cut off while she is still little.'

But the Queen cried that she would far rather have her own head cut off, and that he had better think of something else, for she would never consent to such a thing. So they thought and thought, but they could not tell what to do, until at last the Queen heard that in a great forest near the castle there was an old hermit, who lived in a hollow tree, and that people came from far and near to consult him; so she said:

'I had better go and ask his advice; perhaps he will know what to do to prevent the misfortunes which the fairies foretold.'

She set out very early the next morning, mounted upon a pretty little white mule, which was shod with solid gold, and two of her ladies rode behind her on beautiful horses. When they reached the forest they dismounted, for the trees grew so thickly that the horses could not pass, and made their way on foot to the hollow tree where the hermit lived. At first when he saw them coming he was vexed, for he was not fond of ladies; but when he recognised the Queen, he said:

'You are welcome, Queen. What do you come to ask of me?'

Then the Queen told him all the fairies had foreseen for Rosette, and asked what she should do, and the hermit answered that she must shut the Princess up in a tower and never let her come out of it again. The Queen thanked and rewarded him, and hastened back to the castle to tell the King. When he heard the news he had a great tower built as quickly as possible, and there the Princess was shut up, and the King and Queen and her two brothers went to see her every day that she might not be dull. The eldest brother was called 'the Great Prince,' and the second 'the Little Prince.' They loved their sister dearly, for she was the sweetest, prettiest princess who was ever seen, and the least little smile from her was worth more than a hundred pieces of gold. When Rosette was fifteen years old the Great Prince went to the King and asked if it would not soon be time for her to be married, and the Little Prince put the same question to the Queen.

Their majesties were amused at them for thinking of it, but did

not make any reply, and soon after both the King and the Queen were taken ill, and died on the same day. Everybody was sorry, Rosette especially, and all the bells in the kingdom were tolled.

Then all the dukes and counsellors put the Great Prince upon a golden throne, and crowned him with a diamond crown, and they all cried, 'Long live the King!' And after that there was nothing but feasting and rejoicing.

The new King and his brother said to one another:

' Now that we are the masters, let us take our sister out of that dull tower which she is so tired of.'

They had only to go across the garden to reach the tower, which was very high, and stood up in a corner. Rosette was busy at her embroidery, but when she saw her brothers she got up, and taking the King's hand cried :

' Good morning, dear brother. Now that you are King, please take me out of this dull tower, for I am so tired of it.'

Then she began to cry, but the King kissed her and told her to dry her tears, as that was just what they had come for, to take her out of the tower and bring her to their beautiful castle, and the Prince showed her the pocketful of sugar plums he had brought for her, and said :

' Make haste, and let us get away from this ugly tower, and very soon the King will arrange a grand marriage for you.'

When Rosette saw the beautiful garden, full of fruit and flowers, with green grass and sparkling fountains, she was so astonished that not a word could she say, for she had never in her life seen anything like it before. She looked about her, and ran hither and thither gathering fruit and flowers, and her little dog Frisk, who was bright green all over, and had but one ear, danced before her, crying ' Bow-wow-wow,' and turning head over heels in the most enchanting way.

Everybody was amused at Frisk's antics, but all of a sudden he ran away into a little wood, and the Princess was following him, when, to her great delight, she saw a peacock, who was spreading his tail in the sunshine. Rosette thought she had never seen anything so pretty. She could not take her eyes off him, and there she stood entranced until the King and the Prince came up and asked what was amusing her so much. She showed them the peacock, and asked what it was, and they answered that it was a bird which people sometimes ate.

' What ! ' said the Princess, ' do they dare to kill that beautiful creature and eat it ? I declare that I will never marry any one but the King of the Peacocks, and when I am Queen I will take very good care that nobody eats any of my subjects.'

At this the King was very much astonished.

' But, little sister,' said he, ' where shall we find the King of the Peacocks ? '

' Oh ! wherever you like, sire,' she answered, ' but I will never marry any one else.'

After this they took Rosette to the beautiful castle, and the peacock was brought with her, and told to walk about on the terrace outside her windows, so that she might always see him, and then the ladies of the court came to see the Princess, and they brought her beautiful presents—dresses and ribbons and sweetmeats, diamonds and pearls and dolls and embroidered slippers, and she was so well brought up, and said, 'Thank you!' so prettily, and was so gracious, that everyone went away delighted with her.

Meanwhile the King and the Prince were considering how they should find the King of the Peacocks, if there was such a person in the world. And first of all they had a portrait made of the Princess, which was so like her that you really would not have been surprised if it had spoken to you. Then they said to her :

'Since you will not marry anyone but the King of the Peacocks, we are going out together into the wide world to search for him. If we find him for you we shall be very glad. In the meantime, mind you take good care of our kingdom.'

Rosette thanked them for all the trouble they were taking on her account, and promised to take great care of the kingdom, and only to amuse herself by looking at the peacock, and making Frisk dance while they were away.

So they set out, and asked everyone they met—

'Do you know the King of the Peacocks?'

But the answer was always, 'No, no.'

Then they went on and on, so far that no one has ever been farther, and at last they came to the Kingdom of the Cockchafers.

They had never before seen such a number of cockchafers, and the buzzing was so loud that the King was afraid he should be deafened by it. He asked the most distinguished-looking cockchafer they met if he knew where they could find the King of the Peacocks.

'Sire,' replied the cockchafer, 'his kingdom is thirty thousand leagues from this ; you have come the longest way.'

'And how do you know that ?' said the King.

'Oh!' said the cockchafer, 'we all know you very well, since we spend two or three months in your garden every year.'

Thereupon the King and the Prince made great friends with him, and they all walked arm-in-arm and dined together, and afterwards the cockchafer showed them all the curiosities of his strange country, where the tiniest green leaf costs a gold piece and more. Then they set out again to finish their journey, and this time, as they knew the way, they were not long upon the road. It was easy to guess that they had come to the right place, for they saw peacocks in every tree, and their cries could be heard a long way off.

When they reached the city they found it full of men and women who were dressed entirely in peacocks' feathers, which were evidently thought prettier than anything else.

They soon met the King, who was driving about in a beautiful little golden carriage which glittered with diamonds, and was drawn

at full speed by twelve peacocks. The King and the Prince were delighted to see that the King of the Peacocks was as handsome as possible. He had curly golden hair and was very pale, and he wore a crown of peacocks' feathers.

When he saw Rosette's brothers he knew at once that they were strangers, and stopping his carriage he sent for them to speak to him. When they had greeted him they said:

'Sire, we have come from very far away to show you a beautiful portrait.'

So saying they drew from their travelling bag the picture of Rosette.

The King looked at it in silence a long time, but at last he said :

'I could not have believed that there was such a beautiful Princess in the world!'

'Indeed, she is really a hundred times as pretty as that,' said her brothers.

'I think you must be making fun of me,' replied the King of the Peacocks.

'Sire,' said the Prince, 'my brother is a King, like yourself. He is called "the King," I am called "the Prince," and that is the portrait of our sister, the Princess Rosette. We have come to ask if you would like to marry her. She is as good as she is beautiful, and we will give her a bushel of gold pieces for her dowry.'

'Oh! with all my heart,' replied the King, 'and I will make her very happy. She shall have whatever she likes, and I shall love her dearly ; only I warn you that if she is not as pretty as you have told me, I will have your heads cut off.'

'Oh! certainly, we quite agree to that,' said the brothers in one breath.

'Very well. Off with you into prison, and stay there until the Princess arrives,' said the King of the Peacocks.

And the Princes were so sure that Rosette was far prettier than her portrait that they went without a murmur. They were very kindly treated, and that they might not feel dull the King came often to see them. As for Rosette's portrait that was taken up to the palace, and the King did nothing but gaze at it all day and all night.

As the King and the Prince had to stay in prison, they sent a letter to the Princess telling her to pack up all her treasures as quickly as possible, and come to them, as the King of the Peacocks was waiting to marry her ; but they did not say that they were in prison, for fear of making her uneasy.

When Rosette received the letter she was so delighted that she ran about telling everyone that the King of the Peacocks was found, and she was going to marry him.

Guns were fired, and fireworks let off. Everyone had as many cakes and sweetmeats as he wanted. And for three days everybody who came to see the Princess was presented with a slice of bread-and-jam, a nightingale's egg, and some hippocras. After having thus entertained her friends, she distributed her dolls among them, and left her brother's kingdom to the care of the wisest old men of the city, telling them to take charge of everything, not to spend any money, but save it all up until the King should return, and above all, not to forget to feed her peacock. Then she set out, only taking with her her nurse, and the nurse's daughter, and the little green dog Frisk.

They took a boat and put out to sea, carrying with them the bushel of gold pieces, and enough dresses to last the Princess ten years if she wore two every day, and they did nothing but laugh and sing. The nurse asked the boatman:

'Can you take us, can you take us to the kingdom of the peacocks?'

But he answered:

'Oh no! oh no!'

Then she said:

'You must take us, you must take us.'

And he answered:

'Very soon, very soon.'

Then the nurse said:

'Will you take us? will you take us?'

And the boatman answered:

'Yes, yes.'

Then she whispered in his ear:

'Do you want to make your fortune?'

And he said:

'Certainly I do.'

'I can tell you how to get a bag of gold,' said she.

'I ask nothing better,' said the boatman.

'Well,' said the nurse, 'to-night, when the Princess is asleep, you must help me to throw her into the sea, and when she is drowned I will put her beautiful clothes upon my daughter, and we will take her to the King of the Peacocks, who will be only too glad to marry her, and as your reward you shall have your boat full of diamonds.'

The boatman was very much surprised at this proposal, and said:

'But what a pity to drown such a pretty Princess!'

However, at last the nurse persuaded him to help her, and when the night came and the Princess was fast asleep as usual, with Frisk curled up on his own cushion at the foot of her bed, the wicked nurse fetched the boatman and her daughter, and between them they picked up the Princess, feather bed, mattress, pillows, blankets and all, and threw her into the sea, without even waking her. Now, luckily, the Princess's bed was entirely stuffed with phœnix feathers, which are very rare, and have the property of always floating upon water, so Rosette went on swimming about as if she had been in a boat. After a little while she began to feel very cold, and turned round so often that she woke Frisk, who started up, and, having a very good nose, smelt the soles and herrings so close to him that he began to bark. He barked so long and so loud that he woke all the other fish, who came swimming up round the Princess's bed, and poking at it with their great heads. As for her, she said to herself:

'How our boat does rock upon the water! I am really glad that I am not often as uncomfortable as I have been to-night.'

The wicked nurse and the boatman, who were by this time quite a long way off, heard Frisk barking, and said to each other:

'That horrid little animal and his mistress are drinking our health in sea-water now. Let us make haste to land, for we must be quite near the city of the King of the Peacocks.'

The King had sent a hundred carriages to meet them, drawn by every kind of strange animal. There were lions, bears, wolves, stags, horses, buffaloes, eagles, and peacocks. The carriage intended for the Princess Rosette had six blue monkeys, which could turn summersaults, and dance on a tight-rope, and do many other charming tricks. Their harness was all of crimson velvet with gold buckles, and behind the carriage walked sixty beautiful ladies chosen by the King to wait upon Rosette and amuse her.

The nurse had taken all the pains imaginable to deck out her daughter. She put on her Rosette's prettiest frock, and covered her with diamonds from head to foot. But she was so ugly that nothing could make her look nice, and what was worse, she was sulky and ill-tempered, and did nothing but grumble all the time.

When she stepped from the boat and the escort sent by the King of the Peacocks caught sight of her, they were so surprised that they could not say a single word.

'Now then, look alive,' cried the false Princess. 'If you don't bring me something to eat I will have all your heads cut off!'

Then they whispered one to another:

'Here's a pretty state of things! she is as wicked as she is ugly. What a bride for our poor King! She certainly was not worth bringing from the other end of the world!'

But she went on ordering them all about, and for no fault at all would give slaps and pinches to everyone she could reach.

As the procession was so long it advanced but slowly, and the nurse's daughter sat up in her carriage trying to look like a Queen. But the peacocks, who were sitting upon every tree waiting to salute her, and who had made up their minds to cry, 'Long live our beautiful Queen!' when they caught sight of the false bride could not help crying instead:

'Oh! how ugly she is!'

Which offended her so much that she said to the guards:

'Make haste and kill all these insolent peacocks who have dared to insult me.'

But the peacocks only flew away, laughing at her.

The rogue of a boatman, who noticed all this, said softly to the nurse:

'This is a bad business for us, gossip; your daughter ought to have been prettier.'

But she answered:

'Be quiet, stupid, or you will spoil everything.'

Now they told the King that the Princess was approaching.

'Well,' said he, 'did her brothers tell me truly? Is she prettier than her portrait?'

'Sire,' they answered, 'if she were as pretty that would do very well.'

' That's true,' said the King ; ' I for one shall be quite satisfied if she is. Let us go and meet her.' For they knew by the uproar that she had arrived, but they could not tell what all the shouting was about. The King thought he could hear the words :

' How ugly she is ! How ugly she is ! ' and he fancied they must refer to some dwarf the Princess was bringing with her. It never occurred to him that they could apply to the bride herself.

The Princess Rosette's portrait was carried at the head of the procession, and after it walked the King surrounded by his courtiers. He was all impatience to see the lovely Princess, but when he caught sight of the nurse's daughter he was furiously angry, and would not advance another step. For she was really ugly enough to have frightened anybody.

' What ! ' he cried, ' have the two rascals who are my prisoners dared to play me such a trick as this ? Do they propose that I shall marry this hideous creature ? Let her be shut up in my great tower, with her nurse and those who brought her here ; and as for them, I will have their heads cut off.'

Meanwhile the King and the Prince, who knew that their sister must have arrived, had made themselves smart, and sat expecting every minute to be summoned to greet her. So when the gaoler came with soldiers, and carried them down into a black dungeon which swarmed with toads and bats, and where they were up to their necks in water, nobody could have been more surprised and dismayed than they were.

' This is a dismal kind of wedding,' they said ; ' what can have happened that we should be treated like this ? They must mean to kill us.'

And this idea annoyed them very much. Three days passed before they heard any news, and then the King of the Peacocks came and berated them through a hole in the wall.

' You have called yourselves King and Prince,' he cried, ' to try and make me marry your sister, but you are nothing but beggars, not worth the water you drink. I mean to make short work with you, and the sword is being sharpened that will cut off your heads ! '

' King of the Peacocks,' answered the King angrily, ' you had better take care what you are about. I am as good a King as yourself, and have a splendid kingdom and robes and crowns, and plenty of good red gold to do what I like with. You are pleased to jest about having our heads cut off; perhaps you think we have stolen something from you ? '

At first the King of the Peacocks was taken aback by this bold speech, and had half a mind to send them all away together; but his Prime Minister declared that it would never do to let such a trick as that pass unpunished, everybody would laugh at him; so the accusation was drawn up against them, that they were impostors, and that they had promised the King a beautiful Princess in marriage who, when she arrived, proved to be an ugly peasant girl.

This accusation was read to the prisoners, who cried out that they had spoken the truth, that their sister was indeed a Princess more beautiful than the day, and that there was some mystery about all this which they could not fathom. Therefore they demanded seven days in which to prove their innocence, The King of the Peacocks was so angry that he would hardly even grant them this favour, but at last he was persuaded to do so.

While all this was going on at court, let us see what had been happening to the real Princess. When the day broke she and Frisk were equally astonished at finding themselves alone upon the sea, with no boat and no one to help them. The Princess cried and cried, until even the fishes were sorry for her.

'Alas!' she said, 'the King of the Peacocks must have ordered me to be thrown into the sea because he had changed his mind and did not want to marry me. But how strange of him, when I should have loved him so much, and we should have been so happy together!'

And then she cried harder than ever, for she could not help still loving him. So for two days they floated up and down the sea, wet and shivering with the cold, and so hungry that when the Princess saw some oysters she caught them, and she and Frisk both ate some, though they didn't like them at all. When night came the Princess was so frightened that she said to Frisk:

'Oh! Do please keep on barking for fear the soles should come and eat us up!'

Now it happened that they had floated close in to the shore, where a poor old man lived all alone in a little cottage. When he heard Frisk's barking he thought to himself:

'There must have been a shipwreck!' (for no dogs ever passed that way by any chance), and he went out to see if he could be of any use. He soon saw the Princess and Frisk floating up and down, and Rosette, stretching out her hands to him, cried:

'Oh! Good old man, do save me, or I shall die of cold and hunger!'

When he heard her cry out so piteously he was very sorry for her, and ran back into his house to fetch a long boat-hook. Then he waded into the water up to his chin, and after being nearly drowned once or twice he at last succeeded in getting hold of the Princess's bed and dragging it on shore.

Rosette and Frisk were joyful enough to find themselves once more on dry land, and the Princess thanked the old man heartily; then, wrapping herself up in her blankets, she daintily picked her way up to the cottage on her little bare feet. There the old man lighted a fire of straw, and then drew from an old box his wife's dress and

shoes, which the Princess put on, and thus roughly clad looked as charming as possible, and Frisk danced his very best to amuse her.

The old man saw that Rosette must be some great lady, for her bed coverings were all of satin and gold. He begged that she would tell him all her history, as she might safely trust him. The Princess told him everything, weeping bitterly again at the thought that it was by the King's orders that she had been thrown overboard.

'And now, my daughter, what is to be done?' said the old man. 'You are a great Princess, accustomed to fare daintily, and I have nothing to offer you but black bread and radishes, which will not suit you at all. Shall I go and tell the King of the Peacocks that you are here? If he sees you he will certainly wish to marry you.'

'Oh no!' cried Rosette, 'he must be wicked, since he tried to drown me. Don't let us tell him, but if you have a little basket give it to me.'

The old man gave her a basket, and tying it round Frisk's neck she said to him : ' Go and find out the best cooking-pot in the town and bring the contents to me.'

Away went Frisk, and as there was no better dinner cooking in all the town than the King's, he adroitly took the cover off the pot and brought all it contained to the Princess, who said:

' Now go back to the pantry, and bring the best of everything you find there.'

So Frisk went back and filled his basket with white bread, and red wine, and every kind of sweetmeat, until it was almost too heavy for him to carry.

When the King of the Peacocks wanted his dinner there was nothing in the pot and nothing in the pantry. All the courtiers looked at one another in dismay, and the King was terribly cross.

' Oh well ! ' he said, ' if there is no dinner I cannot dine, but take care that plenty of things are roasted for supper.'

When evening came the Princess said to Frisk :

' Go into the town and find out the best kitchen, and bring me all the nicest morsels that are being roasted upon the spit.'

Frisk did as he was told, and as he knew of no better kitchen than the King's, he went in softly, and when the cook's back was turned took everything that was upon the spit, As it happened it was all done to a turn, and looked so good that it made him hungry only to see it. He carried his basket to the Princess, who at once sent him back to the pantry to bring all the tarts and sugar plums that had been prepared for the King's supper.

The King, as he had had no dinner, was very hungry and wanted his supper early, but when he asked for it, lo and behold it was all gone, and he had to go to bed half-starved and in a terrible temper. The next day the same thing happened, and the next, so that for three days the King got nothing at all to eat, because just when the dinner or the supper was ready to be served it mysteriously disappeared. At last the Prime Minister began to be afraid that the King would be starved to death, so he resolved to hide himself in some dark corner of the kitchen, and never take his eyes off the cooking-pot. His surprise was great when he presently saw a little green dog with one ear slip softly into the kitchen, uncover the pot, transfer all its contents to his basket, and run off. The Prime Minister followed hastily, and tracked him all through the town to the cottage of the good old man ; then he ran back to the King and told him that he had found out where all his dinners and suppers went. The King, who was very much astonished, said he should like to go and see for himself. So he set out, accompanied by the Prime Minister and a guard of archers, and arrived just in time to find the old man and the Princess finishing his dinner.

The King ordered that they should be seized and bound with ropes, and Frisk also.

When they were brought back to the palace some one told the King, who said :

' To-day is the last day of the respite granted to those impostors ; they shall have their heads cut off at the same time as these stealers of my dinner.' Then the old man went down on his knees before the King and begged for time to tell him everything. While he spoke the King for the first time looked attentively at the Princess, because he was sorry to see how she cried, and when he heard the old man saying that her name was Rosette, and that she had been treacherously thrown into the sea, he turned head over heels three times without stopping, in spite of being quite weak from hunger, and ran to embrace her, and untied the ropes which bound her with his own hands, declaring that he loved her with all his heart.

Messengers were sent to bring the Princes out of prison, and they came very sadly, believing that they were to be executed at once : the nurse and her daughter and the boatman were brought also. As soon as they came in Rosette ran to embrace her brothers, while the traitors threw themselves down before her and begged for mercy. The King and the Princess were so happy that they freely forgave them, and as for the good old man he was splendidly rewarded, and spent the rest of his days in the palace. The King of the Peacocks made ample amends to the King and Prince for the way in which they had been treated, and did everything in his power to show how sorry he was.

The nurse restored to Rosette all her dresses and jewels, and the bushel of gold pieces ; the wedding was held at once, and they all lived happily ever after—even to Frisk, who enjoyed the greatest luxury, and never had anything worse than the wing of a partridge for dinner all the rest of his life.[1]

[1] Madame d'Aulnoy.

THE ENCHANTED PIG

ONCE upon a time there lived a King who had three daughters. Now it happened that he had to go out to battle, so he called his daughters and said to them:

'My dear children, I am obliged to go to the wars. The enemy is approaching us with a large army. It is a great grief to me to leave you all. During my absence take care of yourselves and be good girls; behave well and look after everything in the house. You may walk in the garden, and you may go into all the rooms in the palace, except the room at the back in the right-hand corner; into that you must not enter, for harm would befall you.'

'You may keep your mind easy, father,' they replied. 'We have never been disobedient to you. Go in peace, and may heaven give you a glorious victory!'

When everything was ready for his departure, the King gave them the keys of all the rooms and reminded them once more of what he had said. His daughters kissed his hands with tears in their eyes, and wished him prosperity, and he gave the eldest the keys.

Now when the girls found themselves alone they felt so sad and dull that they did not know what to do. So, to pass the time, they decided to work for part of the day, to read for part of the day, and to enjoy themselves in the garden for part of the day. As long as they did this all went well with them. But this happy state of things did not last long. Every day they grew more and more curious, and you will see what the end of that was.

'Sisters,' said the eldest Princess, 'all day long we sew, spin, and read. We have been several days quite alone, and there is no corner of the garden that we have not explored. We have been in all the rooms of our father's palace, and have admired the rich and beautiful furniture: why should not we go into the room that our father forbad us to enter?'

Sister,' said the youngest, 'I cannot think how you can tempt us to break our father's command. When he told us not to go into that room he must have known what he was saying, and have had a good reason for saying it.'

'Surely the sky won't fall about our heads if we *do* go in,' said the second Princess. 'Dragons and such like monsters that would devour us will not be hidden in the room. And how will our father ever find out that we have gone in ? '

While they were speaking thus, encouraging each other, they had reached the room ; the eldest fitted the key into the lock, and snap ! the door stood open.

The three girls entered, and what do you think they saw ?

The room was quite empty, and without any ornament, but in the middle stood a large table, with a gorgeous cloth, and on it lay a big open book.

Now the Princesses were curious to know what was written in the book, especially the eldest, and this is what she read :

'The eldest daughter of this King will marry a prince from the East.'

Then the second girl stepped forward, and turning over the page she read :

'The second daughter of this King will marry a prince from the West.'

The girls were delighted, and laughed and teased each other.

But the youngest Princess did not want to go near the table or to open the book. Her elder sisters however left her no peace, and will she, nill she, they dragged her up to the table, and in fear and trembling she turned over the page and read :

'The youngest daughter of this King will be married to a pig from the North.'

Now if a thunderbolt had fallen upon her from heaven it would not have frightened her more.

She almost died of misery, and if her sisters had not held her up, she would have sunk to the ground and cut her head open.

When she came out of the fainting fit into which she had fallen in her terror, her sisters tried to comfort her, saying :

'How can you believe such nonsense ? When did it ever happen that a king's daughter married a pig ? '

'What a baby you are ! ' said the other sister ; 'has not our father enough soldiers to protect you, even if the disgusting creature did come to woo you ? '

The youngest Princess would fain have let herself be convinced by her sisters' words, and have believed what they said, but her heart was heavy. Her thoughts kept turning to the book, in which stood written that great happiness waited her sisters, but that a fate was in store for her such as had never before been known in the world.

Besides, the thought weighed on her heart that she had been guilty of disobeying her father. She began to get quite ill, and in a few days she was so changed that it was difficult to recognise her; formerly she had been rosy and merry, now she was pale and nothing gave her any pleasure. She gave up playing with her sisters in the garden, ceased to gather flowers to put in her hair, and never sang when they sat together at their spinning and sewing.

In the meantime the King won a great victory, and having completely defeated and driven off the enemy, he hurried home to his daughters, to whom his thoughts had constantly turned. Everyone went out to meet him with cymbals and fifes and drums, and there was great rejoicing over his victorious return. The King's first act on reaching home was to thank Heaven for the victory he had gained over the enemies who had risen against him. He then entered his palace, and the three Princesses stepped forward to meet him. His joy was great when he saw that they were all well, for the youngest did her best not to appear sad.

In spite of this, however, it was not long before the King noticed that his third daughter was getting very thin and sad-looking. And all of a sudden he felt as if a hot iron were entering his soul, for it flashed through his mind that she had disobeyed his word. He felt sure he was right; but to be quite certain he called his daughters to him, questioned them, and ordered them to speak the truth. They confessed everything, but took good care not to say which had led the other two into temptation.

The King was so distressed when he heard it that he was almost overcome by grief. But he took heart and tried to comfort his daughters, who looked frightened to death. He saw that what had happened had happened, and that a thousand words would not alter matters by a hair's-breadth.

Well, these events had almost been forgotten when one fine day a prince from the East appeared at the Court and asked the King for the hand of his eldest daughter. The King gladly gave his consent. A great wedding banquet was prepared, and after three days of feasting the happy pair were accompanied to the frontier with much ceremony and rejoicing.

After some time the same thing befell the second daughter, who was wooed and won by a prince from the West.

Now when the young Princess saw that everything fell out exactly as had been written in the book, she grew very sad. She refused to eat, and would not put on her fine clothes nor go out walking, and declared that she would rather die than become a laughing-stock to the world. But the King would not allow her to do anything so wrong, and he comforted her in all possible ways.

So the time passed, till lo and behold! one fine day an enormous pig from the North walked into the palace, and going straight

up to the King said, 'Hail! oh King. May your life be as prosperous and bright as sunrise on a clear day!'

'I am glad to see you well, friend,' answered the King, 'but what wind has brought you hither?'

'I come a-wooing,' replied the Pig.

Now the King was astonished to hear so fine a speech from a Pig, and at once it occurred to him that something strange was the matter. He would gladly have turned the Pig's thoughts in another direction, as he did not wish to give him the Princess for a wife; but when he heard that the Court and the whole street were full of all the pigs in the world he saw that there was no escape, and that he must give his consent. The Pig was not satisfied with mere promises, but insisted that the wedding should take place within a week, and would not go away till the King had sworn a royal oath upon it.

The King then sent for his daughter, and advised her to submit to fate, as there was nothing else to be done. And he added:

' My child, the words and whole behaviour of this Pig are quite unlike those of other pigs. I do not myself believe that he always *was* a pig. Depend upon it some magic or witchcraft has been at work. Obey him, and do everything that he wishes, and I feel sure that Heaven will shortly send you release.'

' If you wish me to do this, dear father, I will do it,' replied the girl.

In the meantime the wedding-day drew near. After the marriage, the Pig and his bride set out for his home in one of the royal carriages. On the way they passed a great bog, and the Pig ordered the carriage to stop, and got out and rolled about in the mire till he was covered with mud from head to foot; then he got back into the carriage and told his wife to kiss him. What was the poor girl to do ? She bethought herself of her father's words, and, pulling out her pocket handkerchief, she gently wiped the Pig's snout and kissed it.

By the time they reached the Pig's dwelling, which stood in a thick wood, it was quite dark. They sat down quietly for a little, as they were tired after their drive ; then they had supper together, and lay down to rest. During the night the Princess noticed that the Pig had changed into a man. She was not a little surprised, but remembering her father's words, she took courage, determined to wait and see what would happen.

And now she noticed that every night the Pig became a man, and every morning he was changed into a Pig before she awoke. This happened several nights running, and the Princess could not understand it at all. Clearly her husband must be bewitched. In time she grew quite fond of him, he was so kind and gentle.

One fine day as she was sitting alone she saw an old witch go past. She felt quite excited, as it was so long since she had seen a human being, and she called out to the old woman to come and talk to her. Among other things the witch told her that she understood all magic arts, and that she could foretell the future, and knew the healing powers of herbs and plants.

' I shall be grateful to you all my life, old dame,' said the Princess, ' if you will tell me what is the matter with my husband. Why is he a Pig by day and a human being by night ? '

' I was just going to tell you that one thing, my dear, to show you what a good fortune-teller I am. If you like, I will give you a herb to break the spell.'

' If you will only give it to me,' said the Princess, ' I will give you anything you choose to ask for, for I cannot bear to see him in this state.'

' Here, then, my dear child,' said the witch, ' take this thread, but do not let him know about it, for if he did it would lose its healing power. At night, when he is asleep, you must get up very quietly, and fasten the thread round his left foot as firmly as possible ; and you will see in the morning he will not have changed back into a Pig, but will still be a man. I do not want any reward. I shall be sufficiently repaid by knowing that you are happy. It almost breaks my heart to think of all you have suffered, and I only wish I had known it sooner, as I should have come to your rescue at once.'

When the old witch had gone away the Princess hid the thread very carefully, and at night she got up quietly, and with a beating heart she bound the thread round her husband's foot. Just as she was pulling the knot tight there was a crack, and the thread broke, for it was rotten.

Her husband awoke with a start, and said to her, ' Unhappy woman, what have you done ? Three days more and this unholy spell would have fallen from me, and now, who knows how long I may have to go about in this disgusting shape ? I must leave you at once, and we shall not meet again until you have worn out three pairs of iron shoes and blunted a steel staff in your search for me.' So saying he disappeared.

Now, when the Princess was left alone she began to weep and moan in a way that was pitiful to hear ; but when she saw that her tears and groans did her no good, she got up, determined to go wherever fate should lead her.

On reaching a town, the first thing she did was to order three pairs of iron sandals and a steel staff, and having made these preparations for her journey, she set out in search of her husband. On and on she wandered over nine seas and across nine continents ; through forests with trees whose stems were as thick as beer-barrels ; stumbling and knocking herself against the fallen branches, then picking herself up and going on; the boughs of the trees hit her face, and the shrubs tore her hands, but on she went, and never looked back.   At last, wearied with her long journey and worn out and overcome with sorrow, but still with hope at her heart, she reached a house.

Now who do you think lived there ?   The Moon.

The Princess knocked at the door, and begged to be let in that she might rest a little.   The mother of the Moon, when she saw her sad plight, felt a great pity for her, and took her in and nursed and tended her.   And while she was here the Princess had a little baby.

One day the mother of the Moon asked her:

' How was it possible for you, a mortal, to get hither to the house of the Moon ? '

Then the poor Princess told her all that happened to her, and added : ' I shall always be thankful to Heaven for leading me hither, and grateful to you that you took pity on me and on my baby, and did not leave us to die.   Now I beg one last favour of you ; can your daughter, the Moon, tell me where my husband is ? '

' She cannot tell you that, my child,' replied the goddess, ' but, if you will travel towards the East until you reach the dwelling of the Sun, he may be able to tell you something.'

Then she gave the Princess a roast chicken to eat, and warned her to be very careful not to lose any of the bones, because they might be of great use to her.

When the Princess had thanked her once more for her hospitality and for her good advice, and had thrown away one pair of shoes that were worn out, and had put on a second pair, she tied up the chicken bones in a bundle, and taking her baby in her arms and her staff in her hand, she set out once more on her wanderings.

On and on and on she went across bare sandy deserts, where the roads were so heavy that for every two steps that she took forwards she fell back one ; but she struggled on till she had passed these dreary plains ; next she crossed high rocky mountains, jumping from crag to crag and from peak to peak.   Sometimes she would rest for a little on a mountain, and then start afresh always farther and farther on.   She had to cross swamps and to scale mountain peaks covered with flints, so that her feet and knees and elbows were all torn and bleeding, and sometimes she came to a precipice across which she could not jump, and she had to crawl round on hands and knees, helping herself along with her staff.

At length, wearied to death, she reached the palace in which the Sun lived. She knocked and begged for admission. The mother of the Sun opened the door, and was astonished at beholding a mortal from the distant earthly shores, and wept with pity when she heard of all she had suffered. Then, having promised to ask her son about the Princess's husband, she hid her in the cellar, so that the Sun might notice nothing on his return home, for he was always in a bad temper when he came in at night.

The next day the Princess feared that things would not go well with her, for the Sun had noticed that some one from the other world had been in the palace. But his mother had soothed him with soft words, assuring him that this was not so. So the Princess took heart when she saw how kindly she was treated, and asked:

'But how in the world is it possible for the Sun to be angry? He is so beautiful and so good to mortals.'

'This is how it happens,' replied the Sun's mother. 'In the morning when he stands at the gates of paradise he is happy, and smiles on the whole world, but during the day he gets cross, because he sees all the evil deeds of men, and that is why his heat becomes so scorching; but in the evening he is both sad and angry, for he stands at the gates of death; that is his usual course. From there he comes back here.'

She then told the Princess that she had asked about her husband, but that her son had replied that he knew nothing about him, and that her only hope was to go and inquire of the Wind.

Before the Princess left the mother of the Sun gave her a roast chicken to eat, and advised her to take great care of the bones, which she did, wrapping them up in a bundle. She then threw away her second pair of shoes, which were quite worn out, and with her child on her arm and her staff in her hand, she set forth on her way to the Wind.

In these wanderings she met with even greater difficulties than before, for she came upon one mountain of flints after another, out of which tongues of fire would flame up; she passed through woods which had never been trodden by human foot, and had to cross fields of ice and avalanches of snow. The poor woman nearly died of these hardships, but she kept a brave heart, and at length she reached an enormous cave in the side of a mountain. This was where the Wind lived. There was a little door in the railing in front of the cave, and here the Princess knocked and begged for admission. The mother of the Wind had pity on her and took her in, that she might rest a little. Here too she was hidden away, so that the Wind might not notice her.

The next morning the mother of the Wind told her that her husband was living in a thick wood, so thick that no axe had been able to cut a way through it; here he had built himself a sort of house by placing trunks of trees together and fastening them with withes and here he lived alone, shunning human kind.

After the mother of the Wind had given the Princess a chicken to eat, and had warned her to take care of the bones, she advised her to go by the Milky Way, which at night lies across the sky, and to wander on till she reached her goal.

Having thanked the old woman with tears in her eyes for her hospitality, and for the good news she had given her, the Princess set out on her journey and rested neither night nor day, so great was her longing to see her husband again. On and on she walked until her last pair of shoes fell in pieces. So she threw them away and went on with bare feet, not heeding the bogs nor the thorns that wounded her, nor the stones that bruised her. At last she reached a beautiful green meadow on the edge of a wood. Her heart was cheered by the sight of the flowers and the soft cool grass, and she sat down and rested for a little. But hearing the birds chirping to their mates among the trees made her think with longing of her husband, and she wept bitterly, and taking her child in her arms, and her bundle of chicken bones on her shoulder, she entered the wood.

For three days and three nights she struggled through it, but could find nothing. She was quite worn out with weariness and hunger, and even her staff was no further help to her, for in her many wanderings it had become quite blunted. She almost gave up in despair, but made one last great effort, and suddenly in a thicket she came upon the sort of house that the mother of the Wind had described. It had no windows, and the door was up in the roof. Round the house she went, in search of steps, but could find none. What was she to do? How was she to get in? She thought and thought, and tried in vain to climb up to the door. Then suddenly she bethought her of the chicken bones that she had dragged all that weary way, and she said to herself: 'They would not all have told me to take such good care of these bones if they had not had some good reason for doing so. Perhaps now, in my hour of need, they may be of use to me.'

So she took the bones out of her bundle, and having thought for a moment, she placed the two ends together. To her surprise they stuck tight; then she added the other bones, till she had two long poles the height of the house; these she placed against the wall, at a distance of a yard from one another. Across them she placed the other bones, piece by piece, like the steps of a ladder. As soon as one step was finished she stood upon it and made the next one, and then the next, till she was close to the door. But just as she got near the top she noticed that there were no bones left for the last rung of the ladder. What was she to do? Without that last step

the whole ladder was useless. She must have lost one of the bones.
Then suddenly an idea came to her. Taking a knife she chopped
off her little finger, and placing it on the last step, it stuck as the
bones had done. The ladder was complete, and with her child on
her arm she entered the door of the house. Here she found everything in perfect order. Having taken some food, she laid the child
down to sleep in a trough that was on the floor, and sat down herself to rest.

When her husband, the Pig, came back to his house, he was
startled by what he saw. At first he could not believe his eyes,
and stared at the ladder of bones, and at the little finger on the top
of it. He felt that some fresh magic must be at work, and in his
terror he almost turned away from the house; but then a better
idea came to him, and he changed himself into a dove, so that no
witchcraft could have power over him, and flew into the room
without touching the ladder. Here he found a woman rocking a
child. At the sight of her, looking so changed by all that she had
suffered for his sake, his heart was moved by such love and longing
and by so great a pity that he suddenly became a man.

The Princess stood up when she saw him, and her heart beat
with fear, for she did not know him. But when he had told her
who he was, in her great joy she forgot all her sufferings, and they
seemed as nothing to her. He was a very handsome man, as
straight as a fir tree. They sat down together and she told
him all her adventures, and he wept with pity at the tale. And
then he told her his own history.

'I am a King's son. Once when my father was fighting against
some dragons, who were the scourge of our country, I slew the
youngest dragon. His mother, who was a witch, cast a spell over me
and changed me into a Pig. It was she who in the disguise of an
old woman gave you the thread to bind round my foot. So that
instead of the three days that had to run before the spell was broken,
I was forced to remain a Pig for three more years. Now that we
have suffered for each other, and have found each other again, let
us forget the past.'

And in their joy they kissed one another.

Next morning they set out early to return to his father's kingdom. Great was the rejoicing of all the people when they saw him
and his wife; his father and his mother embraced them both, and
there was feasting in the palace for three days and three nights.

Then they set out to see her father. The old King nearly went out of his mind with joy at beholding his daughter again. When she had told him all her adventures, he said to her:

'Did not I tell you that I was quite sure that that creature who wooed and won you as his wife had not been born a Pig? You see, my child, how wise you were in doing what I told you.'

And as the King was old and had no heirs, he put them on the throne in his place. And they ruled as only kings rule who have suffered many things. And if they are not dead they are still living and ruling happily.[1]

---

[1] Rumänische Märchen übersetzt von Nite Kremnitz.

THE NORKA

ONCE upon a time there lived a King and Queen. They had three sons, two of them with their wits about them, but the third a simpleton. Now the King had a deer park in which were quantities of wild animals of different kinds. Into that park there used to come a huge beast—Norka was its name—and do fearful mischief, devouring some of the animals every night. The King did all he could, but he was unable to destroy it. So at last he called his sons together and said, ' Whoever will destroy the Norka, to him will I give the half of my kingdom.'

Well, the eldest son undertook the task. As soon as it was night, he took his weapons and set out. But before he reached the park, he went into a *traktir* (or tavern), and there he spent the whole night in revelry. When he came to his senses it was too late ; the day had already dawned. He felt himself disgraced in the eyes of his father, but there was no help for it. The next day the second son went, and did just the same. Their father scolded them both soundly, and there was an end of it.

Well, on the third day the youngest son undertook the task. They all laughed him to scorn, because he was so stupid, feeling sure he wouldn't do anything. But he took his arms, and went straight into the park, and sat down on the grass in such a position that the moment he went asleep his weapons would prick him, and he would awake.

Presently the midnight hour sounded. The earth began to shake, and the Norka came rushing up, and burst right through the fence into the park, so huge was it. The Prince pulled himself together, leapt to his feet, crossed himself, and went straight at the beast. It fled back, and the Prince ran after it. But he soon saw that he couldn't catch it on foot, so he hastened to the stable, laid his hands on the best horse there, and set off in pursuit. Presently he came up with the beast, and they began a fight. They fought

and fought; the Prince gave the beast three wounds. At last they
were both utterly exhausted, so they lay down to take a short rest.
But the moment the Prince closed his eyes, up jumped the beast
and took to flight. The Prince's horse awoke him; up he jumped
in a moment, and set off again in pursuit, caught up the beast, and
again began fighting with it. Again the Prince gave the beast
three wounds, and then he and the beast lay down again to rest.
Thereupon away fled the beast as before. The Prince caught it up,
and again gave it three wounds. But all of a sudden, just as the
Prince began chasing it for the fourth time, the beast fled to a great
white stone, tilted it up, and escaped into the other world, crying
out to the Prince: 'Then only will you overcome me, when you
enter here.'

The Prince went home, told his father all that had happened,
and asked him to have a leather rope plaited, long enough to reach
to the other world. His father ordered this to be done. When the
rope was made, the Prince called for his brothers, and he and they,
having taken servants with them, and everything that was needed
for a whole year, set out for the place where the beast had disappeared under the stone. When they got there, they built a palace
on the spot, and lived in it for some time. But when everything
was ready, the youngest brother said to the others: ' Now, brothers,
who is going to lift this stone ? '

Neither of them could so much as stir it, but as soon as he
touched it, away it flew to a distance, though it was ever so big —
big as a hill. And when he had flung the stone aside, he spoke a
second time to his brothers, saying:

' Who is going into the other world, to overcome the Norka ? '

Neither of them offered to do so. Then he laughed at them for
being such cowards, and said:

' Well, brothers, farewell ! Lower me into the other world, and
don't go away from here, but as soon as the cord is jerked, pull it
up.'

His brothers lowered him accordingly, and when he had
reached the other world, underneath the earth, he went on his way.
He walked and walked. Presently he espied a horse with rich
trappings, and it said to him :

' Hail, Prince Ivan ! Long have I awaited thee ! '

He mounted the horse and rode on—rode and rode, until he saw
standing before him a palace made of copper. He entered the
courtyard, tied up his horse, and went indoors. In one of the rooms

a dinner was laid out.   He sat down and dined, and then went into
a bedroom.   There he found a bed, on which he lay down to rest.
Presently there came in a lady, more beautiful than can be imagined
anywhere but in a fairy tale, who said :

' Thou who art in my house, name thyself!   If thou art an old
man, thou shalt be my father ; if a middle-aged man, my brother ;
but if a young man, thou shalt be my husband dear.   And if thou
art a woman, and an old one, thou shalt be my grandmother ; if

middle-aged, my mother ; and if a girl, thou shalt be my own
sister.'

Thereupon he came forth.   And when she saw him she was
delighted with him, and said :

' Wherefore, O Prince Ivan—my husband dear shalt thou be !—
wherefore hast thou come hither ? '

Then he told her all that had happened, and she said :

' That beast which thou wishest to overcome is my brother.
He is staying just now with my second sister, who lives not far from
here in a silver palace.   I bound up three of the wounds which thou
didst give him.'

Well, after this they drank, and enjoyed themselves, and held sweet converse together, and then the Prince took leave of her, and went on to the second sister, the one who lived in the silver palace, and with her also he stayed awhile. She told him that her brother Norka was then at her youngest sister's. So he went on to the youngest sister, who lived in a golden palace. She told him that her brother was at that time asleep on the blue sea, and she gave him a sword of steel and a draught of the Water of Strength, and she told him to cut off her brother's head at a single stroke. And when he had heard these things, he went his way.

And when the Prince came to the blue sea, he looked—there slept the Norka on a stone in the middle of the sea ; and when it snored, the water was agitated for seven miles around. The Prince crossed himself, went up to it, and smote it on the head with his sword. The head jumped off, saying the while, 'Well, I'm done for now ! ' and rolled far away into the sea.

After killing the beast, the Prince went back again, picking up all the three sisters by the way, with the intention of taking them out into the upper world : for they all loved him and would not be separated from him. Each of them turned her palace into an egg —for they were all enchantresses—and they taught him how to turn the eggs into palaces, and back again, and they handed over the eggs to him. And then they all went to the place from which they had to be hoisted into the upper world. And when they came to where the rope was, the Prince took hold of it and made the maidens fast to it. Then he jerked away at the rope and his brothers began to haul it up. And when they had hauled it up, and had set eyes on the wondrous maidens, they went aside and said : 'Let's lower the rope, pull our brother part of the way up, and then cut the rope. Perhaps he'll be killed ; but then if he isn't, he'll never give us these beauties as wives.'

So when they had agreed on this, they lowered the rope. But their brother was no fool ; he guessed what they were at, so he fastened the rope to a stone, and then gave it a pull. His brothers hoisted the stone to a great height, and then cut the rope. Down fell the stone and broke in pieces ; the Prince poured forth tears and went away. Well, he walked and walked. Presently a storm arose ; the lightning flashed, the thunder roared, the rain fell in torrents. He went up to a tree in order to take shelter under it, and on that tree he saw some young birds which were being thoroughly drenched. So he took off his coat and covered them over with it, and he himself sat down under the tree. Presently there came flying a bird—such a big one that the light was blotted out by it. It had been dark there before, but now it became darker still. Now this was the mother of those small birds which the Prince had covered up. And when the bird had come flying up,

she perceived that her little ones were covered over, and she said, ' Who has wrapped up my nestlings ? ' and presently, seeing the Prince, she added : ' Didst thou do that ? Thanks ! In return, ask of me anything thou desirest. I will do anything for thee.'

' Then carry me into the other world,' he replied.

' Make me a large vessel with a partition in the middle,' she said; ' catch all sorts of game, and put them into one half of it, and into the other half pour water; so that there may be meat and drink for me.'

All this the Prince did. Then the bird—having taken the vessel on her back, with the Prince sitting in the middle of it—began to fly. And after flying some distance she brought him to his journey's end, took leave of him, and flew away back. But he went to the house of a certain tailor, and engaged himself as his servant. So much the worse for wear was he, so thoroughly had he altered in appearance, that nobody would have suspected him of being a Prince.

Having entered into the service of this master, the Prince began to ask what was going on in that country. And his master replied: ' Our two Princes—for the third one has disappeared—have brought away brides from the other world, and want to marry them, but those brides refuse. For they insist on having all their wedding-clothes made for them first, exactly like those which they used to have in the other world, and that without being measured for them. The King has called all the workmen together, but not one of them will undertake to do it.'

The Prince, having heard all this, said, ' Go to the King, master, and tell him that you will provide everything that's in your line.'

' However can I undertake to make clothes of that sort ? I work for quite common folks,' says his master.

' Go along, master! I will answer for everything,' says the Prince.

So the tailor went. The King was delighted that at least one good workman had been found, and gave him as much money as ever he wanted. When his tailor had settled everything, he went home. And the Prince said to him :

' Now then, pray to God, and lie down to sleep; to-morrow all will be ready.' And the tailor followed his lad's advice, and went to bed.

Midnight sounded. The Prince arose, went out of the city into the fields, took out of his pocket the eggs which the maidens had given him, and, as they had taught him, turned them into three palaces. Into each of these he entered, took the maidens' robes, went out again, turned the palaces back into eggs, and went home. And when he got there he hung up the robes on the wall, and lay down to sleep.

Early in the morning his master awoke, and behold! there hung such robes as he had never seen before, all shining with gold and silver and precious stones. He was delighted, and he seized them and carried them off to the King. When the Princesses saw that the clothes were those which had been theirs in the other world, they guessed that Prince Ivan was in this world, so they exchanged glances with each other, but they held their peace. And the master, having handed over the clothes, went home, but he no longer found his dear journeyman there. For the Prince had gone to a shoemaker's, and him too he sent to work for the King; and in the same way he went the round of all the artificers, and they all proffered him thanks, inasmuch as through him they were enriched by the King.

By the time the princely workman had gone the round of all the artificers, the Princesses had received what they had asked for; all their clothes were just like what they had been in the other world. Then they wept bitterly because the Prince had not come, and it was impossible for them to hold out any longer; it was necessary that they should be married. But when they were ready for the wedding, the youngest bride said to the King:

' Allow me, my father, to go and give alms to the beggars.'

He gave her leave, and she went and began bestowing alms upon them, and examining them closely. And when she had come to one of them, and was going to give him some money, she caught sight of the ring which she had given to the Prince in the other world, and her sisters' rings too—for it really was he. So she seized him by the hand, and brought him into the hall, and said to the King:

' Here is he who brought us out of the other world. His brothers forbade us to say that he was alive, threatening to slay us if we did.'

Then the King was wroth with those sons, and punished them as he thought best. And afterwards three weddings were celebrated.

THE WONDERFUL BIRCH

ONCE upon a time there were a man and a woman, who had an only daughter. Now it happened that one of their sheep went astray, and they set out to look for it, and searched and searched, each in a different part of the wood. Then the good wife met a witch, who said to her :

' If you spit, you miserable creature, if you spit into the sheath of my knife, or if you run between my legs, I shall change you into a black sheep.'

The woman neither spat, nor did she run between her legs, but yet the witch changed her into a sheep. Then she made herself look exactly like the woman, and called out to the good man :

' Ho, old man, halloa ! I have found the sheep already ! '

The man thought the witch was really his wife, and he did not know that his wife was the sheep ; so he went home with her, glad at heart because his sheep was found. When they were safe at home the witch said to the man :

'Look here, old man, we must really kill that sheep lest it run away to the wood again.'

The man, who was a peaceable quiet sort of fellow, made no objections, but simply said :

' Good, let us do so.'

The daughter, however, had overheard their talk, and she ran to the flock and lamented aloud :

' Oh, dear little mother, they are going to slaughter you ! '

' Well, then, if they do slaughter me,' was the black sheep's answer, ' eat you neither the meat nor the broth that is made of me, but gather all my bones, and bury them by the edge of the field.'

Shortly after this they took the black sheep from the flock and slaughtered it. The witch made pease-soup of it, and set it before the daughter. But the girl remembered her mother's warning.

She did not touch the soup, but she carried the bones to the edge of the field and buried them there; and there sprang up on the spot a birch tree—a very lovely birch tree.

Some time had passed away—who can tell how long they might have been living there?—when the witch, to whom a child had been born in the meantime, began to take an ill-will to the man's daughter, and to torment her in all sorts of ways.

Now it happened that a great festival was to be held at the palace, and the King had commanded that all the people should be invited, and that this proclamation should be made:

> ' Come, people all!
> Poor and wretched, one and all!
> Blind and crippled though ye be,
> Mount your steeds or come by sea.'

And so they drove into the King's feast all the outcasts, and the maimed, and the halt, and the blind. In the good man's house, too, preparations were made to go to the palace. The witch said to the man:

' Go you on in front, old man, with our youngest; I will give the elder girl work to keep her from being dull in our absence.'

So the man took the child and set out. But the witch kindled a fire on the hearth, threw a potful of barleycorns among the cinders, and said to the girl:

' If you have not picked the barley out of the ashes, and put it all back in the pot before nightfall, I shall eat you up!'

Then she hastened after the others, and the poor girl stayed at home and wept. She tried to be sure to pick up the grains of barley, but she soon saw how useless her labour was; and so she went in her sore trouble to the birch tree on her mother's grave, and cried and cried, because her mother lay dead beneath the sod and could help her no longer. In the midst of her grief she suddenly heard her mother's voice speak from the grave, and say to her:

' Why do you weep, little daughter?'

' The witch has scattered barleycorns on the hearth, and bid me pick them out of the ashes,' said the girl; ' that is why I weep, dear little mother.'

' Do not weep,' said her mother consolingly. ' Break off one of my branches, and strike the hearth with it crosswise, and all will be put right.'

The girl did so. She struck the hearth with the birchen branch, and lo! the barleycorns flew into the pot, and the hearth was clean. Then she went back to the birch tree and laid the branch upon the grave. Then her mother bade her bathe on one side of the stem, dry herself on another, and dress on the third. When the girl had done all that, she had grown so lovely that no one on earth could rival her. Splendid clothing was given to her, and a horse, with hair partly of gold, partly of silver, and partly of something more precious

still. The girl sprang into the saddle, and rode as swift as an arrow to the palace. As she turned into the courtyard of the castle the King's son came out to meet her, tied her steed to a pillar, and led her in. He never left her side as they passed through the castle rooms; and all the people gazed at her, and wondered who the lovely maiden was, and from what castle she came; but no one knew her—no one knew anything about her. At the banquet the Prince invited her to sit next him in the place of honour; but the witch's daughter gnawed the bones under the table. The Prince

did not see her, and thinking it was a dog, he gave her such a push
with his foot that her arm was broken. Are you not sorry for the
witch's daughter? It was not her fault that her mother was a
witch.

Towards evening the good man's daughter thought it was time
to go home; but as she went, her ring caught on the latch of the
door, for the King's son had had it smeared with tar. She did not
take time to pull it off, but, hastily unfastening her horse from the
pillar, she rode away beyond the castle walls as swift as an arrow.
Arrived at home, she took off her clothes by the birch tree, left her
horse standing there, and hastened to her place behind the stove.
In a short time the man and the woman came home again too, and
the witch said to the girl:

'Ah! you poor thing, there you are to be sure! You don't
know what fine times we have had at the palace! The King's son
carried my daughter about, but the poor thing fell and broke her
arm.'

The girl knew well how matters really stood, but she pretended
to know nothing about it, and sat dumb behind the stove.

The next day they were invited again to the King's banquet.

'Hey! old man,' said the witch, 'get on your clothes as quick
as you can; we are bidden to the feast. Take you the child; I will
give the other one work, lest she weary.'

She kindled the fire, threw a potful of hemp seed among the
ashes, and said to the girl:

'If you do not get this sorted, and all the seed back into the pot,
I shall kill you!'

The girl wept bitterly; then she went to the birch tree, washed
herself on one side of it and dried herself on the other; and this
time still finer clothes were given to her, and a very beautiful
steed. She broke off a branch of the birch tree, struck the hearth
with it, so that the seeds flew into the pot, and then hastened to the
castle.

Again the King's son came out to meet her, tied her horse to a
pillar, and led her into the banqueting hall. At the feast the girl sat
next him in the place of honour, as she had done the day before.
But the witch's daughter gnawed bones under the table, and the
Prince gave her a push by mistake, which broke her leg—he had
never noticed her crawling about among the people's feet. She
was *very* unlucky!

The good man's daughter hastened home again betimes, but the

King's son had smeared the door-posts with tar, and the girl's golden circlet stuck to it. She had not time to look for it, but sprang to the saddle and rode like an arrow to the birch tree. There she left her horse and her fine clothes, and said to her mother :

'I have lost my circlet at the castle ; the door-post was tarred, and it stuck fast.'

'And even had you lost two of them,' answered her mother, 'I would give you finer ones.'

Then the girl hastened home, and when her father came home from the feast with the witch, she was in her usual place behind the stove. Then the witch said to her :

'You poor thing! what is there to see here compared with what *we* have seen at the palace ? The King's son carried my daughter from one room to another ; he let her fall, 'tis true, and my child's foot was broken.'

The man's daughter held her peace all the time, and busied herself about the hearth.

The night passed, and when the day began to dawn, the witch awakened her husband, crying :

'Hi! get up, old man ! We are bidden to the royal banquet.'

So the old man got up. Then the witch gave him the child, saying :

'Take you the little one ; I will give the other girl work to do, else she will weary at home alone.'

She did as usual. This time it was a dish of milk she poured upon the ashes, saying :

'If you do not get all the milk into the dish again before I come home, you will suffer for it.'

How frightened the girl was this time ! She ran to the birch tree, and by its magic power her task was accomplished ; and then she rode away to the palace as before. When she got to the court-yard she found the Prince waiting for her. He led her into the hall, where she was highly honoured ; but the witch's daughter sucked the bones under the table, and crouching at the people's feet she got an eye knocked out, poor thing ! Now no one knew any more than before about the good man's daughter, no one knew whence she came ; but the Prince had had the threshold smeared with tar, and as she fled her gold slippers stuck to it. She reached the birch tree, and laying aside her finery, she said :

'Alas ! dear little mother, I have lost my gold slippers ! '

'Let them be,' was her mother's reply; 'if you need them I shall give you finer ones.'

Scarcely was she in her usual place behind the stove when her father came home with the witch. Immediately the witch began to mock her, saying :

'Ah! you poor thing, there is nothing for you to see here, and *we*—ah : what great things we have seen at the palace ! My little girl was carried about again, but had the ill-luck to fall and get her eye knocked out. You stupid thing, you, what do you know about anything ? '

'Yes, indeed, what can I know ? ' replied the girl; 'I had enough to do to get the hearth clean.'

Now the Prince had kept all the things the girl had lost, and he soon set about finding the owner of them. For this purpose a great banquet was given on the fourth day, and all the people were invited to the palace. The witch got ready to go too. She tied a wooden beetle on where her child's foot should have been, a log of wood instead of an arm, and stuck a bit of dirt in the empty socket for an eye, and took the child with her to the castle. When all the people were gathered together, the King's son stepped in among the crowd and cried :

'The maiden whose finger this ring slips over, whose head this golden hoop encircles, and whose foot this shoe fits, shall be my bride.'

What a great trying on there was now among them all ! The things would fit no one, however.

'The cinder wench is not here,' said the Prince at last; 'go and fetch her, and let her try on the things.'

So the girl was fetched, and the Prince was just going to hand the ornaments to her, when the witch held him back, saying :

'Don't give them to her; she soils everything with cinders; give them to my daughter rather.'

Well, then the Prince gave the witch's daughter the ring, and the woman filed and pared away at her daughter's finger till the ring fitted. It was the same with the circlet and the shoes of gold. The witch would not allow them to be handed to the cinder wench; she worked at her own daughter's head and feet till she got the things forced on. What was to be done now ? The Prince had to take the witch's daughter for his bride whether he would or no ; he sneaked away to her father's house with her, however, for he was ashamed to hold the wedding festivities at the palace with so strange a bride. Some days passed, and at last he had to take his bride home to the palace, and he got ready to do so. Just as they were taking leave, the kitchen wench sprang down from her place by the stove, on the pretext of fetching something from the cowhouse, and in going by she whispered in the Prince's ear as he stood in the yard :

'Alas! dear Prince, do not rob me of my silver and my gold.'

Thereupon the King's son recognised the cinder wench ; so he took both the girls with him, and set out. After they had gone some little way they came to the bank of a river, and the Prince threw the witch's daughter across to serve as a bridge, and so got over with the cinder wench. There lay the witch's daughter then, like a bridge over the river, and could not stir, though her heart was consumed with grief. No help was near, so she cried at last in her anguish :

'May there grow a golden hemlock out of my body! perhaps my mother will know me by that token.'

Scarcely had she spoken when a golden hemlock sprang up from her, and stood upon the bridge.

Now, as soon as the Prince had got rid of the witch's daughter he greeted the cinder wench as his bride, and they wandered together to the birch tree which grew upon the mother's grave. There they received all sorts of treasures and riches, three sacks full of gold, and as much silver, and a splendid steed, which bore them home to the palace. There they lived a long time together, and the young wife bore a son to the Prince. Immediately word was brought to the witch that her daughter had borne a son—for they all believed the young King's wife to be the witch's daughter.

'So, so,' said the witch to herself; 'I had better away with my gift for the infant, then.'

And so saying she set out. Thus it happened that she came to the bank of the river, and there she saw the beautiful golden hemlock growing in the middle of the bridge, and when she began to cut it down to take to her grandchild, she heard a voice moaning :

'Alas! dear mother, do not cut me so !'

'Are you here ? ' demanded the witch.

'Indeed I am, dear little mother,' answered the daughter ' They threw me across the river to make a bridge of me.'

In a moment the witch had the bridge shivered to atoms, and then she hastened away to the palace. Stepping up to the young Queen's bed, she began to try her magic arts upon her, saying :

' Spit, you wretch, on the blade of my knife ; bewitch my knife's blade for me, and I shall change you into a reindeer of the forest.'

' Are you there again to bring trouble upon me ? ' said the young woman.

She neither spat nor did anything else, but still the witch changed her into a reindeer, and smuggled her own daughter into her place as the Prince's wife. But now the child grew restless and cried, because it missed its mother's care. They took it to the court, and tried to pacify it in every conceivable way, but its crying never ceased.

' What makes the child so restless ? ' asked the Prince, and he went to a wise widow woman to ask her advice.

' Ay, ay, your own wife is not at home,' said the widow woman ; ' she is living like a reindeer in the wood ; you have the witch's daughter for a wife now, and the witch herself for a mother-in-law.'

' Is there any way of getting my own wife back from the wood again ? ' asked the Prince.

' Give me the child,' answered the widow woman. ' I'll take it with me to-morrow when I go to drive the cows to the wood. I'll make a rustling among the birch leaves and a trembling among the aspens—perhaps the boy will grow quiet when he hears it.'

' Yes, take the child away, take it to the wood with you to quiet it,' said the Prince, and led the widow woman into the castle.

' How now ? you are going to send the child away to the wood ? ' said the witch in a suspicious tone, and tried to interfere.

But the King's son stood firm by what he had commanded, and said :

' Carry the child about the wood ; perhaps that will pacify it.'

So the widow woman took the child to the wood. She came to the edge of a marsh, and seeing a herd of reindeer there, she began all at once to sing—

> ' Little Bright-eyes, little Redskin,
>   Come nurse the child you bore !
>   That bloodthirsty monster,
>   That man-eater grim,
>   Shall nurse him, shall tend him no more.
>   They may threaten and force as they will,
>   He turns from her, shrinks from her still,'

and immediately the reindeer drew near, and nursed and tended the child the whole day long; but at nightfall it had to follow the herd, and said to the widow woman:

'Bring me the child to-morrow, and again the following day; after that I must wander with the herd far away to other lands.'

The following morning the widow woman went back to the castle to fetch the child. The witch interfered, of course, but the Prince said:

'Take it, and carry it about in the open air; the boy is quieter at night, to be sure, when he has been in the wood all day.'

So the widow took the child in her arms, and carried it to the marsh in the forest. There she sang as on the preceding day—

'Little Bright-eyes, little Redskin,
Come nurse the child you bore!
That bloodthirsty monster,
That man-eater grim,
Shall nurse him, shall tend him no more.
They may threaten and force as they will,
He turns from her, shrinks from her still,'

and immediately the reindeer left the herd and came to the child, and tended it as on the day before. And so it was that the child throve, till not a finer boy was to be seen anywhere. But the King's son had been pondering over all these things, and he said to the widow woman:

'Is there no way of changing the reindeer into a human being again?'

'I don't rightly know,' was her answer. 'Come to the wood with me, however; when the woman puts off her reindeer skin I shall comb her head for her; whilst I am doing so you must burn the skin.'

Thereupon they both went to the wood with the child; scarcely were they there when the reindeer appeared and nursed the child as before. Then the widow woman said to the reindeer:

'Since you are going far away to-morrow, and I shall not see you again, let me comb your head for the last time, as a remembrance of you.'

Good; the young woman stript off the reindeer skin, and let the widow woman do as she wished. In the meantime the King's son threw the reindeer skin into the fire unobserved.

'What smells of singeing here?' asked the young woman, and looking round she saw her own husband. 'Woe is me! you have burnt my skin. Why did you do that?'

' To give you back your human form again.'

' Alack-a-day ! I have nothing to cover me now, poor creature that I am ! ' cried the young woman, and transformed herself first into a distaff, then into a wooden beetle, then into a spindle, and into all imaginable shapes.   But all these shapes the King's son went on destroying till she stood before him in human form again.

Alas ! wherefore take me home with you again,' cried the young woman, ' since the witch is sure to eat me up ? '

' She will not eat you up,' answered her husband ; and they started for home with the child.

But when the witch wife saw them she ran away with her daughter, and if she has not stopped she is running still, though at a great age.   And the Prince, and his wife, and the baby lived happy ever afterwards.[1]

                    [1] From the Russo-Karelian.

JACK AND THE BEANSTALK

JACK SELLS THE COW

ONCE upon a time there was a poor widow who lived in a little cottage with her only son Jack.

Jack was a giddy, thoughtless boy, but very kind-hearted and affectionate. There had been a hard winter, and after it the poor woman had suffered from fever and ague. Jack did no work as yet, and by degrees they grew dreadfully poor. The widow saw that there was no means of keeping Jack and herself from starvation but by selling her cow; so one morning she said to her son, 'I am too weak to go myself, Jack, so you must take the cow to market for me, and sell her.'

Jack liked going to market to sell the cow very much; but as he was on the way, he met a butcher who had some beautiful beans in his hand. Jack stopped to look at them, and the butcher told the boy that they were of great value, and persuaded the silly lad to sell the cow for these beans.

When he brought them home to his mother instead of the money she expected for her nice cow, she was very vexed and shed many tears, scolding Jack for his folly. He was very sorry, and mother and son went to bed very sadly that night; their last hope seemed gone.

At daybreak Jack rose and went out into the garden.

' At least,' he thought, ' I will sow the wonderful beans. Mother says that they are just common scarlet-runners, and nothing else; but I may as well sow them.'

So he took a piece of stick, and made some holes in the ground, and put in the beans.

That day they had very little dinner, and went sadly to bed, knowing that for the next day there would be none and Jack, unable to sleep from grief and vexation, got up at day-dawn and went out into the garden.

What was his amazement to find that the beans had grown up in the night, and climbed up and up till they covered the high cliff that sheltered the cottage, and disappeared above it! The stalks had twined and twisted themselves together till they formed quite a ladder.

'It would be easy to climb it,' thought Jack.

And, having thought of the experiment, he at once resolved to carry it out, for Jack was a good climber. However, after his late mistake about the cow, he thought he had better consult his mother first.

WONDERFUL GROWTH OF THE BEANSTALK

So Jack called his mother, and they both gazed in silent wonder at the Beanstalk, which was not only of great height, but was thick enough to bear Jack's weight.

' I wonder where it ends,' said Jack to his mother; ' I think I will climb up and see.'

His mother wished him not to venture up this strange ladder, but Jack coaxed her to give her consent to the attempt, for he was certain there must be something wonderful in the Beanstalk; so at last she yielded to his wishes.

Jack instantly began to climb, and went up and up on the ladder-like bean till everything he had left behind him—the cottage, the village, and even the tall church tower—looked quite little, and still he could not see the top of the Beanstalk.

Jack felt a little tired, and thought for a moment that he would go back again; but he was a very persevering boy, and he knew that the way to succeed in anything is not to give up. So after resting for a moment he went on.

After climbing higher and higher, till he grew afraid to look down for fear he should be giddy, Jack at last reached the top of the Beanstalk, and found himself in a beautiful country, finely wooded, with beautiful meadows covered with sheep. A crystal stream ran through the pastures; not far from the place where he had got off the Beanstalk stood a fine, strong castle.

Jack wondered very much that he had never heard of or seen this castle before; but when he reflected on the subject, he saw that it was as much separated from the village by the perpendicular rock on which it stood as if it were in another land.

While Jack was standing looking at the castle, a very strange-looking woman came out of the wood, and advanced towards him.

She wore a pointed cap of quilted red satin turned up with ermine, her hair streamed loose over her shoulders, and she walked with a staff. Jack took off his cap and made her a bow.

' If you please, ma'am,' said he, ' is this your house ? '

' No,' said the old lady. ' Listen, and I will tell you the story of that castle.

' Once upon a time there was a noble knight, who lived in this castle, which is on the borders of Fairyland. He had a fair and beloved wife and several lovely children : and as his neighbours, the little people, were very friendly towards him, they bestowed on him many excellent and precious gifts.

' Rumour whispered of these treasures; and a monstrous giant, who lived at no great distance, and who was a very wicked being, resolved to obtain possession of them.

' So he bribed a false servant to let him inside the castle, when the knight was in bed and asleep, and he killed him as he lay. Then he went to the part of the castle which was the nursery, and also killed all the poor little ones he found there.

' Happily for her, the lady was not to be found. She had gone with her infant son, who was only two or three months old, to visit her old nurse, who lived in the valley ; and she had been detained all night there by a storm.

' The next morning, as soon as it was light, one of the servants at the castle, who had managed to escape, came to tell the poor lady of the sad fate of her husband and her pretty babes. She could scarcely believe him at first, and was eager at once to go back and share the fate of her dear ones ; but the old nurse, with many tears, besought her to remember that she had still a child, and that it was her duty to preserve her life for the sake of the poor innocent.

' The lady yielded to this reasoning, and consented to remain at her nurse's house as the best place of concealment ; for the servant told her that the giant had vowed, if he could find her, he would kill both her and her baby. Years rolled on. The old nurse died, leaving her cottage and the few articles of furniture it contained to her poor lady, who dwelt in it, working as a peasant for her daily bread. Her spinning-wheel and the milk of a cow, which she had purchased with the little money she had with her, sufficed for the scanty subsistence of herself and her little son. There was a nice little garden attached to the cottage, in which they cultivated peas, beans, and cabbages, and the lady was not ashamed to go out at harvest time, and glean in the fields to supply her little son's wants.

'Jack, that poor lady is your mother. This castle was once your father's, and must again be yours.'

Jack uttered a cry of surprise.

'My mother! oh, madam, what ought I to do? My poor father! My dear mother!'

'Your duty requires you to win it back for your mother. But the task is a very difficult one, and full of peril, Jack. Have you courage to undertake it?'

'I fear nothing when I am doing right,' said Jack.

'Then,' said the lady in the red cap, 'you are one of those who slay giants. You must get into the castle, and if possible possess yourself of a hen that lays golden eggs, and a harp that talks. Remember, all the giant possesses is really yours.' As she ceased speaking, the lady of the red hat suddenly disappeared, and of course Jack knew she was a fairy.

Jack determined at once to attempt the adventure; so he advanced, and blew the horn which hung at the castle portal. The door was opened in a minute or two by a frightful giantess, with one great eye in the middle of her forehead.

As soon as Jack saw her he turned to run away, but she caught him, and dragged him into the castle.

'Ho, ho!' she laughed terribly. 'You didn't expect to see *me* here, that is clear! No, I shan't let you go again. I am weary of my life. I am so overworked, and I don't see why I should not have a page as well as other ladies. And you shall be my boy. You shall clean the knives, and black the boots, and make the fires, and help me generally when the giant is out. When he is at home I must hide you, for he has eaten up all my pages hitherto, and you would be a dainty morsel, my little lad.'

While she spoke she dragged Jack right into the castle. The poor boy was very much frightened, as I am sure you and I would have been in his place. But he remembered that fear disgraces a man; so he struggled to be brave and make the best of things.

'I am quite ready to help you, and do all I can to serve you, madam,' he said, 'only I beg you will be good enough to hide me from your husband, for I should not like to be eaten at all.'

'That's a good boy,' said the Giantess, nodding her head; 'it is lucky for you that you did not scream out when you saw me, as the other boys who have been here did, for if you had done so my husband would have awakened and have eaten you, as he did them, for breakfast. Come here, child; go into my wardrobe: he never ventures to open *that*; you will be safe there.'

And she opened a huge wardrobe which stood in the great hall, and shut him into it. But the keyhole was so large that it ad-

mitted plenty of air, and he could see everything that took place through it. By-and-by he heard a heavy tramp on the stairs, like the lumbering along of a great cannon, and then a voice like thunder cried out:

' Fe, fa, fi-fo-fum,
I smell the breath of an Englishman.
Let him be alive or let him be dead,
I'll grind his bones to make my bread.'

' Wife,' cried the Giant, ' there is a man in the castle.   Let me have him for breakfast.'

' You are grown old and stupid,' cried the lady in her loud tones.   ' It is only a nice fresh steak off an elephant, that I have cooked for you, which you smell.   There, sit down and make a good breakfast.'

And she placed a huge dish before him of savoury steaming meat, which greatly pleased him, and made him forget his idea of an Englishman being in the castle.   When he had breakfasted he went out for a walk ; and then the Giantess opened the door, and made Jack come out to help her.   He helped her all day.   She fed him well, and when evening came put him back in the wardrobe.

The Hen that lays Golden Eggs.

The Giant came in to supper.   Jack watched him through the keyhole, and was amazed to see him pick a wolf's bone, and put half a fowl at a time into his capacious mouth.

When the supper was ended he bade his wife bring him his hen that laid the golden eggs.

' It lays as well as it did when it belonged to that paltry knight,' he said ; ' indeed I think the eggs are heavier than ever.'

The Giantess went away, and soon returned with a little brown hen, which she placed on the table before her husband.   ' And now, my dear,' she said, ' I am going for a walk, if you don't want me any longer.'

' Go,' said the Giant ; ' I shall be glad to have a nap by-and-by.'

Then he took up the brown hen and said to her :

' Lay ! ' And she instantly laid a golden egg.

' Lay ! ' said the Giant again.   And she laid another.

' Lay ! ' he repeated the third time.   And again a golden egg lay on the table.

Now Jack was sure this hen was that of which the fairy had spoken.

By-and-by the Giant put the hen down on the floor, and soon after went fast asleep, snoring so loud that it sounded like thunder.

Directly Jack perceived that the Giant was fast asleep, he

pushed open the door of the wardrobe and crept out; very softly he stole across the room, and, picking up the hen, made haste to quit the apartment. He knew the way to the kitchen, the door of which he found was left ajar; he opened it, shut and locked it after him, and flew back to the Beanstalk, which he descended as fast as his feet would move.

When his mother saw him enter the house she wept for joy, for she had feared that the fairies had carried him away, or that the Giant had found him. But Jack put the brown hen down before her, and told her how he had been in the Giant's castle, and all his adventures. She was very glad to see the hen, which would make them rich once more.

THE MONEY BAGS.

Jack made another journey up the Beanstalk to the Giant's castle one day while his mother had gone to market; but first he dyed his hair and disguised himself. The old woman did not know him again, and dragged him in as she had done before, to help her to do the work; but she heard her husband coming, and hid him in the wardrobe, not thinking that it was the same boy who had stolen the hen. She bade him stay quite still there, or the Giant would eat him.

Then the Giant came in saying:

' Fe, fa, fi-fo-fum,
I smell the breath of an Englishman.
Let him be alive or let him be dead,
I'll grind his bones to make my bread.'

' Nonsense ! ' said the wife, ' it is only a roasted bullock that I thought would be a tit-bit for your supper; sit down and I will bring it up at once.' The Giant sat down, and soon his wife brought up a roasted bullock on a large dish, and they began their supper. Jack was amazed to see them pick the bones of the bullock as if it had been a lark. As soon as they had finished their meal, the Giantess rose and said :

' Now, my dear, with your leave I am going up to my room to finish the story I am reading. If you want me call for me.'

' First,' answered the Giant, ' bring me my money bags, that I may count my golden pieces before I sleep.' The Giantess obeyed. She went and soon returned with two large bags over her shoulders, which she put down by her husband.

'There,' she said; 'that is all that is left of the knight's money. When you have spent it you must go and take another baron's castle.'

'That he shan't, if I can help it,' thought Jack.

The Giant, when his wife was gone, took out heaps and heaps of golden pieces, and counted them, and put them in piles, till he was tired of the amusement. Then he swept them all back into their bags, and leaning back in his chair fell fast asleep, snoring so loud that no other sound was audible.

Jack stole softly out of the wardrobe, and taking up the bags of money (which were his very own, because the Giant had stolen them from his father), he ran off, and with great difficulty descending the Beanstalk, laid the bags of gold on his mother's table. She had just returned from town, and was crying at not finding Jack.

'There, mother, I have brought you the gold that my father lost.'

'Oh, Jack! you are a very good boy, but I wish you would not risk your precious life in the Giant's castle. Tell me how you came to go there again.'

And Jack told her all about it.

Jack's mother was very glad to get the money, but she did not like him to run any risk for her.

But after a time Jack made up his mind to go again to the Giant's castle.

The Talking Harp.

So he climbed the Beanstalk once more, and blew the horn at the Giant's gate. The Giantess soon opened the door; she was very stupid, and did not know him again, but she stopped a minute before she took him in. She feared another robbery; but Jack's fresh face looked so innocent that she could not resist him, and so she bade him come in, and again hid him away in the wardrobe.

By-and-by the Giant came home, and as soon as he had crossed the threshold he roared out:

'Fe, fa, fi-fo-fum,
I smell the breath of an Englishman.
Let him be alive or let him be dead,
I'll grind his bones to make my bread.'

'You stupid old Giant,' said his wife, 'you only smell a nice sheep, which I have grilled for your dinner.'

And the Giant sat down, and his wife brought up a whole sheep for his dinner. When he had eaten it all up, he said:

'Now bring me my harp, and I will have a little music while you take your walk.'

The Giantess obeyed, and returned with a beautiful harp. The framework was all sparkling with diamonds and rubies, and the strings were all of gold.

'This is one of the nicest things I took from the knight,' said the Giant. 'I am very fond of music, and my harp is a faithful servant.'

So he drew the harp towards him, and said:

'Play!'

And the harp played a very soft, sad air.

' Play something merrier ! ' said the Giant.

And the harp played a merry tune.

' Now play me a lullaby,' roared the Giant ; and the harp played a sweet lullaby, to the sound of which its master fell asleep.

Then Jack stole softly out of the wardrobe, and went into the huge kitchen to see if the Giantess had gone out; he found no one there, so he went to the door and opened it softly, for he thought he could not do so with the harp in his hand.

Then he entered the Giant's room and seized the harp and ran away with it; but as he jumped over the threshold the harp called out :

' Master ! Master ! '

And the Giant woke up.

With a tremendous roar he sprang from his seat, and in two strides had reached the door.

But Jack was very nimble.   He fled like lightning with the harp, talking to it as he went (for he saw it was a fairy), and telling it he was the son of its old master, the knight.

Still the Giant came on so fast that he was quite close to poor Jack, and had stretched out his great hand to catch him.   But, luckily, just at that moment he stepped upon a loose stone, stumbled, and fell flat on the ground, where he lay at his full length.

This accident gave Jack time to get on the Beanstalk and hasten down it ; but just as he reached their own garden he beheld the Giant descending after him.

' Mother ! mother! ' cried Jack, ' make haste and give me the axe.'

His mother ran to him with a hatchet in her hand, and Jack with one tremendous blow cut through all the Beanstalks except one.

' Now, mother, stand out of the way ! ' said he.

THE GIANT BREAKS HIS NECK.

Jack's mother shrank back, and it was well she did so, for just as the Giant took hold of the last branch of the Beanstalk, Jack cut the stem quite through and darted from the spot.

Down came the Giant with a terrible crash, and as he fell on his head, he broke his neck, and lay dead at the feet of the woman he had so much injured.

Before Jack and his mother had recovered from their alarm and agitation, a beautiful lady stood before them.

'Jack,' said she, 'you have acted like a brave knight's son, and deserve to have your inheritance restored to you. Dig a grave and bury the Giant, and then go and kill the Giantess.'

'But,' said Jack, 'I could not kill anyone unless I were fighting with him ; and I could not draw my sword upon a woman. Moreover, the Giantess was very kind to me.'

The Fairy smiled on Jack.

'I am very much pleased with your generous feeling,' she said. 'Nevertheless, return to the castle, and act as you will find needful.'

Jack asked the Fairy if she would show him the way to the castle, as the Beanstalk was now down. She told him that she would drive him there in her chariot, which was drawn by two peacocks. Jack thanked her, and sat down in the chariot with her.

The Fairy drove him a long distance round, till they reached a village which lay at the bottom of the hill. Here they found a number of miserable-looking men assembled. The Fairy stopped her carriage and addressed them :

'My friends,' said she, 'the cruel giant who oppressed you and ate up all your flocks and herds is dead, and this young gentleman was the means of your being delivered from him, and is the son of your kind old master, the knight.'

The men gave a loud cheer at these words, and pressed forward to say that they would serve Jack as faithfully as they had served his father. The Fairy bade them follow her to the castle, and they marched thither in a body, and Jack blew the horn and demanded admittance.

The old Giantess saw them coming from the turret loop-hole. She was very much frightened, for she guessed that something had happened to her husband ; and as she came downstairs very fast she caught her foot in her dress, and fell from the top to the bottom and broke her neck.

When the people outside found that the door was not opened to them, they took crowbars and forced the portal. Nobody was to be seen, but on leaving the hall they found the body of the Giantess at the foot of the stairs.

Thus Jack took possession of the castle. The Fairy went and brought his mother to him, with the hen and the harp. He had the Giantess buried, and endeavoured as much as lay in his power to do right to those whom the Giant had robbed.

Before her departure for fairyland, the Fairy explained to Jack that she had sent the butcher to meet him with the beans, in order to try what sort of lad he was.

If you had looked at the gigantic Beanstalk and only stupidly wondered about it,' she said, 'I should have left you where misfortune had placed you, only restoring her cow to your mother. But you showed an inquiring mind, and great courage and enterprise, therefore you deserve to rise; and when you mounted the Beanstalk you climbed the Ladder of Fortune.'

She then took her leave of Jack and his mother.

THE LITTLE GOOD MOUSE

ONCE upon a time there lived a King and Queen who loved each
other so much that they were never happy unless they were
together. Day after day they went out hunting or fishing; night
after night they went to balls or to the opera; they sang, and danced,
and ate sugar-plums, and were the gayest of the gay, and all their
subjects followed their example so that the kingdom was called the
Joyous Land. Now in the next kingdom everything was as different
as it could possibly be. The King was sulky and savage, and never
enjoyed himself at all. He looked so ugly and cross that all his
subjects feared him, and he hated the very sight of a cheerful face;
so if he ever caught anyone smiling he had his head cut off that
very minute. This kingdom was very appropriately called the Land
of Tears. Now when this wicked King heard of the happiness of
the Jolly King, he was so jealous that he collected a great army
and set out to fight him, and the news of his approach was soon
brought to the King and Queen. The Queen, when she heard of it,
was frightened out of her wits, and began to cry bitterly. 'Sire,'
she said, 'let us collect all our riches and run away as far as ever
we can, to the other side of the world.'

But the King answered:

'Fie, madam! I am far too brave for that. It is better to die
than to be a coward.'

Then he assembled all his armed men, and after bidding the
Queen a tender farewell, he mounted his splendid horse and rode
away. When he was lost to sight the Queen could do nothing but
weep, and wring her hands, and cry.

'Alas! If the King is killed, what will become of me and of my
little daughter?' and she was so sorrowful that she could neither eat
nor sleep.

The King sent her a letter every day, but at last, one morning, as she looked out of the palace window, she saw a messenger approaching in hot haste.

' What news, courier ? What news ? ' cried the Queen, and he answered :

' The battle is lost and the King is dead, and in another moment the enemy will be here.'

The poor Queen fell back insensible, and all her ladies carried her to bed, and stood round her weeping and wailing. Then began a tremendous noise and confusion, and they knew that the enemy had arrived, and very soon they heard the King himself stamping about the palace seeking the Queen. Then her ladies put the little Princess into her arms, and covered her up, head and all, in the bedclothes, and ran for their lives, and the poor Queen lay there shaking, and hoping she would not be found. But very soon the wicked King clattered into the room, and in a fury because the Queen would not answer when he called to her, he tore back her silken coverings and tweaked off her lace cap, and when all her lovely hair came tumbling down over her shoulders, he wound it three times round his hand and threw her over his shoulder, where he carried her like a sack of flour.

The poor Queen held her little daughter safe in her arms and shrieked for mercy, but the wicked King only mocked her, and begged her to go on shrieking, as it amused him, and so mounted his great black horse, and rode back to his own country. When he got there he declared that he would have the Queen and the little Princess hanged on the nearest tree ; but his courtiers said that seemed a pity, for when the baby grew up she would be a very nice wife for the King's only son.

The King was rather pleased with this idea, and shut the Queen up in the highest room of a tall tower, which was very tiny, and miserably furnished with a table and a very hard bed upon the floor. Then he sent for a fairy who lived near his kingdom, and after receiving her with more politeness than he generally showed, and entertaining her at a sumptuous feast, he took her up to see the Queen. The fairy was so touched by the sight of her misery that when she kissed her hand she whispered :

' Courage, madam ! I think I see a way to help you.'

The Queen, a little comforted by these words, received her graciously, and begged her to take pity upon the poor little Princess, who had met with such a sudden reverse of fortune. But the King got very cross when he saw them whispering together, and cried harshly :

' Make an end of these fine speeches, madam. I brought you here to tell me if the child will grow up pretty and fortunate.'

Then the Fairy answered that the Princess would be as pretty, and clever, and well brought up as it was possible to be, and the old King growled to the Queen that it was lucky for her that it was so, as they would certainly have been hanged if it were otherwise. Then he stamped off, taking the Fairy with him, and leaving the poor Queen in tears.

' How can I wish my little daughter to grow up pretty if she is to be married to that horrid little dwarf, the King's son,' she said to herself, 'and yet, if she is ugly we shall both be killed. If I could only hide her away somewhere, so that the cruel King could never find her.'

As the days went on, the Queen and the little Princess grew thinner and thinner, for their hard-hearted gaoler gave them every day only three boiled peas and a tiny morsel of black bread, so they were always terribly hungry. At last, one evening, as the Queen sat at her spinning-wheel—for the King was so avaricious that she was made to work day and night—she saw a tiny, pretty little mouse creep out of a hole, and said to it :

' Alas, little creature ! what are you coming to look for here ? I only have three peas for my day's provision, so unless you wish to fast you must go elsewhere.'

But the mouse ran hither and thither, and danced and capered so prettily, that at last the Queen gave it her last pea, which she was keeping for her supper, saying : 'Here, little one, eat it up ; I have nothing better to offer you, but I give this willingly in return for the amusement I have had from you.'

She had hardly spoken when she saw upon the table a delicious little roast partridge, and two dishes of preserved fruit. ' Truly,' said she, ' a kind action never goes unrewarded ; ' and she and the little Princess ate their supper with great satisfaction, and then the Queen gave what was left to the little mouse, who danced better than ever afterwards. The next morning came the gaoler with the Queen's allowance of three peas, which he brought in upon a large dish to make them look smaller ; but as soon as he set it down the little mouse came and ate up all three, so that when the Queen wanted her dinner there was nothing left for her. Then she was quite provoked, and said :

' What a bad little beast that mouse must be ! If it goes on like this I shall be starved.' But when she glanced at the dish again

it was covered with all sorts of nice things to eat, and the Queen
made a very good dinner, and was gayer than usual over it. But
afterwards as she sat at her spinning-wheel she began to consider
what would happen if the little Princess did not grow up pretty
enough to please the King, and she said to herself:

' Oh ! if I could only think of some way of escaping.'

As she spoke she saw the little mouse playing in a corner with
some long straws. The Queen took them and began to plait them,
saying :

' If only I had straws enough I would make a basket with them,
and let my baby down in it from the window to any kind passer-
by who would take care of her.'

By the time the straws were all plaited the little mouse had
dragged in more and more, until the Queen had plenty to make
her basket, and she worked at it day and night, while the little
mouse danced for her amusement ; and at dinner and supper time
the Queen gave it the three peas and the bit of black bread, and
always found something good in the dish in their place. She
really could not imagine where all the nice things came from.
At last one day when the basket was finished, the Queen was looking out of the window to see how long a cord she must make to
lower it to the bottom of the tower, when she noticed a little old
woman who was leaning upon her stick and looking up at her.
Presently she said :

' I know your trouble, madam. If you like I will help you.'

' Oh ! my dear friend,' said the Queen. ' If you really wish to
be of use to me you will come at the time that I will appoint, and
I will let down my poor little baby in a basket. If you will take
her, and bring her up for me, when I am rich I will reward you
splendidly.'

' I don't care about the reward,' said the old woman, ' but there
is one thing I should like. You must know that I am very particular about what I eat, and if there is one thing that I fancy
above all others, it is a plump, tender little mouse. If there is
such a thing in your garret just throw it down to me, and in
return I will promise that your little daughter shall be well taken
care of.'

The Queen when she heard this began to cry, but made no
answer, and the old woman after waiting a few minutes asked her
what was the matter.

' Why,' said the Queen, ' there is only one mouse in this garret, and that is such a dear, pretty little thing that I cannot bear to think of its being killed.'

What!' cried the old woman, in a rage. 'Do you care more for a miserable mouse than for your own baby ? Good-bye, madam ! I leave you to enjoy its company, and for my own part I thank my stars that I can get plenty of mice without troubling you to give them to me.'

And she hobbled off grumbling and growling. As to the Queen, she was so disappointed that, in spite of finding a better dinner than usual, and seeing the little mouse dancing in its merriest mood, she could do nothing but cry. That night when her baby was fast asleep she packed it into the basket, and wrote on a slip of paper, 'This unhappy little girl is called Delicia ! ' This she pinned to its robe, and then very sadly she was shutting the basket, when in sprang the little mouse and sat on the baby's pillow.

' Ah ! little one,' said the Queen, 'it cost me dear to save your life. How shall I know now whether my Delicia is being taken care of or no ? Anyone else would have let the greedy old woman have you, and eat you up, but I could not bear to do it.' Whereupon the Mouse answered :

' Believe me, madam, you will never repent of your kindness.'

The Queen was immensely astonished when the Mouse began to speak, and still more so when she saw its little sharp nose turn to a beautiful face, and its paws to hands and feet ; then it suddenly grew tall, and the Queen recognised the Fairy who had come with the wicked King to visit her.

The Fairy smiled at her astonished look, and said:

' I wanted to see if you were faithful and capable of feeling a real friendship for me, for you see we fairies are rich in everything but friends, and those are hard to find.'

' It is not possible that *you* should want for friends, you charming creature,' said the Queen, kissing her.

' Indeed it is so,' the Fairy said. ' For those who are only friendly with me for their own advantage, I do not count at all. But when you cared for the poor little mouse you could not have known there was anything to be gained by it, and to try you further I took the form of the old woman whom you talked to from the window, and then I was convinced that you really loved me.' Then, turning to the little Princess, she kissed her rosy lips three times, saying :

' Dear little one, I promise that you shall be richer than your

father, and shall live a hundred years, always pretty and happy,
without fear of old age and wrinkles.'

The Queen, quite delighted, thanked the Fairy gratefully, and
begged her to take charge of the little Delicia and bring her up as
her own daughter. This she agreed to do, and then they shut the
basket and lowered it carefully, baby and all, to the ground at the
foot of the tower. The Fairy then changed herself back into the
form of a mouse, and this delayed her a few seconds, after which
she ran nimbly down the straw rope, but only to find when she got
to the bottom that the baby had disappeared.

In the greatest terror she ran up again to the Queen, crying:

'All is lost! my enemy Cancaline has stolen the Princess away.
You must know that she is a cruel fairy who hates me, and as
she is older than I am and has more power, I can do nothing against
her. I know no way of rescuing Delicia from her clutches.'

When the Queen heard this terrible news she was heart-broken,
and begged the Fairy to do all she could to get the poor little Princess
back again. At this moment in came the gaoler, and when he
missed the little Princess he at once told the King, who came in a
great fury asking what the Queen had done with her. She answered
that a fairy, whose name she did not know, had come and carried
her off by force. Upon this the King stamped upon the ground, and
cried in a terrible voice:

'You shall be hung! I always told you you should.' And without another word he dragged the unlucky Queen out into the nearest
wood, and climbed up into a tree to look for a branch to which he
could hang her. But when he was quite high up, the Fairy, who
had made herself invisible and followed them, gave him a sudden
push, which made him lose his footing and fall to the ground with
a crash and break four of his teeth, and while he was trying to
mend them the fairy carried the Queen off in her flying chariot to a
beautiful castle, where she was so kind to her that but for the loss of
Delicia the Queen would have been perfectly happy. But though
the good little mouse did her very utmost, they could not find out
where Cancaline had hidden the little Princess.

Thus fifteen years went by, and the Queen had somewhat recovered from her grief, when the news reached her that the son of
the wicked King wished to marry the little maiden who kept the
turkeys, and that she had refused him; the wedding-dresses had been
made, nevertheless, and the festivities were to be so splendid that
all the people for leagues round were flocking in to be present at

them.   The Queen felt quite curious about a little turkey-maiden who did not wish to be a Queen, so the little mouse conveyed herself to the poultry-yard to find out what she was like.

She found the turkey-maiden sitting upon a big stone, barefooted, and miserably dressed in an old, coarse linen gown and cap ; the

1 Speed

ground at her feet was all strewn with robes of gold and silver, ribbons and laces, diamonds and pearls, over which the turkeys were stalking to and fro, while the King's ugly, disagreeable son stood opposite her, declaring angrily that if she would not marry him she should be killed.

The Turkey-maiden answered proudly:

' I never will marry you! you are too ugly and too much like your cruel father. Leave me in peace with my turkeys, which I like far better than all your fine gifts.'

The little mouse watched her with the greatest admiration, for she was as beautiful as the spring; and as soon as the wicked Prince was gone, she took the form of an old peasant woman and said to her:

' Good-day, my pretty one! you have a fine flock of turkeys there.'

The young Turkey-maiden turned her gentle eyes upon the old woman, and answered:

' Yet they wish me to leave them to become a miserable Queen! what is your advice upon the matter? '

' My child,' said the Fairy, ' a crown is a very pretty thing, but you know neither the price nor the weight of it.'

' I know so well that I have refused to wear one,' said the little maiden, ' though I don't know who was my father, or who was my mother, and I have not a friend in the world.'

' You have goodness and beauty, which are of more value than ten kingdoms,' said the wise Fairy. ' But tell me, child, how came you here, and how is it you have neither father, nor mother, nor friend? '

' A Fairy called Cancaline is the cause of my being here,' answered she, ' for while I lived with her I got nothing but blows and harsh words, until at last I could bear it no longer, and ran away from her without knowing where I was going, and as I came through a wood the wicked Prince met me, and offered to give me charge of the poultry-yard. I accepted gladly, not knowing that I should have to see him day by day. And now he wants to marry me, but that I will never consent to.'

Upon hearing this the Fairy became convinced that the little Turkey-maiden was none other than the Princess Delicia.

' What is your name, my little one? ' said she.

' I am called Delicia, if it please you,' she answered.

Then the Fairy threw her arms round the Princess's neck, and nearly smothered her with kisses, saying:

' Ah, Delicia! I am a very old friend of yours, and I am truly glad to find you at last; but you might look nicer than you do in that old gown, which is only fit for a kitchen-maid. Take this pretty dress and let us see the difference it will make.'

So Delicia took off the ugly cap, and shook out all her fair shining hair, and bathed her hands and face in clear water from the nearest spring till her cheeks were like roses, and when she was adorned with the diamonds and the splendid robe the Fairy had given her, she looked the most beautiful Princess in the world, and the Fairy with great delight cried :

' Now you look as you ought to look, Delicia : what do you think about it yourself ? '

And Delicia answered :

' I feel as if I were the daughter of some great king.'

' And would you be glad if you were ? ' said the Fairy.

' Indeed I should,' answered she.

' Ah, well,' said the Fairy, ' to-morrow I may have some pleasant news for you.'

So she hurried back to her castle, where the Queen sat busy with her embroidery, and cried :

' Well, madam ! will you wager your thimble and your golden needle that I am bringing you the best news you could possibly hear ? '

' Alas ! ' sighed the Queen, ' since the death of the Jolly King and the loss of my Delicia, all the news in the world is not worth a pin to me.

' There, there, don't be melancholy,' said the Fairy. ' I assure you the Princess is quite well, and I have never seen her equal for beauty.   She might be a Queen to-morrow if she chose ; ' and then she told all that had happened, and the Queen first rejoiced over the thought of Delicia's beauty, and then wept at the idea of her being a Turkey-maiden.

' I will not hear of her being made to marry the wicked King's son,' she said.   ' Let us go at once and bring her here.'

In the meantime the wicked Prince, who was very angry with Delicia, had sat himself down under a tree, and cried and howled with rage and spite until the King heard him, and cried out from the window :

' What is the matter with you, that you are making all this disturbance ? '

The Prince replied :

' It is all because our Turkey-maiden will not love me ! '

' Won't love you ? eh ! ' said the King.   ' We'll very soon see about that ! '   So he called his guards and told them to go and fetch Delicia.   ' See if I don't make her change her mind pretty soon ! ' said the wicked King with a chuckle.

Then the guards began to search the poultry-yard, and could find nobody there but Delicia, who, with her splendid dress and her crown of diamonds, looked such a lovely Princess that they hardly dared to speak to her. But she said to them very politely:

' Pray tell me what you are looking for here ? '

' Madam,' they answered, ' we are sent for an insignificant little person called Delicia.'

' Alas ! ' said she, ' that is my name. What can you want with me ? '

So the guards tied her hands and feet with thick ropes, for fear

S. Krohon se

she might run away, and brought her to the King, who was waiting with his son.

When he saw her he was very much astonished at her beauty, which would have made anyone less hard-hearted sorry for her. But the wicked King only laughed and mocked at her, and cried : ' Well, little fright, little toad ! why don't you love my son, who is far too handsome and too good for you ? Make haste and begin to love him this instant, or you shall be tarred and feathered.'

Then the poor little Princess, shaking with terror, went down on her knees, crying:

'Oh, don't tar and feather me, please! It would be so uncomfortable. Let me have two or three days to make up my mind, and then you shall do as you like with me.'

The wicked Prince would have liked very much to see her tarred and feathered, but the King ordered that she should be shut up in a dark dungeon. It was just at this moment that the Queen and the Fairy arrived in the flying chariot, and the Queen was dreadfully distressed at the turn affairs had taken, and said miserably that she was destined to be unfortunate all her days. But the Fairy bade her take courage.

'I'll pay them out yet,' said she, nodding her head with an air of great determination.

That very same night, as soon as the wicked King had gone to bed, the Fairy changed herself into the little mouse, and creeping up on to his pillow nibbled his ear, so that he squealed out quite loudly and turned over on his other side; but that was no good, for the little mouse only set to work and gnawed away at the second ear until it hurt more than the first one.

Then the King cried 'Murder!' and 'Thieves!' and all his guards ran to see what was the matter, but they could find nothing and nobody, for the little mouse had run off to the Prince's room and was serving him in exactly the same way. All night long she ran from one to the other, until at last, driven quite frantic by terror and want of sleep, the King rushed out of the palace crying:

'Help! help! I am pursued by rats.'

The Prince when he heard this got up also, and ran after the King, and they had not gone far when they both fell into the river and were never heard of again.

Then the good Fairy ran to tell the Queen, and they went together to the black dungeon where Delicia was imprisoned. The Fairy touched each door with her wand, and it sprang open instantly, but they had to go through forty before they came to the Princess, who was sitting on the floor looking very dejected. But when the Queen rushed in, and kissed her twenty times in a minute, and laughed, and cried, and told Delicia all her history, the Princess was wild with delight. Then the Fairy showed her all the wonderful dresses and jewels she had brought for her, and said:

'Don't let us waste time; we must go and harangue the people.'

So she walked first, looking very serious and dignified, and wearing a dress the train of which was at least ten ells long. Behind her came the Queen wearing a blue velvet robe embroidered with gold, and a diamond crown that was brighter than the sun itself. Last of all walked Delicia, who was so beautiful that it was nothing short of marvellous.

They proceeded through the streets, returning the salutations of all they met, great or small, and all the people turned and followed them, wondering who these noble ladies could be.

When the audience hall was quite full, the Fairy said to the subjects of the Wicked King that if they would accept Delicia, who was the daughter of the Jolly King, as their Queen, she would undertake to find a suitable husband for her, and would promise that during their reign there should be nothing but rejoicing and merry-making, and all dismal things should be entirely banished. Upon this the people cried with one accord, ' We will, we will! we have been gloomy and miserable too long already.' And they all took hands and danced round the Queen, and Delicia, and the good Fairy, singing: ' Yes, yes; we will, we will! '

Then there were feasts and fireworks in every street in the town, and early the next morning the Fairy, who had been all over the world in the night, brought back with her, in her flying chariot, the most handsome and good-tempered Prince she could find anywhere. He was so charming that Delicia loved him from the moment their eyes met, and as for him, of course he could not help thinking himself the luckiest Prince in the world. The Queen felt that she had really come to the end of her misfortunes at last, and they all lived happily ever after.[1]

La bonne vetite Souris, par Madame d'Aulnoy.

GRACIOSA AND PERCINET

ONCE upon a time there lived a King and Queen who had one charming daughter. She was so graceful and pretty and clever that she was called Graciosa, and the Queen was so fond of her that she could think of nothing else.

Every day she gave the Princess a lovely new frock of gold brocade, or satin, or velvet, and when she was hungry she had bowls full of sugar-plums, and at least twenty pots of jam. Everybody said she was the happiest Princess in the world. Now there lived at this same court a very rich old duchess whose name was Grumbly. She was more frightful than tongue can tell; her hair was red as fire, and she had but one eye, and that not a pretty one! Her face was as broad as a full moon, and her mouth was so large that everybody who met her would have been afraid they were going to be eaten up, only she had no teeth. As she was as cross as she was ugly, she could not bear to hear everyone saying how pretty and how charming Graciosa was; so she presently went away from the court to her own castle, which was not far off. But if anybody who went to see her happened to mention the charming Princess, she would cry angrily :

' It's not true that she is lovely. I have more beauty in my little finger than she has in her whole body.'

Soon after this, to the great grief of the Princess, the Queen was taken ill and died, and the King became so melancholy that for a whole year he shut himself up in his palace. At last his physicians, fearing that he would fall ill, ordered that he should go out and amuse himself; so a hunting party was arranged, but as it was very hot weather the King soon got tired, and said he would dismount and rest at a castle which they were passing.

This happened to be the Duchess Grumbly's castle, and when she heard that the King was coming she went out to meet him, and said that the cellar was the coolest place in the whole castle if he

would condescend to come down into it. So down they went together, and the King seeing about two hundred great casks ranged
side by side, asked if it was only for herself that she had this immense store of wine.

'Yes, sire,' answered she, 'it is for myself alone, but I shall be
most happy to let you taste some of it. Which do you like, canary,
St. Julien, champagne, hermitage sack, raisin, or cider?'

'Well,' said the King, 'since you are so kind as to ask me, I
prefer champagne to anything else.'

Then Duchess Grumbly took up a little hammer and tapped
upon the cask twice, and out came at least a thousand crowns.

'What's the meaning of this?' said she smiling.

Then she tapped the next cask, and out came a bushel of gold
pieces.

'I don't understand this at all,' said the Duchess, smiling more
than before.

Then she went on to the third cask, tap, tap, and out came such
a stream of diamonds and pearls that the ground was covered with
them.

'Ah!' she cried, 'this is altogether beyond my comprehension,
sire. Someone must have stolen my good wine and put all this
rubbish in its place.'

'Rubbish, do you call it, Madam Grumbly?' cried the King.
'Rubbish! why there is enough there to buy ten kingdoms.'

'Well,' said she, 'you must know that all those casks are full
of gold and jewels, and if you like to marry me it shall all be
yours.'

Now the King loved money more than anything else in the world,
so he cried joyfully:

'Marry you? why with all my heart! to-morrow if you like.'

'But I make one condition,' said the Duchess; 'I must have
entire control of your daughter to do as I please with her.'

'Oh certainly, you shall have your own way; let us shake hands
upon the bargain,' said the King.

So they shook hands and went up out of the cellar of treasure
together, and the Duchess locked the door and gave the key to the
King.

When he got back to his own palace Graciosa ran out to meet
him, and asked if he had had good sport.

'I have caught a dove,' answered he.

'Oh! do give it to me,' said the Princess, 'and I will keep it and
take care of it.'

'I can hardly do that,' said he, 'for, to speak more plainly, I
mean that I met the Duchess Grumbly, and have promised to
marry her.'

'And you call her a dove?' cried the Princess. '*I* should have
called her a screech owl.'

'Hold your tongue,' said the King, very crossly. 'I intend you
to behave prettily to her. So now go and make yourself fit to be
seen, as I am going to take you to visit her.'

So the Princess went very sorrowfully to her own room, and her
nurse, seeing her tears, asked what was vexing her.

'Alas! who would not be vexed?' answered she, 'for the King
intends to marry again, and has chosen for his new bride my
enemy, the hideous Duchess Grumbly.'

'Oh, well!' answered the nurse, 'you must remember that you
are a Princess, and are expected to set a good example in making
the best of whatever happens. You must promise me not to let the
Duchess see how much you dislike her.'

At first the Princess would not promise, but the nurse showed
her so many good reasons for it that in the end she agreed to be
amiable to her step-mother.

Then the nurse dressed her in a robe of pale green and gold

brocade, and combed out her long fair hair till it floated round her
like a golden mantle, and put on her head a crown of roses and
jasmine with emerald leaves.

When she was ready nobody could have been prettier, but she
still could not help looking sad.

Meanwhile the Duchess Grumbly was also occupied in attiring
herself. She had one of her shoe heels made an inch or so higher
than the other, that she might not limp so much, and put in a cunningly made glass eye in the place of the one she had lost. She
dyed her red hair black, and painted her face. Then she put on a
gorgeous robe of lilac satin lined with blue, and a yellow petticoat
trimmed with violet ribbons, and because she had heard that queens
always rode into their new dominions, she ordered a horse to be
made ready for her to ride.

While Graciosa was waiting until the King should be ready to
set out, she went down all alone through the garden into a little
wood, where she sat down upon a mossy bank and began to think.
And her thoughts were so doleful that very soon she began to cry,
and she cried, and cried, and forgot all about going back to the
palace, until she suddenly saw a handsome page standing before
her. He was dressed in green, and the cap which he held in his
hand was adorned with white plumes. When Graciosa looked at
him he went down on one knee, and said to her :

' Princess, the King awaits you.'

The Princess was surprised, and, if the truth must be told, very
much delighted at the appearance of this charming page, whom she
could not remember to have seen before. Thinking he might belong
to the household of the Duchess, she said :

' How long have you been one of the King's pages ? '

' I am not in the service of the King, madam,' answered he, ' but
in yours.'

' In mine ? ' said the Princess with great surprise. ' Then how
is it that I have never seen you before ? '

' Ah, Princess ! ' said he, ' I have never before dared to present
myself to you, but now the King's marriage threatens you with so
many dangers that I have resolved to tell you at once how much I
love you already, and I trust that in time I may win your regard. I
am Prince Percinet, of whose riches you may have heard, and whose
fairy gift will, I hope, be of use to you in all your difficulties, if you
will permit me to accompany you under this disguise.'

' Ah, Percinet ! ' cried the Princess, ' is it really you ? I have so often heard of you and wished to see you. If you will indeed be my friend, I shall not be afraid of that wicked old Duchess any more.'

So they went back to the palace together, and there Graciosa found a beautiful horse which Percinet had brought for her to ride. As it was very spirited he led it by the bridle, and this arrangement enabled him to turn and look at the Princess often, which he did not fail to do. Indeed, she was so pretty that it was a real pleasure to look at her. When the horse which the Duchess was to ride appeared beside Graciosa's, it looked no better than an old cart horse, and as to their trappings, there was simply no comparison between them, as the Princess's saddle and bridle were one glittering mass of diamonds. The King had so many other things to think of that he did not notice this, but all his courtiers were entirely taken up with admiring the Princess and her charming Page in green, who was more handsome and distinguished-looking than all the rest of the court put together.

When they met the Duchess Grumbly she was seated in an open carriage trying in vain to look dignified. The King and the Princess saluted her, and her horse was brought forward for her to mount. But when she saw Graciosa's she cried angrily :

'If that child is to have a better horse than mine, I will go back to my own castle this very minute. What is the good of being a Queen if one is to be slighted like this ? '

Upon this the King commanded Graciosa to dismount and to beg the Duchess to honour her by mounting her horse. The Princess obeyed in silence, and the Duchess, without looking at her or thanking her, scrambled up upon the beautiful horse, where she sat looking like a bundle of clothes, and eight officers had to hold her up for fear she should fall off.

Even then she was not satisfied, and was still grumbling and muttering, so they asked her what was the matter.

'I wish that Page in green to come and lead the horse, as he did when Graciosa rode it,' said she very sharply.

And the King ordered the Page to come and lead the Queen's horse. Percinet and the Princess looked at one another, but said never a word, and then he did as the King commanded, and the procession started in great pomp. The Duchess was greatly elated, and as she sat there in state would not have wished to change places even with Graciosa. But at the moment when it was least expected the beautiful horse began to plunge and rear and kick, and finally to run away at such a pace that it was impossible to stop him.

At first the Duchess clung to the saddle, but she was very soon thrown off and fell in a heap among the stones and thorns, and there they found her, shaken to a jelly, and collected what was left of her as if she had been a broken glass. Her bonnet was here and her shoes there, her face was scratched, and her fine clothes were covered with mud. Never was a bride seen in such a dismal plight. They carried her back to the palace and put her to bed, but as soon as she recovered enough to be able to speak, she began to scold and rage, and declared that the whole affair was Graciosa's fault, that she had contrived it on purpose to try and get rid of her, and that if the King would not have her punished, she would go back to her castle and enjoy her riches by herself.

At this the King was terribly frightened, for he did not at all want to lose all those barrels of gold and jewels. So he hastened to appease the Duchess, and told her she might punish Graciosa in any way she pleased.

Thereupon she sent for Graciosa, who turned pale and trembled at the summons, for she guessed that it promised nothing agreeable for her. She looked all about for Percinet, but he was nowhere to be seen; so she had no choice but to go to the Duchess Grumbly's room. She had hardly got inside the door when she was seized by four waiting women, who looked so tall and strong and cruel that the Princess shuddered at the sight of them, and still more when she saw them arming themselves with great bundles of rods, and heard the Duchess call out to them from her bed to beat the Princess without mercy. Poor Graciosa wished miserably that Percinet could only know what was happening and come to rescue her. But no sooner did they begin to beat her than she found, to her great relief, that the rods had changed to bundles of peacock's feathers, and though the Duchess's women went on till they were so tired that they could no longer raise their arms from their sides, yet she was not hurt in the least. However, the Duchess thought she must be black and blue after such a beating; so Graciosa, when she was released, pretended to feel very bad, and went away into her own room, where she told her nurse all that had happened, and then the nurse left her, and when the Princess turned round there stood Percinet beside her. She thanked him gratefully for helping her so cleverly, and they laughed and were very merry over the way they had taken in the Duchess and her waiting-maids; but Percinet advised her still to pretend to be ill for a few days, and after promising to come to her aid whenever she needed him, he disappeared as suddenly as he had come.

The Duchess was so delighted at the idea that Graciosa was really ill, that she herself recovered twice as fast as she would have done otherwise, and the wedding was held with great magnificence. Now as the King knew that, above all other things, the Queen loved to be told that she was beautiful, he ordered that her portrait should be painted, and that a tournament should be held, at which all the bravest knights of his court should maintain against all comers that Grumbly was the most beautiful princess in the world.

Numbers of knights came from far and wide to accept the challenge, and the hideous Queen sat in great state in a balcony hung with cloth of gold to watch the contests, and Graciosa had to stand up behind her, where her loveliness was so conspicuous that the combatants could not keep their eyes off her. But the Queen was so vain that she thought all their admiring glances were for herself, especially as, in spite of the badness of their cause, the King's knights were so brave that they were the victors in every combat.

However, when nearly all the strangers had been defeated, a young unknown knight presented himself. He carried a portrait, enclosed in a box encrusted with diamonds, and he declared himself willing to maintain against them all that the Queen was the ugliest creature in the world, and that the Princess whose portrait he carried was the most beautiful.

So one by one the knights came out against him, and one by one he vanquished them all, and then he opened the box, and said that, to console them, he would show them the portrait of his Queen of Beauty, and when he did so everyone recognised the Princess Graciosa. The unknown knight then saluted her gracefully and retired, without telling his name to anybody. But Graciosa had no difficulty in guessing that it was Percinet.

As to the Queen, she was so furiously angry that she could hardly speak ; but she soon recovered her voice, and overwhelmed Graciosa with a torrent of reproaches.

' What ! ' she said, ' do you dare to dispute with me for the prize of beauty, and expect me to endure this insult to my knights ? But I will not bear it, proud Princess. I will have my revenge.'

' I assure you, Madam,' said the Princess, ' that I had nothing to do with it and am quite willing that you shall be declared Queen of Beauty

'Ah! you are pleased to jest, popinjay!' said the Queen, 'but it will be my turn soon!'

The King was speedily told what had happened, and how the Princess was in terror of the angry Queen, but he only said:

'The Queen must do as she pleases. Graciosa belongs to her!'

The wicked Queen waited impatiently until night fell, and then she ordered her carriage to be brought. Graciosa, much against her will, was forced into it, and away they drove, and never stopped until they reached a great forest, a hundred leagues from the palace. This forest was so gloomy, and so full of lions, tigers, bears and wolves, that nobody dared pass through it even by daylight, and here they set down the unhappy Princess in the middle of the black night, and left her in spite of all her tears and entreaties. The Princess stood quite still at first from sheer bewilderment, but when the last sound of the retreating carriages died away in the distance she began to run aimlessly hither and thither, sometimes knocking herself against a tree, sometimes tripping over a stone, fearing every minute that she would be eaten up by the lions. Presently she was too tired to advance another step, so she threw herself down upon the ground and cried miserably:

'Oh, Percinet! where are you? Have you forgotten me altogether?'

She had hardly spoken when all the forest was lighted up with a sudden glow. Every tree seemed to be sending out a soft radiance, which was clearer than moonlight and softer than daylight, and at the end of a long avenue of trees opposite to her the Princess saw a palace of clear crystal which blazed like the sun. At that moment a slight sound behind her made her start round, and there stood Percinet himself.

'Did I frighten you, my Princess?' said he. 'I come to bid you welcome to our fairy palace, in the name of the Queen, my mother, who is prepared to love you as much as I do.' The Princess joyfully mounted with him into a little sledge, drawn by two stags, which bounded off and drew them swiftly to the wonderful palace, where the Queen received her with the greatest kindness, and a splendid banquet was served at once. Graciosa was so happy to have found Percinet, and to have escaped from the gloomy forest and all its terrors, that she was very hungry and very merry, and they were a gay party. After supper they went into another lovely room, where the crystal walls were covered with pictures, and the Princess saw with great surprise that her own history was represented, even down to the moment when Percinet found her in the forest.

'Your painters must indeed be diligent,' she said, pointing out the last picture to the Prince.

'They are obliged to be, for I will not have anything forgotten that happens to you,' he answered.

When the Princess grew sleepy, twenty-four charming maidens put her to bed in the prettiest room she had ever seen, and then sang to her so sweetly that Graciosa's dreams were all of mermaids,

and cool sea waves, and caverns, in which she wandered with Percinet; but when she woke up again her first thought was that, delightful as this fairy palace seemed to her, yet she could not stay in it, but must go back to her father. When she had been dressed by the four-and-twenty maidens in a charming robe which the Queen had sent for her, and in which she looked prettier than ever, Prince Percinet came to see her, and was bitterly disappointed when she told him what she had been thinking. He begged her to consider again how unhappy the wicked Queen would make her, and

how, if she would but marry him, all the fairy palace would be
hers, and his one thought would be to please her.   But, in spite of
everything he could say, the Princess was quite determined to go
back, though he at last persuaded her to stay eight days, which were
so full of pleasure and amusement that they passed like a few
hours.   On the last day, Graciosa, who had often felt anxious to
know what was going on in her father's palace, said to Percinet
that she was sure that he could find out for her, if he would, what
reason the Queen had given her father for her sudden disappear-
ance.   Percinet at first offered to send his courier to find out, but
the Princess said:

'Oh! isn't there a quicker way of knowing than that?'

'Very well,' said Percinet, 'you shall see for yourself.'

So up they went together to the top of a very high tower, which,
like the rest of the castle, was built entirely of rock-crystal.

There the Prince held Graciosa's hand in his, and made her put
the tip of her little finger into her mouth, and look towards the town,
and immediately she saw the wicked Queen go to the King, and
heard her say to him, 'That miserable Princess is dead, and no
great loss either.   I have ordered that she shall be buried at once.'

And then the Princess saw how she dressed up a log of wood
and had it buried, and how the old King cried, and all the people
murmured that the Queen had killed Graciosa with her cruelties,
and that she ought to have her head cut off.   When the Princess
saw that the King was so sorry for her pretended death that he
could neither eat nor drink, she cried:

'Ah, Percinet! take me back quickly if you love me.'

And so, though he did not want to at all, he was obliged to
promise that he would let her go.

'You may not regret me, Princess,' he said sadly, 'for I fear
that you do not love me well enough; but I foresee that you will
more than once regret that you left this fairy palace where we
have been so happy.'

But, in spite of all he could say, she bade farewell to the Queen,
his mother, and prepared to set out; so Percinet, very unwillingly,
brought the little sledge with the stags and she mounted beside him.
But they had hardly gone twenty yards when a tremendous noise
behind her made Graciosa look back, and she saw the palace of crystal
fly into a million splinters, like the spray of a fountain, and vanish.

'Oh, Percinet!' she cried, 'what has happened?   The palace is
gone.'

'Yes,' he answered, 'my palace is a thing of the past ; you will see it again, but not until after you have been buried.'

'Now you are angry with me,' said Graciosa in her most coaxing voice, 'though after all I am more to be pitied than you are.'

When they got near the palace the Prince made the sledge and themselves invisible, so the Princess got in unobserved, and ran up to the great hall where the King was sitting all by himself. At first he was very much startled by Graciosa's sudden appearance, but she told him how the Queen had left her out in the forest, and how she had caused a log of wood to be buried. The King, who did not know what to think, sent quickly and had it dug up, and sure enough it was as the Princess had said. Then he caressed Graciosa, and made her sit down to supper with him, and they were as happy as possible. But someone had by this time told the wicked Queen that Graciosa had come back, and was at supper with the King, and in she flew in a terrible fury. The poor old King quite trembled before her, and when she declared that Graciosa was not the Princess at all, but a wicked impostor, and that if the King did not give her up at once she would go back to her own castle and never see him again, he had not a word to say, and really seemed to believe that it was not Graciosa after all. So the Queen in great triumph sent for her waiting women, who dragged the unhappy Princess away and shut her up in a garret ; they took away all her jewels and her pretty dress, and gave her a rough cotton frock, wooden shoes, and a little cloth cap. There was some straw in a corner, which was all she had for a bed, and they gave her a very little bit of black bread to eat. In this miserable plight Graciosa did indeed regret the fairy palace, and she would have called Percinet to her aid, only she felt sure he was still vexed with her for leaving him, and thought that she could not expect him to come.

Meanwhile the Queen had sent for an old Fairy, as malicious as herself, and said to her :

'You must find me some task for this fine Princess which she cannot possibly do, for I mean to punish her, and if she does not do what I order, she will not be able to say that I am unjust.' So the old Fairy said she would think it over, and come again the next day. When she returned she brought with her a skein of thread, three times as big as herself; it was so fine that a breath of air would break it, and so tangled that it was impossible to see the beginning or the end of it.

The Queen sent for Graciosa, and said to her :

' Do you see this skein ?   Set your clumsy fingers to work upon
it, for I must have it disentangled by sunset, and if you break a
single thread it will be the worse for you.'   So saying she left her,
locking the door behind her with three keys.

The Princess stood dismayed at the sight of the terrible skein.
If she did but turn it over to see where to begin, she broke a
thousand threads, and not one could she disentangle.   At last she
threw it into the middle of the floor, crying :

' Oh, Percinet ! this fatal skein will be the death of me if you
will not forgive me and help me once more.'

And immediately in came Percinet as easily as if he had all the
keys in his own possession.

' Here I am, Princess, as much as ever at your service,' said he,
' though really you are not very kind to me.'

Then he just stroked the skein with his wand, and all the broken
threads joined themselves together, and the whole skein wound

itself smoothly off in the most surprising manner, and the Prince, turning to Graciosa, asked if there was nothing else that she wished him to do for her, and if the time would never come when she would wish for him for his own sake.

'Don't be vexed with me, Percinet,' she said. ' I am unhappy enough without that.'

' But why should you be unhappy, my Princess ? ' cried he. ' Only come with me and we shall be as happy as the day is long together.'

' But suppose you get tired of me ? ' said Graciosa.

The Prince was so grieved at this want of confidence that he left her without another word.

The wicked Queen was in such a hurry to punish Graciosa that she thought the sun would never set ; and indeed it was before the appointed time that she came with her four Fairies, and as she fitted the three keys into the locks she said :

' I'll venture to say that the idle minx has not done anything at all—she prefers to sit with her hands before her to keep them white.'

But, as soon as she entered, Graciosa presented her with the ball of thread in perfect order, so that she had no fault to find, and could only pretend to discover that it was soiled, for which imaginary fault she gave Graciosa a blow on each cheek, that made her white and pink skin turn green and yellow. And then she sent her back to be locked into the garret once more.

Then the Queen sent for the Fairy again and scolded her furiously. ' Don't make such a mistake again ; find me something that it will be quite impossible for her to do,' she said.

So the next day the Fairy appeared with a huge barrel full of the feathers of all sorts of birds. There were nightingales, canaries, goldfinches, linnets, tomtits, parrots, owls, sparrows, doves, ostriches, bustards, peacocks, larks, partridges, and everything else that you can think of. These feathers were all mixed up in such confusion that the birds themselves could not have chosen out their own. ' Here,' said the Fairy, ' is a little task which it will take all your prisoner's skill and patience to accomplish. Tell her to pick out and lay in a separate heap the feathers of each bird. She would need to be a fairy to do it.'

The Queen was more than delighted at the thought of the despair this task would cause the Princess. She sent for her, and with the same threats as before locked her up with the three keys, ordering that all the feathers should be sorted by sunset. Graciosa set to work at once, but before she had taken out a dozen feathers she found that it was perfectly impossible to know one from another.

' Ah ! well,' she sighed, ' the Queen wishes to kill me, and if I must die I must. I cannot ask Percinet to help me again, for if he really loved me he would not wait till I called him, he would come without that.'

' I am here, my Graciosa,' cried Percinet, springing out of the barrel where he had been hiding. ' How can you still doubt that I love you with all my heart ? '

Then he gave three strokes of his wand upon the barrel, and all the feathers flew out in a cloud and settled down in neat little separate heaps all round the room.

' What should I do without you, Percinet ? ' said Graciosa gratefully. But still she could not quite make up her mind to go with him and leave her father's kingdom for ever ; so she begged him to give her more time to think of it, and he had to go away disappointed once more.

When the wicked Queen came at sunset she was amazed and infuriated to find the task done. However, she complained that the heaps of feathers were badly arranged, and for that the Princess was beaten and sent back to her garret. Then the Queen sent for the Fairy once more, and scolded her until she was fairly terrified, and promised to go home and think of another task for Graciosa, worse than either of the others.

At the end of three days she came again, bringing with her a box.

' Tell your slave,' said he, ' to carry this wherever you please, but on no account to open it. She will not be able to help doing so, and then you will be quite satisfied with the result.' So the Queen came to Graciosa, and said :

' Carry this box to my castle, and place it upon the table in my own room. But I forbid you on pain of death to look at what it contains.'

Graciosa set out, wearing her little cap and wooden shoes and the old cotton frock, but even in this disguise she was so beautiful that all the passers-by wondered who she could be. She had not gone far before the heat of the sun and the weight of the box tired her so much that she sat down to rest in the shade of a little wood which lay on one side of a green meadow. She was carefully holding the box upon her lap when she suddenly felt the greatest desire to open it.

'What could possibly happen if I did?' she said to herself. 'I should not take anything out. I should only just see what was there.'

And without farther hesitation she lifted the cover.

Instantly out came swarms of little men and women, no taller than her finger, and scattered themselves all over the meadow, singing and dancing, and playing the merriest games, so that at

first Graciosa was delighted and watched them with much amusement. But presently, when she was rested and wished to go on her way, she found that, do what she would, she could not get them back into their box. If she chased them in the meadow they fled into the wood, and if she pursued them into the wood they dodged round trees and behind sprigs of moss, and with peals of elfin laughter scampered back again into the meadow.

At last, weary and terrified, she sat down and cried.

'It is my own fault,' she said sadly. 'Percinet, if you can still care for such an imprudent Princess, do come and help me once more.'

Immediately Percinet stood before her.

'Ah, Princess!' he said, 'but for the wicked Queen I fear you would never think of me at all.'

'Indeed I should,' said Graciosa; 'I am not so ungrateful as you think. Only wait a little and I believe I shall love you quite dearly.'

Percinet was pleased at this, and with one stroke of his wand compelled all the wilful little people to come back to their places in the box, and then rendering the Princess invisible he took her with him in his chariot to the castle.

When the Princess presented herself at the door, and said that the Queen had ordered her to place the box in her own room, the governor laughed heartily at the idea.

'No, no, my little shepherdess,' said he, 'that is not the place for you. No wooden shoes have ever been over that floor yet.'

Then Graciosa begged him to give her a written message telling the Queen that he had refused to admit her. This he did, and she went back to Percinet, who was waiting for her, and they set out together for the palace. You may imagine that they did not go the shortest way, but the Princess did not find it too long, and before they parted she had promised that if the Queen was still cruel to her, and tried again to play her any spiteful trick, she would leave her and come to Percinet for ever.

When the Queen saw her returning she fell upon the Fairy, whom she had kept with her, and pulled her hair, and scratched her face, and would really have killed her if a Fairy could be killed. And when the Princess presented the letter and the box she threw them both upon the fire without opening them, and looked very much as if she would like to throw the Princess after them. However, what she really did do was to have a great hole as deep as a well dug in her garden, and the top of it covered with a flat stone. Then she went and walked near it, and said to Graciosa and all her ladies who were with her:

'I am told that a great treasure lies under that stone; let us see if we can lift it.'

So they all began to push and pull at it, and Graciosa among the others, which was just what the Queen wanted; for as soon as the stone was lifted high enough, she gave the Princess a push which sent her down to the bottom of the well, and then the stone was let fall again, and there she was a prisoner. Graciosa felt that now indeed she was hopelessly lost, surely not even Percinet could find her in the heart of the earth.

'This is like being buried alive,' she said with a shudder. 'Oh, Percinet! if you only knew how I am suffering for my want of trust in you! But how could I be sure that you would not be like other men and tire of me from the moment you were sure I loved you?'

As she spoke she suddenly saw a little door open, and the sunshine blazed into the dismal well. Graciosa did not hesitate an instant, but passed through into a charming garden. Flowers and fruit grew on every side, fountains plashed, and birds sang in the branches overhead, and when she reached a great avenue of trees and looked up to see where it would lead her, she found herself close to the palace of crystal. Yes! there was no mistaking it, and the Queen and Percinet were coming to meet her.

'Ah, Princess!' said the Queen, 'don't keep this poor Percinet in suspense any longer. You little guess the anxiety he has suffered while you were in the power of that miserable Queen.'

The Princess kissed her gratefully, and promised to do as she wished in everything, and holding out her hand to Percinet, with a smile, she said:

'Do you remember telling me that I should not see your palace again until I had been buried? I wonder if you guessed then that, when that happened, I should tell you that I love you with all my heart, and will marry you whenever you like?'

Prince Percinet joyfully took the hand that was given him, and, for fear the Princess should change her mind, the wedding was held at once with the greatest splendour, and Graciosa and Percinet lived happily ever after.[1]

---

[1] *Gracieuse et Percinet.* Mdme. d'Aulnoy.

THE THREE PRINCESSES OF WHITELAND

THERE was once upon a time a fisherman, who lived hard by a palace and fished for the King's table. One day he was out fishing, but caught nothing at all. Let him do what he might with rod and line, there was never even so much as a sprat on his hook; but when the day was well nigh over, a head rose up out of the water, and said: 'If you will give me what your wife shows you when you go home, you shall catch fish enough.'

So the man said 'Yes' in a moment, and then he caught fish in plenty; but when he got home at night, and his wife showed him a baby which had just been born, and fell a-weeping and wailing when he told her of the promise which he had given, he was very unhappy.

All this was soon told to the King up at the palace, and when he heard what sorrow the woman was in, and the reason of it, he said that he himself would take the child and see if he could not save it. The baby was a boy, and the King took him at once and brought him up as his own son until the lad grew up. Then one day he begged to have leave to go out with his father to fish; he had a strong desire to do this, he said. The King was very unwilling to permit it, but at last the lad got leave. He stayed with his father, and all went prosperously and well with them the whole day, until they came back to land in the evening. Then the lad found that he had lost his pocket-handkerchief, and would go out in the boat after it; but no sooner had he got into the boat than it began to move off with him so quickly that the water foamed all round about, and all that the lad did to keep the boat back with the oars was done to no purpose, for it went on and on the whole night through, and at last he came to a white strand that lay far, far away. There he landed, and when he had walked on for some distance he met an old man with a long white beard.

'What is the name of this country?' said the youth.

'Whiteland,' answered the man, and then he begged the youth to tell him whence he came and what he was going to do, and the youth did so.

'Well, then,' said the man, 'if you walk on farther along the sea-shore here, you will come to three princesses who are standing in the earth so that their heads alone are out of it. Then the first of them will call you—she is the eldest—and will beg you very prettily to come to her and help her, and the second will do the same, but you must not go near either of them. Hurry past, as if you neither saw nor heard them ; but you shall go to the third and do what she bids you ; it will bring you good fortune.'

When the youth came to the first princess, she called to him and begged him to come to her very prettily, but he walked on as if he did not even see her, and he passed by the second in the same way, but he went up to the third.

'If thou wilt do what I tell thee, thou shalt choose among us three,' said the Princess.

So the lad said that he was most willing, and she told him that three Trolls had planted them all three there in the earth, but that formerly they had dwelt in the castle which he could see at some distance in the wood.

'Now,' she said, 'thou shalt go into the castle, and let the Trolls beat thee one night for each of us, and if thou canst but endure that, thou wilt set us free.'

'Yes,' answered the lad, 'I will certainly try to do so.'

'When thou goest in,' continued the Princess, 'two lions will stand by the doorway, but if thou only goest straight between them they will do thee no harm ; go straight forward into a small dark chamber ; there thou shalt lie down. Then the Troll will come and beat thee, but thou shalt take the flask which is hanging on the wall, and anoint thyself wheresoever he has wounded thee, after which thou shalt be as well as before. Then lay hold of the sword which is hanging by the side of the flask, and smite the Troll dead.'

So he did what the Princess had told him. He walked straight in between the lions just as if he did not see them, and then into the small chamber, and lay down on the bed.

The first night a Troll came with three heads and three rods, and beat the lad most unmercifully ; but he held out until the Troll was done with him, and then he took the flask and rubbed himself. Having done this, he grasped the sword and smote the Troll dead.

In the morning when he went to the sea-shore the Princesses were out of the earth as far as their waists.

The next night everything happened in the same way, but the Troll who came then had six heads and six rods, and he beat him

much more severely than the first had done   but when the lad went out of doors next morning, the Princesses were out of the earth as far as their knees.

On the third night a Troll came who had nine heads and nine rods, and he struck the lad and flogged him so long, that at last he swooned away ; so the Troll took him up and flung him against the wall, and this made the flask of ointment fall down, and it splashed all over him, and he became as strong as ever again.

Then, without loss of time, he grasped the sword and struck the Troll dead, and in the morning when he went out of the castle the Princesses were standing there entirely out of the earth. So he took the youngest for his Queen, and lived with her very happily for a long time.

At last, however, he took a fancy to go home for a short time to see his parents. His Queen did not like this, but when his longing grew so great that he told her he must and would go, she said to him :

'One thing shalt thou promise me, and that is, to do what thy father bids thee, but not what thy mother bids thee,' and this he promised.

So she gave him a ring, which enabled him who wore it to obtain two wishes.

He wished himself at home, and instantly found himself there ; but his parents were so amazed at the splendour of his apparel that their wonder never ceased.

When he had been at home for some days his mother wanted him to go up to the palace, to show the King what a great man he had become.

The father said, ' No ; he must not do that, for if he does we shall have no more delight in him this time ; ' but he spoke in vain, for the mother begged and prayed until at last he went.

When he arrived there he was more splendid, both in raiment and in all else, than the other King, who did not like it, and said :

' Well, you can see what kind of Queen mine is, but I can't see yours. I do not believe you have such a pretty Queen as I have.'

' Would to heaven she were standing here, and then you would be able to see ! ' said the young King, and in an instant she was standing there.

But she was very sorrowful, and said to him, ' Why didst thou not remember my words, and listen only to what thy father said ? Now must I go home again at once, and thou hast wasted both thy wishes.'

Then she tied a ring in his hair, which had her name upon it, and wished herself at home again.

And now the young King was deeply afflicted, and day out and day in went about thinking of naught else but how to get back again to his Queen. 'I will try to see if there is any place where I can learn how to find Whiteland,' he thought, and journeyed forth out into the world.

When he had gone some distance he came to a mountain, where he met a man who was Lord over all the beasts in the forest —for they all came to him when he blew a horn which he had. So the King asked where Whiteland was.

'I do not know that,' he answered, 'but I will ask my beasts.'

Then he blew his horn and inquired whether any of them knew where Whiteland lay, but there was not one who knew that.

So the man gave him a pair of snow shoes. 'When you have these on,' he said, 'you will come to my brother, who lives hundreds of miles from here ; he is Lord over all the birds in the air—ask him. When you have got there, just turn the shoes so that the toes point this way, and then they will come home again of their own accord.'

When the King arrived there he turned the shoes as the Lord of the beasts had bidden him, and they went back.

And now he once more asked after Whiteland, and the man summoned all the birds together, and inquired if any of them knew where Whiteland lay. No, none knew this. Long after the others there came an old eagle. He had been absent ten whole years, but he too knew no more than the rest.

' Well, well,' said the man, ' then you shall have the loan of a pair of snow shoes of mine. If you wear them you will get to my brother, who lives hundreds of miles from here. He is Lord of all the fish in the sea—you can ask him. But do not forget to turn the shoes round.'

The King thanked him, put on the shoes, and when he had got to him who was Lord of all the fish in the sea, he turned the snow shoes round, and back they went just as the others had gone, and he asked once more where Whiteland was.

The man called the fish together with his horn, but none of them knew anything about it. At last came an old, old pike, which he had great difficulty in bringing home to him.

When he asked the pike, it said, ' Yes, Whiteland is well known to me, for I have been cook there these ten years. To-morrow morning I have to go back there, for now the Queen, whose King is staying away, is to marry some one else.'

' If that be the case I will give you a piece of advice,' said the man. ' Not far from here on a moor stand three brothers, who have stood there a hundred years fighting for a hat, a cloak, and a pair of boots ; if any one has these three things he can make himself invisible, and if he desires to go to any place, he has but to wish and he is there. You may tell them that you have a desire to try these things, and then you will be able to decide which of the men is to have them.'

So the King thanked him and went, and did what he had said.

' What is this that you are standing fighting about for ever and ever ? ' said he to the brothers ; ' let me make a trial of these things, and then I will judge between you.'

They willingly consented to this, but when he had got the hat, the cloak, and the boots, he said, ' Next time we meet you shall have my decision,' and hereupon he wished himself away.

While he was going quickly through the air he fell in with the North Wind.

' And where may you be going ? ' said the North Wind.

'To Whiteland,' said the King, and then he related what had happened to him.

'Well,' said the North Wind, 'you can easily go a little quicker than I can, for I have to puff and blow into every corner; but when you get there, place yourself on the stairs by the side of the door, and then I will come blustering in as if I wanted to blow down the whole castle, and when the Prince who is to have your Queen comes out to see what is astir, just take him by the throat and fling him out, and then I will try to carry him away from court.'

As the North Wind had said, so did the King. He stood on the stairs, and when the North Wind came howling and roaring, and caught the roof and walls of the castle till they shook again, the Prince went out to see what was the matter; but as soon as he came the King took him by the neck and flung him out, and then the North Wind laid hold of him and carried him off. And when he was rid of him the King went into the castle. At first the Queen did not know him, because he had grown so thin and pale from having travelled so long and so sorrowfully; but when she saw her ring she was heartily glad, and then the rightful wedding was held, and held in such a way that it was talked about far and wide.[1]

[1] From J. Moe.

THE VOICE OF DEATH

ONCE upon a time there lived a man whose one wish and prayer was to get rich. Day and night he thought of nothing else, and at last his prayers were granted, and he became very wealthy. Now being so rich, and having so much to lose, he felt that it would be a terrible thing to die and leave all his possessions behind; so he made up his mind to set out in search of a land where there was no death. He got ready for his journey, took leave of his wife, and started. Whenever he came to a new country the first question that he asked was whether people died in that land, and when he heard that they did, he set out again on his quest. At last he reached a country where he was told that the people did not even know the meaning of the word death. Our traveller was delighted when he heard this, and said:

'But surely there are great numbers of people in your land, if no one ever dies?'

'No,' they replied, 'there are not great numbers, for you see from time to time a voice is heard calling first one and then another, and whoever hears that voice gets up and goes away, and never comes back.'

'And do they see the person who calls them,' he asked, 'or do they only hear his voice?'

'They both see and hear him,' was the answer.

Well, the man was amazed when he heard that the people were stupid enough to follow the voice, though they knew that if they went when it called them they would never return. And he went back to his own home and got all his possessions together, and, taking his wife and family, he set out resolved to go and live in that country where the people did not die, but where instead they heard a voice calling them, which they followed into a land from which they never returned. For he had made up his own mind that when he or any of his family heard that voice they would pay no heed to it, however loudly it called.

After he had settled down in his new home, and had got everything in order about him, he warned his wife and family that, unless they wanted to die, they must on no account listen to a voice which they might some day hear calling them.

For some years everything went well with them, and they lived happily in their new home. But one day, while they were all sit-

ting together round the table, his wife suddenly started up, exclaiming in a loud voice :

' I am coming! I am coming ! '

And she began to look round the room for her fur coat, but her husband jumped up, and taking firm hold of her by the hand, held her fast, and reproached her, saying :

' Don't you remember what I told you ? Stay where you are unless you wish to die.'

' But don't you hear that voice calling me ? ' she answered. ' I am merely going to see why I am wanted. I shall come back directly.'

So she fought and struggled to get away from her husband, and to go where the voice summoned. But he would not let her go, and had all the doors of the house shut and bolted. When she saw that he had done this, she said :

' Very well, dear husband, I shall do what you wish, and remain where I am.'

So her husband believed that it was all right, and that she had thought better of it, and had got over her mad impulse to obey the voice. But a few minutes later she made a sudden dash for one of the doors, opened it and darted out, followed by her husband. He caught her by the fur coat, and begged and implored her not to go, for if she did she would certainly never return. She said nothing, but let her arms fall backwards, and suddenly bending herself forward, she slipped out of the coat, leaving it in her husband's hands. He, poor man, seemed turned to stone as he gazed after her hurrying away from him, and calling at the top of her voice, as she ran :

' I am coming ! I am coming ! '

When she was quite out of sight her husband recovered his wits and went back into his house, murmuring :

' If she is so foolish as to wish to die, I can't help it. I warned and implored her to pay no heed to that voice, however loudly it might call.'

Well, days and weeks and months and years passed, and nothing happened to disturb the peace of the household. But one day the man was at the barber's as usual, being shaved. The shop was full of people, and his chin had just been covered with a lather of soap, when, suddenly starting up from the chair, he called out in a loud voice :

' I won't come, do you hear ? I won't come ! '

The barber and the other people in the shop listened to him with amazement. But again looking towards the door, he exclaimed :

' I tell you, once and for all, I do not mean to come, so go away.'

And a few minutes later he called out again :

' Go away, I tell you, or it will be the worse for you. You may call as much as you like but you will never get me to come.'

And he got so angry that you might have thought that some

one was actually standing at the door, tormenting him. At last he jumped up, and caught the razor out of the barber's hand, exclaiming:

'Give me that razor, and I'll teach him to let people alone for the future.'

And he rushed out of the house as if he were running after some one, whom no one else saw. The barber, determined not to lose his razor, pursued the man, and they both continued running at full speed till they had got well out of the town, when all of a sudden the man fell head foremost down a precipice, and never was seen again. So he too, like the others, had been forced against his will to follow the voice that called him.

The barber, who went home whistling and congratulating himself on the escape he had made, described what had happened, and it was noised abroad in the country that the people who had gone away, and had never returned, had all fallen into that pit; for till then they had never known what had happened to those who had heard the voice and obeyed its call.

But when crowds of people went out from the town to examine the ill-fated pit that had swallowed up such numbers, and yet never seemed to be full, they could discover nothing. All that they could see was a vast plain, that looked as if it had been there since the beginning of the world. And from that time the people of the country began to die like ordinary mortals all the world over.[1]

[1] Roumanian Tales from the German of Mite Thremnitz.

THE SIX SILLIES

ONCE upon a time there was a young girl who reached the age of thirty-seven without ever having had a lover, for she was so foolish that no one wanted to marry her.

One day, however, a young man arrived to pay his addresses to her, and her mother, beaming with joy, sent her daughter down to the cellar to draw a jug of beer.

As the girl never came back the mother went down to see what had become of her, and found her sitting on the stairs, her head in her hands, while by her side the beer was running all over the floor, as she had forgotten to close the tap. ' What are you doing there ? ' asked the mother.

' I was thinking what I shall call my first child after I am married to that young man. All the names in the calendar are taken already.'

The mother sat down on the staircase beside her daughter and said, ' I will think about it with you, my dear.'

The father who had stayed upstairs with the young man was surprised that neither his wife nor his daughter came back, and in his turn went down to look for them. He found them both sitting on the stairs, while beside them the beer was running all over the ground from the tap, which was wide open.

' What are you doing there ? The beer is running all over the cellar.'

' We were thinking what we should call the children that our daughter will have when she marries that young man. All the names in the calendar are taken already.'

' Well,' said the father, ' I will think about it with you.'

As neither mother nor daughter nor father came upstairs again, the lover grew impatient, and went down into the cellar to see what they could all be doing. He found them all three sitting on

the stairs, while beside them the beer was running all over the
ground from the tap, which was wide open.

'What in the world are you all doing that you don't come
upstairs, and that you let the beer run all over the cellar?'

'Yes, I know, my boy,' said the father, 'but if you marry our
daughter what shall you call your children? All the names in the
calendar are taken.'

When the young man heard this answer he replied:

'Well! good-bye, I am going away. When I shall have found
three people sillier than you I will come back and marry your
daughter.'

So he continued his journey, and after walking a long way he
reached an orchard. Then he saw some people knocking down
walnuts, and trying to throw them into a cart with a fork.

' What are you doing there ? ' he asked.

' We want to load the cart with our walnuts, but we can't manage to do it.'

The lover advised them to get a basket and to put the walnuts in it, so as to turn them into the cart.

' Well,' he said to himself, ' I have already found someone more foolish than those three.'

So he went on his way, and by-and-by he came to a wood. There he saw a man who wanted to give his pig some acorns to eat, and was trying with all his might to make him climb up the oak-tree.

' What are you doing, my good man ? ' asked he.

' I want to make my pig eat some acorns, and I can't get him to go up the tree.'

' If you were to climb up and shake down the acorns the pig would pick them up.'

' Oh, I never thought of that.'

' Here is the second idiot,' said the lover to himself.

Some way farther along the road he came upon a man who had never worn any trousers, and who was trying to put on a pair. So he had fastened them to a tree and was jumping with all his might up in the air so that he should hit the two legs of the trousers as he came down.

' It would be much better if you held them in your hands,' said the young man, ' and then put your legs one after the other in each hole.'

' Dear me, to be sure ! You are sharper than I am, for that never occurred to me.'

And having found three people more foolish than his bride, or her father or her mother, the lover went back to marry the young lady.

And in course of time they had a great many children.

Story from Hainaut.

(M. Lemoine. *La Tradition*. No. 34.)

KARI WOODENGOWN

THERE was once upon a time a King who had become a widower. His Queen had left one daughter behind her, and she was so wise and so pretty that it was impossible for any one to be wiser or prettier. For a long time the King went sorrowing for his wife, for he had loved her exceedingly; but at last he grew tired of living alone, and married a Queen who was a widow, and she also had a daughter, who was just as ill-favoured and wicked as the other was good and beautiful. The stepmother and her daughter were envious of the King's daughter because she was so pretty, but so long as the King was at home they dared do her no harm, because his love for her was so great.

Then there came a time when he made war on another King and went away to fight, and then the new Queen thought that she could do what she liked; so she both hungered and beat the King's daughter and chased her about into every corner. At last she thought that everything was too good for her, and set her to work to look after the cattle. So she went about with the cattle, and herded them in the woods and in the fields. Of food she got little or none, and grew pale and thin, and was nearly always weeping and sad. Among the herd there was a great blue bull, which always kept itself very smart and sleek, and often came to the King's daughter and let her stroke him. So one day, when she was again sitting crying and sorrowing, the Bull came up to her and asked why she was always so full of care? She made no answer, but continued to weep.

'Well,' said the Bull, 'I know what it is, though you will not tell me; you are weeping because the Queen is unkind to you, and because she wants to starve you to death. But you need be under no concern about food, for in my left ear there lies a cloth, and if you will but take it and spread it out, you can have as many dishes as you like.'

So she did this, and took the cloth and spread it out upon the grass, and then it was covered with the daintiest dishes that any one could desire, and there was wine, and mead, and cake. And now she became brisk and well again, and grew so rosy, and plump, and fair that the Queen and her scraggy daughter turned blue and white with vexation at it. The Queen could not imagine how her step-daughter could look so well on such bad food, so she ordered one of her handmaidens to follow her into the wood and watch her, and see how it was, for she thought that some of the servants must be giving her food. So the maid followed her into the wood and watched, and saw how the step-daughter took the cloth out of the

Blue Bull's ear, and spread it out, and how the cloth was then covered with the most delicate dishes, which the step-daughter ate and re-galed herself with. So the waiting-maid went home and told the Queen.

And now the King came home, and he had conquered the other King with whom he had been at war. So there was great gladness in the palace, but no one was more glad than the King's daughter. The Queen, however, pretended to be ill, and gave the doctor much money to say that she would never be well again unless she had some of the flesh of the Blue Bull to eat. Both the King's daughter and the people in the palace asked the doctor if there were no other means of saving her, and begged for the Bull's life, for they were all fond of him, and they all declared that there was no such Bull in the whole country; but it was all in vain, he was to be killed, and should be killed, and nothing else would serve. When the King's daughter heard it she was full of sorrow, and went down to the byre to the Bull. He too was standing there hanging his head, and looking so downcast that she fell a-weeping over him.

'What are you weeping for?' said the Bull.

So she told him that the King had come home again, and that the Queen had pretended to be ill, and that she had made the doctor say that she could never be well again unless some of the flesh of the Blue Bull was given her to eat, and that now he was to be killed.

'When once they have taken my life they will soon kill you also,' said the Bull. 'If you are of the same mind with me, we will take our departure this very night.'

The King's daughter thought that it was bad to go and leave her father, but that it was worse still to be in the same house with the Queen, so she promised the Bull that she would come.

At night, when all the others had gone to bed, the King's daughter stole softly down to the byre to the Bull, and he took her on his back and got out of the courtyard as quickly as he could. So at cock-crow next morning, when the people came to kill the Bull, he was gone, and when the King got up and asked for his daughter she was gone too. He sent forth messengers to all parts of the kingdom to search for them, and published his loss in all the parish churches, but there was no one who had seen anything of them.

In the meantime the Bull travelled through many lands with the King's daughter on his back, and one day they came to a great copper-wood, where the trees, and the branches, and the leaves, and the flowers, and everything else was of copper.

But before they entered the wood the Bull said to the King's daughter:

'When we enter into this wood, you must take the greatest care not to touch a leaf of it, or all will be over both with me and with you, for a Troll with three heads, who is the owner of the wood, lives here.'

So she said she would be on her guard, and not touch anything. And she was very careful, and bent herself out of the way of the branches, and put them aside with her hands; but it was so thickly wooded that it was all but impossible to get forward, and do what she might, she somehow or other tore off a leaf which got into her hand.

'Oh! oh! What have you done now?' said the Bull. 'It will now cost us a battle for life or death; but do be careful to keep the leaf!'

Very soon afterwards they came to the end of the wood, and the Troll with three heads came rushing up to them.

'Who is that who is touching my wood?' said the Troll.

'The wood is just as much mine as yours!' said the Bull.

'We shall have a tussle for that!' shrieked the Troll.

'That may be,' said the Bull.

So they rushed on each other and fought, and as for the Bull he butted and kicked with all the strength of his body, but the Troll fought quite as well as he did, and the whole day went by before the Bull put an end to him, and then he himself was so full of wounds and so worn out that he was scarcely able to move. So they had to wait a day, and the Bull told the King's daughter to take the horn of ointment which hung at the Troll's belt, and rub him with it; then he was himself again, and the next day they set off once more. And now they journeyed on for many, many days, and then after a long, long time they came to a silver wood. The trees, and the boughs, and the leaves, and the flowers, and everything else was of silver.

Before the Bull went into the wood, he said to the King's daughter: 'When we enter into this wood you must, for Heaven's sake, be very careful not to touch anything at all, and not to pluck off even so much as one leaf, or else all will be over both with you and with me. A Troll with six heads lives here, who is the owner of the wood, and I do not think I should be able to overcome him.'

'Yes,' said the King's daughter, 'I will take good care not to touch what you do not wish me to touch.'

But when they got into the wood it was so crowded, and the trees so close together, that they could scarcely get forward. She was as careful as she could be, and bent aside to get out of the way of the branches, and thrust them away from before her with her hands; but every instant a branch struck against her eyes, and in spite of all her care, she happened to pull off one leaf.

'Oh! oh! What have you done now?' said the Bull. 'It will now cost us a battle for life or death, for this Troll has six heads and is twice as strong as the other, but do be careful to keep the leaf.'

Just as he said this came the Troll. 'Who is that who is touching my wood ?' he said.

' It is just as much mine as yours ! '

' We shall have a tussle for that ! ' screamed the Troll.

' That may be,' said the Bull, and rushed at the Troll, and gored out his eyes, and drove his horns right through him so that his entrails gushed out, but the Troll fought just as well as he did, and it was three whole days before the Bull got the life out of him. But the Bull was then so weak and worn out that it was only with pain and effort that he could move, and so covered with wounds that the blood streamed from him. So he told the King's daughter to take the horn of ointment that was hanging at the Troll's belt, and anoint him with it. She did this, and then he came to himself again, but they had to stay there and rest for a week before the Bull was able to go any farther.

At last they set forth on their way again, but the Bull was still weak, and at first could not go quickly. The King's daughter wished to spare him, and said that she was so young and light of foot that she would willingly walk, but he would not give her leave to do that, and she was forced to seat herself on his back again. So they travelled for a long time, and through many lands, and the King's daughter did not at all know where he was taking her, but after a long, long time they came to a gold wood. It was so golden that the gold dripped off it, and the trees, and the branches, and the flowers, and the leaves were all of pure gold. Here all happened just as it had happened in the copper wood and silver wood. The Bull told the King's daughter that on no account was she to touch it, for there was a Troll with nine heads who was the owner, and that he was much larger and stronger than both the others put together, and that he did not believe that he could overcome him. So she said that she would take great care not to touch anything, and he should see that she did. But when they got into the wood it was still thicker than the silver wood, and the farther they got into it the worse it grew. The wood became thicker and thicker, and closer and closer, and at last she thought there was no way whatsoever by which they could get forward ; she was so terrified lest she should break anything off, that she sat and twisted, and turned herself on this side and on that, to get out of the way of the branches, and pushed them away from her with her hands, but every moment they struck against her eyes, so that she could not see what she was clutching at, and before she knew what she was doing she had a golden apple in her hands. She was now in such terror that she began to cry, and wanted to throw it away, but the Bull said that she was to keep it, and take the greatest care of it, and comforted her as well as he could, but he believed that it would

be a hard struggle, and he doubted whether it would go well with him.

Just then the Troll with nine heads came, and he was so frightful that the King's daughter scarcely dared to look at him.

'Who is this who is breaking my wood?' he screamed.

'It is as much mine as yours!' said the Bull.

' We shall have a tussle for that ! ' screamed the Troll.

' That may be,' said the Bull ; so they rushed at each other, and fought, and it was such a dreadful sight that the King's daughter very nearly swooned. The Bull gored the Troll's eyes out and ran his horns right through him, but the Troll fought as well as he did, and when the Bull had gored one head to death the other heads breathed life into it again, so it was a whole week before the Bull was able to kill him. But then he himself was so worn out and weak that he could not move at all. His body was all one wound, and he could not even so much as tell the King's daughter to take the horn of ointment out of the Troll's belt and rub him with it. She did this without being told ; so he came to himself again, but he had to lie there for three weeks and rest before he was in a state to move.

Then they journeyed onwards by degrees, for the Bull said that they had still a little farther to go, and in this way they crossed many high hills and thick woods. This lasted for a while, and then they came upon the fells.

' Do you see anything ? ' asked the Bull.

' No, I see nothing but the sky above and the wild fell side,' said the King's daughter.

Then they climbed up higher, and the fell grew more level, so that they could see farther around them.

' Do you see anything now ? ' said the Bull.

' Yes, I see a small castle, far, far away,' said the Princess.

' It is not so very little after all,' said the Bull.

After a long, long time they came to a high hill, where there was a precipitous wall of rock.

' Do you see nothing now ? ' said the Bull.

' Yes, now I see the castle quite near, and now it is much, much larger,' said the King's daughter.

' Thither shall you go,' said the Bull ; ' immediately below the castle there is a pig-sty, where you shall dwell. When you get there, you will find a wooden gown which you are to put on, and then go to the castle and say that you are called Kari Woodengown, and that you are seeking a place. But now you must take out your little knife and cut off my head with it, and then you must flay me and roll up my hide and put it there under the rock, and beneath the hide you must lay the copper leaf, and the silver leaf, and the golden apple. Close beside the rock a stick is standing, and when you want me for anything you have only to knock at the wall of rock with that.'

At first she would not do it, but when the Bull said that this was the only reward that he would have for what he had done for her, she could do no otherwise. So though she thought it very cruel, she slaved on and cut at the great animal with the knife till she had cut off his head and hide, and then she folded up the hide and laid it beneath the mountain wall, and put the copper leaf, and the silver leaf, and the golden apple inside it.

When she had done that she went away to the pig-sty, but all the way as she went she wept, and was very sorrowful. Then she put on the wooden gown, and walked to the King's palace. When she got there she went into the kitchen and begged for a place, saying that her name was Kari Woodengown.

The cook told her that she might have a place and leave to stay there at once and wash up, for the girl who had done that before had just gone away. 'And as soon as you get tired of being here you will take yourself off too,' said he.

'No,' said she, 'that I shall certainly not.'

And then she washed up, and did it very tidily.

On Sunday some strangers were coming to the King's palace, so Kari begged to have leave to carry up the water for the Prince's bath, but the others laughed at her and said, 'What do you want there? Do you think the Prince will ever look at such a fright as you?'

She would not give it up, however, but went on begging until at last she got leave. When she was going upstairs her wooden gown made such a clatter that the Prince came out and said, ' What sort of a creature may you be ? '

' I was to take this water to you,' said Kari.

' Do you suppose that I will have any water that you bring ? ' said the Prince, and emptied it over her.

She had to bear that, but then she asked permission to go to church. She got that, for the church was very near. But first she went to the rock and knocked at it with the stick which was standing there, as the Bull had told her to do. Instantly a man came forth and asked what she wanted. The King's daughter said that she had got leave to go to church and listen to the priest, but that she had no clothes to go in. So he brought her a gown that was as bright as the copper wood, and she got a horse and saddle too from him. When she reached the church she was so pretty and so splendidly dressed that every one wondered who she could be, and hardly anyone listened to what the priest was saying, for they were all looking far too much at her, and the Prince himself liked her so well that he could not take his eyes off her for an instant. As she was walking out of church the Prince followed her and shut the church door after her, and thus he kept one of her gloves in his hand. Then she went away and mounted her horse again ; the Prince again followed her, and asked her whence she came.

' Oh ! I am from Bathland,' said Kari. And when the Prince took out the glove and wanted to give it back to her, she said :

' Darkness behind me, but light on my way,
That the Prince may not see where I'm going to-day ! '

The Prince had never seen the equal of that glove, and he went far and wide, asking after the country which the proud lady, who rode away without her glove, had said that she came from, but there was no one who could tell him where it lay.

Next Sunday some one had to take up a towel to the Prince.

' Ah ! may I have leave to go up with that ? ' said Kari.

' What would be the use of that ? ' said the others who were in the kitchen ; ' you saw what happened last time.'

Kari would not give in, but went on begging for leave till she got it, and then she ran up the stairs so that her wooden gown clattered again. Out came the Prince, and when he saw that it was Kari, he snatched the towel from her and flung it right in her eyes.

'Be off at once, you ugly Troll,' said he ; 'do you think that I will have a towel that has been touched by your dirty fingers ? '

After that the Prince went to church, and Kari also asked leave to go. They all asked how she could want to go to church when she had nothing to wear but that wooden gown, which was so black and hideous. But Kari said she thought the priest was such a good man at preaching that she got so much benefit from what he said, and at last she got leave.

She went to the rock and knocked, whereupon out came the man and gave her a gown which was much more magnificent than the first. It was embroidered with silver all over it, and it shone like the silver wood, and he gave her also a most beautiful horse, with housings embroidered with silver, and a bridle of silver too.

When the King's daughter got to church all the people were standing outside upon the hillside, and all of them wondered who on earth she could be, and the Prince was on the alert in a moment, and came and wanted to hold her horse while she alighted. But she jumped off and said that there was no need for that, for the horse was so well broken in that it stood still when she bade it and came when she called it. So they all went into the church together, but there was scarcely any one who listened to what the priest was saying, for they were all looking far too much at her, and the Prince fell much more deeply in love with her than he had been before.

When the sermon was over and she went out of the church, and was just going to mount her horse, the Prince again came and asked her where she came from.

'I am from Towelland,' said the King's daughter, and as she spoke she dropped her riding-whip, and while the Prince was stooping to pick it up she said :

'Darkness behind me, but light on my way,
   That the Prince may not see where I'm going to-day ! '

And she was gone again, neither could the Prince see what had become of her. He went far and wide to inquire for that country from whence she had said that she came, but there was no one who could tell him where it lay, so he was forced to have patience once more.

Next Sunday some one had to go to the Prince with a comb. Kari begged for leave to go with it, but the others reminded her of what had happened last time, and scolded her for wanting to let the

Prince see her when she was so black and so ugly in her wooden gown, but she would not give up asking until they gave her leave to go up to the Prince with the comb. When she went clattering up the stairs again, out came the Prince and took the comb and flung it at her, and ordered her to be off as fast as she could. After that the Prince went to church, and Kari also begged for leave to go. Again they all asked what she would do there, she who was so black and ugly, and had no clothes that she could be seen in by other people. The Prince or some one else might very easily catch sight of her, they said, and then both she and they would suffer for it; but Kari said that they had something else to do than to look at her, and she never ceased begging until she got leave to go.

And now all happened just as it had happened twice already. She went away to the rock and knocked at it with the stick, and then the man came out and gave her a gown which was very much more magnificent than either of the others. It was almost entirely made of pure gold and diamonds, and she also got a noble horse with housings embroidered with gold, and a golden bridle.

When the King's daughter came to the church the priest and people were all standing on the hillside waiting for her, and the Prince ran up and wanted to hold the horse, but she jumped off, saying :

'No, thank you, there is no need; my horse is so well broken in that it will stand still when I bid it.'

So they all hastened into the church together and the priest got into the pulpit, but no one listened to what he said, for they were looking far too much at her and wondering whence she came; and the Prince was far more in love than he had been on either of the former occasions, and he was mindful of nothing but of looking at her.

When the sermon was over and the King's daughter was about to leave the church, the Prince had caused a firkin of tar to be emptied out in the porch in order that he might go to help her over it; she, however, did not trouble herself in the least about the tar, but set her foot down in the middle of it and' jumped over it, and thus one of her gold shoes was left sticking in it. When she had seated herself on the horse the Prince came running out of the church and asked her whence she came.

'From Combland,' said Kari. But when the Prince wanted to reach her her gold shoe, she said :

'Darkness behind me, but light on my way,
That the Prince may not see where I'm going to-day ! '

The Prince did not know what had become of her, so he travelled for a long and wearisome time all over the world, asking where Combland was; but when no one could tell him where that country was, he caused it to be made known everywhere that he would marry any woman who could put on the gold shoe.　So fair maidens and ugly maidens came thither from all regions, but there was none who had a foot so small that she could put on the gold shoe.　After a long, long while came Kari Woodengown's wicked stepmother, with her daughter too, and the shoe fitted her.　But she was so

ugly and looked so loathsome that the Prince was very unwilling to do what he had promised.　Nevertheless all was got ready for the wedding, and she was decked out as a bride, but as they were riding to church a little bird sat upon a tree and sang:

> 'A slice off her heel
> And a slice off her toes,
> Kari Woodengown's shoe
> Fills with blood as she goes!'

And when they looked to it the bird had spoken the truth, for blood was trickling out of the shoe. So all the waiting-maids, and all the womenkind in the castle had to come and try on the shoe, but there was not one whom it would fit.

'But where is Kari Woodengown, then?' asked the Prince, when all the others had tried on the shoe, for he understood the song of birds and it came to his mind what the bird had said.

'Oh! that creature!' said the others; 'it's not the least use for her to come here, for she has feet like a horse!'

'That may be,' said the Prince, 'but as all the others have tried it, Kari may try it too.'

'Kari!' he called out through the door, and Kari came upstairs, and her wooden gown clattered as if a whole regiment of dragoons were coming up.

'Now, you are to try on the gold shoe and be a Princess,' said the other servants, and they laughed at her and mocked her. Kari took up the shoe, put her foot into it as easily as possible, and then threw off her wooden gown, and there she stood in the golden gown which flashed like rays of sunshine, and on her other foot she had the fellow to the gold shoe. The Prince knew her in a moment, and was so glad that he ran and took her in his arms and kissed her, and when he heard that she was a King's daughter he was gladder still, and then they had the wedding.[1]

From P. C. Asbjørnsen.

DRAKESTAIL

DRAKESTAIL was very little, that is why he was called Drakestail; but tiny as he was he had brains, and he knew what he was about, for having begun with nothing he ended by amassing a hundred crowns. Now the King of the country, who was very extravagant and never kept any money, having heard that Drakestail had some, went one day in his own person to borrow his hoard, and, my word, in those days Drakestail was not a little proud of having lent money to the King. But after the first and second year, seeing that they never even dreamed of paying the interest, he became uneasy, so much so that at last he resolved to go and see His Majesty himself, and get repaid. So one fine morning Drakestail, very spruce and fresh, takes the road, singing: ' Quack, quack, quack, when shall I get my money back ? '

He had not gone far when he met friend Fox, on his rounds that way.

' Good-morning, neighbour,' says the friend, ' where are you off to so early ? '

' I am going to the King for what he owes me.'

' Oh ! take me with thee ! '

Drakestail said to himself: ' One can't have too many friends.' . . . ' I will,' says he, ' but going on all-fours you will soon be tired. Make yourself quite small, get into my throat—go into my gizzard and I will carry you.'

' Happy thought ! ' says friend Fox.

He takes bag and baggage, and, presto ! is gone like a letter into the post.

And Drakestail is off again, all spruce and fresh, still singing : ' Quack, quack, quack, when shall I have my money back ? '

He had not gone far when he met his lady-friend Ladder, leaning on her wall.

' Good-morning, my duckling,' says the lady friend, ' whither away so bold ? '

' I am going to the King for what he owes me.'

' Oh! take me with thee! '

Drakestail said to himself : ' One can't have too many friends.' . . . ' I will,' says he, ' but with your wooden legs you will soon be tired. Make yourself quite small, get into my throat—go into my gizzard and I will carry you.'

' Happy thought! ' says my friend Ladder, and nimble, bag and baggage, goes to keep company with friend Fox.

And ' Quack, quack, quack.' Drakestail is off again, singing and spruce as before. A little farther he meets his sweetheart, my friend River, wandering quietly in the sunshine.

' Thou, my cherub,' says she, ' whither so lonesome, with arching tail, on this muddy road ? '

' I am going to the King, you know, for what he owes me.'

' Oh! take me with thee ! '

Drakestail said to himself : ' We can't be too many friends.' . . . ' I will,' says he, ' but you who sleep while you walk will soon be tired. Make yourself quite small, get into my throat—go into my gizzard and I will carry you.'

' Ah ! happy thought ! ' says my friend River.

She takes bag and baggage, and glou, glou, glou, she takes her place between friend Fox and my friend Ladder.

And ' Quack, quack, quack.' Drakestail is off again singing.

A little farther on he meets comrade Wasp's-nest, manœuvring his wasps.

' Well, good-morning, friend Drakestail,' said comrade Wasp's-nest, ' where are we bound for so spruce and fresh ? '

' I am going to the King for what he owes me.'

' Oh! take me with thee ! '

Drakestail said to himself, ' One can't have too many friends.' . . . ' I will,' says he, ' but with your battalion to drag along, you will soon be tired. Make yourself quite small, go into my throat—get into my gizzard and I will carry you.'

' By Jove ! that's a good idea ! ' says comrade Wasp's-nest.

And left file ! he takes the same road to join the others with all his party. There was not much more room, but by closing up a bit they managed. . . . And Drakestail is off again singing.

He arrived thus at the capital, and threaded his way straight up the High Street, still running and singing ' Quack, quack, quack, when shall I get my money back ? ' to the great astonishment of the good folks, till he came to the King's palace.

He strikes with the knocker : ' Toc ! toc ! '

' Who is there ? ' asks the porter, putting his head out of the wicket.

' 'Tis I, Drakestail. I wish to speak to the King.'

' Speak to the King ! . . . That's easily said. The King is dining, and will not be disturbed.'

' Tell him that it is I, and I have come he well knows why.'

The porter shuts his wicket and goes up to say it to the King, who was just sitting down to dinner with a napkin round his neck, and all his ministers.

' Good, good ! ' said the King laughing. ' I know what it is ! Make him come in, and put him with the turkeys and chickens.'

The porter descends.

' Have the goodness to enter.'

' Good ! ' says Drakestail to himself, ' I shall now see how they eat at court.'

' This way, this way,' says the porter. ' One step further. . . . There, there you are.'

' How ? what ? in the poultry yard ? '

Fancy how vexed Drakestail was !

' Ah ! so that's it,' says he. ' Wait ! I will compel you to receive me. Quack, quack, quack, when shall I get my money back ? ' But turkeys and chickens are creatures who don't like people that are not as themselves. When they saw the new-comer and how he was made, and when they heard him crying too, they began to look black at him.

' What is it ? what does he want ? '

Finally they rushed at him all together, to overwhelm him with pecks.

' I am lost ! ' said Drakestail to himself, when by good luck he remembers his comrade friend Fox, and he cries :

> ' Reynard, Reynard, come out of your earth,
>   Or Drakestail's life is of little worth.'

Then friend Fox, who was only waiting for these words, hastens out, throws himself on the wicked fowls, and quick ! quack ! he tears them to pieces ; so much so that at the end of five minutes there was not one left alive. And Drakestail, quite content, began to sing again, ' Quack, quack, quack, when shall I get my money back ? '

DRAKESTAIL, WITH HIS FRIENDS STOWED AWAY IN HIS GIZZARD,
DEMANDS SPEECH OF THE KING.

When the King who was still at table heard this refrain, and the poultry woman came to tell him what had been going on in the yard, he was terribly annoyed.

He ordered them to throw this tail of a drake into the well, to make an end of him.

And it was done as he commanded. Drakestail was in despair of getting himself out of such a deep hole, when he remembered his lady friend, the Ladder.

'Ladder, Ladder, come out of thy hold,
  Or Drakestail's days will soon be told.'

My friend Ladder, who was only waiting for these words, hastens out, leans her two arms on the edge of the well, then Drakestail climbs nimbly on her back, and hop! he is in the yard, where he begins to sing louder than ever.

When the King, who was still at table and laughing at the good trick he had played his creditor, heard him again reclaiming his money, he became livid with rage.

He commanded that the furnace should be heated, and this tail of a drake thrown into it, because he must be a sorcerer.

The furnace was soon hot, but this time Drakestail was not so afraid; he counted on his sweetheart, my friend River.

'River, River, outward flow,
  Or to death Drakestail must go.'

My friend River hastens out, and errouf! throws herself into the furnace, which she floods, with all the people who had lighted it; after which she flowed growling into the hall of the palace to the height of more than four feet.

And Drakestail, quite content, begins to swim, singing deafeningly, ' Quack, quack, quack, when shall I get my money back? '

The King was still at table, and thought himself quite sure of his game; but when he heard Drakestail singing again, and when they told him all that had passed, he became furious and got up from table brandishing his fists.

' Bring him here, and I'll cut his throat! bring him here quick! ' cried he.

And quickly two footmen ran to fetch Drakestail.

' At last,' said the poor chap, going up the great stairs, ' they have decided to receive me.'

Imagine his terror when on entering he sees the King as red as

a turkey cock, and all his ministers attending him standing sword
in hand. He thought this time it was all up with him. Happily,
he remembered that there was still one remaining friend, and he
cried with dying accents :

> ' Wasp's-nest, Wasp's-nest, make a sally,
>   Or Drakestail nevermore may rally.'

Hereupon the scene changes.

' Bs, bs, bayonet them ! '   The brave Wasp's-nest rushes out

with all his wasps.   They threw themselves on the infuriated King
and his ministers, and stung them so fiercely in the face that they
lost their heads, and not knowing where to hide themselves they all
jumped pell-mell from the window and broke their necks on the
pavement.

Behold Drakestail much astonished, all alone in the big saloon
and master of the field. He could not get over it.

Nevertheless, he remembered shortly what he had come for to
the palace, and improving the occasion, he set to work to hunt for

his dear money. But in vain he rummaged in all the drawers ; he found nothing; all had been spent.

And ferreting thus from room to room he came at last to the one with the throne in it, and feeling fatigued, he sat himself down on it to think over his adventure. In the meanwhile the people had found their King and his ministers with their feet in the air on the pavement, and they had gone into the palace to know how it had occurred. On entering the throne-room, when the crowd saw that there was already someone on the royal seat, they broke out in cries of surprise and joy :

'The King is dead, long live the King !
Heaven has sent us down this thing.'

Drakestail, who was no longer surprised at anything, received the acclamations of the people as if he had never done anything else all his life.

A few of them certainly murmured that a Drakestail would make a fine King; those who knew him replied that a knowing Drakestail was a more worthy King than a spendthrift like him who was lying on the pavement. In short, they ran and took the crown off the head of the deceased, and placed it on that of Drakestail, whom it fitted like wax.

Thus he became King.

' And now,' said he after the ceremony, ' ladies and gentlemen, let's go to supper. I am so hungry ! ' [1]

---

[1] *Contes* of Ch. Marelles.

THE RATCATCHER

A VERY long time ago the town of Hamel in Germany was invaded by bands of rats, the like of which had never been seen
before nor will ever be again.

They were great black creatures that ran boldly in broad daylight through the streets, and swarmed so, all over the houses, that
people at last could not put their hand or foot down anywhere without touching one. When dressing in the morning they found them
in their breeches and petticoats, in their pockets and in their boots ;
and when they wanted a morsel to eat, the voracious horde had
swept away everything from cellar to garret. The night was even
worse. As soon as the lights were out, these untiring nibblers set
to work. And everywhere, in the ceilings, in the floors, in the cupboards, at the doors, there was a chase and a rummage, and so furious
a noise of gimlets, pincers, and saws, that a deaf man could not have
rested for one hour together.

Neither cats nor dogs, nor poison nor traps, nor prayers nor
candles burnt to all the saints—nothing would do anything. The
more they killed the more came. And the inhabitants of Hamel
began to go to the dogs (not that *they* were of much use), when one
Friday there arrived in the town a man with a queer face, who
played the bagpipes and sang this refrain :

> ' Qui vivra verra :
> Le voilà,
> Le preneur des rats.'

He was a great gawky fellow, dry and bronzed, with a crooked
nose, a long rat-tail moustache, two great yellow piercing and
mocking eyes, under a large felt hat set off by a scarlet cock's feather.
He was dressed in a green jacket with a leather belt and red breeches,
and on his feet were sandals fastened by thongs passed round his
legs in the gipsy fashion.

That is how he may be seen to this day, painted on a window of the cathedral of Hamel.

He stopped on the great market-place before the town hall, turned his back on the church and went on with his music, singing:

> ' Who lives shall see:
> This is he,
> The ratcatcher.'

The town council had just assembled to consider once more this plague of Egypt, from which no one could save the town.

The stranger sent word to the counsellors that, if they would make it worth his while, he would rid them of all their rats before night, down to the very last.

' Then he is a sorcerer!' cried the citizens with one voice; 'we must beware of him.'

The Town Counsellor, who was considered clever, reassured them.

He said: ' Sorcerer or no, if this bagpiper speaks the truth, it was he who sent us this horrible vermin that he wants to rid us of to-day for money. Well, we must learn to catch the devil in his own snares. You leave it to me.'

' Leave it to the Town Counsellor,' said the citizens one to another.

And the stranger was brought before them.

' Before night,' said he, ' I shall have despatched all the rats in Hamel if you will but pay me a *gros* a head.'

' A *gros* a head!' cried the citizens, ' but that will come to millions of florins!'

The Town Counsellor simply shrugged his shoulders and said to the stranger:

' A bargain! To work; the rats will be paid one *gros* a head as you ask.'

The bagpiper announced that he would operate that very evening when the moon rose. He added that the inhabitants should at that hour leave the streets free, and content themselves with looking out of their windows at what was passing, and that it would be a pleasant spectacle. When the people of Hamel heard of the bargain, they too exclaimed: 'A *gros* a head! but this will cost us a deal of money!'

' Leave it to the Town Counsellor,' said the town council with a malicious air. And the good people of Hamel repeated with their counsellors, ' Leave it to the Town Counsellor.'

Towards nine at night the bagpiper re-appeared on the market-place.   He turned, as at first, his back to the church, and the moment the moon rose on the horizon, 'Trarira, trari!' the bagpipes re-sounded.

It was first a slow, caressing sound, then more and more lively

and urgent, and so sonorous and piercing that it penetrated as far as the farthest alleys and retreats of the town.

Soon from the bottom of the cellars, the top of the garrets, from under all the furniture, from all the nooks and corners of the houses, out come the rats, search for the door, fling themselves into the street, and trip, trip, trip, begin to run in file towards the front of the town hall, so squeezed together that they covered the pavement like the waves of flooded torrent.

When the square was quite full the bagpiper faced about, and, still playing briskly, turned towards the river that runs at the foot of the walls of Hamel.

Arrived there he turned round ; the rats were following.

' Hop ! hop !' he cried, pointing with his finger to the middle of the stream, where the water whirled and was drawn down as if through a funnel. And hop ! hop ! without hesitating, the rats took the leap, swam straight to the funnel, plunged in head foremost and disappeared.

The plunging continued thus without ceasing till midnight.

At last, dragging himself with difficulty, came a big rat, white with age, and stopped on the bank.

It was the king of the band.

'Are they all there, friend Blanchet ? ' asked the bagpiper.

' They are all there,' replied friend Blanchet.

' And how many were they ? '

' Nine hundred and ninety thousand, nine hundred and ninety-nine.'

' Well reckoned ? '

' Well reckoned.'

' Then go and join them, old sire, and *au revoir*.'

Then the old white rat sprang in his turn into the river, swam to the whirlpool and disappeared.

When the bagpiper had thus concluded his business he went to bed at his inn. And for the first time during three months the people of Hamel slept quietly through the night.

The next morning, at nine o'clock, the bagpiper repaired to the town hall, where the town council awaited him.

' All your rats took a jump into the river yesterday,' said he to the counsellors, ' and I guarantee that not one of them comes back. They were nine hundred and ninety thousand, nine hundred and ninety-nine, at one *gros* a head. Reckon ! '

' Let us reckon the heads first. One *gros* a head is one head the *gros*. Where are the heads ? '

The ratcatcher did not expect this treacherous stroke. He paled with anger and his eyes flashed fire.

' The heads ! ' cried he, ' if you care about them, go and find them in the river.'

'So,' replied the Town Counsellor, 'you refuse to hold to the terms of your agreement? We ourselves could refuse you all payment. But you have been of use to us, and we will not let you go without a recompense,' and he offered him fifty crowns.

'Keep your recompense for yourself,' replied the ratcatcher proudly. 'If you do not pay me I will be paid by your heirs.'

Thereupon he pulled his hat down over his eyes, went hastily out of the hall, and left the town without speaking to a soul.

When the Hamel people heard how the affair had ended they rubbed their hands, and with no more scruple than their Town Counsellor, they laughed over the ratcatcher, who, they said, was caught in his own trap. But what made them laugh above all was his threat of getting himself paid by their heirs. Ha! they wished that they only had such creditors for the rest of their lives.

Next day, which was a Sunday, they all went gaily to church, thinking that after Mass they would at last be able to eat some good thing that the rats had not tasted before them.

They never suspected the terrible surprise that awaited them on their return home. No children anywhere, they had all disappeared!

'Our children! where are our poor children?' was the cry that was soon heard in all the streets.

Then through the east door of the town came three little boys, who cried and wept, and this is what they told:

While the parents were at church a wonderful music had resounded. Soon all the little boys and all the little girls that had been left at home had gone out, attracted by the magic sounds, and had rushed to the great market-place. There they found the ratcatcher playing his bagpipes at the same spot as the evening before. Then the stranger had begun to walk quickly, and they had followed, running, singing and dancing to the sound of the music, as far as the foot of the mountain which one sees on entering Hamel. At their approach the mountain had opened a little, and the bagpiper had gone in with them, after which it had closed again. Only the three little ones who told the adventure had remained outside, as if by a miracle. One was bandy-legged and could not run fast enough; the other, who had left the house in haste, one foot shod the other bare, had hurt himself against a big stone and could not walk without difficulty; the third had arrived in time, but in hurrying to go in with the others had struck so violently against the wall of the mountain that he fell backwards at the moment it closed upon his comrades.

At this story the parents redoubled their lamentations. They ran with pikes and mattocks to the mountain, and searched till evening to find the opening by which their children had disappeared, without being able to find it. At last, the night falling, they returned desolate to Hamel.

But the most unhappy of all was the Town Counsellor, for he lost three little boys and two pretty little girls, and to crown all, the people of Hamel overwhelmed him with reproaches, forgetting that the evening before they had all agreed with him.

What had become of all these unfortunate children ?

The parents always hoped they were not dead, and that the rat-

catcher, who certainly must have come out of the mountain, would have taken them with him to his country. That is why for several years they sent in search of them to different countries, but no one ever came on the trace of the poor little ones.

It was not till much later that anything was to be heard of them.

About one hundred and fifty years after the event, when there was no longer one left of the fathers, mothers, brothers or sisters of that day, there arrived one evening in Hamel some merchants of Bremen returning from the East, who asked to speak with the citizens. They told that they, in crossing Hungary, had sojourned in a mountainous country called Transylvania, where the inhabitants only spoke German, while all around them nothing was spoken but Hungarian. These people also declared that they came from Germany, but they did not know how they chanced to be in this strange country. 'Now,' said the merchants of Bremen, 'these Germans cannot be other than the descendants of the lost children of Hamel.'

The people of Hamel did not doubt it ; and since that day they regard it as certain that the Transylvanians of Hungary are their country folk, whose ancestors, as children, were brought there by the ratcatcher. There are more difficult things to believe than that.[1]

[1] Ch. Marelles.

THE TRUE HISTORY OF LITTLE GOLDEN-HOOD

YOU know the tale of poor Little Red Riding-hood, that the Wolf deceived and devoured, with her cake, her little butter can, and her Grandmother; well, the true story happened quite differently, as we know now. And first of all the little girl was called and is still called Little Golden-hood; secondly, it was not she, nor the good grand-dame, but the wicked Wolf who was, in the end, caught and devoured.

Only listen.

The story begins something like the tale.

There was once a little peasant girl, pretty and nice as a star in its season. Her real name was Blanchette, but she was more often called Little Golden-hood, on account of a wonderful little cloak with a hood, gold- and fire-coloured, which she always had on. This little hood was given her by her Grandmother, who was so old that she did not know her age; it ought to bring her good luck, for it was made of a ray of sunshine, she said. And as the good old woman was considered something of a witch, everyone thought the little hood rather bewitched too.

And so it was, as you will see.

One day the mother said to the child: 'Let us see, my little Golden-hood, if you know now how to find your way by yourself. You shall take this good piece of cake to your Grandmother for a Sunday treat to-morrow. You will ask her how she is, and come back at once, without stopping to chatter on the way with people you don't know. Do you quite understand?'

'I quite understand,' replied Blanchette gaily. And off she went with the cake, quite proud of her errand.

But the Grandmother lived in another village, and there was a big wood to cross before getting there. At a turn of the road under the trees, suddenly 'Who goes there?'

' Friend Wolf.'

He had seen the child start alone, and the villain was waiting to devour her; when at the same moment he perceived some wood-cutters who might observe him, and he changed his mind. Instead of falling upon Blanchette he came frisking up to her like a good dog.

' 'Tis you! my nice Little Golden-hood,' said he. So the little girl stops to talk with the Wolf, who, for all that, she did not know in the least.

' You know me, then!' said she; 'what is your name?'

' My name is friend Wolf. And where are you going thus, my pretty one, with your little basket on your arm?'

' I am going to my Grandmother, to take her a good piece of cake for her Sunday treat to-morrow.'

' And where does she live, your Grandmother?'

' She lives at the other side of the wood, in the first house in the village, near the windmill, you know.'

' Ah! yes! I know now,' said the Wolf. ' Well, that's just where I'm going; I shall get there before you, no doubt, with your little bits of legs, and I'll tell her you're coming to see her; then she'll wait for you.'

Thereupon the Wolf cuts across the wood, and in five minutes arrives at the Grandmother's house.

He knocks at the door: toc, toc.

No answer.

He knocks louder.

Nobody.

Then he stands up on end, puts his two fore-paws on the latch and the door opens.

Not a soul in the house.

The old woman had risen early to sell herbs in the town, and she had gone off in such haste that she had left her bed unmade, with her great night-cap on the pillow.

' Good!' said the Wolf to himself, 'I know what I'll do.'

He shuts the door, pulls on the Grandmother's night-cap down to his eyes, then he lies down all his length in the bed and draws the curtains.

In the meantime the good Blanchette went quietly on her way, as little girls do, amusing herself here and there by picking Easter daisies, watching the little birds making their nests, and running after the butterflies which fluttered in the sunshine.

At last she arrives at the door.

Knock, knock.

' Who is there ? ' says the Wolf, softening his rough voice as best he can.

' It's me, Granny, your little Golden-hood.   I'm bringing you a big piece of cake for your Sunday treat to-morrow.'

' Press your finger on the latch, then push and the door opens.'

' Why, you've got a cold, Granny,' said she, coming in.

'Ahem ! a little, a little . . .' replies the Wolf, pretending to cough.   ' Shut the door well, my little lamb.   Put your basket on the table, and then take off your frock and come and lie down by me : you shall rest a little.'

The good child undresses, but observe this !   She kept her little hood upon her head.   When she saw what a figure her Granny cut in bed, the poor little thing was much surprised.

' Oh ! ' cries she, ' how like you are to friend Wolf, Grandmother ! '

' That's on account of my night-cap, child,' replies the Wolf.

' Oh! what hairy arms you've got, Grandmother ! '

' All the better to hug you, my child.'

' Oh ! what a big tongue you've got, Grandmother ! '

' All the better for answering, child.'

' Oh! what a mouthful of great white teeth you have, Grand-mother ! '

' That's for crunching little children with ! '   And the Wolf opened his jaws wide to swallow Blanchette.

But she put down her head crying :

' Mamma ! Mamma ! ' and the Wolf only caught her little hood.

Thereupon, oh dear ! oh dear ! he draws back, crying and shaking his jaw as if he had swallowed red-hot coals.

It was the little fire-coloured hood that had burnt his tongue right down his throat.

The little hood, you see, was one of those magic caps that they used to have in former times, in the stories, for making oneself invisible or invulnerable.

So there was the Wolf with his throat burnt, jumping off the bed and trying to find the door, howling and howling as if all the dogs in the country were at his heels.

Just at this moment the Grandmother arrives, returning from the town with her long sack empty on her shoulder.

' Ah, brigand ! ' she cries, ' wait a bit ! '   Quickly she opens her sack wide across the door, and the maddened Wolf springs in head downwards.

It is he now that is caught, swallowed like a letter in the post.

For the brave old dame shuts her sack, so ; and she runs and empties it in the well, where the vagabond, still howling, tumbles in and is drowned.

'Ah, scoundrel ! you thought you would crunch my little grand-child !   Well, to-morrow we will make her a muff of your skin, and

you yourself shall be crunched, for we will give your carcass to the dogs.'

Thereupon the Grandmother hastened to dress poor Blanchette, who was still trembling with fear in the bed.

'Well,' she said to her, 'without my little hood where would you be now, darling ? '   And, to restore heart and legs to the child, she made her eat a good piece of her cake, and drink a good draught of wine, after which she took her by the hand and led her back to the house.

And then, who was it who scolded her when she knew all that had happened ?

It was the mother.

But Blanchette promised over and over again that she would never more stop to listen to a Wolf, so that at last the mother forgave her.

And Blanchette, the Little Golden-hood, kept her word. And in fine weather she may still be seen in the fields with her pretty little hood, the colour of the sun.

But to see her you must rise early.[1]

[1] Ch. Marelles

THE GOLDEN BRANCH

ONCE upon a time there was a King who was so morose and disagreeable that he was feared by all his subjects, and with good reason, as for the most trifling offences he would have their heads cut off. This King Grumpy, as he was called, had one son, who was as different from his father as he could possibly be. No prince equalled him in cleverness and kindness of heart, but unfortunately he was most terribly ugly. He had crooked legs and squinting eyes, a large mouth all on one side, and a hunchback. Never was there a beautiful soul in such a frightful little body, but in spite of his appearance everybody loved him. The Queen, his mother, called him Curlicue, because it was a name she rather liked, and it seemed to suit him.

King Grumpy, who cared a great deal more for his own grandeur than for his son's happiness, wished to betroth the Prince to the daughter of a neighbouring King, whose great estates joined his own, for he thought that this alliance would make him more powerful than ever, and as for the Princess she would do very well for Prince Curlicue, for she was as ugly as himself. Indeed, though she was the most amiable creature in the world, there was no concealing the fact that she was frightful, and so lame that she always went about with a crutch, and people called her Princess Cabbage-Stalk.

The King, having asked for and received a portrait of this Princess, had it placed in his great hall under a canopy, and sent for Prince Curlicue, to whom he said that as this was the portrait of his future bride, he hoped the Prince found it charming.

The Prince after one glance at it turned away with a disdainful air, which greatly offended his father.

'Am I to understand that you are not pleased?' he said very sharply.

'No, sire,' replied the Prince. 'How could I be pleased to marry an ugly, lame Princess?'

' Certainly it is becoming in *you* to object to that,' said King Grumpy, ' since you are ugly enough to frighten anyone yourself.'

' That is the very reason,' said the Prince, ' that I wish to marry someone who is not ugly. I am quite tired enough of seeing myself.'

' I tell you that you shall marry her,' cried King Grumpy angrily.

And the Prince, seeing that it was of no use to remonstrate, bowed and retired.

As King Grumpy was not used to being contradicted in anything, he was very much displeased with his son, and ordered that he should be imprisoned in the tower that was kept on purpose for rebellious Princes, but had not been used for about two hundred years, because there had not been any. The Prince thought all the rooms looked strangely old-fashioned, with their antique furniture, but as there was a good library he was pleased, for he was very fond of reading, and he soon got permission to have as many books as he liked. But when he looked at them he found that they were written in a forgotten language, and he could not understand a single word, though he amused himself with trying.

King Grumpy was so convinced that Prince Curlicue would soon get tired of being in prison, and so consent to marry the Princess Cabbage-Stalk, that he sent ambassadors to her father proposing that she should come and be married to his son, who would make her perfectly happy.

The King was delighted to receive so good an offer for his un-lucky daughter, though, to tell the truth, he found it impossible to admire the Prince's portrait which had been sent to him. How-ever, he had it placed in as favourable a light as possible, and sent for the Princess, but the moment she caught sight of it she looked the other way and began to cry. The King, who was very much annoyed to see how greatly she disliked it, took a mirror, and hold-ing it up before the unhappy Princess, said :

' I see you do not think the Prince handsome, but look at your-self, and see if you have any right to complain about that.'

' Sire,' she answered, ' I do not wish to complain, only I beg of you do not make me marry at all. I had rather be the unhappy Princess Cabbage-Stalk all my life than inflict the sight of my ugliness on anyone else.'

But the King would not listen to her, and sent her away with the ambassadors.

In the meantime the Prince was kept safely locked up in his tower, and, that he might be as dull as possible, King Grumpy ordered that no one should speak to him, and that they should give him next to nothing to eat. But all the Prince's guards were so fond of him that they did everything they dared, in spite of the King, to make the time pass pleasantly.

One day, as the Prince was walking up and down the great gallery, thinking how miserable it was to be so ugly, and to be forced to marry an equally frightful Princess, he looked up suddenly and noticed that the painted windows were particularly bright and beautiful, and for the sake of doing something that would change his sad thoughts he began to examine them attentively. He found that the pictures seemed to be scenes from the life of a man who appeared in every window, and the Prince, fancying that he saw in this man some resemblance to himself, began to be deeply interested. In the first window there was a picture of him in one of the turrets of the tower, farther on he was seeking something in a chink in the wall, in the next picture he was opening an old cabinet with a golden key, and so it went on through numbers of scenes, and presently the Prince noticed that another figure occupied the most important place in each scene, and this time it was a tall handsome young man : poor Prince Curlicue found it a pleasure to look at him, he was so straight and strong. By this time it had grown dark, and the Prince had to go back to his own room, and to amuse him-self he took up a quaint old book and began to look at the pictures. But his surprise was great to find that they represented the same scenes as the windows of the gallery, and what was more, that they seemed to be alive. In looking at pictures of musicians he saw their hands move and heard sweet sounds ; there was a picture of a ball, and the Prince could watch the little dancing people come and go. He turned a page, and there was an excellent smell of a savoury dinner, and one of the figures who sat at the feast looked at him and said :

' We drink your health, Curlicue. Try to give us our Queen again, for if you do you will be rewarded ; if not, it will be the worse for you.'

At these words the Prince, who had been growing more and more astonished, was fairly terrified, and dropping the book with a crash he sank back insensible. The noise he made brought his guards to his aid, and as soon as he revived they asked him what was the matter. He answered that he was so faint and giddy with hunger that he had imagined he saw and heard all sorts of strange things. Thereupon, in spite of the King's orders, the guards gave him an excellent supper, and when he had eaten it he again opened his book, but could see none of the wonderful pictures, which convinced him that he must have been dreaming before.

However, when he went into he gallery next day and looked at the painted windows again, he found that they moved, and the figures came and went as if they had been alive, and after watching the one who was like himself find the key in the crack of the turret wall and open the old cabinet, he determined to go and examine the place himself, and try to find out what the mystery was. So he went up into the turret and began to search about and tap upon the walls, and all at once he came upon a place that sounded hollow. Taking a hammer he broke away a bit of the stone, and found behind it a little golden key. The next thing to do was to find the cabinet, and the Prince soon came to it, hidden away in a dark corner, though indeed it was so old and battered-looking that he would never have noticed it of his own accord. At first he could not see any keyhole, but after a careful search he found one hidden in the carving, and the golden key just fitted it ; so the Prince gave it a vigorous turn and the doors flew open.

Ugly and old as the cabinet was outside, nothing could have been more rich and beautiful than what met the Prince's astonished eyes. Every drawer was made of crystal, of amber, or of some precious stone, and was quite full of every kind of treasure. Prince Curlicue was delighted ; he opened one after another, until at last he came to one tiny drawer which contained only an emerald key.

'I believe that this must open that little golden door in the middle,' said the Prince to himself. And he fitted in the little key and turned it. The tiny door swung back, and a soft crimson light gleamed over the whole cabinet. The Prince found that it proceeded from an immense glowing carbuncle, made into a box, which lay before him. He lost no time in opening it, but what was his horror when he found that it contained a man's hand, which was holding a portrait. His first thought was to put back the terrible box and fly from the turret ; but a voice in his ear said, ' This hand belonged to one whom you can help and restore. Look at this beautiful portrait, the original of which was the cause of all my misfortunes, and if you wish to help me, go without a moment's delay to the great gallery, notice where the sun's rays fall most brightly, and if you seek there you will find my treasure.'

The voice ceased, and though the Prince in his bewilderment asked various questions, he received no answer. So he put back the box and locked the cabinet up again, and, having replaced the key in the crack in the wall, hastened down to the gallery.

When he entered it all the windows shook and clattered in the strangest way, but the Prince did not heed them; he was looking so carefully for the place where the sun shone most brightly, and it seemed to him that it was upon the portrait of a most splendidly handsome young man.

He went up and examined it, and found that it rested against the ebony and gold panelling, just like any of the other pictures in the gallery. He was puzzled, not knowing what to do next, until it occurred to him to see if the windows would help him, and, looking at the nearest, he saw a picture of himself lifting the picture from the wall.

The Prince took the hint, and lifting aside the picture without difficulty, found himself in a marble hall adorned with statues; from this he passed on through numbers of splendid rooms, until at last he reached one all hung with blue gauze. The walls were of turquoises, and upon a low couch lay a lovely lady, who seemed to be asleep. Her hair, black as ebony, was spread across the pillows, making her face look ivory white, and the Prince noticed that she was unquiet; and when he softly advanced, fearing to wake her, he could hear her sigh, and murmur to herself:

'Ah! how dared you think to win my love by separating me from my beloved Florimond, and in my presence cutting off that dear hand that even you should have feared and honoured?'

And then the tears rolled slowly down the lovely lady's cheeks, and Prince Curlicue began to comprehend that she was under an enchantment, and that it was the hand of her lover that he had found.

At this moment a huge Eagle flew into the room, holding in its talons a Golden Branch, upon which were growing what looked like clusters of cherries, only every cherry was a single glowing ruby.

This he presented to the Prince, who guessed by this time that he was in some way to break the enchantment that surrounded the sleeping lady. Taking the branch he touched her lightly with it, saying:

'Fair one, I know not by what enchantment thou art bound, but in the name of thy beloved Florimond I conjure thee to come back to the life which thou hast lost, but not forgotten.'

Instantly the lady opened her lustrous eyes, and saw the Eagle hovering near.

'Ah! stay, dear love, stay,' she cried.   But the Eagle, uttering a dolorous cry, fluttered his broad wings and disappeared.   Then the lady turned to Prince Curlicue, and said:

'I know that it is to you I owe my deliverance from an enchantment which has held me for two hundred years.   If there is anything that I can do for you in return, you have only to tell me, and all my fairy power shall be used to make you happy.'

'Madam,' said Prince Curlicue, 'I wish to be allowed to restore your beloved Florimond to his natural form, since I cannot forget the tears you shed for him.'

'That is very amiable of you, dear Prince,' said the Fairy, 'but it is reserved for another person to do that.   I cannot explain more at present.   But is there nothing you wish for yourself?'

'Madam,' cried the Prince, flinging himself down at her feet, 'only look at my ugliness. I am called Curlicue, and am an object of derision; I entreat you to make me less ridiculous.'

' Rise, Prince,' said the Fairy, touching him with the Golden Branch. ' Be as accomplished as you are handsome, and take the name of Prince Peerless, since that is the only title which will suit you now.'

Silent from joy, the Prince kissed her hand to express his thanks, and when he rose and saw his new reflection in the mirrors which surrounded him, he understood that Curlicue was indeed gone for ever.

' How I wish,' said the Fairy, ' that I dared to tell you what is in store for you, and warn you of the traps which lie in your path, but I must not. Fly from the tower, Prince, and remember that the Fairy Douceline will be your friend always.'

When she had finished speaking, the Prince, to his great aston-ishment, found himself no longer in the tower, but set down in a thick forest at least a hundred leagues away from it. And there we must leave him for the present, and see what was happening elsewhere.

When the guards found that the Prince did not ask for his supper as usual, they went into his room, and not finding him there, were very much alarmed, and searched the tower from turret to dungeon, but without success. Knowing that the King would certainly have their heads cut off for allowing the Prince to escape, they then agreed to say that he was ill, and after making the smallest among them look as much like Prince Curlicue as possible, they put him into his bed and sent to inform the King.

King Grumpy was quite delighted to hear that his son was ill, for he thought that he would all the sooner be brought to do as he wished, and marry the Princess. So he sent back to the guards to say that the Prince was to be treated as severely as before, which was just what they had hoped he would say. In the meantime the Princess Cabbage-Stalk had reached the palace, travelling in a litter.

King Grumpy went out to meet her, but when he saw her, with a skin like a tortoise's, her thick eyebrows meeting above her large nose, and her mouth from ear to ear, he could not help crying out :

' Well, I must say Curlicue is ugly enough, but I don't think *you* need have thought twice before consenting to marry him.'

' Sire,' she replied, ' I know too well what I am like to be hurt by what you say, but I assure you that I have no wish to marry your son I had rather be called Princess Cabbage-Stalk than Queen Curlicue.'

This made King Grumpy very angry.

'Your father has sent you here to marry my son,' he said, 'and you may be sure that I am not going to offend him by altering his arrangements.' So the poor Princess was sent away in disgrace to her own apartments, and the ladies who attended upon her were charged to bring her to a better mind.

At this juncture the guards, who were in great fear that they would be found out, sent to tell the King that his son was dead, which annoyed him very much. He at once made up his mind that it was entirely the Princess's fault, and gave orders that she should be mprisoned in the tower in Prince Curlicue's place. The

Princess Cabbage-Stalk was immensely astonished at this unjust proceeding, and sent many messages of remonstrance to King Grumpy, but he was in such a temper that no one dared to deliver them, or to send the letters which the Princess wrote to her father. However, as she did not know this, she lived in hope of soon going back to her own country, and tried to amuse herself as well as she could until the time should come. Every day she walked up and down the long gallery, until she too was attracted and fascinated by the ever-changing pictures in the windows, and recognised herself in one of the figures. 'They seem to have taken a great delight in painting me since I came to this country,' she said to herself. 'One would think that I and my crutch were put in on purpose to make that slim, charming young shepherdess in the next picture look prettier by contrast. Ah! how nice it would be to be as pretty as that.' And then she looked at herself in a mirror, and turned away quickly with tears in her eyes from the doleful sight. All at once she became aware that she was not alone, for behind her stood a tiny old woman in a cap, who was as ugly again as herself and quite as lame.

'Princess,' she said, 'your regrets are so piteous that I have come to offer you the choice of goodness or beauty. If you wish to be pretty you shall have your way, but you will also be vain, capricious, and frivolous. If you remain as you are now, you shall be wise and amiable and modest.'

'Alas! madam,' cried the Princess, 'is it impossible to be at once wise and beautiful?'

'No, child,' answered the old woman, 'only to you it is decreed that you must choose between the two. See, I have brought with me my white and yellow muff. Breathe upon the yellow side and you will become like the pretty shepherdess you so much admire, and you will have won the love of the handsome shepherd whose picture I have already seen you studying with interest. Breathe upon the white side and your looks will not alter, but you will grow better and happier day by day. Now you may choose.'

'Ah well,' said the Princess, 'I suppose one can't have everything, and it's certainly better to be good than pretty.'

And so she breathed upon the white side of the muff and thanked the old fairy, who immediately disappeared. The Princess Cabbage-Stalk felt very forlorn when she was gone, and began to think that it was quite time her father sent an army to rescue her.

'If I could but get up into the turret,' she thought, 'to see if anyone is coming.' But to climb up there seemed impossible. Never-theless she presently hit upon a plan. The great clock was in the turret, as she knew, though the weights hung down into the gallery. Taking one of them off the rope, she tied herself on in its place, and when the clock was wound, up she went triumphantly into the turret. She looked out over the country the first thing, but seeing nothing she sat down to rest a little, and accidentally leant back against the wall which Curlicue, or rather Prince Peerless, had so hastily mended. Out fell the broken stone, and with it the golden key. The clatter it made upon the floor attracted the Princess Cabbage-Stalk's attention.

She picked it up, and after a moment's consideration decided that it must belong to the curious old cabinet in the corner, which had no visible keyhole. And then it was not long before she had it open, and was admiring the treasures it contained as much as Prince Peerless had done before her, and at last she came to the carbuncle box. No sooner had she opened it than with a shudder of horror she tried to throw it down, but found that some mysterious power compelled her to hold it against her will. And at this moment a voice in her ear said softly:

' Take courage, Princess; upon this adventure your future happi-ness depends.'

' What am I to do ? ' said the Princess trembling.

' Take the box,' replied the voice, ' and hide it under your pillow, and when you see an Eagle, give it to him without losing a moment.'

Terrified as the Princess was, she did not hesitate to obey, and hastened to put back all the other precious things precisely as she had found them. By this time her guards were seeking her every-where, and they were amazed to find her up in the turret, for they said she could only have got there by magic. For three days nothing happened, but at last in the night the Princess heard something flutter against her window, and drawing back her curtains she saw in the moonlight that it was an Eagle.

Limping across at her utmost speed she threw the window open, and the great Eagle sailed in beating with his wings for joy. The Princess lost no time in offering it the carbuncle box, which it grasped in its talons, and instantly disappeared, leaving in its place the most beautiful Prince she had ever seen, who was splendidly dressed, and wore a diamond crown.

' Princess,' said he, ' for two hundred years has a wicked en-chanter kept me here. We both loved the same Fairy, but she preferred me.   However, he was more powerful than I, and succeeded, when for a moment I was off my guard, in changing me into an Eagle, while my Queen was left in an enchanted sleep.   I knew that after two hundred years a Prince would recall her to the light of day, and a Princess, in restoring to me the hand which my enemy had cut off, would give me back my natural form.   The Fairy who watches over your destiny told me this, and it was she who guided you to the cabinet in the turret, where she had placed my hand.   It is she also who permits me to show my gratitude to you by granting whatever favour you may ask of me.   Tell me, Princess, what is it that you wish for most ?   Shall I make you as beautiful as you deserve to be ? '

' Ah, if you only would ! ' cried the Princess, and at the same moment she heard a crick-cracking in all her bones.   She grew tall and straight and pretty, with eyes like shining stars, and a skin as white as milk.

' Oh, wonderful ! can this really be my poor little self ? ' she exclaimed, looking down in amazement at her tiny worn-out crutch as it lay upon the floor.

' Indeed, Princess,' replied Florimond, ' it is yourself, but you must have a new name, since the old one does not suit you now. Be called Princess Sunbeam, for you are bright and charming enough to deserve the name.'

And so saying he disappeared, and the Princess, without knowing how she got there, found herself walking under shady trees by a clear river.   Of course, the first thing she did was to look at her own reflection in the water, and she was extremely surprised to find that she was exactly like the shepherdess she had so much admired, and wore the same white dress and flowery wreath that she had seen in the painted windows.   To complete the resemblance, her flock of sheep appeared, grazing round her, and she found a gay crook adorned with flowers upon the bank of the river.   Quite tired out by so many new and wonderful experiences, the Princess sat down to rest at the foot of a tree, and there she fell fast asleep.   Now it happened that it was in this very country that Prince Peerless had been set down, and while the Princess Sunbeam was still sleeping peacefully, he came strolling along in search of a shady pasture for his sheep.

The moment he caught sight of the Princess he recognised her as the charming shepherdess whose picture he had seen so often in the tower, and as she was far prettier than he had remembered her, he was delighted that chance had led him that way.

He was still watching her admiringly when the Princess opened her eyes, and as she also recognised him they were soon great friends. The Princess asked Prince Peerless, as he knew the country better than she did, to tell her of some peasant who would give her a lodging, and he said he knew of an old woman whose cottage would be the very place for her, it was so nice and so pretty. So they went there together, and the Princess was charmed with the old woman and everything belonging to her. Supper was soon spread for her under a shady tree, and she invited the Prince to share the cream and brown bread which the old woman provided. This he was delighted to do, and having first fetched from his own garden all the strawberries, cherries, nuts and flowers he could find, they sat down together and were very merry. After this they met every day as they guarded their flocks, and were so happy that Prince Peerless begged the Princess to marry him, so that they might never be parted again. Now though the Princess Sunbeam appeared to be only a poor shepherdess, she never forgot that she was a real Princess, and she was not at all sure that she ought to marry a humble shepherd, though she knew she would like to do so very much.

So she resolved to consult an Enchanter of whom she had heard a great deal since she had been a shepherdess, and without saying a word to anybody she set out to find the castle in which he lived with his sister, who was a powerful Fairy. The way was long, and lay through a thick wood, where the Princess heard strange voices calling to her from every side, but she was in such a hurry that she stopped for nothing, and at last she came to the courtyard of the Enchanter's castle.

The grass and briers were growing as high as if it were a hundred years since anyone had set foot there, but the Princess got through at last, though she gave herself a good many scratches by the way, and then she went into a dark, gloomy hall, where there was but one tiny hole in the wall through which the daylight could enter. The hangings were all of bats' wings, and from the ceiling hung twelve cats, who filled the hall with their ear piercing yells. Upon the long table twelve mice were fastened by the tail, and just in front of each one's nose, but quite beyond its reach, lay a tempting morsel of fat bacon. So the cats could always see the mice, but could not touch them, and the hungry mice were tormented by the sight and smell of the delicious morsels which they could never seize.

The Princess was looking at the poor creatures in dismay, when
the Enchanter suddenly entered, wearing a long black robe and
with a crocodile upon his head. In his hand he carried a whip
made of twenty long snakes, all alive and writhing, and the Princess

was so terrified at the sight that she heartily wished she had never
come. Without saying a word she ran to the door, but it was
covered with a thick spider's web, and when she broke it she found
another, and another, and another. In fact, there was no end to

them; the Princess's arms ached with tearing them down, and yet she was no nearer to getting out, and the wicked Enchanter behind her laughed maliciously. At last he said:

'You might spend the rest of your life over that without doing any good, but as you are young, and quite the prettiest creature I have seen for a long time, I will marry you if you like, and I will give you those cats and mice that you see there for your own. They are princes and princesses who have happened to offend me. They used to love one another as much as they now hate one another. Aha! It's a pretty little revenge to keep them like that.'

'Oh! If you would only change me into a mouse too,' cried the Princess.

'Oh! so you won't marry me?' said he. 'Little simpleton, you should have everything heart can desire.'

'No, indeed; nothing should make me marry you; in fact, I don't think I shall ever love anyone,' cried the Princess.

'In that case,' said the Enchanter, touching her, 'you had better become a particular kind of creature that is neither fish nor fowl; you shall be light and airy, and as green as the grass you live in. Off with you, Madam Grasshopper.' And the Princess, rejoicing to find herself free once more, skipped out into the garden, the prettiest little green Grasshopper in the world. But as soon as she was safely out she began to be rather sorry for herself.

'Ah! Florimond,' she sighed, 'is this the end of your gift? Certainly beauty is short-lived, and this funny little face and a green crape dress are a comical end to it. I had better have married my amiable shepherd. It must be for my pride that I am condemned to be a Grasshopper, and sing day and night in the grass by this brook, when I feel far more inclined to cry.'

In the meantime Prince Peerless had discovered the Princess's absence, and was lamenting over it by the river's brim, when he suddenly became aware of the presence of a little old woman. She was quaintly dressed in a ruff and farthingale, and a velvet hood covered her snow-white hair.

'You seem sorrowful, my son,' she said. 'What is the matter?'

'Alas! mother,' answered the Prince, 'I have lost my sweet shepherdess, but I am determined to find her again, though I should have to traverse the whole world in search of her.'

'Go that way, my son,' said the old woman, pointing towards the path that led to the castle. 'I have an idea that you will soon overtake her.'

The Prince thanked her heartily and set out. As he met with no hindrance, he soon reached the enchanted wood which surrounded the castle, and there he thought he saw the Princess Sunbeam gliding before him among the trees. Prince Peerless hastened after her at the top of his speed, but could not get any nearer ; then he called to her :

' Sunbeam, my darling—only wait for me a moment.'

But the phantom did but fly the faster, and the Prince spent the whole day in this vain pursuit. When night came he saw the castle before him all lighted up, and as he imagined that the Princess must be in it, he made haste to get there too. He entered without difficulty, and in the hall the terrible old Fairy met him. She was so thin that the light shone through her, and her eyes glowed like lamps ; her skin was like a shark's, her arms were thin as laths, and her fingers like spindles. Nevertheless she wore rouge and patches, a mantle of silver brocade and a crown of diamonds, and her dress was covered with jewels, and green and pink ribbons.

' At last you have come to see me, Prince,' said she. ' Don't waste another thought upon that little shepherdess, who is unworthy of your notice. I am the Queen of the Comets, and can bring you to great honour if you will marry me.'

' Marry you, Madam,' cried the Prince, in horror. ' No, I will never consent to that.'

Thereupon the Fairy, in a rage, gave two strokes of her wand and filled the gallery with horrible goblins, against whom the Prince had to fight for his life. Though he had only his dagger, he defended himself so well that he escaped without any harm, and presently the old Fairy stopped the fray and asked the Prince if he was still of the same mind. When he answered firmly that he was, she called up the appearance of the Princess Sunbeam to the other end of the gallery, and said :

' You see your beloved there ?   Take care what you are about, for if you again refuse to marry me she shall be torn in pieces by two tigers.'

The Prince was distracted, for he fancied he heard his dear shepherdess weeping and begging him to save her. In despair he cried :

' Oh, Fairy Douceline, have you abandoned me after so many promises of friendship ? Help, help us now ! '

Immediately a soft voice said in his ear :

'Be firm, happen what may, and seek the Golden Branch.'

Thus encouraged, the Prince persevered in his refusal, and at length the old Fairy in a fury cried :

'Get out of my sight, obstinate Prince. Become a Cricket!'

And instantly the handsome Prince Peerless became a poor little

black Cricket, whose only idea would have been to find himself a cosy cranny behind some blazing hearth, if he had not luckily remembered the Fairy Douceline's injunction to seek the Golden Branch.

So he hastened to depart from the fatal castle, and sought shelter in a hollow tree, where he found a forlorn looking little Grasshopper crouching in a corner, too miserable to sing.

Without in the least expecting an answer, the Prince asked it:
'And where may you be going, Gammer Grasshopper?'

'Where are you going yourself, Gaffer Cricket?' replied the Grasshopper.

'What! can you speak?' said he.

'Why should I not speak as well as you? Isn't a Grasshopper as good as a Cricket?' said she.

'I can talk because I was a Prince,' said the Cricket.

'And for that very same reason I ought to be able to talk more than you, for I was a Princess,' replied the Grasshopper.

'Then you have met with the same fate as I have,' said he. 'But where are you going now? Cannot we journey together?'

'I seemed to hear a voice in the air which said: "Be firm, happen what may, and seek the Golden Branch,"' answered the Grasshopper, 'and I thought the command must be for me, so I started at once, though I don't know the way.'

At this moment their conversation was interrupted by two mice, who, breathless from running, flung themselves headlong through the hole into the tree, nearly crushing the Grasshopper and the Cricket, though they got out of the way as fast as they could and stood up in a dark corner.

'Ah, Madam,' said the fatter of the two, 'I have such a pain in my side from running so fast. How does your Highness find yourself?'

'I have pulled my tail off,' replied the younger Mouse, 'but as I should still be on the sorcerer's table unless I had, I do not regret it. Are we pursued, think you? How lucky we were to escape!'

'I only trust that we may escape cats and traps, and reach the Golden Branch soon,' said the fat Mouse.

'You know the way then?' said the other.

'Oh dear, yes! as well as the way to my own house, Madam. This Golden Branch is indeed a marvel, a single leaf from it makes one rich for ever. It breaks enchantments, and makes all who approach it young and beautiful. We must set out for it at the break of day.'

'May we have the honour of travelling with you—this respectable Cricket and myself?' said the Grasshopper, stepping forward. 'We also are on a pilgrimage to the Golden Branch.'

The Mice courteously assented, and after many polite speeches the whole party fell asleep. With the earliest dawn they were on their way, and though the Mice were in constant fear of being overtaken or trapped, they reached the Golden Branch in safety.

It grew in the midst of a wonderful garden, all the paths of which were strewn with pearls as big as peas. The roses were crimson diamonds, with emerald leaves. The pomegranates were garnets, the marigolds topazes, the daffodils yellow diamonds, the violets sapphires, the corn-flowers turquoises, the tulips amethysts, opals and diamonds, so that the garden borders blazed like the sun. The Golden Branch itself had become as tall as a forest tree, and sparkled with ruby cherries to its topmost twig. No sooner had the Grasshopper and the Cricket touched it than they were restored to their natural forms, and their surprise and joy were great when they recognised each other. At this moment Florimond and the Fairy Douceline appeared in great splendour, and the Fairy, as she descended from her chariot, said with a smile:

' So you two have found one another again, I see, but I have still a surprise left for you. Don't hesitate, Princess, to tell your devoted shepherd how dearly you love him, as he is the very Prince your father sent you to marry. So come here both of you and let me crown you, and we will have the wedding at once.'

The Prince and Princess thanked her with all their hearts, and declared that to her they owed all their happiness, and then the two Princesses, who had so lately been Mice, came and begged that the Fairy would use her power to release their unhappy friends who were still under the Enchanter's spell.

' Really,' said the Fairy Douceline, ' on this happy occasion I cannot find it in my heart to refuse you anything.' And she gave three strokes of her wand upon the Golden Branch, and immediately all the prisoners in the Enchanter's castle found themselves free, and came with all speed to the wonderful garden, where one touch of the Golden Branch restored each one to his natural form, and they greeted one another with many rejoicings. To complete her generous work the Fairy presented them with the wonderful cabinet and all the treasures it contained, which were worth at least ten kingdoms. But to Prince Peerless and the Princess Sunbeam she gave the palace and garden of the Golden Branch, where, immensely rich and greatly beloved by all their subjects, they lived happily ever after.[1]

[1] *Le Rameau d'Or.* Par Madame d'Aulnoy.

THE THREE DWARFS

THERE was once upon a time a man who lost his wife, and a woman who lost her husband ; and the man had a daughter and so had the woman. The two girls were great friends and used often to play together. One day the woman turned to the man's daughter and said :

' Go and tell your father that I will marry him, and then you shall wash in milk and drink wine, but my own daughter shall wash in water and drink it too.'

The girl went straight home and told her father what the woman had said.

' What am I to do ? ' he answered. ' Marriage is either a success or it is a failure.'

At last, being of an undecided character and not being able to make up his mind, he took off his boot, and handing it to his daughter, said :

' Take this boot which has a hole in the sole, hang it up on a nail in the hayloft, and pour water into it. If it holds water I will marry again, but if it doesn't I won't.' The girl did as she was bid, but the water drew the hole together and the boot filled up to the very top. So she went and told her father the result. He got up and went to see for himself, and when he saw that it was true and no mistake, he accepted his fate, proposed to the widow, and they were married at once.

On the morning after the wedding, when the two girls awoke, milk was standing for the man's daughter to wash in and wine for her to drink ; but for the woman's daughter, only water to wash in and only water to drink. On the second morning, water to wash in and water to drink was standing for the man's daughter as well. And on the third morning, water to wash in and water to drink was standing for the man's daughter, and milk to wash in and wine to drink for the woman's daughter ; and so it continued ever after. The woman hated her stepdaughter from the bottom of her heart, and did all she could to make her life miserable. She was as jealous as she could possibly be, because the girl was so beautiful and charming, while her own daughter was both ugly and repulsive.

One winter's day when there was a hard frost, and mountain

and valley were covered with snow, the woman made a dress of paper, and calling the girl to her said:

' There, put on this dress and go out into the wood and fetch me a basket of strawberries ! '

'Now Heaven help us,' replied her stepdaughter; ' strawberries don't grow in winter; the earth is all frozen and the snow has covered up everything; and why send me in a paper dress ? it is so cold outside that one's very breath freezes; the wind will whistle through my dress, and the brambles tear it from my body.'

' How dare you contradict me ! ' said her stepmother; ' be off with you at once, and don't show your face again till you have filled the basket with strawberries.'

Then she gave her a hard crust of bread, saying :

' That will be enough for you to-day,' and she thought to herself : ' The girl will certainly perish of hunger and cold outside, and I shan't be bothered with her any more.'

The girl was so obedient that she put on the paper dress and set out with her little basket. There was nothing but snow far and near, and not a green blade of grass to be seen anywhere. When she came to the wood she saw a little house, and out of it peeped three little dwarfs. She wished them good-day, and knocked modestly at the door. They called out to her to enter, so she stepped in and sat down on a seat by the fire, wishing to warm herself and eat her breakfast. The Dwarfs said at once : ' Give us some of your food ! '

' Gladly,' she said, and breaking her crust in two, she gave them the half.

Then they asked her what she was doing in the depths of winter in her thin dress.

' Oh,' she answered, ' I have been sent to get a basketful of strawberries, and I daren't show my face again at home till I bring them with me.'

When she had finished her bread they gave her a broom and told her to sweep away the snow from the back door. As soon as she left the room to do so, the three little men consulted what they should give her as a reward for being so sweet and good, and for sharing her last crust with them.

The first said : ' Every day she shall grow prettier.'

The second : ' Every time she opens her mouth a piece of gold shall fall out.'

And the third : 'A King shall come and marry her.'

The girl in the meantime was doing as the Dwarfs had bidden her, and was sweeping the snow away from the back door, and what do you think she found there ?—heaps of fine ripe strawberries that showed out dark red against the white snow. She joyfully picked

'No better fate than to be put into a barrel lined with sharp nails, and to be rolled in it down the hill into the water.'

'You have pronounced your own doom,' said the King; and he ordered a barrel to be made lined with sharp nails, and in it he put the bad old woman and her daughter. Then it was fastened down securely, and the barrel was rolled down the hill till it fell into the river.[1]

[1] **Grimm.**

DAPPLEGRIM

THERE was once upon a time a couple of rich folks who had twelve sons, and when the youngest was grown up he would not stay at home any longer, but would go out into the world and seek his fortune. His father and mother said that they thought he was very well off at home, and that he was welcome to stay with them; but he could not rest, and said that he must and would go, so at last they had to give him leave. When he had walked a long way, he came to a King's palace. There he asked for a place and got it.

Now the daughter of the King of that country had been carried off into the mountains by a Troll, and the King had no other children, and for this cause both he and all his people were full of sorrow and affliction, and the King had promised the Princess and half his kingdom to anyone who could set her free; but there was no one who could do it, though a great number had tried. So when the youth had been there for the space of a year or so, he wanted to go home again to pay his parents a visit; but when he got there his father and mother were dead, and his brothers had divided everything that their parents possessed between themselves, so that there was nothing at all left for him.

'Shall I, then, receive nothing at all of my inheritance?' asked the youth.

'Who could know that you were still alive—you who have been a wanderer so long?' answered the brothers. 'However, there are twelve mares upon the hills which we have not yet divided among us, and if you would like to have them for your share, you may take them.'

So the youth, well pleased with this, thanked them, and at once set off to the hill where the twelve mares were at pasture. When he got up there and found them, each mare had her foal, and by the side of one of them was a big dapple-grey foal as well, which was so sleek that it shone again.

'Well, my little foal, you are a fine fellow!' said the youth.

'Yes, but if you will kill all the other little foals so that I can suck all the mares for a year, you shall see how big and handsome I shall be then!' said the Foal.

So the youth did this—he killed all the twelve foals, and then went back again.

Next year, when he came home again to look after his mares and the foal, it was as fat as it could be, and its coat shone with brightness, and it was so big that the lad had the greatest difficulty in getting on its back, and each of the mares had another foal.

'Well, it's very evident that I have lost nothing by letting you

suck all my mares,' said the lad to the yearling; 'but now you are quite big enough, and must come away with me.'

'No,' said the Colt, 'I must stay here another year; kill the twelve little foals, and then I can suck all the mares this year also, and you shall see how big and handsome I shall be by summer.'

So the youth did it again, and when he went up on the hill next year to look after his colt and the mares, each of the mares had her foal again; but the dappled colt was so big that when the lad wanted to feel its neck to see how fat it was, he could not reach up to it, it was so high, and it was so bright that the light glanced off its coat.

'Big and handsome you were last year, my colt, but this year you are ever so much handsomer,' said the youth; 'in all the King's court no such horse is to be found. But now you shall come away with me.'

'No,' said the dappled Colt once more; 'here I must stay for another year. Just kill the twelve little foals again, so that I can suck the mares this year also, and then come and look at me in the summer.'

So the youth did it—he killed all the little foals, and then went home again.

But next year, when he returned to look after the dappled colt and the mares, he was quite appalled. He had never imagined that any horse could become so big and overgrown, for the dappled horse had to lie down on all fours before the youth could get on his back, and it was very hard to do that even when it was lying down, and it was so plump that its coat shone and glistened just as if it had been a looking-glass. This time the dappled horse was not unwilling to go away with the youth, so he mounted it, and when he came riding home to his brothers they all smote their hands together and crossed themselves, for never in their lives had they either seen or heard tell of such a horse as that.

'If you will procure me the best shoes for my horse, and the most magnificent saddle and bridle that can be found,' said the youth, 'you may have all my twelve mares just as they are standing out on the hill, and their twelve foals into the bargain.' For this year also each mare had her foal. The brothers were quite willing to do this; so the lad got such shoes for his horse that the sticks and stones flew high up into the air as he rode away over the hills, and such a gold saddle and such a gold bridle that they could be seen glittering and glancing from afar.

'And now we will go to the King's palace,' said Dapplegrim—that was the horse's name, 'but bear in mind that you must ask the King for a good stable and excellent fodder for me.'

So the lad promised not to forget to do that. He rode to the palace, and it will be easily understood that with such a horse as he had he was not long on the way.

When he arrived there, the King was standing out on the steps, and how he did stare at the man who came riding up!

'Nay,' said he, 'never in my whole life have I seen such a man and such a horse.'

And when the youth inquired if he could have a place in the

King's palace, the King was so delighted that he could have danced on the steps where he was standing, and there and then the lad was told that he should have a place.

' Yes ; but I must have a good stable and most excellent fodder for my horse,' said he.

So they told him that he should have sweet hay and oats, and as much of them as the dappled horse chose to have, and all the other riders had to take their horses out of the stable that Dapplegrim might stand alone and really have plenty of room.

But this did not last long, for the other people in the King's Court became envious of the lad, and there was no bad thing that they would not have done to him if they had but dared. At last they bethought themselves of telling the King that the youth had said that, if he chose, he was quite able to rescue the Princess who had been carried off into the mountain a long time ago by the Troll.

The King immediately summoned the lad into his presence, and said that he had been informed that he had said that it was in his power to rescue the Princess, so he was now to do it. If he succeeded in this, he no doubt knew that the King had promised his daughter and half the kingdom to anyone who set her free, which promise should be faithfully and honourably kept, but if he failed he should be put to death. The youth denied that he had said this, but all to no purpose, for the King was deaf to all his words ; so there was nothing to be done but say that he would make the attempt.

He went down into the stable, and very sad and full of care he was. Then Dapplegrim inquired why he was so troubled, and the youth told him, and said that he did not know what to do, ' for as to setting the Princess free, that was downright impossible.'

' Oh, but it might be done,' said Dapplegrim. ' I will help you ; but you must first have me well shod. You must ask for ten pounds of iron and twelve pounds of steel for the shoeing, and one smith to hammer and one to hold.'

So the youth did this, and no one said him nay. He got both the iron and the steel, and the smiths, and thus was Dapplegrim shod strongly and well, and when the youth went out of the King's palace a cloud of dust rose up behind him. But when he came to the mountain into which the Princess had been carried, the difficulty was to ascend the precipitous wall of rock by which he was to get on to the mountain beyond, for the rock stood right up on end, as steep as a house side and as smooth as a sheet of glass. The first time the youth rode at it he got a little way up the precipice, but then both Dapplegrim's fore legs slipped, and down came horse and rider with a sound like thunder among the mountains. The next time that he rode at it he got a little farther up, but then one of Dapplegrim's fore legs slipped, and down they went with the sound of a landslip. But the third time Dapplegrim said : ' Now we must show what we can do,' and went at it once more till the stones sprang up sky high, and thus they got up. Then the lad rode into the mountain cleft at full gallop and caught up the Princess on his

saddle-bow, and then out again before the Troll even had time to stand up, and thus the Princess was set free.

When the youth returned to the palace the King was both happy and delighted to get his daughter back again, as may easily be believed, but somehow or other the people about the Court had so worked on him that he was angry with the lad too. ' Thou shalt have my thanks for setting my Princess free,' he said, when the youth came into the palace with her, and was then about to go away.

She ought to be just as much my Princess as she is yours now, for you are a man of your word,' said the youth.

Yes, yes,' said the King. 'Have her thou shalt, as I have said it; but first of all thou must make the sun shine into my palace here.'

For there was a large and high hill outside the windows which overshadowed the palace so much that the sun could not shine in.

'That was no part of our bargain,' answered the youth. 'But as nothing that I can say will move you, I suppose I shall have to try to do my best, for the Princess I will have.'

So he went down to Dapplegrim again and told him what the King desired, and Dapplegrim thought that it might easily be done; but first of all he must have new shoes, and ten pounds of iron and twelve pounds of steel must go to the making of them, and two smiths were also necessary, one to hammer and one to hold, and then it would be very easy to make the sun shine into the King's palace.

The lad asked for these things and obtained them instantly, for the King thought that for very shame he could not refuse to give them, and so Dapplegrim got new shoes, and they were good ones. The youth seated himself on him, and once more they went their way, and for each hop that Dapplegrim made, down went the hill fifteen ells into the earth, and so they went on until there was no hill left for the King to see.

When the youth came down again to the King's palace he asked the King if the Princess should not at last be his, for now no one could say that the sun was not shining into the palace. But the other people in the palace had again stirred up the King, and he answered that the youth should have her, and that he had never intended that he should not; but first of all he must get her quite as good a horse to ride to the wedding on as that which he had himself. The youth said that the King had never told him he was to do that, and it seemed to him that he had now really earned the Princess; but the King stuck to what he had said, and if the youth were unable to do it he was to lose his life, the King said. The youth went down to the stable again, and very sad and sorrowful he was, as anyone may well imagine. Then he told Dapplegrim that the King had now required that he should get the Princess as good a bridal horse as that which the bridegroom had, or he should lose his life. 'But that will be no easy thing to do,' said he, 'for your equal is not to be found in all the world,'

'Oh yes, there is one to match me,' said Dapplegrim. 'But it will not be easy to get him, for he is underground. However, we will try. Now you must go up to the King and ask for new shoes for me, and for them we must again have ten pounds of iron, twelve pounds of steel, and two smiths, one to hammer and one to hold, but be very particular to see that the hooks are very sharp. And you must also ask for twelve barrels of rye, and twelve slaughtered oxen must we have with us, and all the twelve ox-hides with twelve hundred spikes set in each of them; all these things must we have, likewise a barrel of tar with twelve tons of tar in it. The youth went to the King and asked for all the things that Dapplegrim had named, and once more, as the King thought that it would be disgraceful to refuse them to him, he obtained them all.

So he mounted Dapplegrim and rode away from the Court, and when he had ridden for a long, long time over hills and moors, Dapplegrim asked : ' Do you hear anything ? '

'Yes ; there is such a dreadful whistling up above in the air that I think I am growing alarmed,' said the youth.

'That is all the wild birds in the forest flying about; they are sent to stop us,' said Dapplegrim. 'But just cut a hole in the corn sacks, and then they will be so busy with the corn that they will forget us.'

The youth did it. He cut holes in the corn sacks so that barley and rye ran out on every side, and all the wild birds that were in the forest came in such numbers that they darkened the sun. But when they caught sight of the corn they could not refrain from it, but flew down and began to scratch and pick at the corn and rye, and at last they began to fight among themselves, and forgot all about the youth and Dapplegrim, and did them no harm.

And now the youth rode onwards for a long, long time, over hill and dale, over rocky places and morasses, and then Dapplegrim began to listen again, and asked the youth if he heard anything now.

' Yes; now I hear such a dreadful crackling and crashing in the forest on every side that I think I shall be really afraid,' said the youth.

'That is all the wild beasts in the forest,' said Dapplegrim ; ' they are sent out to stop us. But just throw out the twelve carcasses of the oxen, and they will be so much occupied with them that they will quite forget us.' So the youth threw out the carcasses of the oxen, and then all the wild beasts in the forest, both bears and wolves, and lions, and grim beasts of all kinds, came. But when they caught sight of the carcasses of the oxen they began to fight for them till the blood flowed, and they entirely forgot Dapplegrim and the youth.

So the youth rode onwards again, and many and many were the new scenes they saw, for travelling on Dapplegrim's back was not travelling slowly, as may be imagined, and then Dapplegrim neighed.

'Do you hear anything? he said.

'Yes; I heard something like a foal neighing quite plainly a long, long way off,' answered the youth.

'That's a full-grown colt,' said Dapplegrim, 'if you hear it so plainly when it is so far away from us.'

So they travelled onwards a long time, and saw one new scene after another once more. Then Dapplegrim neighed again.

'Do you hear anything now?' said he.

'Yes; now I heard it quite distinctly, and it neighed like a full-grown horse,' answered the youth.

'Yes, and you will hear it again very soon,' said Dapplegrim;

' and then you will hear what a voice it has.' So ney travelled on through many more different kinds of country, and then Dapplegrim neighed for the third time; but before he could ask the youth if he heard anything, there was such a neighing on the other side of the heath that the youth thought that hills and rocks would be rent in pieces.

'Now he is here!' said Dapplegrim. 'Be quick, and fling over me the ox-hides that have the spikes in them, throw the twelve tons of tar over the field, and climb up into that great spruce fir tree. When he comes, fire will spurt out of both his nostrils, and then the tar will catch fire. Now mark what I say—if the flame ascends I conquer, and if it sinks I fail; but if you see that I am winning, fling the bridle, which you must take off me, over his head, and then he will become quite gentle.'

Just as the youth had flung all the hides with the spikes over Dapplegrim, and the tar over the field, and had got safely up into the spruce fir, a horse came with flame spouting from his nostrils, and the tar caught fire in a moment; and Dapplegrim and the horse began to fight until the stones leapt up to the sky. They bit, and they fought with their fore legs and their hind legs, and sometimes the youth looked at them, and sometimes he looked at the tar, but at last the flames began to rise, for wheresoever the strange horse bit or wheresoever he kicked he hit upon the spikes in the hides, and at length he had to yield. When the youth saw that, he was not long in getting down from the tree and flinging the bridle over the horse's head, and then he became so tame that he might have been led by a thin string.

This horse was dappled too, and so like Dapplegrim that no one could distinguish the one from the other. The youth seated himself on the dappled horse which he had captured, and rode home again to the King's palace, and Dapplegrim ran loose by his side. When he got there, the King was standing outside in the courtyard.

' Can you tell me which is the horse I have caught, and which is the one I had before? ' said the youth. ' If you can't, I think your daughter is mine.'

The King went and looked at both the dappled horses; he looked high and he looked low, he looked before and he looked behind, but there was not a hair's difference between the two.

' No,' said the King; ' that I cannot tell thee, and as thou hast procured such a splendid bridal horse for my daughter thou shalt

have her ; but first we must have one more trial, just to see if thou
art fated to have her. She shall hide herself twice, and then thou
shalt hide thyself twice. If thou canst find her each time that
she hides herself, and if she cannot find thee in thy hiding-places,
then it is fated, and thou shalt have the Princess.'

' That, too, was not in our bargain,' said the youth. ' But we will
make this trial since it must be so.'

So the King's daughter was to hide herself first.

Then she changed herself into a duck, and lay swimming in a
lake that was just outside the palace. But the youth went down
into the stable and asked Dapplegrim what she had done with herself.

' Oh, all that you have to do is to take your gun, and go down to
the water and aim at the duck which is swimming about there,
and she will soon discover herself,' said Dapplegrim.

The youth snatched up his gun and ran to the lake. ' I will
just have a shot at that duck,' said he, and began to aim at it.

' Oh, no, dear friend, don't shoot! It is I,' said the Princess.
So he had found her once.

The second time the Princess changed herself into a loaf, and
laid herself on the table among four other loaves ; and she was so
like the other loaves that no one could see any difference between
them.

But the youth again went down to the stable to Dapplegrim,
and told him that the Princess had hidden herself again, and that
he had not the least idea what had become of her.

' Oh, just take a very large bread-knife, sharpen it, and pretend
that you are going to cut straight through the third of the four
loaves which are lying on the kitchen table in the King's palace
—count them from right to left—and you will soon find her,' said
Dapplegrim.

So the youth went up to the kitchen, and began to sharpen the
largest bread-knife that he could find ; then he caught hold of the
third loaf on the left-hand side, and put the knife to it as if he
meant to cut it straight in two. ' I will have a bit of this bread
for myself,' said he.

' No, dear friend, don't cut, it is I ! ' said the Princess again ;
so he had found her the second time.

And now it was his turn to go and hide himself ; but Dapplegrim
had given him such good instructions that it was not easy to find
him. First he turned himself into a horse-fly, and hid himself in

Dapplegrim's left nostril. The Princess went poking about and searching everywhere, high and low, and wanted to go into Dapplegrim's stall too, but he began to bite and kick about so that she was afraid to go there, and could not find the youth. 'Well,' said she, 'as I am unable to find you, you must show yourself;' whereupon the youth immediately appeared standing there on the stable floor.

Dapplegrim told him what he was to do the second time, and he turned himself into a lump of earth, and stuck himself between the hoof and the shoe on Dapplegrim's left fore foot. Once more the King's daughter went and sought everywhere, inside and outside, until at last she came into the stable, and wanted to go into the stall beside Dapplegrim. So this time he allowed her to go into it, and she peered about high and low, but she could not look under his hoofs, for he stood much too firmly on his legs for that, and she could not find the youth.

'Well, you will just have to show where you are yourself, for I can't find you,' said the Princess, and in an instant the youth was standing by her side on the floor of the stable.

'Now you are mine!' said he to the Princess.

'Now you can see that it is fated that she should be mine,' he said to the King.

'Yes, fated it is,' said the King. 'So what must be, must.'

Then everything was made ready for the wedding with great splendour and promptitude, and the youth rode to church on Dapplegrim, and the King's daughter on the other horse. So everyone must see that they could not be long on their way thither.[1]

---

[1] From J. Moe.

THE ENCHANTED CANARY

I

ONCE upon a time, in the reign of King Cambrinus, there lived at
Avesnes one of his lords, who was the finest man—by which I
mean the fattest—in the whole country of Flanders. He ate four
meals a day, slept twelve hours out of the twenty-four, and the only
thing he ever did was to shoot at small birds with his bow and
arrow.

Still, with all his practice he shot very badly, he was so fat and
heavy, and as he grew daily fatter, he was at last obliged to give up
walking, and be dragged about in a wheel-chair, and the people
made fun of him, and gave him the name of my Lord Tubby.

Now, the only trouble that Lord Tubby had was about his son,
whom he loved very much, although they were not in the least
alike, for the young Prince was as thin as a cuckoo. And what
vexed him more than all was, that though the young ladies throughout all his lands did their best to make the Prince fall in love with
them, he would have nothing to say to any of them, and told his
father he did not wish to marry.

Instead of chatting with them in the dusk, he wandered about
the woods, whispering to the moon. No wonder the young ladies
thought him very odd, but they liked him all the better for that;
and as he had received at his birth the name of Désiré, they all
called him d'Amour Désiré.

'What is the matter with you?' his father often said to him.
'You have everything you can possibly wish for: a good bed, good
food, and tuns full of beer. The only thing you want, in order to
become as fat as a pig, is a wife that can bring you broad, rich
lands. So marry, and you will be perfectly happy.'

'I ask nothing better than to marry,' replied Désiré, 'but I have
never seen a woman that pleases me. All the girls here are pink
and white, and I am tired to death of their eternal lilie and roses.

'My faith!' cried Tubby; 'do you want to marry a negress, and give me grandchildren as ugly as monkeys and as stupid as owls?'

'No, father, nothing of the sort. But there must be women somewhere in the world who are neither pink nor white, and I tell you, once for all, that I will never marry until I have found one exactly to my taste.'

II

Some time afterwards, it happened that the Prior of the Abbey of Saint Amand sent to the Lord of Avesnes a basket of oranges, with a beautifully-written letter saying that these golden fruit, then unknown in Flanders, came straight from a land where the sun always shone.

That evening Tubby and his son ate the golden apples at supper, and thought them delicious.

Next morning as the day dawned, Désiré went down to the stable and saddled his pretty white horse. Then he went, all dressed for a journey, to the bedside of Tubby, and found him smoking his first pipe.

'Father,' he said gravely, 'I have come to bid you farewell. Last night I dreamed that I was walking in a wood, where the trees were covered with golden apples. I gathered one of them, and when I opened it there came out a lovely princess with a golden skin. That is the wife I want, and I am going to look for her.'

The Lord of Avesnes was so much astonished that he let his pipe fall to the ground; then he became so diverted at the notion of his son marrying a yellow woman, and a woman shut up inside an orange, that he burst into fits of laughter.

Désiré waited to bid him good-bye until he was quiet again; but as his father went on laughing and showed no signs of stopping, the young man took his hand, kissed it tenderly, opened the door, and in the twinkling of an eye was at the bottom of the staircase. He jumped lightly on his horse, and was a mile from home before Tubby had ceased laughing.

'A yellow wife! He must be mad! fit for a strait waistcoat!' cried the good man, when he was able to speak. 'Here! quick! bring him back to me.'

The servants mounted their horses and rode after the Prince; but as they did not know which road he had taken, they went all

ways except the right one, and instead of bringing him back they
returned themselves when it grew dark, with their horses worn out
and covered with dust.

III

When Désiré thought they could no longer catch him, he pulled
his horse into a walk, like a prudent man who knows he has far to

go. He travelled in this way for many weeks, passing by villages,
towns, mountains, valleys, and plains, but always pushing south,
where every day the sun seemed hotter and more brilliant.

At last one day at sunset Désiré felt the sun so warm, that he
thought he must now be near the place of his dream. He was at
that moment close to the corner of a wood where stood a little hut,
before the door of which his horse stopped of his own accord. An

old man with a white beard was sitting on the doorstep enjoying the fresh air. The Prince got down from his horse and asked leave to rest.

' Come in, my young friend,' said the old man ; ' my house is not large, but it is big enough to hold a stranger.'

The traveller entered, and his host put before him a simple meal. When his hunger was satisfied the old man said to him :

' If I do not mistake, you come from far. May I ask where you are going ? '

' I will tell you,' answered Désiré, ' though most likely you will laugh at me. I dreamed that in the land of the sun there was a wood full of orange trees, and that in one of the oranges I should find a beautiful princess who is to be my wife. It is she I am seeking.'

' Why should I laugh ? ' asked the old man. ' Madness in youth is true wisdom. Go, young man, follow your dream, and if you do not find the happiness that you seek, at any rate you will have had the happiness of seeking it.'

IV

The next day the Prince arose early and took leave of his host.

' The wood that you saw in your dream is not far from here,' said the old man. ' It is in the depth of the forest, and this road will lead you there. You will come to a vast park surrounded by high walls. In the middle of the park is a castle, where dwells a horrible witch who allows no living being to enter the doors. Behind the castle is the orange grove. Follow the wall till you come to a heavy iron gate. Don't try to press it open, but oil the hinges with this,' and the old man gave him a small bottle.

' The gate will open of itself,' he continued, ' and a huge dog which guards the castle will come to you with his mouth wide open, but just throw him this oat cake. Next, you will see a baking woman leaning over her heated oven. Give her this brush. Lastly, you will find a well on your left ; do not forget to take the cord of the bucket and spread it in the sun. When you have done this, do not enter the castle, but go round it and enter the orange grove. Then gather three oranges, and get back to the gate as fast as you can. Once out of the gate, leave the forest by the opposite ide.

' Now, attend to this : whatever happens, do not open your oranges till you reach the bank of a river, or a fountain. Out of each orange will come a princess, and you can choose which you like for your wife. Your choice once made, be very careful never to leave your bride for an instant, and remember that the danger which is most to be feared is never the danger we are most afraid of.'

V

Désiré thanked his host warmly, and took the road he pointed out. In less than an hour he arrived at the wall, which was very high indeed. He sprang to the ground, fastened his horse to a tree, and soon found the iron gate. Then he took out his bottle and oiled the hinges, when the gate opened of itself, and he saw an old castle standing inside. The Prince entered boldly into the courtyard.

Suddenly he heard fierce howls, and a dog as tall as a donkey, with eyes like billiard balls, came towards him, showing his teeth, which were like the prongs of a fork. Désiré flung him the oat cake, which the great dog instantly snapped up, and the young Prince passed quietly on.

A few yards further he saw a huge oven, with a wide, red-hot gaping mouth. A woman as tall as a giant was leaning over the oven. Désiré gave her the brush, which she took in silence.

Then he went on to the well, drew up the cord, which was half-rotten, and stretched it out in the sun.

Lastly he went round the castle, and plunged into the orange grove. There he gathered the three most beautiful oranges he could find, and turned to go back to the gate.

But just at this moment the sun was darkened, the earth trembled, and Désiré heard a voice crying :

' Baker, baker, take him by his feet, and throw him into the oven ! '

' No,' replied the baker ; ' a long time has passed since I first began to scour this oven with my own flesh. You never cared to give me a brush ; but he has given me one, and he shall go in peace.'

' Rope, O rope ! ' cried the voice again, ' twine yourself round his neck and strangle him.'

' No,' replied the rope ; ' you have left me for many years past to fall to pieces with the damp. He has stretched me out in the sun. Let him go in peace.'

' Dog, my good dog,' cried the voice, more and more angry, ' jump at his throat and eat him up.'

' No,' replied the dog ; ' though I have served you long, you never

gave me any bread. He has given me as much as I want. Let
him go in peace.'

'Iron gate, iron gate,' cried the voice, growling like thunder,
'fall on him and grind him to powder.'

'No,' replied the gate; 'it is a hundred years since you left me
to rust, and he has oiled me. Let him go in peace.'

VI

Once outside, the young adventurer put his oranges into a bag
that hung from his saddle, mounted his horse, and rode quickly out
of the forest.

Now, as he was longing to see the princesses, he was very anxious to come to a river or a fountain, but, though he rode for hours, a river or fountain was nowhere to be seen. Still his heart was light, for he felt that he had got through the most difficult part of his task, and the rest was easy.

About mid-day he reached a sandy plain, scorching in the sun. Here he was seized with dreadful thirst; he took his gourd and raised it to his lips.

But the gourd was empty; in the excitement of his joy he had forgotten to fill it. He rode on, struggling with his sufferings, but at last he could bear it no longer.

He let himself slide to the earth, and lay down beside his horse, his throat burning, his chest heaving, and his head going round. Already he felt that death was near him, when his eyes fell on the bag where the oranges peeped out.

Poor Désiré, who had braved so many dangers to win the lady of his dreams, would have given at this moment all the princesses in the world, were they pink or golden, for a single drop of water.

' Ah ! ' he said to himself. ' If only these oranges were real fruit— fruit as refreshing as what I ate in Flanders ! And, after all, who knows ? '

This idea put some life into him. He had the strength to lift himself up and put his hand into his bag. He drew out an orange and opened it with his knife.

Out of it flew the prettiest little female canary that ever was seen.

' Give me something to drink, I am dying of thirst,' said the golden bird.

' Wait a minute,' replied Désiré, so much astonished that he forgot his own sufferings; and to satisfy the bird he took a second orange, and opened it without thinking what he was doing. Out of it flew another canary, and she too began to cry :

' I am dying of thirst ; give me something to drink.'

Then Tubby's son saw his folly, and while the two canaries flew away he sank on the ground, where, exhausted by his last effort, he lay unconscious.

VII

When he came to himself, he had a pleasant feeling of freshness all about him. It was night, the sky was sparkling with stars, and the earth was covered with a heavy dew.

The traveller having recovered, mounted his horse, and at the first streak of dawn he saw a stream dancing in front of him, and stooped down and drank his fill.

He hardly had courage to open his last orange. Then he remembered that the night before he had disobeyed the orders of the old man. Perhaps his terrible thirst was a trick of the cunning witch, and suppose, even though he opened the orange on the banks of the stream, that he did not find in it the princess that he sought?

He took his knife and cut it open. Alas! out of it flew a little canary, just like the others, who cried:

'I am thirsty; give me something to drink.'

Great was the disappointment of Désiré. However, he was determined not to let this bird fly away; so he took up some water in the palm of his hand and held it to its beak.

Scarcely had the canary drunk when she became a beautiful girl, tall and straight as a poplar tree, with black eyes and a golden skin. Désiré had never seen anyone half so lovely, and he stood gazing at her in delight.

On her side she seemed quite bewildered, but she looked about her with happy eyes, and was not at all afraid of her deliverer.

He asked her name. She answered that she was called the Princess Zizi; she was about sixteen years old, and for ten years of that time the witch had kept her shut up in an orange, in the shape of a canary.

'Well, then, my charming Zizi,' said the young Prince, who was longing to marry her, 'let us ride away quickly so as to escape from the wicked witch.'

But Zizi wished to know where he meant to take her.

'To my father's castle,' he said.

He mounted his horse and took her in front of him, and, holding her carefully in his arms, they began their journey.

VIII

Everything the Princess saw was new to her, and in passing through mountains, valleys, and towns, she asked a thousand questions. Désiré was charmed to answer them. It is so delightful to teach those one loves!

Once she inquired what the girls in his country were like.

'They are pink and white,' he replied, 'and their eyes are blue.'

'Do you like blue eyes?' said the Princess; but Désiré thought it was a good opportunity to find out what was in her heart, so he did not answer.

'And no doubt,' went on the Princess, 'one of them is your intended bride?'

Still he was silent, and Zizi drew herself up proudly.

'No,' he said at last. 'None of the girls of my own country are beautiful in my eyes, and that is why I came to look for a wife in the land of the sun. Was I wrong, my lovely Zizi?'

This time it was Zizi's turn to be silent.

IX

Talking in this way they drew near to the castle. When they were about four stone-throws from the gates they dismounted in the forest, by the edge of a fountain.

'My dear Zizi,' said Tubby's son, 'we cannot present ourselves before my father like two common people who have come back from a walk. We must enter the castle with more ceremony. Wait for me here, and in an hour I will return with carriages and horses fit for a princess.'

'Don't be long,' replied Zizi, and she watched him go with wistful eyes.

When she was left by herself the poor girl began to feel afraid. She was alone for the first time in her life, and in the middle of a thick forest.

Suddenly she heard a noise among the trees. Fearing lest it should be a wolf, she hid herself in the hollow trunk of a willow tree which hung over the fountain. It was big enough to hold her altogether, but she pooped out, and her pretty head was reflected in the clear water.

Then there appeared, not a wolf, but a creature quite as wicked and quite as ugly. Let us see who this creature was.

X

Not far from the fountain there lived a family of bricklayers. Now, fifteen years before this time, the father in walking through the forest found a little girl, who had been deserted by the gypsies. He carried her home to his wife, and the good woman was sorry for her, and brought her up with her own sons. As she grew older, the little gypsy became much more remarkable for strength and cunning than for sense or beauty. She had a low forehead, a flat nose, thick lips, coarse hair, and a skin not golden like that of Zizi, but the colour of clay.

As she was always being teased about her complexion, she got as noisy and cross as a titmouse. So they used to call her Titty.

Titty was often sent by the bricklayer to fetch water from the fountain, and as she was very proud and lazy the gypsy disliked this very much.

It was she who had frightened Zizi by appearing with her pitcher on her shoulder. Just as she was stooping to fill it, she saw reflected in the water the lovely image of the Princess.

'What a pretty face!' she exclaimed, 'Why, it must be mine! How in the world can they call me ugly? I am certainly much too pretty to be their water-carrier!'

So saying, she broke her pitcher and went home.

'Where is your pitcher?' asked the bricklayer.

'Well, what do you expect? The pitcher may go many times to the well. . . .'

'But at last it is broken. Well, here is a bucket that will not break.'

The gypsy returned to the fountain, and addressing once more the image of Zizi, she said:

'No; I don't mean to be a beast of burden any longer.' And she flung the bucket so high in the air that it stuck in the branches of an oak.

'I met a wolf,' she told the bricklayer, 'and I broke the bucket across his nose.'

The bricklayer asked her no more questions, but took down a broom and gave her such a beating that her pride was humbled a little.

Then he handed to her an old copper milk-can, and said:

'If you don't bring it back full, your bones shall suffer for it.'

XI

Titty went off rubbing her sides; but this time she did not dare to disobey, and in a very bad temper stooped down over the well. It was not at all easy to fill the milk-can, which was large and round. It would not go down into the well, and the gypsy had to try again and again.

At last her arms grew so tired that when she did manage to get the can properly under the water she had no strength to pull it up, and it rolled to the bottom.

On seeing the can disappear, she made such a miserable face

that Zizi, who had been watching her all this time, burst into fits of laughter.

Titty turned round and perceived the mistake she had made; and she felt so angry that she made up her mind to be revenged at once.

'What are you doing there, you lovely creature?' she said to Zizi.

'I am waiting for my lover,' Zizi replied; and then, with a simplicity quite natural in a girl who so lately had been a canary, she told all her story.

The gypsy had often seen the young Prince pass by, with his gun on his shoulder, when he was going after crows. She was too ugly and ragged for him ever to have noticed her, but Titty on her side had admired him, though she thought he might well have been a little fatter.

'Dear, dear!' she said to herself. 'So he likes yellow women! Why, I am yellow too, and if I could only think of a way——'

It was not long before she did think of it.

'What!' cried the sly Titty, 'they are coming with great pomp to fetch you, and you are not afraid to show yourself to so many fine lords and ladies with your hair down like that? Get down at once, my poor child, and let me dress your hair for you!'

The innocent Zizi came down at once, and stood by Titty. The gypsy began to comb her long brown locks, when suddenly she drew a pin from her stays, and, just as the titmouse digs its beak into the heads of linnets and larks, Titty dug the pin into the head of Zizi.

No sooner did Zizi feel the prick of the pin than she became a bird again, and, spreading her wings, she flew away.

'That was neatly done,' said the gypsy. 'The Prince will be clever if he finds his bride.' And, arranging her dress, she seated herself on the grass to await Désiré.

XII

Meanwhile the Prince was coming as fast as his horse could carry him. He was so impatient that he was always full fifty yards in front of the lords and ladies sent by Tubby to bring back Zizi.

At the sight of the hideous gypsy he was struck dumb with surprise and horror.

'Ah me!' said Titty, 'so you don't know your poor Zizi? While you were away the wicked witch came, and turned me into this. But if you only have the courage to marry me I shall get back my beauty.' And she began to cry bitterly.

Now the good-natured Désiré was as soft-hearted as he was brave.

' Poor girl,' he thought to himself. ' It is not her fault, after all,
that she has grown so ugly, it is mine. Oh! why did I not follow
the old man's advice? Why did I leave her alone? And besides, it
depends on me to break the spell, and I love her too much to let
her remain like this.'

So he presented the gypsy to the lords and ladies of the Court,
explaining to them the terrible misfortune which had befallen his
beautiful bride.

They all pretended to believe it, and the ladies at once put on
the false princess the rich dresses they had brought for Zizi.

She was then perched on the top of a magnificent ambling
palfrey, and they set forth to the castle.

But unluckily the rich dress and jewels only made Titty look
uglier still, and Désiré could not help feeling hot and uncomfortable
when he made his entry with her into the city.

Bells were pealing, chimes ringing, and the people filling the
streets and standing at their doors to watch the procession go by,
and they could hardly believe their eyes as they saw what a strange
bride their Prince had chosen.

In order to do her more honour, Tubby came to meet her at the foot of the great marble staircase. At the sight of the hideous creature he almost fell backwards.

'What!' he cried. 'Is this the wonderful beauty?'

'Yes, father, it is she,' replied Désiré with a sheepish look. 'But she has been bewitched by a wicked sorceress, and will not regain her beauty until she is my wife.'

'Does she say so? Well, if you believe that, you may drink cold water and think it bacon,' the unhappy Tubby answered crossly.

But all the same, as he adored his son, he gave the gypsy his hand and led her to the great hall, where the bridal feast was spread.

XIII

The feast was excellent, but Désiré hardly touched anything. However, to make up, the other guests ate greedily, and, as for Tubby, nothing ever took away his appetite.

When the moment arrived to serve the roast goose, there was a pause, and Tubby took the opportunity to lay down his knife and fork for a little. But as the goose gave no sign of appearing, he sent his head carver to find out what was the matter in the kitchen.

Now this was what had happened.

While the goose was turning on the spit, a beautiful little canary hopped on to the sill of the open window.

'Good-morning, my fine cook,' she said in a silvery voice to the man who was watching the roast.

'Good-morning, lovely golden bird,' replied the chief of the scullions, who had been well brought up.

'I pray that Heaven may send you to sleep,' said the golden bird, 'and that the goose may burn, so that there may be none left for Titty.'

And instantly the chief of the scullions fell fast asleep, and the goose was burnt to a cinder.

When he awoke he was horrified, and gave orders to pluck another goose, to stuff it with chestnuts, and put it on the spit.

While it was browning at the fire, Tubby inquired for his goose a second time. The Master Cook himself mounted to the hall to make his excuses, and to beg his lord to have a little patience. Tubby showed his patience by abusing his son.

'As if it wasn't enough,' he grumbled between his teeth, 'that the boy should pick up a hag without a penny, but the goose must go and burn now. It isn't a wife he has brought me, it is Famine herself.'

XIV

While the Master Cook was upstairs, the golden bird came again to perch on the window-sill, and called in his clear voice to the head scullion, who was watching the spit :

' Good-morning, my fine Scullion ! '

' Good-morning, lovely Golden Bird,' replied the Scullion, whom the Master Cook had forgotten in his excitement to warn.

' I pray Heaven,' went on the Canary, ' that it will send you to sleep, and that the goose may burn, so that there may be none left for Titty.'

And the Scullion fell fast asleep, and when the Master Cook came back he found the goose as black as the chimney.

In a fury he woke the Scullion, who in order to save himself from blame told the whole story.

'That accursed bird,' said the Cook ; 'it will end by getting me sent away. Come, some of you, and hide yourselves, and if it comes again, catch it and wring its neck.'

He spitted a third goose, lit a huge fire, and seated himself by it.

The bird appeared a third time, and said : 'Good-morning, my fine Cook.'

'Good-morning, lovely Golden Bird,' replied the Cook, as if nothing had happened, and at the moment that the Canary was beginning, 'I pray Heaven that it may send,' a scullion who was hidden outside rushed out and shut the shutters. The bird flew into the kitchen. Then all the cooks and scullions sprang after it, knocking at it with their aprons. At length one of them caught it just at the very moment that Tubby entered the kitchen, waving his sceptre. He had come to see for himself why the goose had never made its appearance.

The Scullion stopped at once, just as he was about to wring the Canary's neck.

XV

'Will some one be kind enough to tell me the meaning of all this ? ' cried the Lord of Avesnes.

'Your Excellency, it is the bird,' replied the Scullion, and he placed it in his hand.

'Nonsense ! What a lovely bird!' said Tubby, and in stroking its head he touched a pin that was sticking between its feathers. He pulled it out, and lo ! the Canary at once became a beautiful girl with a golden skin who jumped lightly to the ground.

'Gracious ! what a pretty girl ! ' said Tubby.

'Father ! it is she ! it is Zizi ! ' exclaimed Désiré, who entered at this moment.

And he took her in his arms, crying: 'My darling Zizi, how happy I am to see you once more ! '

'Well, and the other one ? ' asked Tubby.

The other one was stealing quietly to the door.

'Stop her ! called Tubby. 'We will judge her cause at once.'

And he seated himself solemnly on the oven, and condemned Titty to be burned alive. After which the lords and cooks formed themselves in lines, and Tubby betrothed Désiré to Zizi.

XVI

The marriage took place a few days later. All the boys in the country side were there, armed with wooden swords, and decorated with epaulets made of gilt paper.

Zizi obtained Titty's pardon, and she was sent back to the brick-fields, followed and hooted at by all the boys. And this is why to-day the country boys always throw stones at a titmouse.

On the evening of the wedding-day all the larders, cellars, cupboards and tables of the people, whether rich or poor, were loaded as if by enchantment with bread, wine, beer, cakes and tarts, roast larks, and even geese, so that Tubby could not complain any more that his son had married Famine.

Since that time there has always been plenty to eat in that country, and since that time, too, you see in the midst of the fair-haired blue-eyed women of Flanders a few beautiful girls, whose eyes are black and whose skins are the colour of gold. They are the descendants of Zizi.[1]

[1] Charles Deulin, *Contes du Roi Gambrinus.*

THE TWELVE BROTHERS

THERE were once upon a time a King and a Queen who lived happily together, and they had twelve children, all of whom were boys. One day the King said to his wife:

'If our thirteenth child is a girl, all her twelve brothers must die, so that she may be very rich and the kingdom hers alone.'

Then he ordered twelve coffins to be made, and filled them with shavings, and placed a little pillow in each. These he put away in an empty room, and, giving the key to his wife, he bade her tell no one of it.

The Queen grieved over the sad fate of her sons and refused to be comforted, so much so that the youngest boy, who was always with her, and whom she had christened Benjamin, said to her one day:

'Dear mother, why are you so sad?'

'My child,' she answered, 'I may not tell you the reason.'

But he left her no peace, till she went and unlocked the room and showed him the twelve coffins filled with shavings, and with the little pillow laid in each.

Then she said: 'My dearest Benjamin, your father has had these coffins made for you and your eleven brothers, because if I bring a girl into the world you are all to be killed and buried in them.'

She wept bitterly as she spoke, but her son comforted her and said:

'Don't cry, dear mother; we'll manage to escape somehow, and will fly for our lives.'

'Yes,' replied his mother, 'that is what you must do—go with your eleven brothers out into the wood, and let one of you always sit on the highest tree you can find, keeping watch on the tower of the castle. If I give birth to a little son I will wave a white flag, and then you may safely return; but if I give birth to a little

daughter I will wave a red flag, which will warn you to fly away as
quickly as you can, and may the kind Heaven have pity on you.
Every night I will get up and pray for you, in winter that you may
always have a fire to warm yourselves by, and in summer that you
may not languish in the heat.'

Then she blessed her sons and they set out into the wood.

They found a very high oak tree, and there they sat, turn about,
keeping their eyes always fixed on the castle tower. On the
twelfth day, when the turn came to Benjamin, he noticed a flag
waving in the air, but alas! it was not white, but blood red, the
sign which told them they must all die. When the brothers heard
this they were very angry, and said:

' Shall we forsooth suffer death for the sake of a wretched girl?

Let us swear vengeance, and vow that wherever and whenever we shall meet one of her sex, she shall die at our hands.'

Then they went their way deeper into the wood, and in the middle of it, where it was thickest and darkest, they came upon a little enchanted house which stood empty.

'Here,' they said, 'let us take up our abode, and you, Benjamin, you are the youngest and weakest, you shall stay at home and keep house for us ; we others will go out and fetch food.' So they went forth into the wood, and shot hares and roe-deer, birds and wood-pigeons, and any other game they came across. They always brought their spoils home to Benjamin, who soon learnt to make them into dainty dishes. So they lived for ten years in this little house, and the time slipped merrily away.

In the meantime their little sister at home was growing up quickly. She was kind-hearted and of a fair countenance, and she had a gold star right in the middle of her forehead. One day a big washing was going on at the palace, and the girl looking down from her window saw twelve men's shirts hanging up to dry, and asked her mother :

'Who in the world do these shirts belong to ? Surely they are far too small for my father ? '

And the Queen answered sadly : 'Dear child, they belong to your twelve brothers.'

'But where are my twelve brothers ? ' said the girl. 'I have never even heard of them.'

'Heaven alone knows in what part of the wide world they are wandering,' replied her mother.

Then she took the girl and opened the locked-up room ; she showed her the twelve coffins filled with shavings, and with the little pillow laid in each.

'These coffins,' she said, 'were intended for your brothers, but they stole secretly away before you were born.'

Then she proceeded to tell her all that had happened, and when she had finished her daughter said :

'Do not cry, dearest mother ; I will go and seek my brothers till I find them.'

So she took the twelve shirts and went on straight into the middle of the big wood. She walked all day long, and came in the evening to the little enchanted house. She stepped in and found a youth who, marvelling at her beauty, at the royal robes she wore, and at the golden star on her forehead, asked her where she came from and whither she was going.

' I am a Princess,' she answered, ' and am seeking for my twelve
brothers. I mean to wander as far as the blue sky stretches over
the earth till I find them.'

Then she showed him the twelve shirts which she had taken
with her, and Benjamin saw that it must be his sister, and
said :

' I am Benjamin, your youngest brother.'

So they wept for joy, and kissed and hugged each other again
and again. After a time Benjamin said :

' Dear sister, there is still a little difficulty, for we had all agreed
that any girl we met should die at our hands, because it was for the
sake of a girl that we had to leave our kingdom.'

' But,' she replied, ' I will gladly die if by that means I can restore
my twelve brothers to their own.'

' No,' he answered, ' there is no need for that ; only go and hide
under that tub till our eleven brothers come in, and I'll soon make
matters right with them.'

She did as she was bid, and soon the others came home from
the chase and sat down to supper.

' Well, Benjamin, what's the news ? ' they asked.

But he replied, ' I like that ; have you nothing to tell me ? '

' No,' they answered.

Then he said : ' Well, now, you've been out in the wood all the
day and I've stayed quietly at home, and all the same I know more
than you do.'

' Then tell us,' they cried.

But he answered : ' Only on condition that you promise faithfully that the first girl we meet shall not be killed.'

' She shall be spared,' they promised, ' only tell us the news.'

Then Benjamin said : ' Our sister is here ! ' and he lifted up the
tub and the Princess stepped forward, with her royal robes and with
the golden star on her forehead, looking so lovely and sweet and
charming that they all fell in love with her on the spot.

They arranged that she should stay at home with Benjamin and
help him in the house work, while the rest of the brothers went out
into the wood and shot hares and roe-deer, birds and wood-pigeons.
And Benjamin and his sister cooked their meals for them. She
gathered herbs to cook the vegetables in, fetched the wood, and
watched the pots on the fire, and always when her eleven brothers
returned she had their supper ready for them. Besides this, she
kept the house in order, tidied all the rooms, and made herself so

generally useful that her brothers were delighted, and they all lived happily together.

One day the two at home prepared a fine feast, and when they were all assembled they sat down and ate and drank and made merry.

Now there was a little garden round the enchanted house, in

which grew twelve tall lilies. The girl, wishing to please her brothers, plucked the twelve flowers, meaning to present one to each of them as they sat at supper. But hardly had she plucked the flowers when her brothers were turned into twelve ravens, who flew croaking over the wood, and the house and garden vanished also.

So the poor girl found herself left all alone in the wood, and as she looked round her she noticed an old woman standing close beside her, who said :

' My child, what have you done ? Why didn't you leave the flowers alone ? They were your twelve brothers. Now they are changed for ever into ravens.'

The girl asked, sobbing : ' Is there no means of setting them free ? '

' No,' said the old woman, ' there is only one way in the whole world, and that is so difficult that you won't free them by it, for you would have to be dumb and not laugh for seven years, and if you spoke a single word, though but an hour were wanting to the time, your silence would all have been in vain, and that one word would slay your brothers.'

Then the girl said to herself: 'If that is all I am quite sure I can free my brothers.' So she searched for a high tree, and when she had found one she climbed up it and spun all day long, never laughing or speaking one word.

Now it happened one day that a King who was hunting in the wood had a large greyhound, who ran sniffing to the tree on which the girl sat, and jumped round it, yelping and barking furiously. The King's attention was attracted, and when he looked up and beheld the beautiful Princess with the golden star on her forehead, he was so enchanted by her beauty that he asked her on the spot to be his wife. She gave no answer, but nodded slightly with her head. Then he climbed up the tree himself, lifted her down, put her on his horse and bore her home to his palace.

The marriage was celebrated with much pomp and ceremony, but the bride neither spoke nor laughed.

When they had lived a few years happily together, the King's mother, who was a wicked old woman, began to slander the young Queen, and said to the King :

' She is only a low-born beggar maid that you have married ; who knows what mischief she is up to ? If she is deaf and can't speak, she might at least laugh; depend upon it, those who don't laugh have a bad conscience.' At first the King paid no heed to her words, but the old woman harped so long on the subject, and accused the young Queen of so many bad things, that at last he let himself be talked over, and condemned his beautiful wife to death.

So a great fire was lit in the courtyard of the palace, where she was to be burnt, and the King watched the proceedings from an

upper window, crying bitterly the while, for he still loved his wife
dearly. But just as she had been bound to the stake, and the

flames were licking her garments with their red tongues, the very
last moment of the seven years had come. Then a sudden rushing
sound was heard in the air, and twelve ravens were seen flying

overhead. They swooped downwards, and as soon as they touched the ground they turned into her twelve brothers, and she knew that she had freed them.

They quenched the flames and put out the fire, and, unbinding their dear sister from the stake, they kissed and hugged her again and again. And now that she was able to open her mouth and speak, she told the King why she had been dumb and not able to laugh.

The King rejoiced greatly when he heard she was innocent, and they all lived happily ever afterwards.[1]

[1] Grimm.

RAPUNZEL

ONCE upon a time there lived a man and his wife who were very unhappy because they had no children. These good people had a little window at the back of their house, which looked into the most lovely garden, full of all manner of beautiful flowers and vegetables; but the garden was surrounded by a high wall, and no one dared to enter it, for it belonged to a witch of great power, who was feared by the whole world. One day the woman stood at the window overlooking the garden, and saw there a bed full of the finest rampion: the leaves looked so fresh and green that she longed to eat them. The desire grew day by day, and just because she knew she couldn't possibly get any, she pined away and became quite pale and wretched. Then her husband grew alarmed and said:

'What ails you, dear wife?'

'Oh,' she answered, 'if I don't get some rampion to eat out of the garden behind the house, I know I shall die.'

The man, who loved her dearly, thought to himself, 'Come! rather than let your wife die you shall fetch her some rampion, no matter the cost.' So at dusk he climbed over the wall into the witch's garden, and, hastily gathering a handful of rampion leaves, he returned with them to his wife. She made them into a salad, which tasted so good that her longing for the forbidden food was greater than ever. If she were to know any peace of mind, there was nothing for it but that her husband should climb over the garden wall again, and fetch her some more. So at dusk over he got, but when he reached the other side he drew back in terror, for there, standing before him, was the old witch.

'How dare you,' she said, with a wrathful glance, 'climb into my garden and steal my rampion like a common thief? You shall suffer for your foolhardiness.'

'Oh!' he implored, 'pardon my presumption; necessity alone

drove me to the deed. My wife saw your rampion from her window, and conceived such a desire for it that she would certainly have died if her wish had not been gratified.' Then the Witch's anger was a little appeased, and she said :

' If it's as you say, you may take as much rampion away with you as you like, but on one condition only—that you give me the child your wife will shortly bring into the world. All shall go well with it, and I will look after it like a mother.'

The man in his terror agreed to everything she asked, and as soon as the child was born the Witch appeared, and having given it the name of Rapunzel, which is the same as rampion, she carried it off with her.

Rapunzel was the most beautiful child under the sun. When she was twelve years old the Witch shut her up in a tower, in the middle of a great wood, and the tower had neither stairs nor doors, only high up at the very top a small window. When the old Witch wanted to get in she stood underneath and called out :

> ' Rapunzel, Rapunzel,
> Let down your golden hair,'

for Rapunzel had wonderful long hair, and it was as fine as spun gold. Whenever she heard the Witch's voice she unloosed her plaits, and let her hair fall down out of the window about twenty yards below, and the old Witch climbed up by it.

After they had lived like this for a few years, it happened one day that a Prince was riding through the wood and passed by the tower. As he drew near it he heard someone singing so sweetly that he stood still spell-bound, and listened. It was Rapunzel in her loneliness trying to while away the time by letting her sweet voice ring out into the wood. The Prince longed to see the owner of the voice, but he sought in vain for a door in the tower. He rode home, but he was so haunted by the song he had heard that he returned every day to the wood and listened. One day, when he was standing thus behind a tree, he saw the old Witch approach and heard her call out :

> ' Rapunzel, Rapunzel,
> Let down your golden hair.'

Then Rapunzel let down her plaits, and the Witch climbed up by them.

' So that's the staircase, is it ? ' said the Prince. ' Then I too will climb it and try my luck.'

So on the following day, at dusk, he went to the foot of the tower and cried :

'Rapunzel, Rapunzel,
Let down your golden hair,'

and as soon as she had let it down the Prince climbed up.

At first Rapunzel was terribly frightened when a man came in, for she had never seen one before; but the Prince spoke to her so kindly, and told her at once that his heart had been so touched by her singing, that he felt he should know no peace of mind till he had seen her. Very soon Rapunzel forgot her fear, and when he asked her to marry him she consented at once. 'For,' she thought, 'he is young and handsome, and I'll certainly be happier with him than with the old Witch.' So she put her hand in his and said :

'Yes, I will gladly go with you, only how am I to get down out of the tower ? Every time you come to see me you must bring a skein of silk with you, and I will make a ladder of them, and when it is finished I will climb down by it, and you will take me away on your horse.'

They arranged that, till the ladder was ready, he was to come to her every evening, because the old woman was with her during the day. The old Witch, of course, knew nothing of what was going on, till one day Rapunzel, not thinking of what she was about, turned to the Witch and said :

'How is it, good mother, that you are so much harder to pull up than the young Prince ? He is always with me in a moment.'

'Oh! you wicked child,' cried the Witch. 'What is this I hear ? I thought I had hidden you safely from the whole world, and in spite of it you have managed to deceive me.'

In her wrath she seized Rapunzel's beautiful hair, wound it round and round her left hand, and then grasping a pair of scissors in her right, snip snap, off it came, and the beautiful plaits lay on the ground. And, worse than this, she was so hard-hearted that she took Rapunzel to a lonely desert place, and there left her to live in loneliness and misery.

But on the evening of the day in which she had driven poor Rapunzel away, the Witch fastened the plaits on to a hook in the window, and when the Prince came and called out :

'Rapunzel, Rapunzel,
Let down your golden hair,'

she let them down, and the Prince climbed up as usual, but instead of his beloved Rapunzel he found the old Witch, who fixed her evil, glittering eyes on him, and cried mockingly :

'Ah, ah! you thought to find your lady love, but the pretty bird has flown and its song is dumb ; the cat caught it, and will scratch out your eyes too. Rapunzel is lost to you for ever—you will never see her more.'

The Prince was beside himself with grief, and in his despair he jumped right down from the tower, and, though he escaped with his life, the thorns among which he fell pierced his eyes out. Then he wandered, blind and miserable, through the wood, eating nothing but roots and berries, and weeping and lamenting the loss of his lovely bride. So he wandered about for some years, as wretched and unhappy as he could well be, and at last he came to the desert place where Rapunzel was living. Of a sudden he heard a voice which seemed strangely familiar to him. He walked eagerly in the direction of the sound, and when he was quite close, Rapunzel recognised him and fell on his neck and wept. But two of her tears touched his eyes, and in a moment they became quite clear again, and he saw as well as he had ever done. Then he led her to his kingdom, where they were received and welcomed with great joy, and they lived happily ever after.[1]

[1] Grimm.

THE NETTLE SPINNER

I

ONCE upon a time there lived at Quesnoy, in Flanders, a great lord whose name was Burchard, but whom the country people called Burchard the Wolf. Now Burchard had such a wicked, cruel heart, that it was whispered how he used to harness his peasants to the plough, and force them by blows from his whip to till his land with naked feet.

His wife, on the other hand, was always tender and pitiful to the poor and miserable.

Every time that she heard of another misdeed of her husband's she secretly went to repair the evil, which caused her name to be blessed throughout the whole country-side. This Countess was adored as much as the Count was hated.

II

One day when he was out hunting the Count passed through a forest, and at the door of a lonely cottage he saw a beautiful girl spinning hemp.

' What is your name ? ' he asked her.

' Renelde, my lord.'

' You must get tired of staying in such a lonely place ? '

' I am accustomed to it, my lord, and I never get tired of it.'

' That may be so ; but come to the castle, and I will make you lady's maid to the Countess.'

' I cannot do that, my lord. I have to look after my grandmother, who is very helpless.'

' Come to the castle, I tell you. I shall expect you this evening,' and he went on his way.

But Renelde, who was betrothed to a young wood-cutter called Guilbert, had no intention of obeying the Count, and she had, besides, to take care of her grandmother.

Three days later the Count again passed by.
' Why didn't you come ? ' he asked the pretty spinner.

' I told you, my lord, that I have to look after my grandmother.'
' Come to-morrow, and I will make you lady-in-waiting to the
Countess,' and he went on his way.

This offer produced no more effect than the other, and Renelde did not go to the castle.

'If you will only come,' said the Count to her when next he rode by, 'I will send away the Countess, and will marry you.'

But two years before, when Renelde's mother was dying of a long illness, the Countess had not forgotten them, but had given help when they sorely needed it. So even if the Count had really wished to marry Renelde, she would always have refused.

III

Some weeks passed before Burchard appeared again.

Renelde hoped she had got rid of him, when one day he stopped at the door, his duck-gun under his arm and his game-bag on his shoulder. This time Renelde was spinning not hemp, but flax.

'What are you spinning?' he asked in a rough voice.

'My wedding shift, my lord.'

'You are going to be married, then?'

'Yes, my lord, by your leave.'

For at that time no peasant could marry without the leave of his master.

'I will give you leave on one condition. Do you see those tall nettles that grow on the tombs in the churchyard? Go and gather them, and spin them into two fine shifts. One shall be your bridal shift, and the other shall be my shroud. For you shall be married the day that I am laid in my grave.' And the Count turned away with a mocking laugh.

Renelde trembled. Never in all Locquignol had such a thing been heard of as the spinning of nettles.

And besides, the Count seemed made of iron and was very proud of his strength, often boasting that he should live to be a hundred.

Every evening, when his work was done, Guilbert came to visit his future bride. This evening he came as usual, and Renelde told him what Burchard had said.

'Would you like me to watch for the Wolf, and split his skull with a blow from my axe?'

'No,' replied Renelde, 'there must be no blood on my bridal bouquet. And then we must not hurt the Count. Remember how good the Countess was to my mother.'

An old, old woman now spoke: she was the mother of Renelde's grandmother, and was more than ninety years old. All day long she sat in her chair nodding her head and never saying a word.

'My children,' she said, 'all the years that I have lived in the world, I have never heard of a shift spun from nettles. But what God commands, man can do. Why should not Renelde try it?'

IV

Renelde did try, and to her great surprise the nettles when crushed and prepared gave a good thread, soft and light and firm. Very soon she had spun the first shift, which was for her own wedding. She wove and cut it out at once, hoping that the Count would not force her to begin the other. Just as she had finished sewing it, Burchard the Wolf passed by.

'Well,' said he, 'how are the shifts getting on?'

'Here, my lord, is my wedding garment,' answered Renelde, showing him the shift, which was the finest and whitest ever seen.

The Count grew pale, but he replied roughly, 'Very good. Now begin the other.'

The spinner set to work. As the Count returned to the castle, a cold shiver passed over him, and he felt, as the saying is, that some one was walking over his grave. He tried to eat his supper, but could not; he went to bed shaking with fever. But he did not sleep, and in the morning could not manage to rise.

This sudden illness, which every instant became worse, made him very uneasy. No doubt Renelde's spinning-wheel knew all about it. Was it not necessary that his body, as well as his shroud, should be ready for the burial?

The first thing Burchard did was to send to Renelde and to stop her wheel.

Renelde obeyed, and that evening Guilbert asked her:

'Has the Count given his consent to our marriage?'

'No,' said Renelde.

'Continue your work, sweetheart. It is the only way of gaining it. You know he told you so himself.'

V

The following morning, as soon as she had put the house in order, the girl sat down to spin. Two hours after there arrived some soldiers, and when they saw her spinning they seized her, tied her arms and legs, and carried her to the bank of the river, which was swollen by the late rains.

When they reached the bank they flung her in, and watched her sink, after which they left her. But Renelde rose to the surface, and though she could not swim she struggled to land.

Directly she got home she sat down and began to spin.

Again came the two soldiers to the cottage and seized the girl,

carried her to the river bank, tied a stone to her neck and flung her into the water.

The moment their backs were turned the stone untied itself. Renelde waded the ford, returned to the hut, and sat down to spin.

This time the Count resolved to go to Locquignol himself; but, as he was very weak and unable to walk, he had himself borne in a litter. And still the spinner spun.

When he saw her he fired a shot at her, as he would have fired at a wild beast. The bullet rebounded without harming the spinner, who still spun on.

Burchard fell into such a violent rage that it nearly killed him. He broke the wheel into a thousand pieces, and then fell fainting on the ground. He was carried back to the castle, unconscious.

The next day the wheel was mended, and the spinner sat down to spin. Feeling that while she was spinning he was dying, the Count ordered that her hands should be tied, and that they should not lose sight of her for one instant.

But the guards fell asleep, the bonds loosed themselves, and the spinner spun on.

Burchard had every nettle rooted up for three leagues round. Scarcely had they been torn from the soil when they sowed themselves afresh, and grew as you were looking at them.

They sprung up even in the well-trodden floor of the cottage, and as fast as they were uprooted the distaff gathered to itself a supply of nettles, crushed, prepared, and ready for spinning.

And every day Burchard grew worse, and watched his end approaching.

VI

Moved by pity for her husband, the Countess at last found out the cause of his illness, and entreated him to allow himself to be cured. But the Count in his pride refused more than ever to give his consent to the marriage.

So the lady resolved to go without his knowledge to pray for mercy from the spinner, and in the name of Renelde's dead mother she besought her to spin no more. Renelde gave her promise, but in the evening Guilbert arrived at the cottage. Seeing that the cloth was no farther advanced than it was the evening before, he inquired the reason. Renelde confessed that the Countess had prayed her not to let her husband die.

' Will he consent to our marriage ? '

' No.'

' Let him die then.'

' But what will the Countess say ? '

' The Countess will understand that it is not your fault ; the Count alone is guilty of his own death.'

' Let us wait a little. Perhaps his heart may be softened.'

So they waited for one month, for two, for six, for a year. The spinner spun no more. The Count had ceased to persecute her, but he still refused his consent to the marriage. Guilbert became impatient.

The poor girl loved him with her whole soul, and she was more unhappy than she had been before, when Burchard was only tormenting her body.

'Let us have done with it,' said Guilbert.

'Wait a little still,' pleaded Renelde.

But the young man grew weary. He came more rarely to Locquignol, and very soon he did not come at all. Renelde felt as if her heart would break, but she held firm.

One day she met the Count. She clasped her hands as if in prayer, and cried:

'My lord, have mercy!'

Burchard the Wolf turned away his head and passed on.

She might have humbled his pride had she gone to her spinning-wheel again, but she did nothing of the sort.

Not long after she learnt that Guilbert had left the country. He did not even come to say good-bye to her, but, all the same, she knew the day and hour of his departure, and hid herself on the road to see him once more.

When she came in she put her silent wheel into a corner, and cried for three days and three nights.

VII

So another year went by. Then the Count fell ill, and the Countess supposed that Renelde, weary of waiting, had begun her spinning anew; but when she came to the cottage to see, she found the wheel silent.

However, the Count grew worse and worse till he was given up by the doctors. The passing bell was rung, and he lay expecting Death to come for him. But Death was not so near as the doctors thought, and still he lingered.

He seemed in a desperate condition, but he got neither better nor worse. He could neither live nor die; he suffered horribly, and called loudly on Death to put an end to his pains.

In this extremity he remembered what he had told the little spinner long ago. If Death was so slow in coming, it was because he was not ready to follow him, having no shroud for his burial.

He sent to fetch Renelde, placed her by his bedside, and ordered her at once to go on spinning his shroud.

Hardly had the spinner begun to work when the Count began to feel his pains grow less.

Then at last his heart melted ; he was sorry for all the evil he had done out of pride, and implored Renelde to forgive him. So Renelde forgave him, and went on spinning night and day.

When the thread of the nettles was spun she wove it with her shuttle, and then cut the shroud and began to sew it.

And as before, when she sewed the Count felt his pains grow less, and the life sinking within him, and when the needle made the last stitch he gave his last sigh.

VIII

At the same hour Guilbert returned to the country, and, as he had never ceased to love Renelde, he married her eight days later.

He had lost two years of happiness, but comforted himself with thinking that his wife was a clever spinner, and, what was much more rare, a brave and good woman.[1]

[1] Ch. Deulin.

FARMER WEATHERBEARD

THERE was once upon a time a man and a woman who had an only son, and he was called Jack. The woman thought that it was his duty to go out to service, and told her husband that he was to take him somewhere.

'You must get him such a good place that he will become master of all masters,' she said, and then she put some food and a roll of tobacco into a bag for them.

Well, they went to a great many masters, but all said that they could make the lad as good as they were themselves, but better than that they could not make him. When the man came home to the old woman with this answer, she said, 'I shall be equally well pleased whatever you do with him ; but this I do say, that you are to have him made a master over all masters.' Then she once more put some food and a roll of tobacco into the bag, and the man and his son had to set out again.

When they had walked some distance they got upon the ice, and there they met a man in a carriage who was driving a black horse.

'Where are you going ? ' he said.

'I have to go and get my son apprenticed to someone who will be able to teach him a trade, for my old woman comes of such well-to-do folk that she insists on his being taught to be master of all masters,' said the man.

· 'We are not ill met, then,' said the man who was driving, ' for I am the kind of man who can do that, and I am just looking out for such an apprentice. Get up behind with you,' he said to the boy, and off the horse went with them straight up into the air.

'No, no, wait a little ! ' screamed the father of the boy. ' I ought to know what your name is and where you live.'

'Oh, I am at home both in the north and the south and the east and the west, and I am called Farmer Weatherbeard,' said

the master. 'You may come here again in a year's time, and then
I will tell you if the lad suits me.' And then they set off again
and were gone.

When the man got home the old woman inquired what had
become of the son.

'Ah! Heaven only knows what has become of him!' said the man.
'They went up aloft.' And then he told her what had happened.

But when the woman heard that, and found that the man did
not at all know either when their son would be out of his apprentice-

ship, or where he had gone, she packed him off again to find out,
and gave him a bag of food and a roll of tobacco to take away
with him.

When he had walked for some time he came to a great wood,
and it stretched before him all day long as he went on, and when
night began to fall he saw a great light, and went towards it.
After a long, long time he came to a small hut at the foot of a
rock, outside which an old woman was standing drawing water up
from a well with her nose, it was so long.

'Good-evening, mother,' said the man.

'Good-evening to you too,' said the old woman. 'No one has called me mother this hundred years.'

'Can I lodge here to-night?' said the man.

'No,' said the old woman. But the man took out his roll of tobacco, lighted a little of it, and then gave her a whiff. Then she was so delighted that she began to dance, and thus the man got leave to stay the night there. It was not long before he asked about Farmer Weatherbeard.

She said that she knew nothing about him, but that she ruled over all the four-footed beasts, and some of them might know him. So she gathered them all together by blowing a whistle which she had, and questioned them, but there was not one of them which knew anything about Farmer Weatherbeard.

'Well,' said the old woman, 'there are three of us sisters; it may be that one of the other two knows where he is to be found. You shall have the loan of my horse and carriage, and then you will get there by night; but her house is three hundred miles off, go the nearest way you will.'

The man set out and got there at night. When he arrived, this old woman also was standing drawing water out of the well with her nose.

'Good-evening, mother,' said the man.

'Good-evening to you,' said the old woman. 'No one has ever called me mother this hundred years.'

'Can I lodge here to-night?' said the man.

'No,' said the old woman.

Then he took out the roll of tobacco, took a whiff, and gave the old woman some snuff on the back of her hand. Then she was so delighted that she began to dance, and the man got leave to stay all night. It was not long before he began to ask about Farmer Weatherbeard.

She knew nothing about him, but she ruled over all the fishes, she said, and perhaps some of them might know something. So she gathered them all together by blowing a whistle which she had, and questioned them, but there was not one of them which knew anything about Farmer Weatherbeard.

'Well,' said the old woman, 'I have another sister; perhaps she may know something about him. She lives six hundred miles off, but you shall have my horse and carriage, and then you will get there by nightfall.'

So the man set off and he got there by nightfall. The old woman was standing raking the fire, and she was doing it with her nose, so long it was.

'Good-evening, mother,' said the man.

'Good-evening to you,' said the old woman. 'No one has called me mother this hundred years.'

'Can I lodge here to-night?' said the man.

'No,' said the old woman. But the man pulled out his roll of

tobacco again, and filled his pipe with some of it, and gave the old woman enough snuff to cover the back of her hand. Then she was so delighted that she began to dance, and the man got leave to stay in her house. It was not long before he asked about Farmer Weatherbeard. She knew nothing at all about him, she said, but she governed all the birds; and she gathered them together with her whistle. When she questioned them all, the eagle was not there, but it came soon afterwards, and when asked, it said that it had just come from Farmer Weatherbeard's. Then the old woman said that it was to guide the man to him. But the eagle would have something to eat first, and then it wanted to wait until the next day, for it was so tired with the long journey that it was scarcely able to rise from the earth.

When the eagle had had plenty of food and rest, the old woman plucked a feather out of its tail, and set the man in the feather's place, and then the bird flew away with him, but they did not get to Farmer Weatherbeard's before midnight.

When they got there the Eagle said : ' There are a great many dead bodies lying outside the door, but you must not concern yourself about them. The people who are inside the house are all so sound asleep that it will not be easy to awake them; but you must go straight to the table-drawer, and take out three bits of bread, and if you hear anyone snoring, pluck three feathers from his head; he will not waken for that.'

The man did this; when he had got the bits of bread he first plucked out one feather.

' Oof ! ' screamed Farmer Weatherbeard.

So the man plucked out another, and then Farmer Weatherbeard shrieked 'Oof!' again; but when the man had plucked the third, Farmer Weatherbeard screamed so loudly that the man thought that brick and mortar would be rent in twain, but for all that he went on sleeping. And now the Eagle told the man what he was to do next, and he did it. He went to the stable door, and there he stumbled against a hard stone, which he picked up, and beneath it lay three splinters of wood, which he also picked up. He knocked at the stable door and it opened at once. He threw down the three little bits of bread and a hare came out and ate them. He caught the hare. Then the Eagle told him to pluck three feathers out of its tail, and put in the hare, the stone, the splinters of wood and himself instead of them, and then he would be able to carry them all home.

When the Eagle had flown a long way it alighted on a stone.

' Do you see anything ? ' it asked.

' Yes; I see a flock of crows coming flying after us,' said the man.

' Then we shall do well to fly on a little farther,' said the Eagle, and off it set.

In a short time it asked again, ' Do you see anything now ? '

' Yes ; now the crows are close behind us,' said the man.

' Then throw down the three feathers which you plucked out of his head,' said the Eagle.

So the man did this, and no sooner had he flung them down than the feathers became a flock of ravens, which chased the crows home again. Then the Eagle flew on much farther with the man, but at length it alighted on a stone for a while.

' Do you see anything ? ' it said.

' I am not quite certain,' said the man, ' but I think I see something coming in the far distance.'

' Then we shall do well to fly on a little farther,' said the Eagle, and away it went.

' Do you see anything now ? ' it said, after some time had gone by.

' Yes ; now they are close behind us,' said the man.

' Then throw down the splinters of wood which you took from beneath the gray stone by the stable door,' said the Eagle. The man did this, and no sooner had he flung them down than they grew up into a great thick wood, and Farmer Weatherbeard had to go home for an axe to cut his way through it. So the Eagle flew on a long, long way, but then it grew tired and sat down on a fir tree.

' Do you see anything ? ' it asked.

' Yes ; I am not quite certain,' said the man, ' but I think I can catch a glimpse of something far, far away.'

' Then we shall do well to fly on a little farther,' said the Eagle, and it set off again.

' Do you see anything now ? ' it said after some time had gone by.

' Yes ; he is close behind us now,' said the man.

' Then you must fling down the great stone which you took away from the stable door,' said the Eagle.

The man did so, and it turned into a great high mountain of stone, which Farmer Weatherbeard had to break his way through before he could follow them. But when he had got to the middle of the mountain he broke one of his legs, so he had to go home to get it put right.

While he was doing this the Eagle flew off to the man's home with him, and with the hare, and when they had got home the man went to the churchyard, and had some Christian earth laid upon the hare, and then it turned into his son Jack.

When the time came for the fair the youth turned himself into a light-coloured horse, and bade his father go to the market with him. 'If anyone should come who wants to buy me,' said he, 'you are to tell him that you want a hundred dollars for me ; but you must not forget to take off the halter, for if you do I shall never be able to get away from Farmer Weatherbeard, for he is the man who will come and bargain for me.'

And thus it happened. A horse-dealer came who had a great fancy to bargain for the horse, and the man got a hundred dollars for it, but when the bargain was made, and Jack's father had got the money, the horse-dealer wanted to have the halter.

'That was no part of our bargain,' said the man, 'and the halter you shall not have, for I have other horses which I shall have to sell.'

So each of them went his way. But the horse-dealer had not got very far with Jack before he resumed his own form again, and when the man got home he was sitting on the bench by the stove.

The next day he changed himself into a brown horse and told his father that he was to set off to market with him. 'If a man should come who wants to buy me,' said Jack, 'you are to tell him that you want two hundred dollars, for that he will give, and treat you besides ; but whatsoever you drink, and whatsoever you do, don't forget to take the halter off me, or you will never see me more.'

And thus it happened. The man got his two hundred dollars for the horse, and was treated as well, and when they parted from each other it was just as much as he could do to remember to take off the halter. But the buyer had not got far on his way before the youth took his own form again, and when the man reached home Jack was already sitting on the bench by the stove.

On the third day all happened in the same way. The youth changed himself into a great black horse, and told his father that if a man came and offered him three hundred dollars, and treated him well and handsomely into the bargain, he was to sell him, but whatsoever he did, or how much soever he drank, he must not forget to take off the halter, or else he himself would never get away from Farmer Weatherbeard as long as he lived.

'No,' said the man, 'I will not forget.'

When he got to the market, he received the three hundred dollars, but Farmer Weatherbeard treated him so handsomely that he quite forgot to take off the halter ; so Farmer Weatherbeard went away with the horse.

When he had got some distance he had to go into an inn to get some more brandy ; so he set a barrel full of red-hot nails under his horse's nose, and a trough filled with oats beneath its tail, and then he tied the halter fast to a hook and went away into the inn. So the horse stood there stamping, and kicking, and snorting, and rearing, and out came a girl who thought it a sin and a shame to treat a horse so ill.

'Ah, poor creature, what a master you must have to treat you thus!' she said, and pushed the halter off the hook so that the horse might turn round and eat the oats.

'I am here!' shrieked Farmer Weatherbeard, rushing out of doors. But the horse had already shaken off the halter and flung himself into a goose-pond, where he changed himself into a little fish. Farmer Weatherbeard went after him, and changed himself into a great pike. So Jack turned himself into a dove, and Farmer Weatherbeard turned himself into a hawk, and flew after the dove and struck it. But a Princess was standing at a window in the King's palace watching the struggle.

'If thou didst but know as much as I know, thou wouldst fly in to me through the window,' said the Princess to the dove.

So the dove came flying in through the window and changed itself into Jack again, and told her all as it had happened.

'Change thyself into a gold ring, and set thyself on my finger,' said the Princess.

'No, that will not do,' said Jack, 'for then Farmer Weatherbeard will make the King fall sick, and there will be no one who can make him well again before Farmer Weatherbeard comes and cures him, and for that he will demand the gold ring.'

'I will say that it was my mother's, and that I will not part with it,' said the Princess.

So Jack changed himself into a gold ring, and set himself on the Princess's finger, and Farmer Weatherbeard could not get at him there. But then all that the youth had foretold came to pass.

The King became ill, and there was no doctor who could cure him till Farmer Weatherbeard arrived, and he demanded the ring which was on the Princess's finger as a reward.

So the King sent a messenger to the Princess for the ring. She, however, refused to part with it, because she had inherited it from her mother. When the King was informed of this he fell into a rage, and said that he would have the ring, let her have inherited it from whom she might.

'Well, it's of no use to be angry about it,' said the Princess, 'for

I can't get it off. If you want the ring you will have to take the finger too!'

'I will try, and then the ring will very soon come off,' said Farmer Weatherbeard.

'No, thank you, I will try myself,' said the Princess, and she went away to the fireplace and put some ashes on the ring.

So the ring came off and was lost among the ashes.

Farmer Weatherbeard changed himself into a hare, which scratched and scraped about in the fireplace after the ring until the ashes were up to its ears. But Jack changed himself into a fox, and bit the hare's head off, and if Farmer Weatherbeard was possessed by the evil one all was now over with him.[1]

[1] From P. C. Asbjornsen.

MOTHER HOLLE

ONCE upon a time there was a widow who had two daughters; one of them was pretty and clever, and the other ugly and lazy. But as the ugly one was her own daughter, she liked her far the best of the two, and the pretty one had to do all the work of the house, and was in fact the regular maid of all work. Every day she had to sit by a well on the high road, and spin till her fingers were so sore that they often bled. One day some drops of blood fell on her spindle, so she dipped it into the well meaning to wash it, but, as luck would have it, it dropped from her hand and fell right in. She ran weeping to her stepmother, and told her what had happened, but she scolded her harshly, and was so merciless in her anger that she said :

' Well, since you've dropped the spindle down, you must just go after it yourself, and don't let me see your face again until you bring it with you.'

Then the poor girl returned to the well, and not knowing what she was about, in the despair and misery of her heart she sprang into the well and sank to the bottom. For a time she lost all consciousness, and when she came to herself again she was lying in a lovely meadow, with the sun shining brightly overhead, and a thousand flowers blooming at her feet. She rose up and wandered through this enchanted place, till she came to a baker's oven full of bread, and the bread called out to her as she passed :

' Oh ! take me out, take me out, or I shall be burnt to a cinder. I am quite done enough.'

So she stepped up quickly to the oven and took out all the loaves one after the other. Then she went on a little farther and came to a tree laden with beautiful rosy-cheeked apples, and as she passed by it called out :

' Oh ! shake me, shake me, my apples are all quite ripe.'

She did as she was asked, and shook the tree till the apples fell like rain and none were left hanging. When she had gathered them all up into a heap she went on her way again, and came at length to a little house, at the door of which sat an old woman. The old dame had such large teeth that the girl felt frightened and wanted to run away, but the old woman called after her:

'What are you afraid of, dear child? Stay with me and be my little maid, and if you do your work well I will reward you handsomely; but you must be very careful how you make my bed—you must shake it well till the feathers fly; then people in the world below say it snows, for I am Mother Holle.'

She spoke so kindly that the girl took heart and agreed readily to enter her service. She did her best to please the old woman, and shook her bed with such a will that the feathers flew about like snow-flakes; so she led a very easy life, was never scolded, and lived on the fat of the land. But after she had been some time with Mother Holle she grew sad and depressed, and at first she hardly knew herself what was the matter. At last she discovered that she was homesick, so she went to Mother Holle and said:

'I know I am a thousand times better off here than I ever was in my life before, but notwithstanding, I have a great longing to go home, in spite of all your kindness to me. I can remain with you no longer, but must return to my own people.'

'Your desire to go home pleases me,' said Mother Holle, 'and because you have served me so faithfully, I will show you the way back into the world myself.'

So she took her by the hand and led her to an open door, and as the girl passed through it there fell a heavy shower of gold all over her, till she was covered with it from top to toe.

'That's a reward for being such a good little maid,' said Mother Holle, and she gave her the spindle too that had fallen into the well. Then she shut the door, and the girl found herself back in the world again, not far from her own house; and when she came to the courtyard the old hen, who sat on the top of the wall, called out:

'Click, clock, clack,
Our golden maid's come back.'

Then she went in to her stepmother, and as she had returned covered with gold she was welcomed home.

She proceeded to tell all that had happened to her, and when the mother heard how she had come by her riches, she was most

anxious to secure the same luck for her own idle, ugly daughter ;
so she told her to sit at the well and spin. In order to make her
spindle bloody, she stuck her hand into a hedge of thorns and pricked
her finger. Then she threw the spindle into the well, and jumped
in herself after it. Like her sister she came to the beautiful meadow,

and followed the same path. When she reached the baker's oven
the bread called out as before :

'Oh ! take me out, take me out, or I shall be burnt to a cinder.
I am quite done enough.'

But the good-for-nothing girl answered :

'A pretty joke, indeed; just as if I should dirty my hands for you !'

And on she went. Soon she came to the apple tree, which cried :
' Oh ! shake me, shake me, my apples are all quite ripe.'
' I'll see myself farther,' she replied, ' one of them might fall on
my head.'

And so she pursued her way. When she came to Mother Holle's
house she wasn't the least afraid, for she had been warned about
her big teeth, and she readily agreed to become her maid. The first
day she worked very hard, and did all her mistress told her, for she
thought of the gold she would give her ; but on the second day she
began to be lazy, and on the third she wouldn't even get up in the
morning. She didn't make Mother Holle's bed as she ought to
have done, and never shook it enough to make the feathers fly. So
her mistress soon grew weary of her, and dismissed her, much to the
lazy creature's delight.

' For now,' she thought, ' the shower of golden rain will come.'

Mother Holle led her to the same door as she had done her sister,
but when she passed through it, instead of the gold rain a kettle full
of pitch came showering over her.

' That's a reward for your service,' said Mother Holle, and she
closed the door behind her.

So the lazy girl came home all covered with pitch, and when the
old hen on the top of the wall saw her, it called out :

> ' Click, clock, clack,
> Our dirty slut's come back.'

But the pitch remained sticking to her, and never as long as she
lived could it be got off.[1]

[1] Grimm.

MINNIKIN

THERE was once upon a time a couple of needy folk who lived in a wretched hut, in which there was nothing but black want; so they had neither food to eat nor wood to burn. But if they had next to nothing of all else they had the blessing of God so far as children were concerned, and every year brought them one more. The man was not overpleased at this. He was always going about grumbling and growling, and saying that it seemed to him that there might be such a thing as having too many of these good gifts; so shortly before another baby was born he went away into the wood for some firewood, saying that he did not want to see the new child; he would hear him quite soon enough when he began to squall for some food.

As soon as this baby was born it began to look about the room. ' Ah, my dear mother ! ' said he, ' give me some of my brothers' old clothes, and food enough for a few days, and I will go out into the world and seek my fortune, for, so far as I can see, you have children enough.'

' Heaven help thee, my son ! ' said the mother, ' that will never do ; thou art still far too little.'

But the little creature was determined to do it, and begged and prayed so long that the mother was forced to let him have some old rags, and tie up a little food for him, and then gaily and happily he went out into the world.

But almost before he was out of the house another boy was born, and he too looked about him, and said, ' Ah, my dear mother ! give me some of my brothers' old clothes, and food for some days, and then I will go out into the world and find my twin brother, for you have children enough.'

' Heaven help thee, little creature ! thou art far too little for that,' said the woman ; ' it would never do.'

But she spoke to no purpose, for the boy begged and prayed

until he had got some old rags and a bundle of provisions, and then he set out manfully into the world to find his twin brother.

When the younger had walked for some time he caught sight of his brother a short distance in front of him, and called to him and bade him to stop.

'Wait a minute,' he said; 'you are walking as if for a wager, but you ought to have stayed to see your younger brother before you hurried off into the world.'

So the elder stood still and looked back, and when the younger had got up to him, and had told him that he was his brother, he said : ' But now, let us sit down and see what kind of food our mother has given us,' and that they did.

When they had walked on a little farther they came to a brook which ran through a green meadow, and there the younger said that they ought to christen each other. 'As we had to make such haste, and had no time to do it at home, we may as well do it here,' said he.

' What will you be called ? ' asked the elder.

' I will be called Minnikin,' answered the second ; ' and you, what will you be called ? '

' I will be called King Pippin,' answered the elder.

They christened each other and then went onwards. When they had walked for some time they came to a crossway, and there they agreed to part, and each take his own road. This they did, but no sooner had they walked a short distance than they met again. So they parted once more, and each took his own road, but in a very short time the same thing happened again—they met each other before they were at all aware, and so it happened the third time also. Then they arranged with each other that each should choose his own quarter, and one should go east and the other west.

' But if ever you fall into any need or trouble,' said the elder, ' call me thrice, and I will come and help you; only you must not call me until you are in the utmost need.'

' In that case we shall not see each other for some time,' said Minnikin ; so they bade farewell to each other, and Minnikin went east and King Pippin went west.

When Minnikin had walked a long way alone, he met an old, old crook-backed hag, who had only one eye. Minnikin stole it.

' Oh ! oh ! ' cried the old hag, ' what has become of my eye ? '

' What will you give me to get your eye back ? ' said Minnikin.

' I will give thee a sword which is such a sword that it can con-quer a whole army, let it be ever so great,' replied the woman.

'Let me have it, then,' said Minnikin.

The old hag gave him the sword, so she got her eye back. Then Minnikin went onwards, and when he had wandered on for some time he again met an old, old crook-backed hag, who had only one eye. Minnikin stole it before she was aware.

'Oh! oh! what has become of my eye?' cried the old hag.

'What will you give me to get your eye back?' said Minnikin.

'I will give thee a ship which can sail over fresh water and salt water, over high hills and deep dales,' answered the old woman.

'Let me have it then,' said Minnikin.

So the old woman gave him a little bit of a ship which was no bigger than he could put in his pocket, and then she got her eye back, and she went her way and Minnikin his. When he had walked on for a long time, he met for the third time an old, old crook-backed hag, who had only one eye. This eye also Minnikin stole, and when the woman screamed and lamented, and asked what had become of her eye, Minnikin said, ' What will you give me to get your eye back ? '

' I will give thee the art to brew a hundred lasts of malt in one brewing.'

So, for teaching that art, the old hag got her eye back, and they both went away by different roads.

But when Minnikin had walked a short distance, it seemed to him that it might be worth while to see what his ship could do ; so he took it out of his pocket, and first he put one foot into it, and then the other, and no sooner had he put one foot into the ship than it became much larger, and when he set the other foot into it, it grew as large as ships that sail on the sea.

Then Minnikin said : ' Now go over fresh water and salt water, over high hills and deep dales, and do not stop until thou comest to the King's palace.'

And in an instant the ship went away as swiftly as any bird in the air till it got just below the King's palace, and there it stood still.

From the windows of the King's palace many persons had seen Minnikin come sailing thither, and had stood to watch him ; and they were all so astounded that they ran down to see what manner of man this could be who came sailing in a ship through the air. But while they were running down from the King's palace, Minnikin had got out of the ship and had put it in his pocket again ; for the moment he got out of it, it once more became as small as it had been when he got it from the old woman, and those who came from the King's palace could see nothing but a ragged little boy who was standing down by the sea-shore. The King asked where he had come from, but the boy said he did not know, nor yet could he tell them how he had got there, but he begged very earnestly and prettily for a place in the King's palace. If there was nothing else for him to do, he said he would fetch wood and water for the kitchen-maid, and that he obtained leave to do.

When Minnikin went up to the King's palace he saw that everything there was hung with black both outside and inside, from the bottom to the top ; so he asked the kitchen-maid what that meant.

' Oh, I will tell you that,' answered the kitchen-maid. ' The King's daughter was long ago promised away to three Trolls, and

next Thursday evening one of them is to come to fetch her. Ritter
Red has said that he will be able to set her free, but who knows
whether he will be able to do it ? so you may easily imagine what
grief and distress we are in here.'

So when Thursday evening came, Ritter Red accompanied the
Princess to the sea-shore; for there she was to meet the Troll, and
Ritter Red was to stay with her and protect her. He, however, was
very unlikely to do the Troll much injury, for no sooner had the

Princess seated herself by the sea-shore than Ritter Red climbed
up into a great tree which was standing there, and hid himself as
well as he could among the branches.

The Princess wept, and begged him most earnestly not to go and
leave her; but Ritter Red did not concern himself about that. 'It
is better that one should die than two,' said he.

In the meantime Minnikin begged the kitchen-maid very prettily to give him leave to go down to the strand for a short time.

'Oh, what could you do down at the strand ? ' said the kitchen-maid. 'You have nothing to do there.'

'Oh yes, my dear, just let me go,' said Minnikin. 'I should so like to go and amuse myself with the other children.'

'Well, well, go then ! ' said the kitchen-maid, 'but don't let me find you staying there over the time when the pan has to be set on the fire for supper, and the roast put on the spit; and mind you bring back a good big armful of wood for the kitchen.'

Minnikin promised this, and ran down to the sea-shore.

Just as he got to the place where the King's daughter was sitting, the Troll came rushing up with a great whistling and whirring, and he was so big and stout that he was terrible to see, and he had five heads.

'Fire ! ' screeched the Troll.

'Fire yourself ! ' said Minnikin.

'Can you fight ? ' roared the Troll.

'If not, I can learn,' said Minnikin.

So the Troll struck at him with a great thick iron bar which he had in his fist, till the sods flew five yards up into the air.

'Fie!' said Minnikin. 'That was not much of a blow. Now you shall see one of mine.'

So he grasped the sword which he had got from the old crook-backed woman, and slashed at the Troll, so that all five heads went flying away over the sands.

When the Princess saw that she was delivered she was so delighted that she did not know what she was doing, and skipped and danced.

'Come and sleep a bit with your head in my lap,' she said to Minnikin, and as he slept she put a golden dress on him.

But when Ritter Red saw that there was no longer any danger afoot, he lost no time in creeping down from the tree. He then threatened the Princess, until at length she was forced to promise to say that it was he who had rescued her, for he told her that if she did not he would kill her. Then he took the Troll's lungs and tongue and put them in his pocket-handkerchief, and led the Princess back to the King's palace; and whatsoever had been lacking to him in the way of honour before was lacking no longer, for the King did not know how to exalt him enough, and always set him on his own right hand at table.

As for Minnikin, first he went out on the Troll's ship and took a great quantity of gold and silver hoops away with him, and then he trotted back to the King's palace.

When the kitchen-maid caught sight of all this gold and silver she was quite amazed, and said: 'My dear friend Minnikin, where have you got all that from?' for she was half afraid that he had not come by it honestly.

'Oh,' answered Minnikin, 'I have been home a while, and these hoops had fallen off some of our buckets, so I brought them away with me for you.'

So when the kitchen-maid heard that they were for her, she asked no more questions about the matter. She thanked Minnikin, and everything was right again at once.

Next Thursday evening all went just the same, and everyone was full of grief and affliction, but Ritter Red said that he had been able to deliver the King's daughter from one Troll, so that he could very easily deliver her from another, and he led her down to the sea-shore. But he did not do much harm to this Troll either, for when the time came when the Troll might be expected, he said as he had said before : ' It is better that one should die than two,' and then climbed up into the tree again.

Minnikin once more begged the cook's leave to go down to the sea-shore for a short time.

' Oh, what can you do there ? ' said the cook.

' My dear, do let me go ! ' said Minnikin ; ' I should so like to go down there and amuse myself a little with the other children.'

So this time also she said that he should have leave to go, but he must first promise that he would be back by the time the joint was turned and that he would bring a great armful of wood with him.

No sooner had Minnikin got down to the strand than the Troll came rushing along with a great whistling and whirring, and he was twice as big as the first Troll, and he had ten heads.

' Fire ! ' shrieked the Troll.

' Fire yourself ! ' said Minnikin.

' Can you fight ? ' roared the Troll.

' If not, I can learn,' said Minnikin.

So the Troll struck at him with his iron club—which was still bigger than that which the first Troll had had—so that the earth flew ten yards up in the air.

' Fie ! ' said Minnikin. ' That was not much of a blow. Now you shall see one of my blows.'

Then he grasped his sword and struck at the Troll, so that all his ten heads danced away over the sands.

And again the King's daughter said to him, ' Sleep a while on my lap,' and while Minnikin lay there she drew some silver raiment over him.

As soon as Ritter Red saw that there was no longer any danger afoot, he crept down from the tree and threatened the Princess, until at last she was again forced to promise to say that it was he who had rescued her ; after which he took the tongue and the lungs of the Troll and put them in his pocket-handkerchief, and then he conducted the Princess back to the palace. There was joy and gladness in the palace, as may be imagined, and the King did not know how to show enough honour and respect to Ritter Red.

Minnikin, however, took home with him an armful of gold and silver hoops from the Troll's ship. When he came back to the King's palace the kitchen-maid clapped her hands and wondered where he could have got all that gold and silver ; but Minnikin answered that he had been home for a short time, and that it was only the hoops which had fallen off some pails, and that he had brought them away for the kitchen-maid.

When the third Thursday evening came, everything happened exactly as it had happened on the two former occasions. Everything in the King's palace was hung with black, and everyone was sorrowful and distressed; but Ritter Red said that he did not think that they had much reason to be afraid—he had delivered the King's daughter from two Trolls, so he could easily deliver her from the third as well.

He led her down to the strand, but when the time drew near for the Troll to come, he climbed up into the tree again and hid himself.

The Princess wept and entreated him to stay, but all to no purpose. He stuck to his old speech, ' It is better that one life should be lost than two.'

This evening also, Minnikin begged for leave to go down to the sea-shore.

' Oh, what can you do there ? ' answered the kitchen-maid.

However, he begged until at last he got leave to go, but he was forced to promise that he would be back again in the kitchen when the roast had to be turned.

Almost immediately after he had got down to the sea-shore the Troll came with a great whizzing and whirring, and he was much, much bigger than either of the two former ones, and he had fifteen heads.

' Fire ! ' roared the Troll.

' Fire yourself ! ' said Minnikin.

' Can you fight ? ' screamed the Troll.

' If not, I can learn,' said Minnikin.

' I will teach you,' yelled the Troll, and struck at him with his iron club so that the earth flew up fifteen yards high into the air.

' Fie ! ' said Minnikin. ' That was not much of a blow. Now I will let you see one of my blows.'

So saying he grasped his sword, and cut at the Troll in such a way that all his fifteen heads danced away over the sands.

Then the Princess was delivered, and she thanked Minnikin and blessed him for saving her.

' Sleep a while now on my lap,' said she, and while he lay there she put a garment of brass upon him.

' But now, how shall we have it made known that it was you who saved me ? ' said the King's daughter.

' That I will tell you,' answered Minnikin. ' When Ritter Red has taken you home again, and given out that it was he who rescued you, he will, as you know, have you to wife, and half the kingdom. But when they ask you on your wedding-day whom you will have to be your cup-bearer, you must say, "I will have the ragged boy who is in the kitchen, and carries wood and water for the kitchen-maid; " and when I am filling your cups for you, I will spill a drop upon his plate but none upon yours, and then he will be angry and strike me, and this will take place thrice. But the third time you must say, " Shame on you thus to smite the beloved of mine heart. It is he who delivered me from the Troll, and he is the one whom I will have." '

Then Minnikin ran back to the King's palace as he had done before, but first he went on board the Troll's ship and took a great quantity of gold and silver and other precious things, and out of these he once more gave to the kitchen-maid a whole armful of gold and silver hoops.

No sooner did Ritter Red see that all danger was over than he crept down from the tree, and threatened the King's daughter till he made her promise to say that he had rescued her. Then he conducted her back to the King's palace, and if honour enough had not been done him before it was certainly done now, for the King had no other thought than how to make much of the man who had saved his daughter from the three Trolls ; and it was settled then that Ritter Red should marry her, and receive half the kingdom.

On the wedding-day, however, the Princess begged that she might have the little boy who was in the kitchen, and carried wood and water for the kitchen-maid, to fill the wine-cups at the wedding feast.

' Oh, what can you want with that dirty, ragged boy, in here ? ' said Ritter Red, but the Princess said that she insisted on having him as cup-bearer and would have no one else; and at last she got leave, and then everything was done as had been agreed on between the Princess and Minnikin. He spilt a drop on Ritter Red's plate but none upon hers, and each time that he did it Ritter Red fell into a rage and struck him. At the first blow all the ragged garments which he had worn in the kitchen fell from off Minnikin, at the second blow the brass garments fell off, and at the third the silver raiment, and there he stood in the golden raiment, which was so bright and splendid that light flashed 'from it.

Then the King's daughter said: ' Shame on you thus to smite the beloved of my heart. It is he who delivered me from the Troll, and he is the one whom I will have.'

Ritter Red swore that he was the man who had saved her, but the King said: ' He who delivered my daughter must have some token in proof of it.'

So Ritter Red ran off at once for his handkerchief with the lungs and tongue, and Minnikin went and brought all the gold and silver and precious things which he had taken out of the Trolls' ships; and they each of them laid these tokens before the King.

' He who has such precious things in gold and silver and diamonds,' said the King, ' must be the one who killed the Troll, for such things are not to be had anywhere else.' So Ritter Red was thrown into the snake-pit, and Minnikin was to have the Princess, and half the kingdom.

One day the King went out walking with Minnikin, and Minnikin asked him if he had never had any other children.

' Yes,' said the King, ' I had another daughter, but the Troll carried her away because there was no one who could deliver her. You are going to have one daughter of mine, but if you can set free the other, who has been taken by the Troll, you shall willingly have her too, and the other half of the kingdom as well.'

' I may as well make the attempt,' said Minnikin, ' but I must have an iron rope which is five hundred ells long, and then I must have five hundred men with me, and provisions for five weeks, for I have a long voyage before me.'

So the King said he should have these things, but the King was afraid that he had no ship large enough to carry them all.

' But I have a ship of my own,' said Minnikin, and he took the one which the old woman had given him out of his pocket. The King laughed at him and thought that it was only one of his jokes, but Minnikin begged him just to give him what he had asked for, and then he should see something. Then all that Minnikin had asked for was brought; and first he ordered them to lay the cable in the ship, but there was no one who was able to lift it, and there was only room for one or two men at a time in the little bit of a ship. Then Minnikin himself took hold of the cable, and laid one or two links of it into the ship, and as he threw the links into it the ship grew bigger and bigger, and at last it was so large that the cable, and the five hundred men, and provisions, and Minnikin himself, had room enough.

' Now go over fresh water and salt water, over hill and dale, and do not stop until thou comest to where the King's daughter is,' said Minnikin to the ship, and off it went in a moment over land and water till the wind whistled and moaned all round about it.

When they had sailed thus a long, long way, the ship stopped short in the middle of the sea.

'Ah, now we have got there,' said Minnikin, 'but how we are to get back again is a very different thing.'

Then he took the cable and tied one end of it round his body. 'Now I must go to the bottom,' he said, 'but when I give a good jerk to the cable and want to come up again, you must all pull like one man, or there will be an end of all life both for you and for me.' So saying he sprang into the water, and yellow bubbles rose up all around him. He sank lower and lower, and at last he came to the bottom. There he saw a large hill with a door in it, and in he went. When he had got inside he found the other Princess sitting sewing, but when she saw Minnikin she clapped her hands.

'Ah, heaven be praised!' she cried, 'I have not seen a Christian man since I came here.'

'I have come for you,' said Minnikin.

'Alas! you will not be able to get me,' said the King's daughter. 'It is no use even to think of that; if the Troll catches sight of you he will take your life.'

'You had better tell me about him,' said Minnikin. 'Where is he gone? It would be amusing to see him.'

So the King's daughter told Minnikin that the Troll was out trying to get hold of someone who could brew a hundred lasts of malt at one brewing, for there was to be a feast at the Troll's, at which less than that would not be drunk.

'I can do that,' said Minnikin.

'Ah! if only the Troll were not so quick-tempered I might have told him that,' answered the Princess, 'but he is so ill-natured that he will tear you to pieces, I fear, as soon as he comes in. But I will try to find some way of doing it. Can you hide yourself here in the cupboard? and then we will see what happens.'

Minnikin did this, and almost before he had crept into the cupboard and hidden himself, came the Troll.

'Huf! What a smell of Christian man's blood!' said the Troll.

'Yes, a bird flew over the roof with a Christian man's bone in his bill, and let it fall down our chimney,' answered the Princess. 'I made haste enough to get it away again, but it must be that which smells so, notwithstanding.'

' Yes, it must be that,' said the Troll.

Then the Princess asked if he had got hold of anyone who could brew a hundred lasts of malt at one brewing.

' Nò, there is no one who can do it,' said the Troll.

' A short time since there was a man here who said he could do it,' said the King's daughter.

'How clever you always are!' said the Troll. 'How could you let him go away? You must have known that I was just wanting a man of that kind.'

'Well, but I didn't let him go, after all,' said the Princess; 'but father is so quick-tempered, so I hid him in the cupboard, but if father has not found any one then the man is still here,'

'Let him come in,' said the Troll.

When Minnikin came, the Troll asked if it were true that he could brew a hundred lasts of malt at one brewing.

'Yes,' said Minnikin, 'it is.'

'It is well then that I have lighted on thee,' said the Troll. 'Fall to work this very minute, but Heaven help thee if thou dost not brew the ale strong.'

'Oh, it shall taste well,' said Minnikin, and at once set himself to work to brew.

'But I must have more trolls to help to carry what is wanted,' said Minnikin; 'these that I have are good for nothing.'

So he got more and so many that there was a swarm of them, and then the brewing went on. When the sweet-wort was ready they were all, as a matter of course, anxious to taste it, first the Troll himself and then the others; but Minnikin had brewed the wort so strong that they all fell down dead like so many flies as soon as they had drunk any of it. At last there was no one left but one wretched old hag who was lying behind the stove.

'Oh, poor old creature!' said Minnikin, 'you shall have a taste of the wort too like the rest.' So he went away and scooped up a little from the bottom of the brewing vat in a milk pan, and gave it to her, and then he was quit of the whole of them.

While Minnikin was now standing there looking about him, he cast his eye on a large chest. This he took and filled it with gold and silver, and then he tied the cable round himself and the Princess and the chest, and tugged at the rope with all his might, whereupon his men drew them up safe and sound.

As soon as Minnikin had got safely on his ship again, he said: 'Now go over salt water and fresh water, over hill and dale, and do not stop until thou comest unto the King's palace.' And in a moment the ship went off so fast that the yellow foam rose up all round about it.

When those who were in the King's palace saw the ship, they lost no time in going to meet him with song and music, and thus they marched up towards Minnikin with great rejoicings; but the gladdest of all was the King, for now he had got his other daughter back again.

But now Minnikin was not happy, for both the Princesses wanted to have him, and he wanted to have none other than the one whom he had first saved, and she was the younger. For this cause he was continually walking backwards and forwards, thinking

how he could contrive to get her, and yet do nothing that was unkind
to her sister. One day when he was walking about and thinking
of this, it came into his mind that if he only had his brother, King
Pippin, with him, who was so like himself that no one could distinguish the one from the other, he could let him have the elder
Princess and half the kingdom; as for himself, he thought, the
other half was quite enough. As soon as this thought occurred to
him he went outside the palace and called for King Pippin, but no
one came. So he called a second time, and a little louder, but no!
still no one came. So Minnikin called for the third time, and with
all his might, and there stood his brother by his side.

'I told you that you were not to call me unless you were in the
utmost need,' he said to Minnikin, 'and there is not even so much
as a midge here who can do you any harm!' and with that he
gave Minnikin such a blow that he rolled over on the grass.

'Shame on you to strike me!' said Minnikin. 'First have I won
one Princess and half the kingdom, and then the other Princess
and the other half of the kingdom; and now, when I was just thinking that I would give you one of the Princesses and one of the
halves of the kingdom, do you think you have any reason to give
me such a blow?'

When King Pippin heard that he begged his brother's pardon,
and they were reconciled at once and became good friends.

'Now, as you know,' said Minnikin, 'we are so like each other
that no one can tell one of us from the other; so just change clothes
with me and go up to the palace, and then the Princesses will think
that I am coming in, and the one who kisses you first shall be
yours, and I will have the other.' For he knew that the elder
Princess was the stronger, so he could very well guess how things
would go.

King Pippin at once agreed to this. He changed clothes with
his brother, and went into the palace. When he entered the
Princess's apartments they believed that he was Minnikin, and
both of them ran up to him at once; but the elder, who was bigger
and stronger, pushed her sister aside, and threw her arms round
King Pippin's neck and kissed him; so he got her to wife, and
Minnikin the younger sister. It will be easy to understand that
two weddings took place, and they were so magnificent that they
were heard of and talked about all over seven kingdoms.[1]

[1] From J. Moe.

BUSHY BRIDE

THERE was once on a time a widower who had a son and a daughter by his first wife. They were both good children, and loved each other with all their hearts. After some time had gone by the man married again, and he chose a widow with one daughter who was ugly and wicked, and her mother was ugly and wicked too. From the very day that the new wife came into the house there was no peace for the man's children, and not a corner to be found where they could get any rest; so the boy thought that the best thing he could do was to go out into the world and try to earn his own bread.

When he had roamed about for some time he came to the King's palace, where he obtained a place under the coachman; and very brisk and active he was, and the horses that he looked after were so fat and sleek, that they shone again.

But his sister, who was still at home, fared worse and worse. Both her step-mother and her step-sister were always finding fault with her, whatsoever she did and whithersoever she went, and they scolded her and abused her so that she never had an hour's peace. They made her do all the hard work, and hard words fell to her lot early and late, but little enough food accompanied them.

One day they sent her to the brook to fetch some water home, and an ugly and horrible head rose up out of the water, and said, 'Wash me, girl!'

'Yes, I will wash you with pleasure,' said the girl, and began to wash and scrub the ugly face, but she couldn't help thinking that it was a very unpleasant piece of work. When she had done it, and done it well, another head rose up out of the water, and this one was uglier still.

'Brush me, girl!' said the head.

'Yes, I will brush you with pleasure,' said the girl, and set to work with the tangled hair, and, as may be easily imagined, this too was by no means pleasant work.

When she had got it done, another and a much more ugly and horrible-looking head rose up out of the water.

'Kiss me, girl!' said the head.

'Yes, I will kiss you,' said the man's daughter, and she did it, but she thought it was the worst bit of work that she had ever had to do in her life.

So the heads all began to talk to each other, and to ask what they should do for this girl who was so full of kindliness.

'She shall be the prettiest girl that ever was, and fair and bright as the day,' said the first head.

'Gold shall drop from her hair whenever she brushes it,' said the second.

'Gold shall drop from her mouth whenever she speaks,' said the third head.

So when the man's daughter went home, looking as beautiful and bright as day, the step-mother and her daughter grew much more ill-tempered, and it was worse still when she began to talk, and they saw that golden coins dropped from her mouth. The step-mother fell into such a towering passion that she drove the man's daughter into the pig-stye—she might stay there with her fine show of gold, the step-mother said, but she should not be permitted to set foot in the house.

It was not long before the mother wanted her own daughter to go to the stream to fetch some water.

When she got there with her pails, the first head rose up out of the water close to the bank. 'Wash me, girl!' it said.

'Wash yourself!' answered the woman's daughter.

Then the second head appeared.

'Brush me, girl!' said the head.

'Brush yourself!' said the woman's daughter.

So down it went to the bottom, and the third head came up.

'Kiss me, girl!' said the head.

'As if I would kiss your ugly mouth!' said the girl.

So again the heads talked together about what they should do for this girl who was so ill-tempered and full of her own importance, and they agreed that she should have a nose that was four ells long, and a jaw that was three ells, and a fir bush in the middle of her forehead, and every time she spoke ashes should fall from her mouth.

When she came back to the cottage door with her pails, she called to her mother who was inside, 'Open the door!'

'Open the door yourself, my own dear child!' said the mother.

'I can't get near, because of my nose,' said the daughter.

When the mother came and saw her you may imagine what a state of mind she was in, and how she screamed and lamented, but neither the nose nor the jaw grew any the less for that.

Now the brother, who was in service in the King's palace, had taken a portrait of his sister, and he had carried the picture away with him, and every morning and evening he knelt down before it and prayed for his sister, so dearly did he love her.

The other stable-boys had heard him doing this, so they peeped through the key-hole into his room, and saw that he was kneeling there before a picture; so they told everyone that every morning and evening the youth knelt down and prayed to an idol which he had; and at last they went to the King himself, and begged that he too would peep through the key-hole, and see for himself what the youth did. At first the King would not believe this, but after a long, long time, they prevailed with him, and he crept on tip-toe to the door, peeped through, and saw the youth on his knees, with his hands clasped together before a picture which was hanging on the wall.

'Open the door!' cried the King, but the youth did not hear.

So the King called to him again, but the youth was praying so fervently that he did not hear him this time either.

'Open the door, I say!' cried the King again. 'It is I! I want to come in.'

So the youth sprang to the door and unlocked it, but in his haste he forgot to hide the picture.

When the King entered and saw it, he stood still as if he were in fetters, and could not stir from the spot, for the picture seemed to him so beautiful.

'There is nowhere on earth so beautiful a woman as this!' said the King.

But the youth told him that she was his sister, and that he had painted her, and that if she was not prettier than the picture she was at all events not uglier.

'Well, if she is as beautiful as that, I will have her for my Queen,' said the King, and he commanded the youth to go home and fetch her without a moment's delay, and to lose no time in coming back. The youth promised to make all the haste he could, and set forth from the King's palace.

When the brother arrived at home to fetch his sister, her step-mother and step-sister would go too. So they all set out together, and the man's daughter took with her a casket in which she kept her gold, and a dog which was called Little Snow. These two things were all that she had inherited from her mother. When they had travelled for some time they had to cross the sea, and the brother sat down at the helm, and the mother and the two half-sisters went to the fore-part of the vessel, and they sailed a long, long way. At last they came in sight of land.

'Look at that white strand there; that is where we shall land,' said the brother, pointing across the sea.

'What is my brother saying?' inquired the man's daughter.

'He says that you are to throw your casket out into the sea,' answered the step-mother.

'Well, if my brother says so, I must do it,' said the man's daughter, and she flung her casket into the sea.

When they had sailed for some time longer, the brother once more pointed over the sea. 'There you may see the palace to which we are bound,' said he.

'What is my brother saying?' asked the man's daughter.

'Now he says that you are to throw your dog into the sea,' answered the step-mother.

The man's daughter wept, and was sorely troubled, for Little Snow was the dearest thing she had on earth, but at last she threw him overboard.

'If my brother says that, I must do it, but Heaven knows how unwilling I am to throw thee out, Little Snow!' said she.

So they sailed onwards a long way farther.

'There may'st thou see the King coming out to meet thee,' said the brother, pointing to the sea-shore.

'What is my brother saying?' asked his sister again.

'Now he says that you are to make haste and throw yourself overboard,' answered the step-mother.

She wept and she wailed, but as her brother had said that, she thought she must do it; so she leaped into the sea.

But when they arrived at the palace, and the King beheld the ugly bride with a nose that was four ells long, a jaw that was three ells, and a forehead that had a bush in the middle of it, he was quite terrified; but the wedding feast was all prepared, as regarded brewing and baking, and all the wedding guests were sitting waiting, so, ugly as she was, the King was forced to take her.

But he was very wroth, and none can blame him for that; so he caused the brother to be thrown into a pit full of snakes.

On the first Thursday night after this, a beautiful maiden came into the kitchen of the palace, and begged the kitchen-maid, who slept there, to lend her a brush. She begged very prettily, and got it, and then she brushed her hair, and the gold dropped from it.

A little dog was with her, and she said to it, 'Go out, Little Snow, and see if it will soon be day!'

This she said thrice, and the third time that she sent out the dog to see, it was very near dawn. Then she was forced to depart, but as she went she said:

> 'Out on thee, ugly Bushy Bride,
> Sleeping so soft by the young King's side,
> On sand and stones my bed I make,
> And my brother sleeps with the cold snake,
> Unpitied and unwept.'

I shall come twice more, and then never again,' said she.

In the morning the kitchen-maid related what she had seen and **heard, and the King said that next Thursday night he himself** would watch in the kitchen and see if this were true, and when it had begun to grow dark he went out into the kitchen to the girl. But though he rubbed his eyes and did everything he could to keep himself awake it was all in vain, for the Bushy Bride crooned and sang till his eyes were fast closed, and when the beautiful young maiden came he was sound asleep and snoring.

This time also, as before, she borrowed a brush and brushed her hair with it, and the gold dropped down as she did it; and again she sent the dog out three times, and when day dawned she departed, but as she was going she said as she had said before, ' I shall come once more, and then never again.'

On the third Thursday night the King once more insisted on keeping watch. Then he set two men to hold him; each of them was to take an arm, and shake him and jerk him by the arm whenever he seemed to be going to fall asleep; and he set two men to watch his Bushy Bride. But as the night wore on the Bushy Bride again began to croon and to sing, so that his eyes began to close and his head to droop on one side. Then came the lovely maiden, and got the brush and brushed her hair till the gold dropped from it, and then she sent her Little Snow out to see if it would soon be day, and this she did three times. The third time it was just beginning to grow light, and then she said:

> ' Out on thee, ugly Bushy Bride,
> Sleeping so soft by the young King's side,
> On sand and stones my bed I make,
> And my brother sleeps with the cold snake,
> Unpitied and unwept.'

' Now I shall never come again,' she said, and then she turned to go. But the two men who were holding the King by the arms seized his hands and forced a knife into his grasp, and then made him cut her little finger just enough to make it bleed.

Thus the true bride was freed. The King then awoke, and she told him all that had taken place, and how her step-mother and step-sister had betrayed her. Then the brother was at once taken out of the snake-pit—the snakes had never touched him—and the step-mother and step-sister were flung down into it instead of him.

No one can tell how delighted the King was to get rid of that hideous Bushy Bride, and get a Queen who was bright and beautiful as day itself.

And now the real wedding was held, and held in such a way that it was heard of and spoken about all over seven kingdoms. The King and his bride drove to church, and Little Snow was in the carriage too. When the blessing was given they went home again, and after that I saw no more of them.[1]

[1] From J. Moe.

THE SLEEPING KING, GUIDED BY HIS ATTENDANTS, CUTS THE FINGER
OF THE BEAUTIFUL MAIDEN.

SNOWDROP

ONCE upon a time, in the middle of winter when the snow-flakes were falling like feathers on the earth, a Queen sat at a window framed in black ebony and sewed. And as she sewed and gazed out to the white landscape, she pricked her finger with the needle, and three drops of blood fell on the snow outside, and because the red showed out so well against the white she thought to herself:

' Oh ! what wouldn't I give to have a child as white as snow, as red as blood, and as black as ebony ! '

And her wish was granted, for not long after a little daughter was born to her, with a skin as white as snow, lips and cheeks as red as blood, and hair as black as ebony. They called her Snow-drop, and not long after her birth the Queen died.

After a year the King married again. His new wife was a beautiful woman, but so proud and overbearing that she couldn't stand any rival to her beauty. She possessed a magic mirror, and when she used to stand before it gazing at her own reflection and ask :

' Mirror, mirror, hanging there,
Who in all the land's most fair ? '

it always replied :

'You are most fair, my Lady Queen,
None fairer in the land, I ween.'

Then she was quite happy, for she knew the mirror always spoke the truth.

But Snowdrop was growing prettier and prettier every day, and when she was seven years old she was as beautiful as she could be, and fairer even than the Queen herself. One day when the latter asked her mirror the usual question, it replied :

' My Lady Queen, you are fair, 'tis true,
But Snowdrop is fairer far than you.'

Then the Queen flew into the most awful passion, and turned every shade of green in her jealousy. From this hour she hated poor Snowdrop like poison, and every day her envy, hatred, and

malice grew, for envy and jealousy are like evil weeds which spring up and choke the heart. At last she could endure Snowdrop's presence no longer, and, calling a huntsman to her, she said:

'Take the child out into the wood, and never let me see her face again. You must kill her, and bring me back her lungs and liver, that I may know for certain she is dead.'

The Huntsman did as he was told and led Snowdrop out into the wood, but as he was in the act of drawing out his knife to slay her, she began to cry, and said:

' Oh, dear Huntsman, spare my life, and I will promise to fly forth into the wide wood and never to return home again.'

And because she was so young and pretty the Huntsman had pity on her, and said:

' Well, run along, poor child.' For he thought to himself: ' The wild beasts will soon eat her up.'

And his heart felt lighter because he hadn't had to do the deed himself. And as he turned away a young boar came running past, so he shot it, and brought its lungs and liver home to the Queen as a proof that Snowdrop was really dead. And the wicked woman had them stewed in salt, and ate them up, thinking she had made an end of Snowdrop for ever.

Now when the poor child found herself alone in the big wood the very trees around her seemed to assume strange shapes, and she felt so frightened she didn't know what to do. Then she began to run over the sharp stones, and through the bramble bushes, and the wild beasts ran past her, but they did her no harm. She ran as far as her legs would carry her, and as evening approached she saw a little house, and she stepped inside to rest. Everything was very small in the little house, but cleaner and neater than anything you can imagine. In the middle of the room there stood a little table, covered with a white tablecloth, and seven little plates and forks and spoons and knives and tumblers. Side by side against the wall there were seven little beds, covered with snow-white counterpanes. Snowdrop felt so hungry and so thirsty that she ate a bit of bread and a little porridge from each plate, and drank a drop of wine out of each tumbler. Then feeling tired and sleepy she lay down on one of the beds, but it wasn't comfortable; then she tried all the others in turn, but one was too long, and another too short, and it was only when she got to the seventh that she found one to suit her exactly. So she lay down upon it, said her prayers like a good child, and fell fast asleep.

When it got quite dark the masters of the little house returned.
They were seven dwarfs who worked in the mines, right down deep
in the heart of the mountain.   They lighted their seven little lamps,
and as soon as their eyes got accustomed to the glare they saw that
someone had been in the room, for all was not in the same order as
they had left it.

The first said :

' Who's been sitting on my little chair ? '

The second said :

' Who's been eating my little loaf ? '

The third said :

' Who's been tasting my porridge ? '

The fourth said :

' Who's been eating out of my little plate ? '

The fifth said :

' Who's been using my little fork ? '

The sixth said :

' Who's been cutting with my little knife ? '

The seventh said :

' Who's been drinking out of my little tumbler ? '

Then the first Dwarf looked round and saw a little hollow in his
bed, and he asked again :

' Who's been lying on my bed ? '

The others came running round, and cried when they saw their
beds :

' Somebody has lain on ours too.'

But when the seventh came to his bed, he started back in
amazement, for there he beheld Snowdrop fast asleep.   Then he
called the others, who turned their little lamps full on the bed, and
when they saw Snowdrop lying there they nearly fell down with
surprise.

' Goodness gracious ! ' they cried, ' what a beautiful child ! '

And they were so enchanted by her beauty that they did not
wake her, but let her sleep on in the little bed.   But the seventh
Dwarf slept with his companions one hour in each bed, and in this
way he managed to pass the night.

In the morning Snowdrop awoke, but when she saw the seven
little Dwarfs she felt very frightened.   But they were so friendly
and asked her what her name was in such a kind way, that she
replied :

' I am Snowdrop.'

'Why did you come to our house?' continued the Dwarfs.

Then she told them how her stepmother had wished her put to death, and how the Huntsman had spared her life, and how she had run the whole day till she had come to their little house. The Dwarfs, when they had heard her sad story, asked her:

'Will you stay and keep house for us, cook, make the beds, do the washing, sew and knit? and if you give satisfaction and keep everything neat and clean, you shall want for nothing.'

'Yes,' answered Snowdrop, 'I will gladly do all you ask.'

And so she took up her abode with them. Every morning the Dwarfs went into the mountain to dig for gold, and in the evening, when they returned home, Snowdrop always had their supper ready for them. But during the day the girl was left quite alone, so the good Dwarfs warned her, saying:

'Beware of your step-mother. She will soon find out you are here, and whatever you do don't let anyone into the house.'

Now the Queen, after she thought she had eaten Snowdrop's lungs and liver, never dreamed but that she was once more the most beautiful woman in the world; so stepping before her mirror one day she said:

'Mirror, mirror, hanging there,
Who in all the land's most fair?'

and the mirror replied:

'My Lady Queen, you are fair, 'tis true,
But Snowdrop is fairer far than you.
Snowdrop, who dwells with the seven little men,
Is as fair as you, as fair again.'

When the Queen heard these words she was nearly struck dumb with horror, for the mirror always spoke the truth, and she knew now that the Huntsman must have deceived her, and that Snowdrop was still alive. She pondered day and night how she might destroy her, for as long as she felt she had a rival in the land her jealous heart left her no rest. At last she hit upon a plan. She stained her face and dressed herself up as an old peddler wife, so that she was quite unrecognisable. In this guise she went over the seven hills till she came to the house of the seven Dwarfs. There she knocked at the door, calling out at the same time:

'Fine wares to sell, fine wares to sell!'

Snowdrop peeped out of the window, and called out:

' Good-day, mother, what have you to sell ? '

' Good wares, fine wares,' she answered ; ' laces of every shade and description,' and she held one up that was made of some gay coloured silk.

' Surely I can let the honest woman in,' thought Snowdrop ; so she unbarred the door and bought the pretty lace.

' Good gracious ! child,' said the old woman, ' what a figure you've got. Come ! I'll lace you up properly for once.'

Snowdrop, suspecting no evil, stood before her and let her lace her bodice up, but the old woman laced her so quickly and so tightly that it took Snowdrop's breath away, and she fell down dead.

' Now you are no longer the fairest,' said the wicked old woman, and then she hastened away.

In the evening the seven Dwarfs came home, and you may think what a fright they got when they saw their dear Snowdrop lying on the floor, as still and motionless as a dead person. They lifted her up tenderly, and when they saw how tightly laced she was they cut the lace in two, and she began to breathe a little and gradually came back to life. When the Dwarfs heard what had happened, they said :

' Depend upon it, the old peddler wife was none other than the old Queen. In future you must be sure to let no one in, if we are not at home.'

As soon as the wicked old Queen got home she went straight to her mirror, and said :

> ' Mirror, mirror, hanging there,
> Who in all the land's most fair ? '

and the mirror answered as before :

> ' My Lady Queen, you are fair, 'tis true,
> But Snowdrop is fairer far than you.
> Snowdrop, who dwells with the seven little men,
> Is as fair as you, as fair again.'

When she heard this she became as pale as death, because she saw at once that Snowdrop must be alive again.

' This time,' she said to herself, ' I will think of something that will make an end of her once and for all.'

And by the witchcraft which she understood so well she made a poisonous comb ; then she dressed herself up and assumed the form of another old woman. So she went over the seven hills till she reached the house of the seven Dwarfs, and knocking at the door she called out:

'Fine wares for sale.'

Snowdrop looked out of the window and said:

'You must go away, for I may not let anyone in.'

'But surely you are not forbidden to look out?' said the old woman, and she held up the poisonous comb for her to see.

It-pleased the girl so much that she let herself be taken in, and opened the door. When they had settled their bargain the old woman said:

'Now I'll comb your hair properly for you, for once in the way.'

Poor Snowdrop thought no evil, but hardly had the comb touched her hair than the poison worked and she fell down unconscious.

'Now, my fine lady, you're really done for this time,' said the wicked woman, and she made her way home as fast as she could.

Fortunately it was now near evening, and the seven Dwarfs returned home. When they saw Snowdrop lying dead on the ground, they at once suspected that her wicked step-mother had been at work again; so they searched till they found the poisonous comb, and the moment they pulled it out of her head Snowdrop came to herself again, and told them what had happened. Then they warned her once more to be on her guard, and to open the door to no one.

As soon as the Queen got home she went straight to her mirror, and asked:

> 'Mirror, mirror, hanging there,
> Who in all the land's most fair?'

and it replied as before:

> 'My Lady Queen, you are fair, 'tis true,
> But Snowdrop is fairer far than you.
> Snowdrop, who dwells with the seven little men,
> Is as fair as you, as fair again.'

When she heard these words she literally trembled and shook with rage.

'Snowdrop shall die,' she cried; 'yes, though it cost me my own life.'

Then she went to a little secret chamber, which no one knew or but herself, and there she made a poisonous apple. Outwardly it looked beautiful, white with red cheeks, so that everyone who saw

it longed to eat it, but anyone who might do so would certainly die
on the spot.   When the apple was quite finished she stained her
face and dressed herself up as a peasant, and so she went over
the seven hills to the seven Dwarfs'.   She knocked at the door, as
usual, but Snowdrop put her head out of the window and called
out:

'I may not let anyone in, the seven Dwarfs have forbidden me
to do so.'

'Are you afraid of being poisoned?' asked the old woman. 'See, I
will cut this apple in half. I'll eat the white cheek and you can eat
the red.'

But the apple was so cunningly made that only the red cheek
was poisonous. Snowdrop longed to eat the tempting fruit, and when
she saw that the peasant woman was eating it herself, she couldn't
resist the temptation any longer, and stretching out her hand she
took the poisonous half.   But hardly had the first bite passed her
lips than she fell down dead on the ground.   Then the eyes of the
cruel Queen sparkled with glee, and laughing aloud she cried:

'As white as snow, as red as blood, and as black as ebony, this
time the Dwarfs won't be able to bring you back to life.'

When she got home she asked the mirror:

> 'Mirror, mirror, hanging there,
> Who in all the land's most fair?'

and this time it replied:

> 'You are most fair, my Lady Queen,
> None fairer in the land, I ween.'

Then her jealous heart was at rest—at least, as much at rest
as a jealous heart can ever be.

When the little Dwarfs came home in the evening they found
Snowdrop lying on the ground, and she neither breathed nor stirred.
They lifted her up, and looked round everywhere to see if they
could find anything poisonous about.   They unlaced her bodice,
combed her hair, washed her with water and wine, but all in vain;
the child was dead and remained dead.   Then they placed her on
a bier, and all the seven Dwarfs sat round it, weeping and sobbing
for three whole days.   At last they made up their minds to bury
her, but she looked as blooming as a living being, and her cheeks
were still such a lovely colour, that they said:

'We can't hide her away in the black ground.'

So they had a coffin made of transparent glass, and they laid her in it, and wrote on the lid in golden letters that she was a royal Princess. Then they put the coffin on the top of the mountain, and one of the Dwarfs always remained beside it and kept watch over it.

And the very birds of the air came and bewailed Snowdrop's death, first an owl, and then a raven, and last of all a little dove.

Snowdrop lay a long time in the coffin, and she always looked the same, just as if she were fast asleep, and she remained as white as snow, as red as blood, and her hair as black as ebony.

Now it happened one day that a Prince came to the wood and
passed by the Dwarfs' house. He saw the coffin on the hill, with
the beautiful Snowdrop inside it, and when he had read what was
written on it in golden letters, he said to the Dwarf:

'Give me the coffin. I'll give you whatever you like for it.'

But the Dwarf said: 'No ; we wouldn't part with it for all the
gold in the world.'

'Well, then,' he replied, 'give it to me, because I can't live with-

out Snowdrop. I will cherish
and love it as my dearest possession.'

He spoke so sadly that the
good Dwarfs had pity on him,
and gave him the coffin, and the
Prince made his servants bear
it away on their shoulders. Now
it happened that as they were
going down the hill they stumbled
over a bush, and jolted the coffin
so violently that the poisonous
bit of apple Snowdrop had
swallowed fell out of her throat.
She gradually opened her eyes,
lifted up the lid of the coffin,
and sat up alive and well.

'Oh! dear me, where am I ? '
she cried.

The Prince answered joy-
fully, 'You are with me,' and
he told her all that had happened,
adding, 'I love you better than anyone in the whole wide world.
Will you come with me to my father's palace and be my wife ? '

Snowdrop consented, and went with him, and the marriage was
celebrated with great pomp and splendour.

Now Snowdrop's wicked step-mother was one of the guests
invited to the wedding feast. When she had dressed herself very
gorgeously for the occasion, she went to the mirror, and said:

'Mirror, mirror, hanging there,
Who in all the land's most fair ? '

and the mirror answered :

' My Lady Queen, you are fair, 'tis true,
But Snowdrop is fairer far than you.'

When the wicked woman heard these words she uttered a curse, and was beside herself with rage and mortification. At first she didn't want to go to the wedding at all, but at the same time she felt she would never be happy till she had seen the young Queen. As she entered Snowdrop recognised her, and nearly fainted with fear ; but red-hot iron shoes had been prepared for the wicked old Queen, and she was made to get into them and dance till she fell down dead.[1]

[1] Grimm.

THE GOLDEN GOOSE

THERE was once a man who had three sons. The youngest of them was called Dullhead, and was sneered and jeered at and snubbed on every possible opportunity.

One day it happened that the eldest son wished to go into the forest to cut wood, and before he started his mother gave him a fine rich cake and a bottle of wine, so that he might be sure not to suffer from hunger or thirst.

When he reached the forest he met a little old grey man who wished him 'Good-morning,' and said : ' Do give me a piece of that cake you have got in your pocket, and let me have a draught of your wine—I am so hungry and thirsty.'

But this clever son replied : ' If I give you my cake and wine I shall have none left for myself; you just go your own way ;' and he left the little man standing there and went further on into the forest. There he began to cut down a tree, but before long he made a false stroke with his axe, and cut his own arm so badly that he was obliged to go home and have it bound up.

Then the second son went to the forest, and his mother gave him a good cake and a bottle of wine as she had to his elder brother. He too met the little old grey man, who begged him for a morsel of cake and a draught of wine.

But the second son spoke most sensibly too, and said : ' Whatever I give to you I deprive myself of. Just go your own way, will you ? ' Not long after his punishment overtook him, for no sooner had he struck a couple of blows on a tree with his axe, than he cut his leg so badly that he had to be carried home.

So then Dullhead said : ' Father, let me go out and cut wood.'

But his father answered : ' Both your brothers have injured themselves. You had better leave it alone; you know nothing about it.'

But Dullhead begged so hard to be allowed to go that at last his father said : ' Very well, then—go. Perhaps when you have hurt yourself, you may learn to know better.' His mother only gave him a very plain cake made with water and baked in the cinders, and a bottle of sour beer.

When he got to the forest, he too met the little grey old man, who greeted him and said : ' Give me a piece of your cake and a draught from your bottle ; I am so hungry and thirsty.'

And Dullhead replied : ' I've only got a cinder-cake and some sour beer, but if you care to have that, let us sit down and eat.'

So they sat down, and when Dullhead brought out his cake he found it had turned into a fine rich cake, and the sour beer into excellent wine. Then they ate and drank, and when they had finished the little man said : ' Now I will bring you luck, because you have a kind heart and are willing to share what you have with others.   There stands an old tree ; cut it down, and amongst its roots you'll find something.'   With that the little man took leave.

Then Dullhead fell to at once to hew down the tree, and when it fell he found amongst its roots a goose, whose feathers were all of pure gold.   He lifted it out, carried it off, and took it with him to an inn where he meant to spend the night.

Now the landlord of the inn had three daughters, and when they saw the goose they were filled with curiosity as to what this wonderful bird could be, and each longed to have one of its golden feathers.

The eldest thought to herself : ' No doubt I shall soon find a good opportunity to pluck out one of its feathers,' and the first time Dullhead happened to leave the room she caught hold of the goose by its wing.   But, lo and behold ! her fingers seemed to stick fast to the goose, and she could not take her hand away.

Soon after the second daughter came in, and thought to pluck a golden feather for herself too ; but hardly had she touched her sister than she stuck fast as well.   At last the third sister came with the same intentions, but the other two cried out : ' Keep off ! for Heaven's sake, keep off ! '

The younger sister could not imagine why she was to keep off, and thought to herself : ' If they are both there, why should not I be there too ? '

So she sprang to them ; but no sooner had she touched one of them than she stuck fast to her.   So they all three had to spend the night with the goose.

Next morning Dullhead tucked the goose under his arm and went off, without in the least troubling himself about the three girls who were hanging on to it.   They just had to run after him right or left as best they could.   In the middle of a field they met the parson, and when he saw this procession he cried : ' For shame, you bold girls ! What do you mean by running after a young fellow through the fields like that ?   Do you call that proper behaviour ? ' And with that he caught the youngest girl by the hand to try and draw her away.   But directly he touched her he hung on himself, and had to run along with the rest of them.

Not long after the clerk came that way, and was much surprised to see the parson following the footsteps of three girls. ' Why, where is your reverence going so fast ? ' cried he ; ' don't forget there is to be a christening to-day ; ' and he ran after him, caught him by

the sleeve, and hung on to it himself.   As the five of them trotted
along in this fashion one after the other, two peasants were coming
from their work with their hoes.   On seeing them the parson called
out and begged them to come and rescue him and the clerk.   But
no sooner did they touch the clerk than they stuck on too, and so
there were seven of them running after Dullhead and his goose.

After a time they all came to a town where a King reigned whose
daughter was so serious and solemn that no one could ever manage

to make her laugh.   So the King had decreed that whoever should
succeed in making her laugh should marry her.

When Dullhead heard this he marched before the Princess with
his goose and its appendages, and as soon as she saw these seven
people continually running after each other she burst out laughing,
and could not stop herself.   Then Dullhead claimed her as his
bride, but the King, who did not much fancy him as a son-in-law,
made all sorts of objections, and told him he must first find a man
who could drink up a whole cellarful of wine.

Dullhead bethought him of the little grey man, who could, he felt sure, help him; so he went off to the forest, and on the very spot where he had cut down the tree he saw a man sitting with a most dismal expression of face.

Dullhead asked him what he was taking so much to heart, and the man answered: 'I don't know how I am ever to quench this terrible thirst I am suffering from. Cold water doesn't suit me at all. To be sure I've emptied a whole barrel of wine, but what is one drop on a hot stone?'

'I think I can help you,' said Dullhead. 'Come with me, and you shall drink to your heart's content.' So he took him to the King's cellar, and the man sat down before the huge casks and drank and drank till he drank up the whole contents of the cellar before the day closed.

Then Dullhead asked once more for his bride, but the King felt vexed at the idea of a stupid fellow whom people called 'Dullhead' carrying off his daughter, and he began to make fresh conditions. He required Dullhead to find a man who could eat a mountain of bread. Dullhead did not wait to consider long but went straight off to the forest, and there on the same spot sat a man who was drawing in a strap as tight as he could round his body, and making a most woeful face the while. Said he: 'I've eaten up a whole oven full of loaves, but what's the good of that to anyone who is as hungry as I am? I declare my stomach feels quite empty, and I must draw my belt tight if I'm not to die of starvation.'

Dullhead was delighted, and said: 'Get up and come with me, and you shall have plenty to eat,' and he brought him to the King's Court.

Now the King had given orders to have all the flour in his kingdom brought together, and to have a huge mountain baked of it. But the man from the wood just took up his stand before the mountain and began to eat, and in one day it had all vanished.

For the third time Dullhead asked for his bride, but again the King tried to make some evasion, and demanded a ship 'which could sail on land or water! When you come sailing in such a ship,' said he, 'you shall have my daughter without further delay.'

Again Dullhead started off to the forest, and there he found the little old grey man with whom he had shared his cake, and who said: 'I have eaten and I have drunk for you, and now I will give you the ship. I have done all this for you because you were kind and merciful to me.'

Then he gave Dullhead a ship which could sail on land or water, and when the King saw it he felt he could no longer refuse him his daughter.

So they celebrated the wedding with great rejoicings; and after the King's death Dullhead succeeded to the kingdom, and lived happily with his wife for many years after.[1]

[1] Grimm.

THE SEVEN FOALS

THERE was once upon a time a couple of poor folks who lived in a wretched hut, far away from everyone else, in a wood. They only just managed to live from hand to mouth, and had great difficulty in doing even so much as that, but they had three sons, and the youngest of them was called Cinderlad, for he did nothing else but lie and poke about among the ashes.

One day the eldest lad said that he would go out to earn his living; he soon got leave to do that, and set out on his way into the world. He walked on and on for the whole day, and when night was beginning to fall he came to a royal palace. The King was standing outside on the steps, and asked where he was going.

' Oh, I am going about seeking a place, my father,' said the youth.

' Wilt thou serve me, and watch my seven foals?' asked the King. ' If thou canst watch them for a whole day and tell me at night what they eat and drink, thou shalt have the Princess and half my kingdom, but if thou canst not, I will cut three red stripes on thy back.'

The youth thought that it was very easy work to watch the foals, and that he could do it well enough.

Next morning, when day was beginning to dawn, the King's Master of the Horse let out the seven foals; and they ran away, and the youth after them just as it chanced, over hill and dale, through woods and bogs. When the youth had run thus for a long time he began to be tired, and when he had held on a little longer he was heartily weary of watching at all, and at the same moment he came to a cleft in a rock where an old woman was sitting spinning with her distaff in her hand.

As soon as she caught sight of the youth, who was running after the foals till the perspiration streamed down his face, she cried:

' Come hither, come hither, my handsome son, and let me comb your hair for you.'

The lad was willing enough, so he sat down in the cleft of the rock beside the old hag, and laid his head on her knees, and she combed his hair all day while he lay there and gave himself up to idleness.

When evening was drawing near, the youth wanted to go.

' I may just as well go straight home again,' said he, ' for it is no use to go to the King's palace.'

' Wait till it is dusk,' said the old hag, ' and then the King's foals will pass by this place again, and you can run home with them ; no one will ever know that you have been lying here all day instead of watching the foals.'

So when they came she gave the lad a bottle of water and a bit of moss, and told him to show these to the King and say that this was what his seven foals ate and drank.

' Hast thou watched faithfully and well the whole day long ? ' said the King, when the lad came into his presence in the evening.

' Yes, that I have ! ' said the youth.

' Then you are able to tell me what it is that my seven foals eat and drink,' said the King.

So the youth produced the bottle of water and the bit of moss which he had got from the old woman, saying :

' Here you see their meat, and here you see their drink.'

Then the King knew how his watching had been done, and fell into such a rage that he ordered his people to chase the youth back to his own home at once; but first they were to cut three red stripes in his back, and rub salt into them.

When the youth reached home again, anyone can imagine what a state of mind he was in. He had gone out once to seek a place, he said, but never would he do such a thing again.

Next day the second son said that he would now go out into the world to seek his fortune. His father and mother said ' No,' and bade him look at his brother's back, but the youth would not give up his design, and stuck to it, and after a long, long time he got leave to go, and set forth on his way. When he had walked all day he too came to the King's palace, and the King was standing outside on the steps, and asked where he was going; and when the youth replied that he was going about in search of a place, the King said that he might enter into his service and watch his seven foals. Then the King promised him the same punishment and the same reward that he had promised his brother.

The youth at once consented to this and entered into the King's service, for he thought he could easily watch the foals and inform the King what they ate and drank.

In the grey light of dawn the Master of the Horse let out the seven foals, and off they went again over hill and dale, and off went the lad after them. But all went with him as it had gone with his brother. When he had run after the foals for a long, long time and was hot and tired, he passed by a cleft in the rock where an old woman was sitting spinning with a distaff, and she called to him :

' Come hither, come hither, my handsome son, and let me comb your hair.'

The youth liked the thought of this, let the foals run where they chose, and seated himself in the cleft of the rock by the side of the old hag. So there he sat with his head on her lap, taking his ease the livelong day.

The foals came back in the evening, and then he too got a bit of moss and a bottle of water from the old hag, which things he was to show to the King. But when the King asked the youth : ' Canst thou tell me what my seven foals eat and drink ? ' and the youth showed him the bit of moss and the bottle of water, and said : ' Yes here may you behold their meat, and here their drink,' the King once more became wroth, and commanded that three red stripes should be cut on the lad's back, that salt should be strewn upon them, and that he should then be instantly chased back to his own home. So when the youth got home again he too related all that had happened to him, and he too said that he had gone out in search of a place once, but that never would he do it again.

On the third day Cinderlad wanted to set out. He had a fancy to try to watch the seven foals himself, he said.

The two others laughed at him, and mocked him. 'What! when all went so ill with us, do you suppose that you are going to succeed? You look like succeeding—you who have never done anything else but lie and poke about among the ashes!' said they.

'Yes, I will go too,' said Cinderlad, 'for I have taken it into my head.'

The two brothers laughed at him, and his father and mother begged him not to go, but all to no purpose, and Cinderlad set out on his way. So when he had walked the whole day, he too came to the King's palace as darkness began to fall.

There stood the King outside on the steps, and he asked whither he was bound.

'I am walking about in search of a place,' said Cinderlad.

'From whence do you come, then?' inquired the King, for by this time he wanted to know a little more about the men before he took any of them into his service.

So Cinderlad told him whence he came, and that he was brother to the two who had watched the seven foals for the King, and then he inquired if he might be allowed to try to watch them on the following day.

'Oh, shame on them!' said the King, for it enraged him even to think of them. 'If thou art brother to those two, thou too art not good for much. I have had enough of such fellows.'

'Well, but as I have come here, you might just give me leave to make the attempt,' said Cinderlad.

'Oh, very well, if thou art absolutely determined to have thy back flayed, thou may'st have thine own way if thou wilt,' said the King.

'I would much rather have the Princess,' said Cinderlad.

Next morning, in the grey light of dawn, the Master of the Horse let out the seven foals again, and off they set over hill and dale, through woods and bogs, and off went Cinderlad after them. When he had run thus for a long time, he too came to the cleft in the rock. There the old hag was once more sitting spinning from her distaff, and she cried to Cinderlad:

'Come hither, come hither, my handsome son, and let me comb your hair for you.'

'Come to me, then ; come to me ! ' said Cinderlad, as he passed by jumping and running, and keeping tight hold of one of the foals' tails.

When he had got safely past the cleft in the rock, the youngest foal said :

'Get on my back, for we have still a long way to go.' So the lad did this.

And thus they journeyed onwards a long, long way.

'Dost thou see anything now ? ' said the Foal.

'No,' said Cinderlad.

So they journeyed onwards a good bit farther.

'Dost thou see anything now ? ' asked the Foal.

'Oh, no,' said the lad.

When they had gone thus for a long, long way, the Foal again asked :

'Dost thou see anything now ? '

'Yes, now I see something that is white,' said Cinderlad. 'It looks like the trunk of a great thick birch tree.'

'Yes, that is where we are to go in,' said the Foal.

When they got to the trunk, the eldest foal broke it down on one side, and then they saw a door where the trunk had been standing, and inside this there was a small room, and in the room there was scarcely anything but a small fire-place and a couple of benches, but behind the door hung a great rusty sword and a small pitcher.

'Canst thou wield that sword ? ' asked the Foal.

Cinderlad tried, but could not do it ; so he had to take a draught from the pitcher, and then one more, and after that still another, and then he was able to wield the sword with perfect ease.

'Good,' said the Foal ; ' and now thou must take the sword away with thee, and with it shalt thou cut off the heads of all seven of us on thy wedding-day, and then we shall become princes again as we were before. For we are brothers of the Princess whom thou art to have when thou canst tell the King what we eat and drink, but there is a mighty Troll who has cast a spell over us. When thou hast cut off our heads, thou must take the greatest care to lay each head at the tail of the body to which it belonged before, and then the spell which the Troll has cast upon us will lose all its power.'

Cinderlad promised to do this, and then they went on farther.

When they had travelled a long, long way, the Foal said :
' Dost thou see anything ? '
' No,' said Cinderlad.
So they went on a great distance farther.
' And now ? ' inquired the Foal, ' seest thou nothing now ? '
' Alas ! no,' said Cinderlad.
So they travelled onwards again, for many and many a mile,
over hill and dale.
' Now, then,' said the Foal, ' dost thou not see anything now ? '

' Yes,' said Cinderlad ; ' now I see something like a bluish streak,
far, far away.'
' That is a river,' said the Foal, ' and we have to cross it.'
There was a long, handsome bridge over the river, and when
they had got to the other side of it they again travelled on a long,
long way, and then once more the Foal inquired if Cinderlad saw
anything. Yes, this time he saw something that looked black, far,
far away, and was rather like a church tower.
' Yes,' said the Foal, ' we shall go into that.'
When the Foals got into the churchyard they turned into men
again, and looked like the sons of a king, and their clothes were so

magnificent that they shone with splendour, and they went into the church and received bread and wine from the priest, who was standing before the altar, and Cinderlad went in too. But when the priest had laid his hands on the princes and read the blessing, they went out of the church again, and Cinderlad went out too, but he took with him a flask of wine and some consecrated bread. No sooner had the seven princes come out into the churchyard than they became foals again, and Cinderlad got upon the back of the youngest, and they returned by the way they had come, only they went much, much faster.

First they went over the bridge, and then past the trunk of the birch tree, and then past the old hag who sat in the cleft of the rock spinning, and they went by so fast that Cinderlad could not hear what the old hag screeched after him, but just heard enough to understand that she was terribly enraged.

It was all but dark when they got back to the King at nightfall, and he himself was standing in the courtyard waiting for them.

' Hast thou watched well and faithfully the whole day ? ' said the King to Cinderlad.

' I have done my best,' replied Cinderlad.

' Then thou canst tell me what my seven foals eat and drink ? ' asked the King.

So Cinderlad pulled out the consecrated bread and the flask of wine, and showed them to the King. ' Here may you behold their meat, and here their drink,' said he.

' Yes, diligently and faithfully hast thou watched,' said the King, ' and thou shalt have the Princess and half the kingdom.'

So all was made ready for the wedding, and the King said that it was to be so stately and magnificent that everyone should hear of it, and everyone inquire about it.

But when they sat down to the marriage-feast, the bridegroom arose and went down to the stable, for he said that he had forgotten something which he must go and look to. When he got there, he did what the foals had bidden him, and cut off the heads of all the seven. First the eldest, and then the second, and so on according to their age, and he was extremely careful to lay each head at the tail of the foal to which it had belonged, and when that was done, all the foals became princes again. When he returned to the marriage-feast with the seven princes, the King was so joyful that he both kissed Cinderlad and clapped him on the back, and his bride was still more delighted with him than she had been before.

' Half my kingdom is thine already,' said the King, ' and the other half shall be thine after my death, for my sons can get countries and kingdoms for themselves now that they have become princes again.'

Therefore, as all may well believe, there was joy and merriment at that wedding.[1]

[1] From J. Moe.

THE MARVELLOUS MUSICIAN

THERE was once upon a time a marvellous musician. One day he was wandering through a wood all by himself, thinking now of one thing, now of another, till there was nothing else left to think about. Then he said to himself:

'Time hangs very heavily on my hands when I'm all alone in the wood. I must try and find a pleasant companion.'

So he took his fiddle out, and fiddled till he woke the echoes round. After a time a wolf came through the thicket and trotted up to the musician.

'Oh! it's a Wolf, is it?' said he. 'I've not the smallest wish for his society.'

But the Wolf approached him and said:

'Oh, my dear musician, how beautifully you play! I wish you'd teach me how it's done.'

'That's easily learned,' answered the fiddler; 'you must only do exactly as I tell you.'

'Of course I will,' replied the Wolf. 'I can promise that you will find me a most apt pupil.'

So they joined company and went on their way together, and after a time they came to an old oak tree, which was hollow and had a crack in the middle of the trunk.

'Now,' said the Musician, 'if you want to learn to fiddle, here's your chance. Lay your front paws in this crack.'

The Wolf did as he was told, and the Musician quickly seized a stone, and wedged both his fore paws so firmly into the crack that he was held there, a fast prisoner.

'Wait there till I return,' said the Fiddler, and he went on his way.

After a time he said to himself again:

'Time hangs very heavily on my hands when I'm all alone in th e wood; I must try and find a companion.'

So he drew out his fiddle, and fiddled away lustily. Presently a fox slunk through the trees.

'Aha ! what have we here ? ' said the Musician. 'A fox ; well, I haven't the smallest desire for his company.'

The Fox came straight up to him and said :

'My dear friend, how beautifully you play the fiddle ; I would like to learn how you do it.'

'Nothing easier,' said the Musician. 'if you'll promise to do exactly as I tell you.'

'Certainly,' answered the Fox, ' you have only to say the word.'

'Well, then, follow me,' replied the Fiddler.

When they had gone a bi of the way, they came to a path with high trees on each side. Here the Musician halted, bent a stout hazel bough down to the ground from one side of the path, and put his foot on the end of it to keep it down. Then he bent a branch down from the other side and said :

'Give me your left front paw, my little Fox, if you really wish to learn how it's done.'

The Fox did as he was told, and the Musician tied his front paw to the end of one of the branches.

'Now, my friend,' he said, 'give me your right paw.'

This he bound to the other branch, and having carefully seen that his knots were all secure, he stepped off the ends of the branches, and they sprang back, leaving the poor Fox suspended in mid-air.

'Just you wait where you are till I return,' said the Musician, and he went on his way again.

Once more he said to himself :

'Time hangs heavily on my hands when I'm all alone in the wood ; I must try and find another companion.'

So he took out his fiddle and played as merrily as before. This time a little hare came running up at the sound.

'Oh ! here comes a hare,' said the Musician ; 'I've not the smallest desire for his company.'

'How beautifully you play, dear Mr. Fiddler,' said the little Hare. 'I wish I could learn how you do it.'

'It's easily learnt,' answered the Musician ; 'just do exactly as I tell you.'

'That I will,' said the Hare, 'you will find me a most attentive pupil.'

They went on a bit together, till they came to a thin part of the wood, where they found an aspen tree growing. The Musician bound a long cord round the little Hare's neck, the other end of which he fastened to the tree.

'Now, my merry little friend,' said the Musician, 'run twenty times round the tree.'

The little Hare obeyed, and when it had run twenty times round the tree, the cord had twisted itself twenty times round the trunk, so that the poor little beast was held a fast prisoner, and it might bite and tear as much as it liked, it couldn't free itself, and the cord only cut its tender neck.

'Wait there till I return,' said the Musician, and went on his way.

In the meantime the Wolf had pulled and bitten and scratched at the stone, till at last he succeeded in getting his paws out. Full of anger, he hurried after the Musician, determined when he met him to tear him to pieces. When the Fox saw him running by, he called out as loud as he could :

'Brother Wolf, come to my rescue, the Musician has deceived me too.'

The Wolf pulled the branches down, bit the cord in two, and set the Fox free. So they went on their way together, both vowing vengeance on the Musician. They found the poor imprisoned little Hare, and having set him free also, they all set out to look for their enemy.

During this time the Musician had once more played his fiddle, and had been more fortunate in the result. The sounds pierced to the ears of a poor woodman, who instantly left his work, and with his hatchet under his arm came to listen to the music.

'At last I've got a proper sort of companion,' said the Musician, ' for it was a human being I wanted all along, and not a wild animal.'

And he began playing so enchantingly that the poor man stood there as if bewitched, and his heart leapt for joy as he listened.

And as he stood thus, the Wolf and Fox and little Hare came up, and the woodman saw at once that they meant mischief. He lifted his glittering axe and placed himself in front of the Musician, as much as to say : 'If you touch a hair of his head, beware, for you will have to answer for it to me.'

Then the beasts were frightened, and they all three ran back into the wood, and the Musician played the woodman one of his best tunes, by way of thanks, and then continued his way.[1]

---

[1] Grimm.

THE STORY OF SIGURD

[This is a very old story : the Danes who used to fight with the English in King Alfred's time knew this story. They have carved on the rocks pictures of some of the things that happen in the tale, and those carvings may still be seen. Because it is so old and so beautiful the story is told here again, but it has a sad ending—indeed it is all sad, and all about fighting and killing, as might be expected from the Danes.]

ONCE upon a time there was a King in the North who had won many wars, but now he was old. Yet he took a new wife, and then another Prince, who wanted to have married her, came up against him with a great army. The old King went out and fought bravely, but at last his sword broke, and he was wounded and his men fled. But in the night, when the battle was over, his young wife came out and searched for him among the slain, and at last she found him, and asked whether he might be healed. But he said ' No,' his luck was gone, his sword was broken, and he must die. And he told her that she would have a son, and that son would be a great warrior, and would avenge him on the other King, his enemy. And he bade her keep the broken pieces of the sword, to make a new sword for his son, and that blade should be called *Gram*.

Then he died. And his wife called her maid to her and said, ' Let us change clothes, and you shall be called by my name, and I by yours, lest the enemy finds us.'

So this was done, and they hid in a wood, but there some strangers met them and carried them off in a ship to Denmark. And when they were brought before the King, he thought the maid looked like a Queen, and the Queen like a maid. So he asked the Queen, ' How do you know in the dark of night whether the hours are wearing to the morning ? '

And she said :

' I know because, when I was younger, I used to have to rise and light the fires, and still I waken at the same time.'

' A strange Queen to light the fires,' thought the King.

Then he asked the Queen, who was dressed like a maid, ' How do you know in the dark of night whether the hours are wearing near the dawn ? '

' My father gave me a gold ring,' said she, ' and always, ere the dawning, it grows cold on my finger.'

' A rich house where the maids wore gold,' said the King. ' Truly you are no maid, but a King's daughter.'

So he treated her royally, and as time went on she had a son called Sigurd, a beautiful boy and very strong. He had a tutor to be with him, and once the tutor bade him go to the King and ask for a horse.

' Choose a horse for yourself,' said the King ; and Sigurd went to the wood, and there he met an old man with a white beard, and said, ' Come ! help me in horse-choosing.'

Then the old man said, ' Drive all the horses into the river, and choose the one that swims across.'

So Sigurd drove them, and only one swam across. Sigurd chose him : his name was Grani, and he came of Sleipnir's breed, and was the best horse in the world. For Sleipnir was the horse of Odin, the God of the North, and was as swift as the wind.

But a day or two later his tutor said to Sigurd, ' There is a great treasure of gold hidden not far from here, and it would become you to win it.'

But Sigurd answered, ' I have heard stories of that treasure, and I know that the dragon Fafnir guards it, and he is so huge and wicked that no man dares to go near him.'

' He is no bigger than other dragons,' said the tutor, ' and if you were as brave as your father you would not fear him.'

' I am no coward,' says Sigurd ; ' why do you want me to fight with this dragon ? '

Then his tutor, whose name was Regin, told him that all this great hoard of red gold had once belonged to his own father. And his father had three sons—the first was Fafnir, the Dragon ; the next was Otter, who could put on the shape of an otter when he liked ; and the next was himself, Regin, and he was a great smith and maker of swords.

Now there was at that time a dwarf called Andvari, who lived in a pool beneath a waterfall, and there he had hidden a great hoard of gold. And one day Otter had been fishing there, and had killed a salmon and eaten it, and was sleeping, like an otter, on a stone. Then someone came by, and threw a stone at the otter and killed it, and flayed off the skin, and took it to the house of Otter's father. Then he knew his son was dead, and to punish the person who had killed him he said he must have the Otter's skin filled with gold, and covered all over with red gold, or it should go worse with him. Then the person who had killed Otter went down and caught the Dwarf who owned all the treasure and took it from him.

Only one ring was left, which the Dwarf wore, and even that was taken from him.

Then the poor Dwarf was very angry, and he prayed that the gold might never bring any but bad luck to all the men who might own it, for ever.

Then the otter skin was filled with gold and covered with gold, all but one hair, and that was covered with the poor Dwarf's last ring.

But it brought good luck to nobody. First Fafnir, the Dragon, killed his own father, and then he went and wallowed on the gold, and would let his brother have none, and no man dared go near it.

When Sigurd heard the story he said to Regin :

' Make me a good sword that I may kill this Dragon.'

So Regin made a sword, and Sigurd tried it with a blow on a lump of iron, and the sword broke.

Another sword he made, and Sigurd broke that too.

Then Sigurd went to his mother, and asked for the broken pieces of his father's blade, and gave them to Regin. And he hammered and wrought them into a new sword, so sharp that fire seemed to burn along its edges.

Sigurd tried this blade on the lump of iron, and it did not break, but split the iron in two. Then he threw a lock of wool into the river, and when it floated down against the sword it was cut into two pieces. So Sigurd said that sword would do. But before he went against the Dragon he led an army to fight the men who had killed his father, and he slew their King, and took all his wealth, and went home.

When he had been at home a few days, he rode out with Regin one morning to the heath where the Dragon used to lie. Then he saw the track which the Dragon made when he went to a cliff to drink, and the track was as if a great river had rolled along and left a deep valley.

Then Sigurd went down into that deep place, and dug many pits in it, and in one of the pits he lay hidden with his sword drawn. There he waited, and presently the earth began to shake with the weight of the Dragon as he crawled to the water. And a cloud of venom flew before him as he snorted and roared, so that it would have been death to stand before him.

But Sigurd waited till half of him had crawled over the pit, and then he thrust the sword Gram right into his very heart.

Then the Dragon lashed with his tail till stones broke and trees crashed about him.

Then he spoke, as he died, and said :

' Whoever thou art that hast slain me this gold shall be thy ruin, and the ruin of all who own it.'

Sigurd said :

' I would touch none of it if by losing it I should never die. But all men die, and no brave man lets death frighten him from his desire. Die thou, Fafnir,' and then Fafnir died.

And after that Sigurd was called Fafnir's Bane, and Dragon-slayer.

Then Sigurd rode back, and met Regin, and Regin asked him to roast Fafnir's heart and let him taste of it.

So Sigurd put the heart of Fafnir on a stake, and roasted it. But it chanced that he touched it with his finger, and it burned him. Then he put his finger in his mouth, and so tasted the heart of Fafnir.

Then immediately he understood the language of birds, and he heard the Woodpeckers say :

' There is Sigurd roasting Fafnir's heart for another, when he should taste of it himself and learn all wisdom.'

The next bird said :

' There lies Regin, ready to betray Sigurd, who trusts him.'

The third bird said :

' Let him cut off Regin's head, and keep all the gold to himself.'

The fourth bird said :

' That let him do, and then ride over Hindfell, to the place where Brynhild sleeps.'

When Sigurd heard all this, and how Regin was plotting to betray him, he cut off Regin's head with one blow of the sword Gram.

Then all the birds broke out singing :

> ' We know a fair maid,
>   A fair maiden sleeping ;
>   Sigurd, be not afraid,
>   Sigurd, win thou the maid
>   Fortune is keeping.

> ' High over Hindfell
>   Red fire is flaming,
>   There doth the maiden dwell
>   She that should love thee well,
>   Meet for thy taming.

> ' There must she sleep till thou
>   Comest for her waking
>   Rise up and ride, for now
>   Sure she will swear the vow
>   Fearless of breaking.'

Then Sigurd remembered how the story went that somewhere, far away, there was a beautiful lady enchanted. She was under a spell, so that she must always sleep in a castle surrounded by flaming fire ; there she must sleep for ever till there came a knight who would ride through the fire and waken her. There he determined to go, but first he rode right down the horrible trail of Fafnir. And Fafnir had lived in a cave with iron doors, a cave dug deep down in the earth, and full of gold bracelets, and crowns, and rings ; and there, too, Sigurd found the Helm of Dread, a golden helmet, and whoever wears it is invisible. All these he piled on the back of the good horse Grani, and then he rode south to Hindfell.

Now it was night, and on the crest of the hill Sigurd saw a red fire blazing up into the sky, and within the flame a castle, and a banner on the topmost tower. Then he set the horse Grani at the fire, and he leaped through it lightly, as if it had been through the heather. So Sigurd went within the castle door, and there he saw someone sleeping, clad all in armour. Then he took the helmet off the head of the sleeper, and behold, she was a most beautiful lady. And she wakened and said, ' Ah ! is it Sigurd, Sigmund's son, who has broken the curse, and comes here to waken me at last ? '

This curse came upon her when the thorn of the tree of sleep ran into her hand long ago as a punishment because she had displeased Odin the God. Long ago, too, she had vowed never to marry a man who knew fear, and dared not ride through the fence of flaming fire. For she was a warrior maid herself, and went armed into the battle like a man. But now she and Sigurd loved

each other, and promised to be true to each other, and he gave her a ring, and it was the last ring taken from the dwarf Andvari. Then Sigurd rode away, and he came to the house of a King who had a fair daughter. Her name was Gudrun, and her mother was a witch. Now Gudrun fell in love with Sigurd, but he was always talking of Brynhild, how beautiful she was and how dear. So one day Gudrun's witch mother put poppy and forgetful drugs in a magical cup, and bade Sigurd drink to her health, and he drank, and instantly he forgot poor Brynhild and he loved Gudrun, and they were married with great rejoicings.

Now the witch, the mother of Gudrun, wanted her son Gunnar to marry Brynhild, and she bade him ride out with Sigurd and go and woo her. So forth they rode to her father's house, for Brynhild had quite gone out of Sigurd's mind by reason of the witch's wine, but she remembered him and loved him still. Then Brynhild's father told Gunnar that she would marry none but him who could ride the flame in front of her enchanted tower, and thither they rode, and Gunnar set his horse at the flame, but he would not face it. Then Gunnar tried Sigurd's horse Grani, but he would not move with Gunnar on his back. Then Gunnar remembered witchcraft that his mother had taught him, and by his magic he made Sigurd look exactly like himself, and he looked exactly like Gunnar. Then Sigurd, in the shape of Gunnar and in his mail, mounted on Grani, and Grani leaped the fence of fire, and Sigurd went in and found Brynhild, but he did not remember her yet, because of the forgetful medicine in the cup of the witch's wine.

Now Brynhild had no help but to promise she would be his wife, the wife of Gunnar as she supposed, for Sigurd wore Gunnar's shape, and she had sworn to wed whoever should ride the flames. And he gave her a ring, and she gave him back the ring he had given her before in his own shape as Sigurd, and it was the last ring of that poor dwarf Andvari. Then he rode out again, and he and Gunnar changed shapes, and each was himself again, and they went home to the witch Queen's, and Sigurd gave the dwarf's ring to his wife, Gudrun. And Brynhild went to her father, and said that a King had come called Gunnar, and had ridden the fire, and she must marry him. ' Yet I thought,' she said, ' that no man could have done this deed but Sigurd, Fafnir's bane, who was my true love. But he has forgotten me, and my promise I must keep.'

So Gunnar and Brynhild were married, though it was not Gunnar but Sigurd in Gunnar's shape, that had ridden the fire.

And when the wedding was over and all the feast, then the magic of the witch's wine went out of Sigurd's brain, and he remembered all. He remembered how he had freed Brynhild from the spell, and how she was his own true love, and how he had forgotten and had married another woman, and won Brynhild to be the wife of another man.

But he was brave, and he spoke not a word of it to the others to make them unhappy. Still he could not keep away the curse which was to come on every one who owned the treasure of the dwarf Andvari, and his fatal golden ring.

And the curse soon came upon all of them. For one day, when Brynhild and Gudrun were bathing, Brynhild waded farthest out into the river, and said she did that to show she was Gudrun's superior. For her husband, she said, had ridden through the flame when no other man dared face it.

Then Gudrun was very angry, and said that it was Sigurd, not Gunnar, who had ridden the flame, and had received from Brynhild that fatal ring, the ring of the dwarf Andvari.

Then Brynhild saw the ring which Sigurd had given to Gudrun, and she knew it and knew all, and she turned as pale as a dead

woman, and went home. All that evening she never spoke. Next day she told Gunnar, her husband, that he was a coward and a liar, for he had never ridden the flame, but had sent Sigurd to do it for him, and pretended that he had done it himself. And she said he would never see her glad in his hall, never drinking wine, never playing chess, never embroidering with the golden thread, never speaking words of kindness. Then she rent all her needlework asunder and wept aloud, so that everyone in the house heard her.

For her heart was broken, and her pride was broken in the same hour. She had lost her true love, Sigurd, the slayer of Fafnir, and she was married to a man who was a liar.

Then Sigurd came and tried to comfort her, but she would not listen, and said she wished the sword stood fast in his heart.

' Not long to wait,' he said, ' till the bitter sword stands fast in my heart, and thou will not live long when I am dead. But, dear Brynhild, live and be comforted, and love Gunnar thy husband, and I will give thee all the gold, the treasure of the dragon Fafnir.'

Brynhild said :

' It is too late.'

Then Sigurd was so grieved and his heart so swelled in his breast that it burst the steel rings of his shirt of mail.

Sigurd went out and Brynhild determined to slay him. She mixed serpent's venom and wolf's flesh, and gave them in one dish to her husband's younger brother, and when he had tasted them he was mad, and he went into Sigurd's chamber while he slept and pinned him to the bed with a sword. But Sigurd woke, and caught the sword Gram into his hand, and threw it at the man as he fled, and the sword cut him in twain. Thus died Sigurd, Fafnir's bane, whom no ten men could have slain in fair fight. Then Gudrun wakened and saw him dead, and she moaned aloud, and Brynhild heard her and laughed; but the kind horse Grani lay down and died of very grief. And then Brynhild fell a-weeping till her heart broke. So they attired Sigurd in all his golden armour, and built a great pile of wood on board his ship, and at night laid on it the dead Sigurd and the dead Brynhild, and the good horse, Grani, and set fire to it, and launched the ship. And the wind bore it blazing out to sea, flaming into the dark. So there were Sigurd and Brynhild burned together, and the curse of the dwarf Andvari was fulfilled.[1]

---

[1] The *Volsunga Saga*.